# CJ DUGGAN

# PARADISE CITY

AUSTRALIA

hachette
AUSTRALIA

Published in Australia and New Zealand in 2015
by Hachette Australia
(an imprint of Hachette Australia Pty Limited)
Level 17, 207 Kent Street, Sydney NSW 2000
www.hachette.com.au

10 9 8 7 6 5 4 3 2

National Library of Australia
Cataloguing-in-Publication data:

Duggan, C.J.
Paradise city/C.J. Duggan.

ISBN 978 0 7336 3386 7 (pbk)

Teenagers – Australia – Fiction.
Man–woman relationships – Fiction.

A823.4

Cover design by XOU Creative
Cover photographs courtesy of iStock
Author photograph by Craig Peihopa
Text design by Bookhouse, Sydney
Typeset in 11/14 pt Minion Pro
Printed and bound in Australia by McPherson's Printing Group

MIX
Paper from
responsible sources
FSC
www.fsc.org
FSC® C001695

The paper this book is printed on is certified against the
Forest Stewardship Council® Standards. McPherson's Printing
Group holds FSC® chain of custody certification SA-COC-005379.
FSC® promotes environmentally responsible, socially beneficial
and economically viable management of the world's forests.

*For my dad, who always believed*

# I dreamed of Paradise

f there is one thing I have learned in my short little life, it is to take advice from the least likely of sources.

'Have low expectations, kid, and you'll never be disappointed.' My Uncle Eddie delivered his words of wisdom with a wink and a double-barrelled shooting finger.

At the time, I hadn't taken it too seriously because, firstly, I was only nine and, secondly, he was wearing mission-brown stubbies with thongs. I mean, really? Sure, all those things could have very well been the reason why Uncle Eddie's words didn't sink in. But it was more the fact that after he had delivered his wise words, he then tripped backwards over his own esky, rolling like a human pinball down the front steps and landing, spread-eagled, on the lawn, wailing about soft tissue damage and needing an ambulance.

Eight years later, it was still one of the most talked about of Uncle Eddie's drunken antics resulting in cringe-worthy accounts of public humiliation, not just limited to our front lawn.

Uncle Eddie, while at times hilarious, was also the resident drunk, who cycled his way around town on his punting, drinking expeditions sporting his crisscrossed fluoro safety vest (courtesy of Al, the local policeman). He would wear it even in the daytime – mortifying! He was almost like the town mascot, which pretty much paints an accurate picture of my hometown.

Red Hill.

The European explorers who named it obviously had a sense of humour because, unlike the name suggested, there was no hill in sight. Just a flat, desolate whole-lot-of-nothing. Well, that's not exactly true. There were three pubs and a club, a Caltex petrol station, an IGA supermarket, a post office and a newsagent. And when you're seventeen and trapped in a place nicknamed 'Red Hole', the only thing left to do is dream of a life less ordinary.

In my room I had a bookshelf that housed my entire Holy Grail collection: a crystal angel from my Aunty Deb, a jasmine-scented candle that was too pretty to use and a stack of penpal letters from around the world. I kept writing to my penpals vigilantly with the idea of scoring free accommodation when I travelled abroad someday. I stashed the truly sacred stuff on the top shelf, like the tattered postcard from my cousin Amanda. It was slightly frayed around the edges from the countless times I had picked it up and flipped the glossed square over in my hands, reading the exciting account of the new life she had found in a place nothing like Red Hole.

For the past year I had been set a challenge: maintain my good grades and Mum and Dad would 'entertain' the thought of me finishing my VCE in a real school, not one that involved a satellite connection to a virtual teacher. That's right, Red Hole had three pubs and no school and I, for one, was not revelling in a future as an uneducated drunk, slurring my words and tripping over myself. No way.

I hoped it was just a matter of time before they would let me venture out to further my education. Whether they liked it or not, that change was what I needed to 'experience' the big bad world. And even though I had a long-standing wish that maybe it could be so, it was never anything more than a crazy pipe dream. So come the time we had the family roundtable discussion, never in my wildest dreams did I think it would come true.

Dad's lips were pressed together in a grim line, his arms folded over his broad chest as he let Mum break it to me.

'We've talked it over and if you agree,' she said, smiling to herself as she traced her finger along the patterned wood grain of the tabletop, 'we think –' Dad coughed. 'Okay, *I* think that straight A grades deserve nothing less than destination Paradise.'

My head snapped up, my eyes widening in disbelief. 'Are you serious?'

Mum laughed. 'I spoke to Aunty Karen, and they would love to have you.'

I flung myself against my parents, hugging the life out of them. Thanking all the gods in all the universe that my prayers had been answered. 'Thank you! Thank you! Thank you!'

A smile spread across my face as I re-read Amanda's postcard; her elegant, cursive writing described how her life was all about sun, surf, sand and boys (shhhh), which wasn't exactly the smartest thing to write on the back of a postcard. It was the first and only postcard she had sent, and four years had passed since I'd received it, but when you're thirteen and a seed is planted, and you have no clear future other than becoming betrothed to one of the local farming boys, you take solace in alternative future possibilities. Glancing at the front of the postcard, I absorbed the beach landscape peppered with sky-high buildings along the foreshore, and an embossed golden font that read 'Paradise City'.

Sorry, Uncle Eddie, but I ignored your advice. My expectations were as epic as those high-rises and, knowing my grades had earned me a ticket to the beach, to a real school, with real people, I was determined. Yes, I'd dreamed of Paradise City. From the day that postcard arrived I knew I was destined to be there.

And just as I thought the likes of Red Hill ironic in all its flat mundaneness, I came to realise you should never judge a place by its name.

Maybe Uncle Eddie was a genius?

# Chapter One

'Where's Ballantine?'

That was the first time I heard his name. I was sitting outside the principal's office, wedged between Mum and Dad, seeking an audience with Mr Fitzgibbons, the bow tie–wearing man with a balding head and high blood pressure, if his scarlet-tinged complexion was anything to go by.

His flushed face-off was with a woman sitting behind a desk in the opposite room. She had 'Counsellor' mounted in front of her, one of those removable plaques she probably popped into her handbag at the end of each day.

Mr Fitzgibbons' fire-breathing question was met with a sigh and half-hearted shoulder shrug. Obviously not the answer he was looking for as he closed his eyes briefly – as if he was silently counting to three, or perhaps praying for strength. 'That boy will be the death of me,' he said to himself, before turning on his polished heel and heading back into his office, slamming the door so hard that the staff photos along the wall lifted with a violent jolt.

'Geez, looks like someone needs to loosen his bow tie,' murmured Dad from the side of his mouth, in that inconspicuous way people do, thinking no-one would suspect they were speaking at all. We giggled like naughty school kids until Mum elbowed me in the side, cutting us both a warning flash of her steel-blue eyes.

Mum leant forward. 'Nice, Rick. Real nice. Remember, you never get a second chance to make a first impression.'

Poor Mum. She had been brushing off imaginary dust, picking at a loose thread on her cardigan, and fidgeting with a nervous anticipation I had rarely seen in her.

'Relax, Mum, I'm in.'

'Yeah. Relax, Jen, she's in. And what school wouldn't want someone with her grades?' Dad slung his arm around my shoulder, giving me a squeeze. I cringed away from his hug. I was grateful that Dad had warmed to the idea of me coming here, but seriously.

'Cool it, Toto, we're not in Kansas anymore.' I quickly looked up the hall, hoping no-one had seen. It was bad enough that I was going to have my orientation being walked around by the principal while my parents ooohed and ahhhed about the state-of-the-art facilities; I could have thought of less subtle ways to be tortured publicly. On our way to the principal's office my dad had even commented on how impressive the touch-free drinking taps outside the boys' toilets were. I pressed the back of my head against the wall with a sigh.

*Yep, it was going to be a long day.*

I'd had grand visions of walking through the school gates with my cousin Amanda, cool, calm and with an air of mystery as I sauntered under the ornate archway, while Destiny's Child's 'Independent Women' played softly in the background, perhaps with an industrial-strength fan blowing my hair back. A smoke machine would have been a bit much. I was all about keeping my fantasies real.

Mr Fitzgibbons' door whooshed open, shunting me out of my daydream. I blinked into the here and now as he paused, clasping his hands with joy.

'You must be Lexie.' He beamed. 'I am so happy to meet you,' he said, stepping forward and shaking my hand in a series of shoulder-dislocating tugs. I peered past him into his empty office, wondering if this had been the same man from moments before.

Bald, coffee-stained teeth, hideous bow tie. Yep, this was him.

Another none-too-subtle elbow from my mum had me standing instantly to attention. 'That's me,' I managed, smiling politely.

'And you must be Mr and Mrs Atkinson.'

'Oh, please. Call us Rick and Jen.' My dad laughed. Mum laughed. Mr Fitzgibbons laughed – it was just an absolute riot.

'Well, you can call me John, but just this once.' He pointed, laughing at his own zany joke, while he ushered us inside his office and closed the door behind him. 'Please, take a seat.'

I had imagined that the principal's office would be like a luxury penthouse, with all the lurks and perks that come with the job. A large modern space with city views and your own parking spot. Instead, the room was cramped; three mismatched chairs had been wedged in where they didn't fit, giving us barely enough room to awkwardly manoeuvre our way to sit without playing a form of musical chairs. Mr Fitzgibbons didn't seem fazed in the slightest with his less-than-humble abode. I daresay the pot plant by the window and his own private kettle facilities in the corner – with a rather impressive selection of Cup a Soups – made him more than happy with his space, even if the walls were covered in seventies wood panelling and the desk was laminate. I could imagine how desperately my dad was trying to contain himself from stating the obvious.

*Looks like they blew the budget on the drinking fountain.*

But he behaved; he sat stoically straight, resting his elbows on the arms of his chair, and linking his fingers over his stomach. I would have relaxed too but my orange plastic bucket seat didn't have arms. Another budget cut?

What I guessed were family photos stood on Mr Fitzgibbons' desk, pointed away from us. My imagination started to wander. No doubt a picture of a pretty teenage daughter who was not a student at this school, probably privy to a spot as a foreign exchange student in France or something. A son on the brink of manhood, sporting a gleaming metallic grin and acne, most likely an interstate hockey champion. And then there would be a dowdy Mrs Fitzgibbons, who was probably a local tax attorney with sensible shoes and a not-too-sensible bob haircut.

I blinked out of my imaginary Fitzgibbons' family character assessments when Mr Fitzgibbons knocked heavily and rather expectantly on the window of his office, scurrying to pull the blind up without taking an eye out.

'Boys!' He yelled a fine mist onto the glass as he gesticulated towards the yard at a group playing basketball. He pointed to his eyes and then back to the group – a rather threatening mime of 'I'm watching you'.

The boys merely laughed, continuing their game. It was becoming obvious to me that Principal John Fitzgibbons wasn't exactly a respected authority figure at Paradise High.

'I have to say, I was pleasantly surprised when I received your application, Lexie,' he said, picking up a manila folder from on top of his keyboard. He went to casually sit on the edge of his desk, opting for the laidback look. He soon leapt up when it was apparent his weight was too much for the flimsy frame, the desk shifting with a violent jolt that had us all flinching in horror.

He cleared his throat and moved to his chair as if nothing had happened, adjusting his bow tie.

My mum straightened nervously in her chair, as if she was dreading Dad or me losing it at any moment.

I bit my lip, suddenly finding my hands in my lap so incredibly interesting.

'It's certainly been a while since we've had a student of your calibre enrol here at Paradise High, and home schooled too? Simply amazing.'

'We're very proud of Lexie,' said Mum, almost bursting with pride.

'Yeah, she gets the brains from her mother and her devilish good looks from me.'

'Dad,' I whined in embarrassment.

Mr Fitzgibbons leaned back in his seat, his belly laughing so over the top that I could barely stop my brow from curving in disdain. He steepled his fingers like a Bond villain. 'Well, we have an excellent curriculum here, and we need upstanding role models like you, Lexie. We have a healthy debate team, a maths club, drama society, and an SRC committee that I will put you forward for, straightaway.'

With every rattled-off program, committee and club, a little piece of me died. It was like I was no longer in the room. He had gone from addressing me solely to addressing my parents, who were smiling and nodding with glee.

It was almost like I was witnessing everything play out in slow motion as Mr Fitzgibbons jotted down notes into that manila folder with my name on it.

*No-no-no-no . . .*

I didn't want to be a representative of any committee or a team leader of an inter-school debate. I just wanted to be normal, to blend in, to infiltrate the life of a local city slicker. Although I was pretty sure people in the city didn't refer to themselves as city slickers.

'Of course, there is good and bad in every school and there seems to be something rather alluring about the beach that has birthed a generation of delinquent, slacking beach bums,' he said.

I straightened in my seat, finally interested in what he was saying.

'That's why we need leaders in academia, to show the way.'

Yeah, to improve your tertiary statistics, I thought bitterly.

Mr Fitzgibbons mercifully put down his pen, which was slowly destroying my life. He closed the folder, clasping his hands over the cover. 'Now, with your permission, and Lexie's, of course,' he smiled, exposing his off-white teeth, 'I think Lexie would benefit from some of our accelerated classes. From what I can see here, you are quite above the state average. I'm thinking Year Eleven might be a bit of a doddle.'

Dad's chest puffed with pride. 'Well, I guess it's up to what Lexie wants to do, what she feels comfortable with. I mean, it's going to be a bit of a culture shock at first.'

'And as much as all that extra-curricular stuff sounds wonderful,' added Mum, 'I think we best just settle her into the final weeks of Year Eleven first; if all goes well, maybe we can look at those things next year when Lexie comes back for Year Twelve.'

*Oh, how I loved my parents.*

I saw the light in Mr Fitzgibbons' eyes dim. His demeanour changed as he picked up his pen and clicked it in deep thought.

I cleared my throat. 'I would be happy to do accelerated classes; I think it would really build my confidence to do other things.' I smiled sweetly.

Mr Fitzgibbons doodled idly on the corner of my folder, taking in my words before lifting his gaze, a smile emerging, but not quite reaching his eyes. 'So tell me, why Paradise High?' he asked with interest. 'You could have chosen St Sebastian's or Noble Park High, for example. Why here?'

'Lexie's cousin is currently doing her Year Twelve here,' said Mum, nodding her head in approval.

This finally had his attention, pushing him forward in his seat. 'Really? And who might that be?'

'Her name's Amanda, my sister's daughter,' replied Mum.

I'd never seen a rabbit caught in headlights before, or the colour drain from someone's face so quickly. I could actually see the bob of Mr Fitzgibbons' Adam's apple as he closed his mouth and swallowed, staring catatonically at my mum.

'Amanda, Amanda Burnsteen?' He repeated her name as if it left a bad taste in his mouth.

'That's her,' said my dad cheerfully, clearly oblivious that this sudden revelation didn't appear to be welcome news.

'Well, what a small world we live in,' Mr Fitzgibbons half-laughed as he casually opened my folder and scribbled a quick note on the inside.

I leant forward, trying to peer at his writing but he jotted the note of importance so fast and slammed the folder shut so quickly, it made me blink.

Mr Fitzgibbons was about to speak when he was cut off by the sudden sounding of the recess bell, ringing for students to return to their holding cells. Exercise time was over.

'Ah, very good. I suggest that now is the time for you to have a look around, while all the students are settled in class.' He grabbed the folder and stood, moving towards the door. 'Forgive me for not showing you myself but I have to see to an urgent matter.' He opened the door, sweeping his hand out to the hall.

Mum, Dad and I stood, throwing uncertain looks at one another as we exited the principal's office. He shook Dad's, mine, and then Mum's hands quickly, smiling and thanking us for our time – good luck, goodbye. It was like Charlie had gone from inheriting the chocolate factory to being dismissed by Willy Wonka himself. We were dazed and confused by the change in Mr Fitzgibbons as he looked past us to make eye contact with the school counsellor, who simply shook her head.

He sighed heavily before returning to his office and closing the door.

We stood there for a long while, stunned, before Dad spoke. 'Well, that went well.'

Mum and I looked at each other, laughing unsurely, as we headed down the hall, the bell drowning out our chatter with its second and final warning followed by a PA announcement as we descended the stairs.

'Luke Ballantine, report to the principal's office immediately.'

And with a small curve of my mouth, I laughed, thinking that Mr Fitzgibbons' day was about to get a whole lot worse.

# Chapter Two

Does anything say family better than rocking up with a bucket of KFC for dinner?

I don't think so, and to make the deal even sweeter, yep, a giant tub of coleslaw; it was the least we could do, plus Aunty Karen was not known for her culinary skills.

The Best Western was not situated in the most prestigious of locations; a fence line of skip bins sat right outside our motel room, and there was an angry dog barking constantly in one of the suburban backyards we so charmingly over-looked. Still, it was the budget-savvy thing to do, even if there were probably chalked outlines of bodies on the pavement around the corner and yellow police tape cordoning off a part of the neighbourhood.

I watched on as Mum pumped hand sanitiser liberally in her palm for the hundredth time that day, and it didn't escape my attention that Dad was clicking the central locking on our doors every time we hopped in the car.

I knew Mum and Dad were massively out of their comfort zone, and I had to admit this wasn't exactly what I had envisioned as Dad cruised past the fibro-sheeted houses and another laneway, thick with coloured graffiti. It was gritty and lively, for sure, but seeing piled-up mattresses and TV sets on the nature strips for hard rubbish collection day – oh God, at least I hoped that's what it was for – didn't exactly scream Paradise. I quickly wiped the thought from my mind. This wasn't Paradise City, this wasn't the hub of my dreams, this was merely a suburb of the city itself: an unfortunate introduction because my parents were always a little tight with the purse strings.

I stretched forward from the back seat. 'Tell me again, why aren't we staying at Aunty Karen and Uncle Peter's?'

'There's just not enough room for us all to stay there,' insisted Mum, massaging the disinfectant into the back of her hands.

It was so great to finally be here, and to actually step foot in what was to be my school, but I was saving most of my excitement for seeing my cousin Amanda again. She was only a few months older than me, but I always had this kind of worshipping thing about Amanda. Before they moved to Paradise City, they only lived a three-hour drive from Red Hill in Sunnyvale, where we used to share birthdays and Christmas holidays. We would play Barbies, bruise our ribs sliding along the slip 'n' slide in our backyard, become death-defying stuntmen by tipping our trampoline on its side before charging from across the yard, latching onto it and pushing it over to slam to the ground again. We used to host our own radio station by recording our voices on cassette tapes, or freak each other out by telling ghost stories with torches pressed up against our chins under the blankets. Amanda was the sister I never had. When her family moved away, it was like they had taken a piece of my childhood with them, and Red Hill suddenly became unbearable with no option of an escape. Aside from that first postcard she had sent and a few phone calls, Amanda had slowly drifted away from me. She was busy with her new friends in her new life, and why wouldn't she be? I mean, they lived in Paradise, literally. I would often comment on her Myspace page, a window into her amazing existence of linked arms around friends and pouty pictures at the beach with heart-shaped glasses on. Long gone were the Barbie dolls and afternoons spent swooning over pictures of Jonathan Taylor Thomas. Amanda had moved on. Whereas I was just the same old Lexie. Until now.

'So, how much longer?' My insides flipped with giddy excitement.

'Are you so eager to be rid of us?' My mum looked at me pointedly in the rearview mirror.

'Of course not,' I lied. 'But I start school on Monday and I need to get my bearings.'

As in, I needed to grill Amanda about who's who and the dos and don'ts of real high school society. Having her as my wing woman would be an invaluable asset if I was going to fit in and furthermore convince my parents that I could live out my final high school year here.

'You'll have plenty of time,' Mum said.

'Time for what?' asked Dad, as usual, coming in on the end of a conversation, while he tuned into the cricket on the radio.

'Lexie's worried her life is flashing before her eyes.'

'Every day is a wasted day,' I groaned, flinging myself back into my seat.

'Don't wish your life away, Lexie.'

*Pfft, what life?*

'Well, I wouldn't say today was a waste; you got to look around the school at least,' said Mum.

I cringed at the memory.

My dad winking and jovially saying g'day to each student he passed in the corridor. More often than not, people would snigger with their friends or look back at him as if he was a mutant, or more accurately, some kind of country bumpkin. He might as well have been wearing a cowboy hat, chewing on a piece of straw. Disguising my mortification as starvation I cut the walk-around short, insisting that we please go . . . now!

Orientation: disaster.

I much preferred my chances with Amanda. I mean, I had to remain the mysterious new girl. I wanted my entrance to be, like my dad would say, bigger than Ben Hur. I sat in the back seat dreaming of slow-motion entrances, whispers and stares from hot surfer boys.

'So, is Aunty Karen going to be home by the time we get there?' I asked.

'Ah, yes, she took the day off for us.'

'Bloody hell, we'll never hear the end of that,' Dad said, rolling his eyes.

The fact that Mum and Dad had pulled the 'we need our own space' card when checking into our motel was not lost on me. And the fact they thought I was immune to their grown-up politics was, well, insulting. I'd innocently earwigged on enough conversations between Mum and Dad to know that there was a definite divide between Mum and her younger sister.

Nothing more telling than Mum's admission. 'They're just trying to keep up with the Joneses.'

'Joneses? They think they *are* the bloody Joneses,' said Dad, laughing.

The differences were pretty clear.

Mum married a country boy.

Aunty Karen married a city boy.

Mum was asset rich but cash poor.

Aunty Karen was just rich.

Mum drove a Patrol.

Aunty Karen drove a Volvo.

Mum's fingernails were chipped, broken from helping Dad on the farm.

Aunty Karen's French-tipped nails dialled for a cleaner to clean her two-storey house.

Worlds apart and none of it had seemed so obvious until their big move to the coast.

'Doesn't Aunty Karen have some big high-flying government job?' I asked with interest, causing Dad to nearly spit out his drink over the steering wheel as he looked at Mum.

'Where did you hear that?' Mum's brows creased.

'I heard Nan telling Mrs Muir at the supermarket.'

'Oh, bloody hell.' Dad shook his head.

'Rick!' Mum warned.

'No, Jen. If Lexie is going to be immersed in this world she needs to know the truth. Aunty Karen works at the local shire council as a glorified receptionist answering phones and taking rates payments. She lives purely on credit that her long-suffering husband has to work seven days a week to pay for.'

*Whoa, go Dad!*

All this I had kind of gathered, but still, Dad always liked to tell it like it was, while Mum chose to live in the 'if you don't have anything nice to say, don't say anything at all' category.

I was somewhere in between, myself.

Mum sighed, clenching the bridge of her nose as if warding off a migraine. 'I'm not doing this now, Rick,' Mum warned.

And when Dad didn't let it go, I took it as a sign to dig out my ear plugs, wedging one in each ear and pressing play, spinning one of my Triple J's Hottest 100 CDs, circa 1995, to life. It was a wonder it still played at all considering the number of times I had listened to it over and over again. The chilling waves of Natalie Merchant's 'Carnival' washed over me, just as the flashes of light from the setting sun over the city blinded me in patches through the buildings. Graffiti-clad fences morphed into bustling streets of Chinese takeaway and two-dollar shops, divided up with traffic lights on every block. The animated gestures of my parents as they continued to argue seemed to play out in slow motion compared to the fast-moving surrounds at peak hour. I pressed my temple against the window, gazing up at some palm trees, a long stretch of them dotted along a concrete jungle. Were we getting nearer to the ocean, I wondered? If we turned a corner would it suddenly be there on the horizon? With no real idea where we were headed or how far away we were, the city scene soon blended into a long stretch of industrial building sites. Long gone were the mystical, towering palm trees, and hello, Bunnings and tyre wholesalers.

The car interior smelt like Colonel Sanders and his secret herbs and spices, which were probably cementing their stench into my hair and clothes. I sniffed the fabric of my top. Impossible to tell. I wasn't sure why a part of me was suddenly so nervous. This was family and we were going over for dinner, just like we had when I was little. But I was always amazed how quickly things changed, how people got older and time moved on, almost as fast as the ever-changing neighbourhoods we drove through. I straightened with interest, noting the very obvious differences and feel of the area we were heading into.

Money.

Single fibro housing commission shacks were exchanged for actual bricks and mortar – some with their own strategically placed palm trees. A good test of wealth, it seemed, was whether you had an impressive concrete driveway and a remote-controlled garage door. We had definitely entered into that territory. A far cry from Red Hill, where fortune was dependent on how many acres you had or how large your rented TV was. This was more like the Paradise I had envisioned: kids playing cricket on the street; a group of women power walking in their three-quarter lycra pants and sunvisor caps; a man hand-mowing his minuscule front yard with earmuffs on.

My heart almost leapt out of my chest when I spotted a surfboard mounted on the wall of an open garage. We had to be close, we just had to be, and as I quickly wound down the window and raised my face up to the sky, the first thing that hit me was the glorious smell of the ocean. Ocean and sunshine, thick in the air that whipped the wisps of hair into my eyes.

Dad turned in to a long sweeping road to the right and just as I was about to announce the assault on my senses to my parents, there it was. There in the distance, as we drove along the winding road, was a deep blue mass of water, cresting up to meet the sand. Just as quickly as it was there it was gone again, as Dad made another sharp right, powering up a ridge of bitumen into another street. I spun around in my seat, grinning like a fool at what was slowly disappearing behind me. Now this was Paradise.

# Chapter Three

'We're here!' Dad sighed.

I love it how parents state the obvious, as if pulling into a driveway and turning the engine off wasn't a giveaway. And of all the houses, in all the streets to pull up in front of, I was oh so happy it was this one. I opened my door, slowly sliding out of the back seat, my eyeline following the impressive Colorbond roofline of the second storey.

Large concrete drive, double automated garage and trees that were actually manicured into balls. Now *that* was luxurious. Somehow, parking behind Aunty Karen's shiny Volvo station wagon in our dust-covered Patrol with a bucket of chicken in hand definitely screamed intruder. I would have let the feeling of unease consume me if it wasn't for the high-pitched screams that were closing in on us.

'Oh my God. OH MY GOD!' Aunty Karen charged out of the front door, arms outstretched.

I didn't have time to process the incoming crazed aunty before I was mooshed with a big set of boobs in my face and engulfed in a backbreaking bear hug. I needn't have worried about passive KFC fumes, my eyes literally watered from the overpowering scent of Aunty Karen's expensive perfume, splashed liberally in the abyss of her cleavage, no doubt. Her gold bracelets jangled as she rocked me from side to side.

'Oh, look how you've grown,' she cried, pulling back only to cup my face and mush my cheeks in between her meticulously manicured hands. 'Oh, Jen, she could be a model,' she said, turning to Mum, who managed a pained smile.

Aunty Karen's eyes fell to the bucket of chicken Mum was holding. 'Oh, you brought KFC, how hysterical,' she said, laughing.

I could tell Dad was trying to avoid the theatrics by busying himself with the luggage.

'Oh, Rick, don't trouble yourself with that. Peter! Peter, come out here and help Rick,' Aunty Karen called out.

There were two things I remembered in particular about my Uncle Peter: one, he was very tall; two, he was not a conversationalist. He was kind of like Mr Darcy, without an endearing happily ever after.

My dad, who was equally tortured by Mum's family, at least had the tact to disguise his sighs and inner burning contempt. Uncle Peter Burnsteen did not. He emerged from his lavish abode with a deep sigh and a weary expression. 'Hello, Jen.' He managed a head nod to my mum. 'Rick.' Handshake.

I wasn't exactly a kid anymore, so a hair ruffle would have just been plain awkward, but I would have given anything for that head rub instead of the mis-timed half hug he gave me, only for the button of his sleeve to snag in my hair as he pulled away.

'Ouch!'

'Oh, um, it's, um, stuck, bloody hell, hang on a sec.' He unravelled my hair and sidestepped away to help Dad with the bags.

Nope. Nothing awkward about that.

Aunty Karen linked her arm through Mum's. 'I'm so happy you're here,' she beamed.

As if reading my mind, Mum looked around. 'Where's Amanda?'

Aunty Karen's smile dimmed. 'Oh.' She turned around, looking up at the top window. I followed her gaze in time to notice there was a slightly parted curtain, which quickly fell back into place as we looked up.

'She's on the computer. Peter, did you tell Amanda to come down?'

Uncle Peter merely scoffed in reply as he took a suitcase and walked back into the house.

Aunty Karen laughed as a way to disguise her husband's lack of social graces. 'Come on, let's get you inside.'

Aunty Karen never drew breath as we walked up the curving terracotta-tiled path, past the ball trees, the immaculately kept ankle-high box hedge and manicured lawn. She sported black heels that click-clacked along the walkway and a figure-hugging charcoal dress with a black belt fastened under her ample bosom; her blonde, curly hair was pulled up into a French twist with enough hair lacquer to put a hole in the ozone layer. Her lipstick was bright, bold like her smoky eyeliner and bronzer. Okay, so maybe describing her makes her sound a bit like a circus clown, but Aunty Karen was very glam and I think my mum felt it, too, because she handed me the chicken bucket to carry. I walked behind her as we followed Aunty Karen to the house.

Mum pulled at her cardigan, adjusted it just like she had waiting outside the principal's office. I felt sad knowing that she was feeling uncomfortable being led into her sister's home for the first time, wearing a denim skirt and Diana Ferrari sandals.

I looked back at Dad, who was carrying the last of my bags. He shook his head in dismay and I had to look away, fearing I would burst into a fit of giggles and earn not one but two filthy looks from the women in front.

We stepped into an enormous entrance hall, with glossed white tiles that flowed through the entire living space. The first thing that hit me was the huge staircase with its wood and wrought iron banister. The second thing that snapped us to attention was the shrill screaming.

'Amanda Nicole Burnsteen, get your toosh down here this instant,' Aunty Karen yelled to the great above.

There was a faint ringing in my ears – my aunty's voice bounced off the walls of the large space – and I swear I saw the floral arrangement vibrate. Yeah, there was a floral arrangement.

Uncle Peter sat with his arms casually resting on the back of the couch, the king of the castle, as he watched cricket on their humungous flat-screen. He didn't so much as acknowledge us as he hissed and jeered at the TV, sipping his Crown Lager. It was the most animated I think I had ever seen him.

Mum motioned with a not-too-subtle nod for Dad to go over and do the man thing and bond over sports. Poor Dad. I could see he would have much preferred to hang with us girls, until Aunty Karen clapped her hands together with joy.

'I'll give you a tour of the house.'

'Um, yeah, I think I'll just check the score.' Dad rubbed the back of his head, stepping away from the luggage he'd left by the door, and headed for the black leather couch to bond with Uncle Peter.

•

I sipped on my Coke, sitting at the large breakfast bar in the kitchen, finding it hard to imagine that this was going to be my new home, that I, Lexie (no middle name) Atkinson, was going to be chillin' in a two-storey mansion with its own pool, and sea views from the top floor. Okay, so it was from their master bedroom; still, the views were there and the beach was near, and that was good enough for me. One of the rooms we hadn't ventured into on our tour was Uncle Peter's study, and we also skipped the one place I had wanted to go to most of all – to see Amanda. But as Aunty Karen gave my mum the lowdown on the wallpaper they had imported from abroad for the powder room, and the price of the Axminster carpet in the master bedroom (Aunty Karen loved to name-drop price tags), we had simply walked past the one closed door upstairs, the one I lingered near in the hope that maybe Amanda might emerge.

And almost as if my wishful thinking had willed it, Aunty Karen's voice broke off as we heard the distant thud of foot-steps coming down the staircase.

'Finally,' she muttered, moving from behind the breakfast bar and out into the lounge. 'Amanda!' she called out.

I tried to lean back on my stool, craning my neck to see a figure appear at the bottom of the steps, but Aunty Karen's body blocked the way.

'Amanda, come say hello.' But aside from the footsteps and then the loud slamming of a door, there was going to be no welcome party.

Aunty Karen breathed in deeply, readying herself before she spun around with a brilliant smile.

'Is she all right?' Mum asked, her uncertain gaze looking towards the direction of the slam.

'Oh, yes, she's just tired.' Aunty Karen waved her words away before clicking her heels along the tiles and, without skipping a beat, picked up her conversation, explaining to Mum about the marbled bench tops.

Maybe I wasn't as easily distracted or, more to the point, couldn't care less about imported Italian marble, and as I continued to look towards the direction in which Amanda had disappeared without so much as a word, I couldn't help but feel a little . . . worried.

Aunty Karen must have taken in my troubled expression – chewing on my bottom lip was a bit of a giveaway.

'I know!' she said, curving her manicured brow and sharing a devious look between me and Mum. 'Why don't you go see Amanda? She's dying to see you, you just need to break the ice; I mean, it's been so long.'

My eyes flicked to Mum, who seemed to nod her approval.
'I don't know . . .'

'Here.' Aunty Karen spun around, opening the pantry and grabbing a giant-sized packet of salt and vinegar Samboy chips. 'Take these to her and she'll be a friend for life.'

'Go on,' mouthed Mum.

I thought about it for a moment, before allowing the giddiness to take over.

*Stop being such a sook, Lexie. It's only Amanda.*

She was probably just as excited and nervous as I was. Of course I'd break the ice. We had so much catching up to do, and I had so much to learn about this alien planet I had landed on.

I smiled, grabbing the chips with much gusto.

*I'm going in.*

The hall was more like a wing – a long extension into a separate part of the house – and having been given the grand tour, it was clear that upstairs was the parents' retreat and down here was the teenagers' domain. Even that in itself was really cool. Amanda's older brother, Gus, had long since moved out and was off at uni, which basically left Amanda an only child. With so much at your doorstep, I doubt there was ever a dull moment in her life. I was bursting out of my skin to find out. The muffled beat of loud music pounded through the door at the end of the hall. I wondered if she would even hear me. I knocked gently at first, and then harder a moment later.

'Amanda? It's me, Le–' Before I even had a chance to finish my sentence, the bedroom door was whipped open. My fist lingered in the air, my eyes widening as my senses were assaulted with the ear-piercing noise – I think it was music – that was pouring out of her room. But more than that, I stood, frozen, my catatonic gaze etching its way up and down the girl who stood before me: tall, slender, with long flowing hair, heavy eye makeup and a lip piercing. She wore a midriff top, exposing her pierced belly button, and yoga pants low on her hips. The only recognisable part of her was her big blue eyes. The very ones that were glaring down at me as she stood there, her hip cocked to the side and her arms crossed. She raised her brows with impatience, as if to say, 'May I help you?'

Did she not recognise me? I hadn't changed at all, not a bit. Taller, yes, but that was about it. I couldn't fathom the creature that stood before me. What had it done with my cousin?

My mouth gaped, trying to speak, to construct a single sentence, but all I could manage was to hold up my peace offering and croak, 'Chip?'

Amanda scoffed, before snatching the packet from my hands, tearing it open and shoving chips into her gob, crunching loudly. She looked at me, shaking her head in dismay. 'Tragic,' she said through a mouthful of chips, before she laughed and stepped back into her room, kicking the door shut with her foot.

I let out a breath, one I wasn't even aware I was holding. I moved away from the door, pressing my back to the wall, blinking rapidly as I tried to process what the hell had just happened.

This was a definite game changer.

# Chapter Four

I couldn't believe it.

Dinnertime arrived, when we all came together to feast on not-KFC – that was somehow 'shelved' by Aunty Karen for baked salmon over a bed of couscous and Mediterranean vegetables. My heart sank, testing the gravelly mound of what looked like sand. The meal wasn't the thing that I was having trouble accepting, though; it was the fact that Amanda, my fire-breathing cousin from only mere moments before, had emerged out of her cave like a beautiful butterfly. I'm not saying she transformed in any physical way as she still had on the belly-exposing tank top and yoga pants, but she was sporting a beaming smile and open arms to my parents. Double blinking and flashing her white teeth at their typical aunty and uncle praises. 'Look at you.' 'Haven't you grown?' Blah, blah, blah.

*Spare me.*

The only other person who didn't seem to be buying it was Uncle Peter, who was looking at his daughter like he didn't have a clue who she was. Not that I think he actually cared. He stood up and opened the door to his stainless steel fridge and grabbed another beer. Probably to numb the pain.

Amanda laughed and smiled and helped her mother with bringing food over to the table; the only time I ever saw a crack in Amanda's facade was on the odd occasion when her eyes met mine and her expression dimmed somewhat.

I frowned. What had she said? Tragic? Was she calling *me* tragic?

I adjusted my top, looking down and trying to work out how a white V-neck and denim mini could be tragic or offensive. I had deliberately gone shopping for a new summer wardrobe knowing I was coming here, and just as I straightened my top, I froze.

*Oh my God.*

I was fidgeting self-consciously like my mother. Oh no, that *was* tragic. My heart sank; I had never felt so incredibly out of place. Even my dad had begun to relax after a few beers. He had managed to strike up a conversation with Uncle Peter about cricket and Mum and Aunty Karen, well, after a few red wines, they were thick as thieves. They may have been worlds apart in a materialistic sense, but they would always have one thing in common – their childhood. A burst of laughter sounded from the kitchen as Aunty Karen topped up Mum's glass. They were talking about old boyfriends or something cringeworthy like that. I turned to look at their carefree, flushed expressions; tears were literally falling from my mum's eyes as Aunty Karen fought to breathe.

That was what I had hoped to have with Amanda, that no matter how much we had changed, we would always have a childhood to cling to, that even though the Barbie dolls were long gone, and yoga pants and piercings were now in vogue, all that could be put aside; we were blood, that meant more than the aesthetics of someone. But there was just one teeny, tiny issue I could foresee being a complication. The

Amanda Burnsteen, the one who sat across from me, smugly shovelling a fork of couscous into her mouth, this Amanda was an absolute bitch!

•

After having said goodnight to my parents, who were too tipsy to drive back to the motel and were looking at a night crashed out in Uncle Peter's office, I readied myself for bed.

I held my toothbrush and toothpaste to my chest like a shield as I stood in the doorway and stared in horror at my new sleeping quarters. In. Amanda's. Room.

'It's only a single bed, but it's a king single we bought from Freedom.' Aunty Karen gave me the décor rundown as she turned down the sheets. It was a beautiful bed, expensive-quality cover striped with greens and blues, nestled under a big window on the opposite side of the room from Amanda's bed. But it didn't matter how beautifully it had been made, I still got this sense that a certain someone was not going to be pleased about this and, as if conjuring her out of my nightmares, Amanda appeared, walking past me, bumping my shoulder as she walked into her bedroom. Yep, definitely not happy.

And neither was I. I'd kind of assumed with Gus having gone to uni, that there would be a spare room now. But apparently his room was sacred and off limits, used as some kind of shrine to their son for whenever he returned, which from what I'd heard, wasn't very often. Surely with such a big house you would think that there would be a space for me? A nook, a cranny, a closet? Anywhere that wouldn't put me at risk of getting smothered in my sleep. Apparently there was another room but that was Aunty Karen's 'studio'. That was her space for whatever phase she went through each month. I had spotted a yoga mat, walking machine, beading station, a potter's wheel from her stint at clay-pot making, and painting materials: a real mishmash of hobbies. Obviously Aunty Karen had commitment issues.

I glanced at Amanda; she had peeled her cover back and jumped into bed, wedging her ear plugs in her ears and turning the volume up.

Looked like there was going to be no late-night ghost stories like the days of old; the only nightmare I would be having tonight would be the thought of my parents actually leaving me here in the morning.

'There you go!' Aunty Karen stepped back, admiring her handiwork. 'You'll sleep like a baby.'

*What? Wet, hungry and awake, screaming my lungs out every hour?*

I smiled. My aunty was trying to make me feel at home; at least someone was.

She came over to me, sweeping my hair from my shoulder. 'Now tomorrow, we'll sort out your uniform for Monday and get you any last-minute things you might need for your big day.'

I pooled all my effort into smiling. 'Great.'

'Oh, I am so happy you're here, Lexie,' she said, embracing me in a huge perfumed hug. 'Don't stress about Amanda, she'll get used to it,' she whispered into my ear before letting me go with a cheek pinch.

Aunty Karen made her way, well, zigzagged her way over to Amanda's bed. It was a few red wines later.

'Goodnight my angel . . . MWAH!'

'Ugh, get off me, Mum,' Amanda yelled.

'Aw, I love you, too,' she laughed, slapping her daughter on the bum as she struggled to get off the bed, zigzagging her way out the door, pausing at the light switch until I slipped into my bed and under the covers.

'Night, girls,' she said, flicking off the light, plunging the room into darkness and closing the door.

I lifted the cover up to my chin, much like a child would do to ward off creatures that go bump in the night. The blackness wasn't entirely consuming; a streetlight outside cast a muted glow through the curtain of the window I lay under. It was the silence that was suffocating. Back in the day, Amanda and I would have pulled our mattresses to the floor, wedging them together and making one giant springy island. We would crawl under our blankets with torches and talk about what we wanted to be when we grew up or about our super secret crushes. Now all that pierced through the dark was the distant, high-pitched noise of the music that was being drummed into Amanda's ears – that and . . . laughing?

*Was she laughing?*

I cocked my head, listening intently, thinking maybe it was just the music playing tricks on me, but it wasn't. Amanda was laughing all right, almost giggling like a school girl. I peered over to her bed.

*Was she laughing at me?*

When I hitched myself onto one elbow to squint her way, there she was. Her smiling face, illuminated by the screen of her mobile.

*Whoa. Amanda had a mobile phone. I didn't even own one.*

Her thumbs made clicking sounds in the dark as she lay on her back, listening to music and texting one of her BFFs, no doubt.

I don't know what it was about that sight, but it made it crystal clear that she didn't in any way, shape or form want me involved in her life. I felt a heaviness in my heart.

I settled back down in my thousand thread-count sheets, and brand-new orthopaedic mattress, and tried to not let every giggle, every click wind me down further into sadness. But as I stared out the window, focusing on the glow of the streetlight, I could feel hot tears well in my eyes, pooling and falling down my temples as I came to a sudden realisation.

Paradise was a lie.

•

It didn't take long for sleep to claim me. The build-up, anticipation, travel and orientation had me bone tired. It might have been the luxurious feather-top mattress as well. I could have slept for a thousand years; well, until I awoke with a foot to my head.

I thought I was dreaming when I felt the searing pain of my hair being ripped out by the roots, my bed springing up and down with violent jolts, before being hit with the sound of scraping metal and a gush of wind. I went to scream as my hand flew up to my trapped hair. My scream was muffled as a hand clamped down on my mouth; plunged fiercely out of my slumber, my eyes blinked wide, my heart threatening to punch a hole through my chest, my nostrils flaring at the sight of Amanda kneeling on my bed.

'Shhhh.' She scowled down at me. 'If you so much as make a sound, I swear to God,' she warned.

'Amanda, come on, let's go,' a hushed voice sounded. My eyes snapped to where the voice had come from, the opened window.

'I'm coming,' she called, momentarily peeling her eyes from me and then back again. She pressed her finger to her lips to mime a warning for silence. When I nodded quickly she slowly lifted her hand from my mouth, watching me like a hawk, warily waiting to see if I would scream or not. I desperately wanted to, I wanted to shout the house down, lash out at her for scaring the shit out of me, for stepping on my head, for pulling my hair. Instead I sat up, pushing myself back and away from her against my bedhead, brushing the hair out of my eyes and staring daggers at Amanda.

'Well, well, well . . . what do we have here then?' A pair of elbows rested on the aluminium frame of the opened sill, a head poking through the window with a cheeky smile and eyes that trailed over me in curious assessment. I pulled the blankets around me, still trying to catch my breath after such a rude awakening.

The boy canted his head towards me. 'Is this her?' he asked Amanda.

Amanda ignored him, readying herself to stand, before locking her burning eyes on me. 'If you breathe a word of this to anyone, I will make your life a living hell!'

She put as much diva-esque emphasis on her warning as she could, most likely because she had an audience. My brows lowered, matching her murderous gaze as she tried to intimidate me; I couldn't contain it any longer.

'Oh, fuck off!'

A burst of laughter came from outside the window, not from the boy standing there, who merely looked on with an open mouth – the loud outburst of deep-bellied, surprised laughter came from behind him. As I peered past boy one, my eyes rested on boy number two. He leant against the house, his shoulders vibrating as he laughed; his profile was highlighted by the glow of the streetlight, and the first thing that struck me was the deep dimple that formed when he smiled. I wondered if his other cheek matched and desperately wanted him to turn around, to look my way. But instead he remained casually slouched beside the house in the semi-shadows, arms crossed against his chest; he was tall, lean and maybe it was the darkness but his hair was dark and ruffled in a devil-may-care way. The only thing that snapped me out of my trance was what would be the second biggest surprise of the night.

Amanda shifted her focus from me and glared towards the tall boy in the shadows; she moved to grab onto the edge of the opened window as boy number one lifted his arms to help her. She was midway out when she addressed the still-laughing boy: 'Shut up, Ballantine!'

# Chapter Five

Ballantine?

  Ballantine . . . Ballantine.

The name rolled over in my mind, time and time again. It had been on repeat ever since the previous night, when I'd stared wide-eyed and stupefied as Amanda snuck out the window and disappeared with the two boys: admittedly, two hot boys. Even in the shadows I could tell that; there was no mistaking the lure of that dimple, and that laugh; the laugh that was a direct result of me telling Amanda where to go. A part of me cringed at the memory, of being such a gutter mouth. Seriously, what would they think of me? What would bad-boy Ballantine, who stood up the principal, think of me? Well, at least he found it funny, much to Amanda's displeasure. I, of course, wondered what my new life would be like now, how she would most certainly make my life a living hell. When the sun rose in the morning, I had tentatively rolled over to squint through sleepy eyes, and there she was. Twisted in a blanketed cocoon, fast asleep. I hadn't even heard her come back in. Oh God, had she climbed back through the window? I blinked at the curtains in horror. Had the boys helped her back in and looked down at me drooling onto my pillow?

I pulled the covers over my head.

*Ugh, I hated sharing her room!*

But then the memory of the smiling boy in the shadows would pop into my mind and somehow that very thought seemed to trump all the negative. My chest puffed out with pride every time I recalled it.

As my spoon clinked against the porcelain of my cereal bowl at breakfast, I remembered the boy in the shadows. Showering, soaping my hair into a bubbly, foamy hive, I remembered the boy in the shadows. Standing on a chair as my mum fixed the hem on my school uniform, I smiled a small smile, thinking of the dimple in the dark and just as I was lost in the dreamy perfection of the memory, a half-asleep, probably half-hungover Amanda shuffled herself into the lounge, looking like death. I lifted my chin with a knowing glint in my eyes, as she sneered my way and went to the pantry.

'Done!' Mum announced. 'Go take a look.'

I hopped down from the chair, running towards the downstairs bathroom mirror. My school dress fitted perfectly – the blue and white checked uniform had me grinning like a fool.

I couldn't believe this was happening. I was going to go to a real school, with lockers, school socials and canteen lunches, and real people who passed notes to each other in class. I had agonised over so many decisions: hair up? Hair down? Half up? My hair was not straight enough to be dead straight and didn't have enough of a curl to be curly. It was just ash-blonde, and kinky. Dull. My nose was not too offensive; it kind of had a ski-jump quality about it that I didn't entirely hate. I was glad I got my mum's nose and not my dad's bulbous one. I had a light smattering of freckles across my nose that I hated. Mum bought me some powder concealer and I didn't go anywhere without a dusting of it across my face; it also helped make me look a bit less pasty. Seeing myself next to Amanda or Aunty Karen – heck, anyone in Paradise – I was painfully aware of how pale I was. My skin was almost translucent in comparison. My mum would tell me I had a peaches-and-cream complexion, like that of an English maiden. I likened it more to Casper the ugly-arsed Ghost! Still, it would now be my summer mission to inject some colour into my life.

I'd posed a million ways in front of the mirror, testing out a million different hypothetical scenarios. 'Hey, I'm Lexie. What's up?' 'Hi, I'm Lex.' I was literally yanking out strands of hair every time I readjusted the elastic band into a new style; I decided to quit while I was ahead, rocking up to school with a comb over would not be a hot look.

'So what do you think?' My mum's voice startled me, as I caught her beaming smile in the reflection.

'Geez, Muuum.' I clutched my chest, reeling in the pounding of my heart.

'Sorry, love,' she said, wrapping her arms around my shoulders. 'You look so lovely.'

A smile tugged at the corners of my mouth. 'How cool is the uniform?'

'Pretty cool,' she agreed.

'Do you think I'll be the only girl at Paradise High who is really excited about things like uniforms, and school bags and lockers?' I laughed.

'I think that's exactly why Paradise High is going to be so lucky to have you. You've already scored an A plus for enthusiasm.'

Ha! I thought, what would Amanda score then? The simple task of breathing in and out seemed to inconvenience her.

Dad appeared in the bathroom doorway, folding his arms across his barrelled chest and drinking in the sight of his girls. He wouldn't say anything but you could tell what he was thinking. I was half expecting him to relay some kind of Dad humour like, 'I'm gonna need a shotgun.' Or 'You take after your old man.' So when he finally spoke and said, 'It's time to go, luv,' I swung around so fast my ponytail whooshed across Mum's face, momentarily blinding her.

'What, already? No, you can't go,' I said in dismay, my eyes bulging and alarmed. I knew today was the day my parents were leaving for home but, I don't know, I just didn't expect the reality of it.

'We've got to, Lexie. It's a long drive and I have to go to work on Monday,' Dad reasoned, his eyes sad.

'But you guys haven't even been to the beach yet; you can't come to Paradise City and not go to the beach. That's just wrong.'

Mum stepped forward, brushing my fringe from my forehead. 'We'll be back, and when we are, you can show us around.'

Mum was implying I would what? Be a local by the time they came back for school holidays, in eleven weeks time? Heat began to creep up my neck again. Seventy-seven whole days coexisting with Amanda, of her hissing and glaring at me, stepping on my hair each and every night. I tried to not let my inner turmoil bubble to the surface.

Instead I smiled, hoping it didn't seem so forced. 'I will, I'll plan a whole agenda for when you come back. Surfing, boogie boarding, beach volleyball, rollerblading.' I counted out the activities on my fingers.

'Oh, for sure; hang gliding, body piercings, you name it,' Dad agreed.

•

After the initial chaotic runabout that seemed rather indic-
ative of the way the Burnsteen household operated, we were
walking Mum and Dad out to the car, doing the usual pouted,
sobbing goodbyes. Actually, that was just Aunty Karen.

'Oh, you sure you can't stay a little longer?' She shuffled
in small, heeled steps towards Mum, throwing her arms
dramatically around her. I was still a bit perplexed as to why
she was wearing heels on a weekend.

I tried to put my big-girl pants on, to not let my mum's
tears affect me and make me want to jump in the car
and go home with them. This would be the first time in,
well, ever, that I would be living away from my parents
for anything longer than a weekend. And now they would
soon be gone and I would be gloriously free, living it up in
the city: new start, new friends, new me. It was the life I'd
imagined I wanted. The only thing was I just wasn't feeling
it yet. I shook off the thought, thinking it would be different
once I started school. That would change everything.

In true Uncle Peter style, he stood idly by, his body
language making it clear that he would prefer to be anywhere
else right now instead of at painful family farewells. Amanda
had said her goodbyes before heading out to who knew where
for the afternoon. Maybe to hang with the boys from last
night? My mind flicked back to Ballantine.

My parents were behaving as if they were sending me off
to the warfront or something. Hugging me so fiercely, tears
staining my mum's cheeks. Even Dad was all misty-eyed as
he focused intently on straightening the car aerial.

'Don't cry. You'll see me in school holidays,' I said, trying
to pacify them in some small way.

Mum gave a small and totally unconvincing smile. 'Home just won't be the same.'

'Are you kidding? It will be even better. Less laundry to do, no more nagging me to keep my room clean or me whingeing that I don't want to watch the ABC. You're going to love it.'

'She has a point, Jen,' said Dad, 'I'm kind of regretting not opting for boarding school earlier.'

I tilted my head as if to say 'Ha-ha' but it was exactly the distraction Mum needed, and I felt less sad about her being upset, because I knew five minutes into their journey Dad would have her laughing again. He was good like that.

'Oh, Lexie. Wait a sec, I almost forgot,' my mum said, sniffing as she moved to the passenger seat and grabbed her handbag, delving into the contents.

My interest piqued; the bag search usually meant money, and any donations to the Lexie Atkinson fund were always greatly appreciated.

'Here, take this.' Mum held out her fist, indicating I should hold out my hand.

Ooh, what's this, I wondered, offering my open hand eagerly as Mum dropped something into my palm.

My brows narrowed, my smile slowly falling as I studied what sat in my hand.

*A whistle?*

'Um, did you sign me up for some sporting team I don't know about?' I eyed the whistle with disdain.

'It's a safety whistle; you wear it around your neck and if anyone tries to mug you, you can alert the neighbourhood you're in trouble.'

*Oh my God. Was this a joke?*

When I didn't so much as move, Mum took it upon herself to step forward, picking it up from my palm and looping the cord around my neck. I looked down at it, studying it with disbelief.

'Why didn't you just ask Uncle Eddie if I could borrow his safety vest?' I asked, horror lining my face.

'Come on, Lexie, you're not in Red Hill anymore.' Dad adopted his disciplinary voice.

Thank God for that, I wanted to say. I wanted to throw the biggest mind-blowing tantrum of my entire seventeen years, but instead I took a deep breath, and tucked the whistle under my t-shirt before Amanda came home. They held all the cards here and I was half convinced that this was some kind of test – a minefield laid out before me so that at any moment they could declare that this wasn't going to happen and then whisk me away, never to see Paradise City again.

I was almost there. Only a few more moments of playing it safe, of saying yes sir, no sir, three bags full, sir. Not long and I would be waving my parents goodbye, home free.

I straightened my shoulders. 'Thanks,' I managed.

My mum blinked in disbelief. I think she had actually mentally prepared herself for Armageddon and when it didn't come, her shoulders relaxed, and that sad look she would break into every so often since my enrolment had been accepted at Paradise High appeared. The tilt of the head, the watering of the eyes and the pout. Followed by a bone-crushing hug.

'Aww, our baby girl is growing up,' she cried.

Well, at least I was trying to.

# Chapter Six

Like many things, I had played this moment over and over in my mind.

I had imagined it in so many ways: me sliding out of Aunty Karen's car, my hair blowing in the wind as I walked in slow motion through the school gate. Low hums and whispers surrounded me as Amanda and I strutted side by side, giving each other knowing glances as the sea of bodies parted, letting us through.

But reality was nothing like that. I inched my way out of the car, self-consciously pulling at my dress, trying to stop it from riding too high and revealing all to the world. I shrugged on my backpack, heavily laden with textbooks – somehow my fantasy didn't include the practicality of a school bag. And instead of Amanda standing diligently by my side, she merely stood in contempt, sighing deeply with a 'let's get this over with' expression.

'Now, remember, Amanda, show Lexie around, and help her meet some people.' Aunty Karen smiled through the open car window. 'Have a great day, girls.'

Amanda and I turned and began to walk through the crowds, but no-one parted: it was a fight to the death to weave our way through the masses. Girls chirping in groups, boys pushing and shoving each other. No-one so much as looked my way until I accidentally stepped on the back of some girl's shoe.

'Sorry.' I grimaced, knowing how hard I had stomped, not paying attention.

The girl, a Year Seven at a guess, spun around, anger flashing in her eyes. 'Watch where you're going, skank.'

My mouth gaped, looking down at her – that's right, looking down, because she was a full half-foot shorter than me, with a serious slathering of freckles across her face, and a heavy layer of black eyeliner on her eyelids, flicked up into little ticks at the corners. I was shocked on so many levels and apparently my reaction was somewhat hilarious to her and her friends as they continued on their way, chucking me filthy looks.

Amanda just walked on, shaking her head. 'You're going to be eaten alive,' she said.

I had gone from a world of slumber parties and giggling about boys to a school where Year Sevens were wearing makeup and weren't afraid to lash out at seniors.

I now wished I had made more of an effort to get my bearings at orientation. Why didn't I locate the locker block, find out what house I was in or where my first class would be? My heart started to race, heat creeping up my neck as my eyes lifted to the imposing greyscale building, its pebbled concrete exterior stretching out like a prison minus the barbed wire.

This wasn't the first day of school for everyone, just me. So every student went along with their own sense of routine, with their own surety. I quickstepped up the concrete steps, aiming to keep up with Amanda as I took the crumpled piece of paper from my pocket that I had studied over and over again. 'Um, where is 11F? Is that a room?' I asked, chasing after her.

She stopped at the top of the steps, looking back towards the front of the school, making sure the Volvo had departed before turning to me with a shrug. 'You're on your own.' And just like that she pushed through the door of the main building and made true on her promise.

I was on my own. That was painfully clear.

*Don't panic, don't panic, don't panic.*

I may have been lost and the bell may have sounded but I did know how to get to one place.

The line was three deep to the main reception, where, from memory, the lady minding the front desk was called Ms Ray, an older woman with military precision for all things admin and a particular fondness for tweed material. It was also to my genuine surprise that she was still rocking the perm, something I didn't know was legally happening in any self-respecting salon. Not since the eighties.

It seemed like all I had done since my arrival at Paradise High was avoid collisions in fear of being abused again. I thought it safest to just opt for a seat against the wall and out of the way until the line cleared; the second bell sounded, causing my heart to spike in anxiety as the last of the stragglers cleared out of the halls.

Great, late on my first day of school, just great. I cursed Amanda. With each lagging student getting served by Ms Ray I watched anxiously as every tick of the clock on the wall made me later and later. At 9.16 a.m. I wanted to give up, to cry, and then Ms Ray called out to me. 'Can I help you?'

I jumped to my feet, approaching the bench and scrabbling for my piece of paper.

'Did you want to sign the late book?' Ms Ray spoke to me without taking her eyes from her computer screen. I paused, before looking down and seeing a blue bound book in front of me, titled, very helpfully, 'Late Book'.

'Oh, um, I actually don't know where I'm meant to be.'

Ms Ray looked up from her chained bifocals.

'It's my first day.' I cringed, sliding over the tattered piece of paper.

'Oh dear.' She pursed her lips.

'I was here last Friday; I had a meeting with Mr Fitzgibbons prior to my orientation.'

'Honey, there are six hundred and forty-three students in this school. It's going to take more than a brief walk-in on a Friday afternoon for me to remember student six hundred and forty-four.'

Okay, so she didn't remember me.

'Do you know which house you belong in?' she asked, continuing to type.

'Um, I don't . . .'

She took the page from me with a sigh, looking at the grids and tracing a finger along the top blue line.

'You're a Gilmore girl,' she said, pointing to a place on the paper that read 11G+. 'The number is your year, the letter is your house, and the plus means acceleration. We like to keep it simple here,' she said.

Yeah, real simple.

She pointed her pencil behind me to the wall. 'We have three houses here, three divisions: Kirkland, Gilmore and Chisholm.'

My eyes followed hers to the framed pictures of three students, all sporting different-coloured polo tops, below a plaque that read, 'House Captains'.

Penny Aldridge was a smiley-faced, perky, ponytailed blonde with a yellow polo – Gilmore captain. James Masters was a green-shirt-clad boy with a monobrow doing it for Chisholm. But my eyes couldn't help but linger on the dimpled image attached to a cocky grin of the boy in red, the gold plaque mounted with his name: Luke Ballantine.

My brows lowered. 'Are these the school captains?' I wondered, thinking it unusual that a school captain was called to the principal's office and was aiding girls sneaking out of their bedroom windows in the middle of the night.

'We don't have school captains here, only house captains voted in by the students themselves.'

'So kind of like a popularity contest,' I said, mainly to myself.

But Ms Ray nodded. 'Something like that,' she said, slipping over a fresh piece of paper. 'Here's a map of the school. I've marked out today's timetable with where you need to be. This is where you should be now,' she said, drawing a big red circle on the sheet. I tilted my head, looking at the mark.

'So is that 11F, Biology?'

'No, that is the main hall. It's Monday and every Monday there's a school assembly.'

*Oh God.*

Ms Ray must have seen the colour drain from my face.

'Yes, I suggest you get a wriggle on.'

I worked fast to fold up my pieces of paper, frantically shouldering my bag, ready to bolt down the empty corridor.

'Wait a minute, the green block on the map is the locker room, and you are 1138,' she said, sliding over my key.

I simply held the key in my palm. 'Oh, okay,' I said, without much conviction.

Ms Ray sighed. 'Leave your bag here and come and collect it after assembly, you're late enough as it is.'

A small bubble of relief lifted my heart. 'Thanks,' I said, handing over my bag as quickly as I could.

'Just don't make a habit of it; new or not, next time you sign the book.'

'Oh, I won't. Promise,' I said, raising a small smile and starting down the corridor.

'Miss Atkinson?'

I slid to a halt, turning on my heel. 'Yes?'

Ms Ray pointed her pencil in the opposite direction. 'That way.'

# Chapter Seven

I stood slightly to the side, peering through a small glass window that looked into the main hall, the main hall being the indoor basketball arena.

My chest heaved, mainly because I had run the equivalent of two football ovals in order to get there, but my laboured breathing didn't lessen when I realised how late I was and worse, that there was no way of delicately slipping in undetected: the entrance was in everyone's direct line of sight. I might as well have had a spotlight shine on me. I bit my lip, frantically looking for Amanda, wondering where she was among the hundreds of students and patrolling teachers. The only thing I could distinguish was the house factions, which was something. The school was divided into three stands. A red banner, a yellow banner and a green banner connected to the front bar of the front row. I just had to make my way to the middle section and find a seat. Desperately searching for a spare spot, I realised I would have to walk right up the back of the tiered stadium. It was such a long way up. While mentally assessing my plan I finally set eyes on Amanda, who was seated in the green section for Chisholm looking bored and as disengaged as ever even among her friends. I bet she'd spark up the moment she saw me do my walk of shame. I made a mental note not to make eye contact with her and just focus on getting to my seat.

Mr Fitzgibbons stood at the microphone; the muffled sounds of the PA system echoed in the large arena as he addressed his minions. Unlike the Friday before, he seemed in good spirits, passionate and bubbly in his body language.

And then as my eyes skimmed to the stands, I froze. There he was, standing to the left of the first section. His arms crossed over his chest, his stance casual as he leant on the front bar of the front row stand. His hair, which I'd thought was as dark as the night was actually a warm brown colour, cropped short and dishevelled. Unlike in his captain photo, he was dressed like everyone else – white shirt, navy tie, his long legs clad in dark denim, something only the seniors were allowed to wear. By the look of things, though, he wasn't there out of choice; the Gilmore captain and Chisholm captain were also front and centre of their houses, a show of leadership no doubt, and they seemed to take it rather seriously, their attention hanging on every word Mr Fitzgibbons delivered, unlike Luke Ballantine, who cricked his neck from side to side and rolled his right shoulder as if struggling to stay awake.

My eyes fixed on his every movement, noticing that when he was serious there was no trace of that gorgeous dimple. I desperately wished something would take his fancy so I could see a flash of that devil-may-care smile, or that hypnotic pucker in his left cheek. And just as if I had willed it, it appeared right after his eyes landed on me. Perving through the window, watching him with a besotted stare, his brown eyes had locked onto mine, pinning me there. His expression changed from a confused frown, into that of recognition and quickly into a crooked grin.

*Shit.*

I ducked. Actually ducked.

I was so lame. Nope, nothing obvious about me, so cool, calm and collected I was; I should have just gone to the locker room and ditched the school assembly, signed the bloody late book and be done with it. Gone down into the history books as the worst first-day student ever. Instead, there I was, hunched over with my eyes closed, praying for the strength not to be physically sick and instead just bite the bullet and walk through the door. What was the worst thing that could happen, people might look at me? They weren't anything to me; besides, I was the new girl, I could play the newbie card for the first week at least, surely. Lexie Atkinson, straight-A student, surely it wouldn't be too bad . . . would it?

There was only one way to find out. I moved to the side of the door, taking a moment to gather myself. I straightened my hair and uniform, took a deep breath and silently counted from three – two, one . . . push.

It was as bad as I had feared. The hall door hinges hadn't been oiled in the last century, so a loud screech as good as announced my entrance. If that wasn't enough for all eyes to shift to me, then Mr Fitzgibbons breaking off mid-speech and craning his head around towards me standing in the doorway sure was. His happy demeanour went down a few notches and I half expected him to scream 'Release the hounds' at the sight of the new girl rocking up late on her first day at school.

I smiled apologetically, keeping my eyes somewhat averted from Mr Fitzgibbons as I quickly made my way along the edge of the main hall. The sound of my new school shoes squeaking painfully loudly was the only thing that – mortifyingly – broke the stony silence of the room. You could seriously have heard a pin drop as the entire school watched me take each agonising step. Squeak, squeak, squeak.

I wanted to die.

Even more so as I made a long line towards a path that would have me basically skimming past Luke Ballantine. I glanced up briefly to see his deep-set eyes glinting with amusement as I neared the first section of Kirkland.

The squeaking seemed less of an issue now that the murmurs had started among the stands. A rowdiness of chatter and laughter swept through the building and I didn't know whether I should be relieved at the fact, knowing that most of it was directed at me. I dropped my eyes to my feet as I walked past Ballantine; I could feel his eyes on me more heavily than anyone else's, mainly because he had caught me spying on him. That had made my cheeks flush before any kind of embarrassment I was facing now. Mercifully Gilmore was the second section so I quickly swung into the aisle and made my way up the steps. Passing comments were not lost on me, no matter how hard I tried to block them out.

'Stupid bitch.'

'Who the hell is she?'

'Fresh meat, bro.'

'I think she's the foreign-exchange student.'

'Another Gilmore nerd.'

It was the longest walk of my life; my sole focus was to not let it get to me, to carry on, take my seat and cry later. Wow, it wasn't even nine-thirty and I already wanted to burst into tears; definitely some kind of record.

'All right settle down, everyone,' Mr Fitzgibbons snapped, his angry voice echoing in the grand space. 'I said, settle down,' he repeated, his eyes darting their warning beams across the stadium. It took a few sweeping glares by neighbouring teachers to finally regain silence, and just when I thought I had done pretty well, my eyes lifted to the right, locking with the big blue eyes of Amanda. To my surprise she didn't look smug, or disgusted. I could have sworn I saw a glimmer of another emotion, one I couldn't quite put my finger on and just as I was trying to identify it, she tore her eyes from my gaze, faced forward and slammed down the stony guard I had come to know so well over the past few days.

There was no-one else on my row aside from a boy who my mum would have referred to as big-boned, but I would say he was just massive in every which way. At least six feet tall with legs the size of tree trunks, he had a rather interestingly large head that was topped by an enormous mop of curly hair. He snacked lazily on a Mars Bar, paying me no mind until he realised I was watching him, but not in the way I had been watching Luke Ballantine.

'First day?' he whispered.

'Is it that obvious?'

He shrugged. 'Everyone knows if you're late for assembly then you come through the back door.'

'There's a back door?'

'Under the stairs.'

*Crap.*

'Oh well, next time,' he said, crumpling up the empty wrapper and letting it fall under the seat.

*There won't be a next time.*

'Shhhhh!'

A teacher who stood in the aisle half-a-dozen steps down glared in our general direction, not entirely figuring out the guilty party. I took the warning though, thinking I was in enough trouble as it was without drawing further attention to myself. Mr Fitzgibbons was raving on about school spirit and God knows what else; all I could think about was how

I fancied a Mars Bar. I brushed out the lines of the fabric on my uniform in my lap, wondering when the assembly would be over and I could just get my first class underway, trying to visualise where the building for my first class was. My eyes lifted, wandering around the tops of the heads of what was the entire school, sweeping across to lock once again with a familiar set of eyes, brown and burning right into me. The only difference was this time I had caught Luke Ballantine staring at me, and, unlike me, he didn't look away; he didn't blush or duck. He looked at me, without apology, the only thing breaking his attention was the sudden burst of cheering from the stands.

I flinched, blinking back into my skin and wondering what had been so interesting in Mr Fitzgibbons' speech that could possibly get such a reaction. I turned to Mars Bar boy next to me, who appeared to be less than thrilled. He groaned, rubbing his thick, sausage-like fingers through his afro.

'What's going on?' I asked above the hoots and the hollers.

He sighed wearily. 'Swimming carnival results.'

'Oh.' And just like that my heart sunk. Red Hill didn't exactly do many sporting activities; instead, our idea of grand water-sports was running under the sprinkler in the summer-time, or going for a dunk in our dam.

I started to think that me and Mars Bar boy were kindred spirits, sitting up the back like the pair of misfits we were. I looked across to find Luke Ballantine was no longer standing down the front. Long before Mr Fitzgibbons called the assembly to a close, he had disappeared, and I smiled to myself thinking he had probably gone out the back door.

# Chapter Eight

So I had not only made an acquaintance, but somehow had inherited a tour guide.

And it was absolutely welcome. Mars Bar boy (or Ben I think he said his name was) walked me to the locker room, to my locker, waited patiently, and then showed me to my first class. He was a good foot taller than me and when we walked down the corridor people moved; I wouldn't have to worry about nasty Year Sevens. Sure, people looked, but we kind of were the odd couple.

'This is 11F,' he said, stopping before an open sliding door.

'Thanks,' I said, suddenly feeling the same pull of anxiety twist in my stomach at the thought of being left on my own again.

'No worries. See you around.'

Mars Bar boy continued on not so much walking as loping down the corridor. My eyes shifted down to my piece of paper: 11F Biology+. Great! My first class would be an accelerated one – thrown in the deep end with the Year Twelves. Using the same tactic as in assembly, I made my way through the classroom, eyes down, only lifting them enough to locate a seat right down the back so no-one could stare at the back of my head, and there was less chance of a missile being launched at me as a few boys were playing cricket across the room with a ruler and ball of paper.

The room was lined with long tables that could each sit half-a-dozen in a row. In my head, I had thought we would be seated two by two at desks where we lifted a lid and retrieved our books, but then I realised this was not TV. This was not Degrassi High and, much to my disappointment, there was no Joey Jeremiah sitting next to me down the back.

Even my locker, which I had fantasised about hanging pictures and posters in, that I thought I would open while chatting to my new BFFs either side of me, was just a tiny box you could barely wedge your bag into. There was someone above me and two below making it an awkward balance of either getting hit in the head by a door or hitting someone in the head with mine. It was a hot mess come the rush of the bell and bitterly disappointing. In fact, everything about my experience to date had been an absolute disaster, one that didn't seem to be getting any better anytime soon as I sensed someone stand by my side.

'You're in my seat.'

I blinked twice. Looking up to see the very tall, and very frowny Ballantine. Long gone was the amused glimmer in his eyes and the boyish dimple that appeared when he smiled. Instead he looked down at me as if I was something that he had stepped in; did he not remember me from the other night? That I was the girl who made him laugh, the one he enjoyed watching squirm under the scrutiny of the entire school? But his gaze held no recollection, not an ounce; just like the rest of the school I was merely another face in the crowd that he had to dodge in the hall. I probably would have jumped and scurried out of his way, apologising profusely, but it was nearly ten and I was a little over the self-righteous smarminess that this city had to offer. I may have been from Red Hole but at least we had the common decency to treat each other with a bit of respect. Even my drunken Uncle Eddie was more friendly to a dog tied up outside the pub than anyone I had stumbled across in the last few days, including my own cousin. Maybe it was something in the water? Maybe the salty sea air robbed people of their sense of humour?

I heard the scraping of a chair against the wood floor nearby. 'Look out, mate, she'll tell you where to go.'

My eyes shifted to the familiar face of the boy who had helped Amanda out the window, who had taken a seat one away from me; he winked at me, all the while taking in the scene with a wide smile.

Ballantine didn't move. He stood next to my chair looking tall and intimidating, especially from my vantage point. I honestly didn't see what the big problem was, there was actually a spare seat next to me. By now we were attracting some attention. People were elbowing each other and spinning around to witness the showdown. They might as well have taken out buckets of popcorn and put on 3D glasses, they were enjoying the show so much.

I had two choices: move and live to fight another day, or hold my ground, stamp my authority and run the risk of my head being flushed at recess. For some inexplicable reason, which I will never, ever truly understand, I chose the latter.

I simply broke from his heated gaze, and shifted my body to sit forward, clasping my hands innocently together over my books, like a choir girl with a halo above her head.

I heard the titters and a catcall instantly, Ballantine's friend wailing, 'Oh no, she d'int!', as if he was some kind of guest on the *Ricki Lake Show* or something. The mocking reactions and the lunacy filled the classroom as everyone caught on to my act of defiance, or more alarmingly, Ballantine's humiliation.

It wasn't too dissimilar to the way I had stood up to Amanda the other night. The major difference was that then Ballantine had been laughing at my reaction, and he was most certainly not laughing now.

I tried not to be alarmed by the stony, angry statue standing next to me, imagining him sliding all my books off the table and getting in my grill – was that the saying in the city? I doubted it. Instead, I was saved by the glorious intervention of the teacher.

'All right, everyone settle down.' A small, moustached man entered the room carrying a stack of books, managing to juggle them and not spill his coffee as he shut the door in a rather fluid motion. 'Come on, everyone, pipe down. Boon, legs off the table, Ballantine, bum on seat.'

In my peripheral vision I saw Ballantine's mate take his feet off the table; Boon, I made a mental note. It took another less-than-patient request from the teacher for Ballantine to rather violently yank out the spare seat and sit down next to me. He was so close our knees were nearly touching. I could feel the anger rolling off him, and the heat of his body burn next to me. I dared not look; it was going to be a long, long fifty minutes. I doodled a circle around and around on a corner of my exercise book.

A hand raised in the row in front. 'Mr Branson, can I go to the toilet?'

My pen stilled. The hairs on the back of my neck prickled as a bone-jarring dread swept through me.

*Mr Branson?*

I slowly shifted the crinkled paper I had slipped inside my Biology book and smoothed it out: Biology – Mr Cranford.

My eyes widened, the sound of Mr Branson's voice became muffled, the whole world seemed to slow right down. I could feel a light sheen of sweat form against my skin, my hands clammy as the beat of my heart thrummed dangerously fast. I had no choice but to slowly and subtly shift my eyes sideways, peering at Ballantine's textbook.

His History book.

*Oh. My. God.*

I was in the wrong class.

# Chapter Nine

How to lose friends and irritate people in less than an hour, by Lexie Atkinson.

I had gone from badass new girl facing off against Ballantine and asserting my authority, to quickly and rather mortifyingly grabbing my Biology book and scurrying towards the teacher, apologising in my lowest voice that I was in the wrong room before walking briskly out the door with not so much as a backwards glance.

Mars Bar boy, bless his soul, had actually walked me to the wrong room; an honest mistake, no doubt, but it didn't make me feel less like throwing myself down the stairs. Maybe breaking my leg and being taken to the sick bay with a doctor's certificate that insisted on weeks of rest, in my own room that is – no distractions, no disrupted sleep, no filthy looks by bullying cousins. Just me, room service and watching reruns of John Stamos in *Full House*; it sounded so tempting. Instead, what little confidence I had left was knocked out of me as I once again found myself slinking into a doorway, late, disrupting the class and earning myself the spotlight for all the wrong reasons.

After Biology, I glanced at my timetable. My next class would be easier; it was a non-accelerated class, so it would be less intimidating, right?

Wrong!

Miss Smith, our Health teacher, actually wanted me to stand up and introduce myself, like I was in some kind of therapy group.

*Hi, I'm Lexie and I am an alcoholic.*

'I'm Lexie from Red Hill.' I managed, sitting down quickly.

'*Hello*, sexy Lexie!' a boy in the back called out.

'That's quite enough, Tommy; one more outcry from you and you will be going on a little holiday.'

Tommy straightened with interest. 'Oh really, Miss? That sounds nice, where am I off to?'

'Sit down,' she warned. 'Right. Welcome, Lexie.' She smiled before turning to the whiteboard and beginning the class.

Miss Smith used the better half of the session writing directly from her textbook onto the whiteboard, which in turn we had to copy into our exercise books. It was her attempt at keeping us quiet for a bit and it was pretty effective; well, except for the girl next to me.

'I'm Laura,' she said out of the blue.

My eyes shifted from the board in surprise. 'Oh, hey. Lexie.'

'I know.' She nodded.

Well, this was going well.

'Have you been in Paradise long?'

It was the first authentic question I'd been asked, and judging by her earnest expression she actually seemed to genuinely want to know the answer. It took me a moment to think, to voice the words.

'We arrived on Friday.'

'We?' Another question. Wow. An actual conversation was unfolding right in between copying off the whiteboard; I was pretty certain Miss Smith was conducting some kind of plagiarism. Still, it made the time go faster, or maybe it was due to the real-life human connection I was finally having. I tried to play down my excitement, tried not to answer her questions so eagerly and talk for too long, but I couldn't help it, it had opened the floodgates and before we knew it we were chatting away like long-lost friends.

Laura had to catch the bus from the western suburbs, which was a half-hour ride to school and back each day. She wished she lived nearer to the beach because when it came to parties and such, that's where all the action was.

At recess, Laura and I lined up in the longest canteen line I had ever seen. Seriously, it was like we were queueing for a Coldplay concert or something.

I wasn't tall by anyone's standards, but Laura was actually smaller than me. She had tanned skin, which was not an uncommon thing in Paradise, but it was very unlike my own. I made a note to purchase some fake tan ASAP. She had dark hair and dark eyes: Greek or Italian heritage, maybe?

'The Gilmore house is where all the smart people get sent; it's a common fact that that's the case.' Laura continued her tuition.

'Oh, and that wouldn't be because you and I happen to be Gilmore, by any chance?' I mused.

'No, for real. As a rule, they put the majority of the academics in Gilmore; the houses are more than just colour-coded division, it's a class system.'

I thought about that, catching sight of Mars Bar boy loping across the asphalt yard in the distance, feasting on a meat pie.

*Could he be some kind of secret genius?*

'Well, what about Chisholm then?'

Amanda's house: maybe it was a division for people diagnosed with chronic evil?

'Band geeks.'

Okay, that didn't make sense.

'Really?' I questioned, shuffling a millimetre forward in the never-ending line of starvation.

'And artsy kind of eccentrics.' Laura shrugged.

Amanda eccentric? Maybe.

'And what about Kirkland?' I inclined my head over to a group of boys, across the way, as if they alone represented the house. To me they kind of did. They were Ballantine's posse. Four of them sitting on a bench, shirts untucked from their jeans, loosened ties, deep tans and wild hair. They looked like trouble. The sort of students you would want to keep an eye on. They just didn't seem like anyone else in the school, they seemed free. Ballantine sat in the middle of them, his eyes alight with amusement as he listened to a tall boy with blond shaggy hair telling him a yarn with wild hand movements and flailing arms that caused them to break out in laughter. I watched on with guarded interest; the last thing I needed was to catch his attention. I was kind of working on avoiding him for the rest of my life. Every time I thought back to my rather inelegant exit from Mr Branson's History class, I wanted the ground to open up.

'Oh, they're the beach bums.'

'Beach bums?'

'Yeah, you know? The sporty types. The surfing delinquents of society.' She leant in. 'Not much between the ears but pretty good between the sheets is the saying.'

*Ew.*

My face twisted.

Laura giggled. 'Tell me about it. My brother is one of them and believe me, that is not something you want to hear.'

Brother?

And before I could question her, a figure jumped towards us, wedging himself between Laura and me in the line.

Boon.

Incredulous angry calls sounded from the back of the line, something Boon chose to ignore.

'Get out, you bloody idiot,' yelled Laura.

My eyes darted between them, trying as I might to see the family resemblance. Boon had lighter hair and a golden-coloured complexion. Looking at them side by side, they were chalk and cheese.

'He's your brother?' I asked in dismay.

Boon turned around as if spotting me for the first time. 'Well, looky here,' he said, flashing a blinding smile. 'You sure you're in the right line?'

I offered him a deadpan stare that only seemed to amuse him more.

Boon turned to his sister. 'I thought Mum told you not to bring any more strays home, creep.' Boon playfully tugged on Laura's ponytail, eliciting a fiery glare.

'Piss off, Boon!'

'Actually, you two are going to get along just fine, I think.'

Laura turned her back, ignoring his taunts.

'Hang on a sec,' he delved into his jeans pocket, 'if I give you the money, can you just get me a small iced coffee Big M and a packet of Samboys?' Coins spilled out and rolled everywhere as he upended his pockets.

Laura glanced around, looking mortified. 'Boon,' she said through gritted teeth.

Poor Laura. I knew all too well what it was like to be embarrassed by family. I sighed, shaking my head as Boon scrambled to stop the rolling coins.

'Here,' I said, holding out my hand, 'I'll bloody get it.'

Boon's eyes snapped up, his whole face lighting up in surprise. 'Really?' he said, grinning from ear to ear.

'Really,' I repeated, with absolutely no enthusiasm.

'Bloody legend!' he shrieked, plunging the coins into my palm.

I rolled my eyes as another coin twanged to the ground. 'What did you want again?' I asked.

Boon picked up the wayward coin, placing it in my hand with a confused line pinching between his brows. 'Oh, it's not for me,' he said in all seriousness, before nodding his head towards the Kirkland boys. 'It's for Ballantine.'

•

'You know what you've done?' said Laura. 'You've opened up the floodgates. Now the boys know they can boss you around you'll be their lackey.'

I watched on as Boon swaggered his way back towards the boys. I could see the mystified look on Ballantine's face as he looked at his mate's empty hands. I couldn't help but smile, watching his expression change into something darker as Boon explained exactly where his goods were coming from. Ballantine's eyes lifted, searching along the line before settling on me. I offered a small wave and a smug little smile.

So much for avoiding him.

'Do you know Ballantine?' Laura's troubled look shifted between us.

'Yes and no,' I said, breaking off the stare.

'Well, remember what I said, as they'll probably think they can bully their way into getting you to do this all the time,' she warned.

'I don't think so, I think they know not to mess with me,' I said, lifting my chin.

'Oh yeah? And why do you think that?'

I glanced behind me, catching the briefest glimpse of a less-than-amused Ballantine.

'Oh, I just know.'

# Chapter Ten

expected him to say something smart, to maybe snatch the food out of my hands, so when he instead asked, 'What's your name?' I wasn't exactly prepared for that.

I blinked. Twice.

Having known of Luke Ballantine even before I had sighted him, I kind of just assumed that he may have known my name. But how could he have? I hadn't been called to the principal's office, or elected as some momentous house captain. Still, I had hoped that maybe Amanda might have explained who the sleeping girl she had stepped on to get out the window was, or might have mentioned my name in passing. But then I thought of the long list of names she probably did refer to me as, and I blushed. Yeah, he probably only knew me as tragic, or scrubber, or the cousin who had ruined her life.

'Lexie,' I said, sounding nowhere near as confident as I had felt earlier.

'Well, Lexie,' he said, ripping open the top of his iced coffee Big M. The straw I had given him rested next to the chips on the bench seat beside him. He had given me a strange look when I'd handed it to him and then I realised, of course, these were the surfing delinquents, the bad boys.

And bad boys don't drink through straws. That really should be on a t-shirt, I mused to myself.

Laura elbowed me, shifting my focus back to Ballantine, who was sitting, looking up at me with interest.

Oh crap, had he said something?

'Um, sorry?'

He held out his hand, an empty hand, and my brows lowered in confusion, my blank stare telling him as much until a small crooked smile tilted the corner of his mouth and I was blinded by that dimple. I felt my chest tighten. It was the first time I had been so close to that smile. It really should've come with a warning label, like when your parents told you never to look directly at the sun; well, it was too late for that.

I blinked. 'Yes?'

*Does he want me to hold his hand?*

'My change?'

*Lexie, you are an idiot!*

'Oh God, sorry!' I delved into my pockets so quickly, reaching and pulling so frantically I spilled coins all over the asphalt, much like Boon had done, except there was nothing graceful or cool about the way I did it. These boys could open milk cartons and chip packets and make it look cool; hell, they just had to exist to be known. If Gilmore were the brainiacs, Chisholm were the misfits, then Kirkland were most certainly the cool kids; let's put all the rotten eggs into the one basket. No doubt a genius ploy from our industrious leader, Mr Fitzgibbons.

I ducked and weaved for the coins, pushing past the boys, excusing myself as I retrieved them from all corners. I could hear Laura openly sigh as she watched on. The rest of the boys cast me weary looks or stared at me like I was some creature from outer space – a look I was most certainly getting used to. But above all that there was one thing that struck me, one clear defined sound that cut through all of the chaos as I picked up the last of the rolling coins. I pushed the wisps of hair that had fallen into my eyes from my ponytail as my eyes came to rest on Ballantine, who was laughing at my money chasing. Oh, yeah, so funny, I thought. I walked back to him and held my hand out, motioning for him to take his bloody change.

Ballantine reached out, scooping up the coins, his fingers ghosting across my palm, sending a tingling sensation right up my arm. My eyes flicked up in surprise, wondering if the same feeling had hit him, or if I was just being sensitive. It was hard to tell, the one thing that was certain was that the laughter had disappeared, and was instead replaced by a sobering look of interest. No smile, no dimple, just a curt head nod right as the recess bell sounded, snapping us into action and moving us away from each other.

•

For the rest of the day, I was very much in the right class after double then triple checking the timetable. At lunchtime I wasn't coerced into any canteen-line antics. In fact, Ballantine, Boon and co. were noticeably absent and, for me at least, it kind of left a huge hole in the schoolyard.

'Where have the boys from Kirkland gone?' I asked Laura, innocently enough.

'Seniors are allowed to leave the school grounds if they have permission from their parents; you'll probably find them getting a gutful of hot chips down the arcade,' she said, as if bored by the subject.

'So, what, no surfing?'

'Oh, they'll be surfing all right: morning, noon and night. Note the perpetual damp collars they have.'

It hadn't gone unnoticed; the boys did have that wet, dishevelled look about them.

We walked across the long stretch of concreted school-yard, making sure to dodge a basketball that sailed passed us.

'Hey, Laura, can I ask you something?'

'Shoot!'

'Is my cousin Amanda the resident mean girl or does she just hate . . . me?' I winced. Laura was proving to be a rather helpful source of information, and although she hadn't provided me with the same essence of cool school domination I had hoped to possess walking around with Amanda, she was still one degree of separation from Ballantine and that intrigued me more than I cared to admit.

Laura took a deep draw of her Prima box, thoughtful. 'She's always nice to me,' she said. 'Mind you, I am Boon's sister, so of course she would be.'

I stopped, looking down at Laura, who was five foot nothing next to me. 'Why should that matter?' I asked, with an air of excitement in my voice. My mind flashed back to Boon and Ballantine helping her escape from my bedroom window.

'Because she is completely in love with Boon,' she said, as if it was the most obvious answer in the world.

Bingo!

The cogs quickly started turning in my head. I didn't know why just yet, but somehow this was very useful information to have.

'So are they like together or . . .'

'Oh, ew! I have no idea and I don't want to know about my brother's love life.' Laura's face screwed up in horror and she kind of had a point there. We neared one of the bench

seats under the shade of a tree overlooking the Year Tens
playing cricket in the nets.

'What's with the questions anyway? I thought for sure
you'd be grilling me about Ballantine.' She smiled, fluttering
her eyelids dramatically.

I straightened a crease out of my skirt, feeling uneasy
about the insinuation. Had I been so obvious? 'Why would
I ask about him?' I scoffed.

'Because you're a girl, and you have a pulse,' she said,
laughing. 'Ballantine is certainly not lacking in female
admirers, that's for sure.'

I shrugged. 'Hadn't noticed.'

'You have to admit, he's fine.' Laura jolted her head side
to side like a diva; it was so ridiculous I had to laugh.

'I suppose he's all right,' I lied.

'Lord of the Beach Bums, he is,' joked Laura.

It got me thinking; he didn't remind me of a stereo-
typical surfer. When I was packing for Paradise City, I had
all these grand visions of bronzed surfers with long blond
hair matted with saltwater and bleached by the sun. They
would say things like dude or bro and drive around in
Kombi vans, covered in name brands like Rip Curl and
Quiksilver. In reality there wasn't any one of them who
really fit that image.

Ballantine had a deeply bronzed tan that highlighted the
stark white flash of his teeth every time he smiled. He was
tall and lean with toned rips of muscle in all the right places.
I could tell this by the way he coolly yet casually had the
sleeves of his shirt rolled up his forearms – the fabric tight
across his square shoulders. He was definitely athletic, but
his thick dark hair wasn't the surfer platinum I'd imagined.
It had a beautiful tinge of brown to it and when he moved his

head a certain way, the sun highlighted the blonder strands. I wondered what it looked like fresh out of the water. What had been a curiosity before had now turned into a burning desire to find out.

# Chapter Eleven

The bus dropped me at the top of our street. I smiled to myself triumphantly as I stepped off, hooking my thumbs into the straps of my backpack. I had survived my first day. Ha! I didn't need Amanda to help me find my way around, I thought, lifting my chin to the sky.

*Nope. Lexie Atkinson: Lone Wolf.*

I could have almost pulled off the confidence that soared within me if, in that very moment, the edge of my shoe hadn't clipped a jagged piece of footpath, causing me to stumble. I quickly straightened, spinning to make sure the school bus was far enough away so that no-one would have seen my clumsy moves. How mortifying.

With the bus safely out of view I bolted along the last stretch of the street, the zips on my school bag clinking as I ran until the manicured ball trees came into sight. Aunty Karen's Volvo was in the drive, and I was unexpectedly excited to tell her about my day. Even in my haste I took care to dodge around the box hedges of the terracotta-tiled path towards the front door. Pulling up short, I almost toppled over in my squeaky new school shoes.

Amanda sat on the front steps. The deep blue of her eyes was accentuated by the heavy eyeliner framing them. Her hair was dark and straightened to within an inch of its life; this I knew for certain seeing as she took over an hour to get ready in the morning and what had awaited me was a trashed bathroom, strands of her hair all over the basin. If she was going to ask me about my day I was seriously going to throw a shoe at her.

'If Mum asks, you had a great day,' said Amanda, not an ounce of emotion in her voice.

Her words slowly registered.

'But I did have a good day,' I said.

Her brows lifted in surprise, her eyes ticking over my face as if assessing whether I was telling the truth. 'Really?' Her question was laced with intrigue, as if me actually enjoying my day was impossible.

And when I thought about the walk of shame in assembly, the showdown with Ballantine, the wrong class saga, and the awkward coin-collecting moment in front of the Kirkland boys, for a minute I actually had to think about what had made my day a good one.

Laura, sure, the fact I was in the smart house, yeah, the fact that Luke Ballantine now knew my name . . . hmmm.

'Why? Are you disappointed?' I said, moving past her and onto the steps.

'I just don't need to hear it from my parents right now,' she said, causing me to pause at the front door.

'What do you mean?'

Amanda moved to stand, giving me her famous head tilt; I've never met anyone who could convey so much with mere body language.

This was saying. *What do you mean, what do I mean?*

'The last thing I need is my parents giving me the third degree because I didn't hold your hand all day.'

It took me back somewhat. Amanda seemed uncharac-
teristically tense; gone was her aloof, whatever attitude and
instead it was replaced by a creature who waited on the steps
to cut me off and try to plant some kind of warning.

I crossed my arms. 'So do you want me to paint a picture
of what an amazing help you were today?'

Amanda's eyes flicked up, a new emotion lining her face;
was that a flash of hope I saw? Wow, was she really needing
brownie points from her parents so badly?

'What's in it for me?' I asked, curving a sceptical brow.

Amanda sighed, as if what she was about to say was
going to cause her immense pain. 'You can hang with me
tomorrow,' she said, with no enthusiasm whatsoever.

I laughed. 'Thanks, but I have my own friends.' Well,
friend.

Amanda crossed her arms to mirror me. 'Who?' she asked
with a cocky little smirk.

I smiled.

'Laura Boon.' I said the words loud and clear. Her eyes
lightened in surprise.

*That's right, your crush's sister.*

For the first time I actually felt like I was in control, that
I had the upper hand for once. But seeing Amanda in this
way, the stunned surprise that soon morphed into a childlike
worry, didn't satisfy me for too long. Damn, I could never
be a mean girl.

'So, as you see, that doesn't make it worth my while.'

The inner workings of Amanda's mind were ticking over
frantically. I could almost hear the cogs turning in her head.

Before her eyes glassed over, her expression shut down in
contempt. 'What do you want?' she asked.

For a moment I felt uneasy. Amanda was asking me a million-dollar question, putting me on the spot and presenting me with an opportunity. If I painted her as a saint to her mum and dad then she would do something in return for me. My heart was racing; I had to think of something before she took the offer off the table and I lost the chance to use it. Just as she was about to walk inside it came to me.

My eyes snapped up to meet hers. 'There is something you can do.'

•

'Oh, Aunty Karen, it was so amazing! Amanda showed me where my locker was and then we went to assembly and even though we're not in the same house Amanda pointed me in the right direction.'

*Lies, lies, lies.*

Aunty Karen positively glowed with pride.

*Hook, line and sinker.*

Uncle Peter, on the other hand, looked rather sceptical, piling a spoonful of couscous onto his plate.

Yes, tonight's menu was grilled barramundi and couscous; what was with these people and their couscous? I was going to waste away living here.

I tried not to look Uncle Peter's way as I was retelling the glorious events of my first day.

'Oh, honey, I'm so thrilled you had such a great day, and to think the first day is always the hardest. Onwards and upwards from here, hey, Peter?'

'Hmm,' he managed, taking a sip of his wine.

'Well, if this is what happened on the first day, I can't wait to hear what happens by the end of the week. How about we celebrate with ice cream after dinner?' Aunty Karen said.

I felt a little kick to my shin from across the table. My eyes locked with Amanda's, thinking maybe I had been a bit over the top with my enthusiastic version of the events of my day, but when Amanda smirked I knew I'd done my job. I shoved down all the remorseful feelings that clawed at my soul, namely the fact that I was lying to the very people who fed and housed me, who were allowing me a chance to coexist in their little piece of Paradise.

I pushed my guilt down, way down, and instead shovelled a forkful of couscous into my mouth, smiling as I chewed on the bland, gravel-like texture before grabbing for my water and washing down what I couldn't quite swallow. Even through the lies, the paranoia and the couscous there was one thing that did spur me on, and that was the thought of Amanda's end of the bargain.

# Chapter Twelve

'Oh no, you d'int!'

Laura snatched the piece of paper out of my outstretched hand. 'They actually gave you permission? Your aunty and uncle are so cool!'

'Well . . .' I said, leaving the word to linger.

'Well, what?'

'I may have got it by some other means,' I said, wincing at the admission.

It took a moment, but then the realisation hit Laura. 'Oh my God, you mean . . . ?'

I nodded.

'Amanda?' Laura lowered her voice, her eyes shifting around the locker room. 'How?'

'Nothing a bit of quid pro quo couldn't fix.'

*And a whole week of wearing her down.*

'Huh?'

'You scratch my back and I scratch yours. I had to make out that she was cousin of the year to win brownie points with her parents, and in exchange she would forge her mum's signature for me.'

Laura laughed, shaking her head. 'Hot chips for everyone!'

'Almost everyone,' I said, pocketing the precious note. 'Now you have to get permission.'

Laura's smile fell away. 'No chance, my brother is such a rat. Because he's always in trouble they're extra strict on me. As if I'm somehow going to follow down the same troubled path as Boon; I mean, as if. It's only because I'm a girl; it's so unfair.'

'I don't expect you to ask your parents,' I said in all seriousness, again amused by the blank expression plastered across her face. But it only took a mere moment for the light bulb to go off.

'No, no way,' she said.

'Oh, come on, Laura, I don't want to go without you.'

'No! I am not asking Boon!' she said, turning to close her locker door.

'Well, can you forge it?'

'Not a chance; believe me, I've tried. Boon's the expert forger in our family.'

'Laura,' I whined, 'please.' I clasped my hands under my chin; I would beg if I had to, this was my golden ticket down to the beach, down to watch the boys surf, to see Ballantine.

Laura's shoulders slumped, her jaw clenched. 'You don't understand, he will use this against me any chance he gets, it will be like a time bomb waiting to explode at any given moment.'

'Well, we'll just make it so the favour is of mutual benefit,' I said with confidence. 'If he does this for us, we'll do something in return.'

Only my second week at Paradise High and I was already getting really good at this stuff, a mastermind of lies and manipulation and what for? Hot chips and hot surfers. Seemed like the right kind of motivation for me.

'Is there anything you can think of that we could use as a bartering tool?' I asked Laura, who was lost in thought, biting her bottom lip. We were running out of time before the morning bell sounded. But then her eyes flashed with a spark of knowledge, a grin spreading from ear to ear.

'I've got it!' she said just as the bell sounded.

As the crowds scurried around us my heart slammed against my chest with the desperation to find out what Laura was about to say before the second warning bell sounded.

'Boon and the boys have been carrying on for weeks about their footy, which got confiscated by Mr Branson. If we got it back for them I'm pretty sure he would do anything we asked him to.'

'Why don't they just buy another footy?' I asked.

'This isn't just any footy, this is Boon's precious St Kilda footy, he's had it for years.'

*Perfect.*

'Well, where's the ball?'

Laura's enthusiasm died some. 'Can you believe in the Year Twelve common room?'

I tried to think if that meant anything to me? It didn't.

Laura rolled her eyes, losing patience. 'The Year Twelve common room is off limits while it's getting renovated. It's where the teachers have been storing confiscated items.'

The second warning bell sounded, propelling us both into motion. 'We get the ball, we get Boon.'

•

I don't know why I did what I did. But I backed out of the long canteen line, leaving Laura to chat with one of her friends and made my way across the yard to where Amanda and her posse sat in a cluster near the Kirkland boys. Much to my amusement, I skimmed past Boon and Ballantine lining up for their own food for once. Two Year Seven girls were giggling behind them, flushed with excitement at being so close to Year Twelve surfing gods. Even though I'd declined her half-hearted invitation to 'hang' with her, if Amanda was surprised by the fact I was approaching her now she didn't let on. In fact, I am pretty sure Amanda didn't do many emotions besides pissed off, really pissed off and anxious. Although today she added bored to the list. I confidently sat down opposite her and her two girlfriends: one a tanned blonde with shiny shoulder-length hair, the other a tall dark-haired girl who looked like she could be on the cover of *Dolly* magazine.

'Want a Tic Tac?' I asked, pulling out a box of the clattering white beads; it was my attempt at an icebreaker.

The blonde held out her hand so I could tap the pack into her palm. 'Thanks,' she said, flicking all three into her mouth at once.

After a moment of reluctance, the tall girl held out her hand too, but she was more discreet, instead placing one into her mouth and pocketing the rest for later. I did the same dance for Amanda, but she just shook her head.

Seeing as Amanda wasn't the most gracious of hosts, I took the lead. 'I'm Lexie,' I said. I could tell there was a certain unease in my presence, as their conversation had died off since my arrival. Now all that could be heard was the occasional outburst from the Kirkland boys on the seats next to us.

'I'm Jess,' said the blonde, 'this is Gemma.' Her eyes shifted to the tall girl. 'And I'm kind of guessing you know who Amanda is,' she said with a knowing smirk.

I tried not to react – but holy crap! Had Amanda mentioned me to her friends? Although the excitement died down a bit when I realised that it probably hadn't been the most glowing character reference. It was up to me now to prove I wasn't the girl they thought I was.

'So is anyone in English with Miss Scott? I have a double next.'

I thought I'd try my luck at aligning myself with one of the Year Twelve girls, but when my question was met with silence, I quickly learned that this was not going to be as easy as I'd hoped, until an unexpected voice trailed over the top of us.

'Miss Scott's class?' Boon was hand-balling chips to one of his mates on the opposite side of the table. 'I'm in that class. Do you want me to save you a seat?' he said with a cheeky wink that made his mates burst into laughter, jeering and pushing him into his seat. Even Ballantine hid his smirk behind the carton of Mr D's Cola he was taking a swig from.

My eyes flicked briefly to Amanda. I made a mental note not to look for her response; I could already feel her eyes burning into my skull.

'Better not. I haven't the best track record for finding the right classes,' I said, trying for a half-hearted joke at my own expense. 'On my first day of school I thought I was in Biology but I was actually in –'

'We know,' said Jess, cutting me off.

'Oh.'

Gemma laughed. 'Everyone knows.'

*Oh.*

I could feel the heat flooding my cheeks; no doubt I had been the butt of many a joke.

'So why aren't you guys hanging in your common room?' I asked innocently enough, also eager to change the subject.

'It's getting renovated,' said Gemma.

'Yeah, some students broke in last school holidays and trashed the place,' added Jess. 'From what I hear it's going to be pretty cool. New carpet, new paintwork, new sofas.'

'Sounds awesome,' I said. 'So where is this common room?'

This was it; this was the intel I needed. The small, yet vital detail I hadn't thought to ask Laura. I waited for the answer, almost holding my breath. To my surprise, it came from the least likely of sources: my cousin.

'It's that building over there, the one with red double doors leading into it,' she said.

Jess followed her gaze before nodding animatedly. 'Oh, yeah, you'll definitely have to take a look, see if the wallpaper is up yet. Rainforest, wasn't it, the new theme?'

'Rainforest,' Amanda agreed.

'Yeah, but best to do it before the recess bell rings, that way the painters won't be in there and you can have a real look around,' Gemma added helpfully.

I checked my watch: five to. 'I'll go now and report back,' I said. Thinking this could be my moment of glory: sneak in, grab the footy, come back to the group, smiling like the cat that got the mouse. I would be a hero, a legend to go down in history. We could deliver the footy to Boon on the proviso he forge a note for Laura and we would all head off for hot chips and beach-time activities.

Brilliant!

I didn't go through the red double doors that led into the corridor though, that would have been too obvious; I didn't plan to merely stick my head in and check out the bloody rainforest wallpaper. No way, I was about to do the one thing that no-one else had thought of doing; I was going to sneak in and liberate the confiscated collection. Swipe the footy and save the day. And to do that I had to be a little more discreet – I needed to find an alternative way in. Rounding the other side of the building, skimming along the edge of the weatherboarded walls, I looked up at the windows, noticing a line of them were left open, probably to let the paint fumes out. There were a few stragglers walking by but luckily the common room looked out over a manicured courtyard near the music room, and aside from band lessons and music classes, the building seemed to be largely unoccupied, meaning the coast was clear.

With the theme to *Mission Impossible* in my head, and adrenalin soaring though my veins, I wedged my foot in the first slat, giving myself enough leverage to pull myself up and latch onto the window ledge, freezing when I thought I heard someone approaching, but no-one came. I decided the only way to do this was to lift and army roll myself into the room, snatch and grab and get out like the ninja I intended to be. All before the bell sounded, all before someone walked around the corner and all before the painters came back.

I silently counted to three and lifted myself up under the window, envisioning I would let gravity do its thing as I rolled forward into a beautifully elegant somersault. But when the curtain got trapped against my face and the sill and my footing unlocked themselves from below, suddenly my planned badass entrance turned into me screaming, and falling forward, face-diving onto the carpet with a gut-heaving oomph, the pain of the ensuing carpet burn on my left elbow was outdone only by the curtain rod that chose to twang down on the back of my head. I barely managed to claw the fabric away from my face, the netting threatening to suffocate me. I rolled onto my back with a groan, trying to regain the breath that had been knocked out of me.

I blinked, clearing the spots from my vision and struggling to gather my thoughts, but those thoughts were interrupted by a rather loud and unexpected voice.

'Miss Atkinson!'

My head snapped around. First I spotted legs, chair legs, table legs, people legs, then I looked upward, wide-eyed and horrified. My mouth gaped as I took in the stern faces of Mr Clarkson, Miss Smith, Mr Anderson, the Drama teacher, the Music teacher, the entire faculty watching on, interrupted from their papers, cups of coffee, conversations. Everyone stalled in horror at the sight of the new girl lying on the floor in what was clearly not the Year Twelve common room, but the teachers' staff room.

My eyes shifted to the voice, to meet the wild and fuming gaze of Mr Fitzgibbons standing over me, his face red, a vein pulsing in his temple.

'My. Office. Now.'

# Chapter Thirteen

There would be no lunchtime hot chips, no beach cartwheels, and no gawking at hot surfers.

I had landed myself on Mr Fitzgibbons' radar, and that was not a place anyone wanted to be. I found myself in the principal's office; this time it wasn't to bask in his compliments about how impressive my grades were. Instead, what followed was a livid principal pacing back and forth in front of me in his tiny office, his movements so animated that it caused the leaves of the pot plant to sway.

'I overlooked the late arrival to assembly last week. I was willing to give you the benefit of the doubt, Miss Atkinson, but I damn well draw the line at breaking and entering into the staff room,' he shouted.

'I'm sorry, it was an accident.' I cringed as the words fell from my mouth.

'So, you just accidentally climbed up, opened a window and "fell" into the staff room, did you?'

Mr Fitzgibbons using sarcastic air quotes just seemed wrong and momentarily put me off my path.

'No, of course not, I just . . .'

Here was the clincher. I couldn't dob Amanda in, even though I inwardly cursed her with every ounce of my soul.

But I had to be smart. I'd seen enough late-night documentaries on doing time in hard prisons, and aside from some differences like manufacturing a shank in metal work, I was sure that schoolyard politics also frowned upon being a snitch.

'I thought it was the Year Twelve common room, I just wanted to take a look.' It wasn't entirely untrue.

'The Year Twelve common room doesn't concern you, Miss Atkinson.' I knew he was mad because he kept referring to me by my last name.

'The Year Twelve common room is a privilege, not a right – a privilege, might I add, that is not for you. Never forget you are still a Year Eleven student.'

I looked down into my hands; I had suffered enough humiliation caused by my own stupidity. The thought of being downgraded from my accelerated classes would have my parents asking questions. Oh God, my parents.

'Are you going to tell my parents about this?' I asked quietly, afraid to look him in the eye.

Maybe it was the completely defeated slump in my shoulders or the fact I fought so hard not to let the tears come, but something in Mr Fitzgibbons' demeanour changed. Maybe he wasn't used to chastising girls; I'm sure this seat I was on was usually reserved for Ballantine.

He sighed, took a seat behind his desk and watched me wearily. 'This is your first warning,' he said. 'Second, you will not be so lucky.'

I exhaled in relief, a smile of gratitude lining my face. 'Oh, thank you, Mr Fitzgibbons, I swear I will be on my best behaviour.'

'Well, to ensure that you are, I'm going to remind you of the consequences of bad behaviour here at Paradise High.

You are to report to Miss Smith and tell her that you will be on yard duty – she will know what that means. And then you are to report to Mr Collins, the cleaner; he will give you the bag you'll be needing. Then, once you have spent your time thinking about why you are cleaning the schoolyard, I want you to report back to Miss Smith at lunch to pick up any homework and lesson notes you have missed.'

Okay, that didn't seem too bad. Skipping class, picking up some rubbish. Could be worse. Mr Fitzgibbons rolled back in his seat, pulling open his bottom drawer, rummaging around before he brought out a bright orange scrap of material. He handed it over to me and I reluctantly took it from him, touching it as if I was afraid it might electrocute me. I held it in front of me; it was a fluoro orange safety vest, with reflectors down the trim, the kind of jacket road workers wore, but all I could think about was how my Uncle Eddie would have loved it. My mouth gaped in horror. This couldn't get any worse. Did Mr Fitzgibbons expect that I might get hit by a bus? Was it a hazard on the barren schoolyard? I tried to think myself lucky that at least he hadn't wanted me to do this in the thick of lunch: a small silver lining in the dark storm cloud of my soul.

Mr Fitzgibbons linked his hands over his stomach, looking on as if he was most proud of his invention. 'Turn it around,' he insisted.

Looking at him warily, I slowly flipped the vest around on the desk in front of me. My blood ran cold.

*Oh-no-no-no-no . . .*

There, in big black permanent texta were the words:

I DID A BAD, BAD THING.

The vest of shame suddenly took on a whole new meaning, and I just wanted to die.

•

Lunchtime reprieve or not, it was amazing how many teachers thought it such a great idea to take their lessons outside. And on this particular occasion, of course it happened to be Miss Gleeson's Lit class. Amanda, Gemma and Ballantine sat around the bench seats underneath the shade of a gum tree. They were the first students my eyes locked on, as I stood there at the top of the stairs, in my fluoro vest, holding my big black garbage bag in one hand, my stick with a spike in the other. I looked back to where Mr Fitzgibbons stood in the open doorway, probably making sure I didn't make a run for it. I had thought about it.

'Off you go,' he said with an adamant head nod. 'All around the main yard.'

There was no alternate route to take; the stairs led down into the heart of the yard, and once the sun's rays glinted off the reflectors on my vest it was only a matter of time before they would see me, and then would come the titters and the sniggers and the laughter and . . . I wanted to be sick.

I tried not to look at them, but then there was something in me that wanted to look, that wanted to cast daggers towards Amanda, complete with silent, pissed-off body language that read:

*You did this, you did this to me!*

The horror of the vest and the severe tongue lashing I had received from Mr Fitzgibbons, was all in the name of teaching me a lesson – this little exercise was allowing me to pause and reflect on my actions. Oh yes! And to ensure it wouldn't be happening anytime in the future, definitely yes. I lifted my chin with an air of stone-cold defiance, making my way proudly down the steps, almost stomping a loud trail, my steps echoing in the silent yard, and sure enough one head, two, three, four heads spun around, taking me in – the bag lady of Paradise High. But their giggles and mutterings were just distant white noise to me; instead, all my focus was directed solely at Amanda. She had flicked her head around, smiling and laughing with Gemma, until her eyes landed on me. Her smile fell away, her eyes widening as they trailed over my attire in horror, as if she was genuinely shocked to see me in 'the vest'.

One of the gangly surfing buddies sitting next to Ballantine started singing Chris Isaacs' 'Baby Did a Bad Bad Thing'. That had everyone in the class laughing, everyone except, to my surprise, Ballantine, who just stared on with his cool, calm gaze.

'All right, Jason, settle down, we don't need to be tortured by your off-key singing,' Miss Gleeson said, attempting to reel in her rowdy class.

I lazily tore my gaze away from Amanda and moved into the yard, imagining every Prima box, chip packet and banana peel was Amanda's stupid, insipid face as I spiked each item.

I wasn't the kind to think of master plans of revenge, but if I was going to hang with the big guns I would have to hold my own, and that is exactly what I decided to do.

•

I peeled off the vest before I did anything else, throwing it to the ground before dousing my hands with a liberal amount of liquid soap, lathering to my elbows and washing the suds off with blistering hot water. I looked as though I was about to perform an operation. Maybe I was? A personality transplant for Amanda would be nice. If there were two things I had learned in my time of punishment they were that, firstly, I was an idiot for trusting Amanda to begin with and, secondly, the students at Paradise High were absolute pigs, who seldom used a rubbish bin. The bell for lunch sounded, causing me to sigh in sheer relief that my time was up; I wouldn't dare seek permission to leave the school grounds, that was for sure. I picked up the vest, slinging it over my shoulder as I dragged my feet out of the girls' toilets.

You had to have your wits about you, ducking and weaving amongst the frenzy of the lunchtime crowds. The seniors whooping and hollering, pushing and nudging each other down the stairs towards their lockers, towards freedom. Having already returned my manky rubbish stick I now had to report to Miss Smith to receive the homework that I had missed. Classroom 7B: I stuck my head through the slightly ajar door, slowly pushing it open.

'Miss Smith?' I called, knocking lightly on the door. 'Hello?'

The room was eerily empty, everything was in its place and desks were free from students' mess, even the whiteboard had been cleaned down; it seemed that the students were not the only ones keen to escape the classroom. An image of Miss Smith hip and shouldering students out of the way through the door made me smile.

I left the classroom, once again entering the chaotic fray of high-pitched screams and chatter where I was always finding myself either stepping on someone or being stepped on. I saw a Year Seven cop an elbow to his temple from a girl who was fixing her hair; he just laughed with his mates and kept on walking. I had not yet acclimatised to the noise, the sea of flailing arms. It was still very much a culture shock for me; I almost felt like an explorer trying to machete my way through the jungle. I learned quickly that saying 'excuse me' would only get me weird looks.

*Oh, yeah, manners, sure. What are those?*

Unless your best friend called you a skank or a mole, your friendship wasn't a true one.

Aside from the tsunami of noise as crazed pubescent weirdos surged through the corridors, you could always be guaranteed of the warnings yelled from teachers trying to navigate the chaos like traffic wardens at a city intersection.

'Pick. It. Up.'

'No running.'

'I'm watching you, Jones.'

'Language!'

'I won't tell you again, Robbie Robinson.'

I didn't know what was more shocking: Mr Branson's screaming or the fact that someone actually named their kid Robbie Robinson.

# Chapter Fourteen

Mercifully I found the principal's door open and Mr Fitzgibbons on the phone.

I tiptoed into his office and placed the folded-up orange vest on his desk, ready to sidestep away, all until his finger lifted up and he mouthed: 'Wait'.

My insides screamed.

*No-no-no-no . . .*

Mr Fitzgibbons nodded thoughtfully, his expression grim with concentration. He was probably speaking to the department about some government grant, or maybe child services about little Robbie Robinson and his poorly chosen name. I bit my lip, trying to think of something else before I lost it. Mr Fitzgibbons scribbled down something on his notepad before speaking.

'Yep, twelve potato cakes, eight pieces of flake, two lamb souvlaki, five dollars worth of chips, and half a dozen dim sims.' He crossed off his list.

*Was he for real?*

'Yep, great, how long will that be, Connie? Right, excellent! Thanks for that.' He put down the phone, jotting another note on his list.

He glanced up, pausing as if he had forgotten I was there.

'Ah, Atkinson.'

Was this how it was going to be now? My criminal activity would have the principal forever referring to me as Atkinson, just like all the other rule breakers. I had only ever heard Boon or Ballantine referred to by their last names, and they were the resident school delinquents.

He followed my eyeline.

'Oh, yeah, it's a Special Lunch Day,' he said sheepishly. 'A few of the staff chip in and we lash out on some takeaway.'

More images of the teachers charging out the doors of their classrooms, pushing students out of the way. No wonder Mr Branson had been so crabby in the corridor: he was thinking 'Hurry up! Hurry up! It's Special Lunch Day!'

'So how did you go?' he asked, reclining lazily in his chair.

'Yeah, good. The yard's clean.' I nodded.

'Hmm, for now it is,' he said, glaring out the window at the screaming basketballers. I kind of wondered if Mr Fitzgibbons was really suited to working with teenagers.

'Now, I have had a talk with some of the other teachers and I think we have all come to the same conclusion about you, Lexie, about the best way to deal with this situation.'

'Oh?' I said, feeling rather concerned that I was deemed a 'situation'.

'Yes, I'm afraid we believe there is only one way to deal with your actions.'

*Oh God, they're going to tell my parents.*

I could feel my stomach churning, the seventies wood-panelled walls were closing in on me, heat flooding my cheeks as the deafening thrums of my heart made it difficult to concentrate.

'I'm afraid I'm going to have to send you to Siberia.'

*Wait, what?*

I blinked. 'Sorry?'

Mr Fitzgibbons' face crinkled with confusion. 'Oh, sorry,' he said with a laugh. 'Siberia is what we call detention. We are sending you to detention.'

'Oh.' I blew out the word in relief. Hang on a minute: detention? My relief was short-lived.

Mr Fitzgibbons pulled a pink slip out of his top drawer. He scribbled his unreadable handwriting across it. 'Hand this slip to Mr Anderson in room C3; I believe he is running Siberia today.' He handed me the slip. 'You are to present yourself every lunchtime for the rest of the week. I suggest you make full use of your time, Miss Atkinson.' He reached for a manila folder in his in-tray. 'Miss Smith asked me to give this to you – this was what was covered in today's lesson.'

'Thanks,' I managed rather unenthusiastically.

His cool grey eyes looked at me with no kindness, until they dipped to his wristwatch – then they lit up. 'Anyway, best get going, I have things to do.'

*Pfft, yeah, wouldn't want your fish 'n' chips to get cold.*

•

My lunchtime pass had gone from a forged note of freedom to a pink slip pass to Siberia.

Life was wicked and cruel sometimes; my mind flashed to Amanda who was probably sitting on the beach watching Boon and Ballantine slicing up the waves. Ballantine's bronzed skin, iridescent droplets of water cascading over his toned stomach as he wedged his board in the sand and towel dried his torso in slow motion. I blinked. . . . almost walking into a rubbish bin.

'Wake up, Lexie!' Mr Branson called. He was still standing in the hall barking orders at people, probably dreaming of his cold dim sims.

Would every day be like this? How had I managed to stuff up so badly and it was only my second week? I was now going to be imprisoned in a classroom all day for the rest of the week. I walked through the corridors dragging my feet and sighing with each step, the very same thing I found myself doing as I handed over my pink slip to Mr Anderson, the head of the Drama department. He had kind hazel eyes and a salt-and-pepper goatee. He also referred to me by my first name, which made me instantly like him.

'Take a seat, Lexie. You got stuff to do?'

'Yeah, some English,' I said, making my way to the back row, before stopping mid-aisle.

*Yeah, that didn't end so well for me last time.*

I about-faced and headed for a middle row near the window. From now on I was going to be a stellar student. I sat down, lifting my chin and straightening my spine. No more crazy, whacky antics daydreaming about surfers or hanging with the cool kids, no more attention-seeking strutting in the schoolyard and playing the new girl card; I mean, it's not like anyone cared anyway. From now on I would spend my time maturely and patiently, I thought, unzipping my pencil case and lining up my red pen, blue pen, grey pencil, rubber, sharpener on top of the desk. From now on there was going to be no distractions, just hard work that would get me the worldly experience I craved and the grades I wanted.

It was all about focus.

But then a binder and pencil case slammed down next to mine, breaking my focus and causing me to blink in fright. I took in that familiar black Quiksilver pencil case and an exercise book graffitied with blue inked waves.

My heart stopped.

Slowly I lifted my eyes to see Ballantine and Boon standing there looking down at me.

Boon with a boyish grin peeking over Ballantine's shoulder, not an easy thing to do considering the fact that Ballantine was a good foot taller than him.

'Bloody hell, new girl. What. Did. You. Do?' asked Boon, laughing hysterically, as he pulled his chair out, scraping the legs against the floorboards, leaving Ballantine still standing, still looking at me with an amused, curious spark in his eyes, as if he was trying to solve a mystery.

I shifted awkwardly under his watchful scrutiny, straightening my already straight line of pens. 'I'm not in your seat, am I?' I asked, cocking my brow and glancing up at him with a challenge.

He tucked in his bottom lip as if to stifle the smile that wanted to come. Instead he shook his head. 'Not today.' He pulled out the chair next to me, taking his seat and shifting himself forward, placing his elbows on the table, almost touching mine.

I swallowed. So much for being focused. If anyone had warned me that I would be spending my lunches in Siberia with bad boys from Kirkland, I wouldn't have believed them.

Never could I have hoped for better; Ballantine sat so close I could sense the rise and fall of his chest in my peripheral vision, actually smell the mind-numbing scent of his aftershave: crisp, clean and mouth-watering.

*Oh God, Lexie, get your head together.*

Not so easy when I was aware of every single move he made, flicking the pages of his exercise book, the deep sighs, his fingers ruffling through his thick, dishevelled hair, rummaging through his pencil case. Why was he sitting next to me? There were plenty of other seats in the room. Why me?

'All right, gang, you know how this works. Heads down, zipped lips and best behaviours, yeah?' Mr Anderson settled in behind his desk stacked with piles of paper, probably using the time to catch up on some marking, I thought, until he pulled a mysterious little ear plug from his top pocket and wedged it in his right ear. Bloody hell, was he looking at a racing guide for the horses?

I couldn't believe it; nothing like a bit of sly gambling on the side to kill the time. My outrage was short-lived when Ballantine leant over to me, so close I could feel his breath against my earlobe.

'Can I borrow a pen?'

I flung into action fast, a desperate attempt at aiming to please. 'Um, yeah, sure,' I said, almost pushing my pencil case off the edge of the desk, catching it just before it fell and pens clattered everywhere. I breathed a big sigh of relief as I pulled the pencil case into my lap, smiling a small smile at Ballantine, who was waiting with amused interest. I nervously tucked a strand of hair behind my ear as I delved into the recess of my case, hunting for the best pen I could find. I opted for a black ink ballpoint with a retractable clicker.

*Nice.*

I held it out to him, my heart rate spiking as he took it from my clasp, his finger once again brushing against me in the simplest and briefest touch, but it was enough to have me replaying and analysing every aspect of it for the rest of the day.

'Thanks,' he whispered, with a crooked smile.

I had an image of me fainting at the sight of that devilish smile, eyes rolling to the back of my head, sliding under the desk unconscious. Instead, I cleared my throat and faced forward, glancing around the room. It suddenly occurred to me that either Paradise City had a school full of impeccably behaved students or we were just the really bad ones, segregated from the rest of the school, kind of maximum security, or maybe this was just the section for seniors? I was dying to know but didn't dare ask. Not that I minded sharing detention solely with Ballantine and Boon. And the fact that, even with a massive empty classroom, they opted to sit next to me was a rather dramatic change after the seating fiasco of my first day.

I pulled out what looked like an English assignment and read through the bullet points of the criteria, trying to focus my mind. Not so easily achievable when a triangular piece of paper flicked into my temple and landed on the back of my hand. I slowly shifted my eyes to the two other students in the class. They sported excellent poker faces, looking down at their books with deep, intense interest.

I glanced up to Mr Anderson, who was intently studying his racing form and pressing in the earbud; it must have been mid-race because he was sitting on the edge of his seat mouthing 'Come on, come on' under his breath. I took the moment of his distraction to slide the paper into my lap and unfold it carefully to read:

*Seriously, what did you do?*

It was Boon. I knew this much because it was scrawled in blue ink, not the black I had given Ballantine.

I bit my lip.

*What did I do?*

In any case, honesty was always the best policy, right? Plus, there was a little part of me – okay, a huge part of me – that wanted to see his reaction.

Mr Anderson fist-pumped the air, well and truly distracted, as I jotted down my response.

*I got caught breaking into the staff room* ☹

I thought the sad face was a nice little touch. I refolded the note and tugged gently on Ballantine's shirt, motioning for the pass down. His head snapped around in surprise as he eyed the piece of paper with interest, taking it from me and discreetly passing it to Boon.

Boon slowly unfolded it much like I had, with an ever-watchful gaze on Mr Anderson. When his serious blue eyes lowered, to tick over my response, the instantaneous rise of both his brows was priceless; I had to force myself not to laugh. Ballantine's interest piqued, he grabbed the note from Boon and a small smile creased the corner of his mouth, his brow kinking in surprise. He glanced my way as if gauging whether I was telling the truth or not.

I merely shrugged, as if to say 'What's a girl to do?' As I returned to study my English assignment I could still feel the full weight of Ballantine's eyes on me, but I just straightened my spine and read on in confidence. I would leave the details up to their imaginations, let them wonder what would possess a new girl to act in such a way, allow myself a certain amount of mystery, I thought. In actual fact, there was more mystery surrounding Ballantine than there was me. Everyone would know by now that I was Amanda's country bumpkin cousin from Hicksville. They would know that there was obviously no love lost between us. I was inducted into the Gilmore brainiacs and was rebelling mere days after starting here.

But what of Ballantine? Why was he here? Why was it that mostly every time I came into contact with him it was to do with some kind of trouble? He was sporty, a surfer – a good one or bad one I was yet to find out. He had an annoying tendency to click the top of his biro while flicking it through his fingers. Actually, that was kind of hot. As was the thick leather bracelet he wore on his right wrist, accompanied by several smaller leather bands, intricately braided in different colours. I wondered what the story was behind them.

His hands were the only thing I could risk a partial glance at, being so close. But they were beautiful hands, so tanned. His sleeves were rolled up to his elbows – a trait quite common among the sporty boys, even their ties were often loose and skew-whiff, no doubt choking from the restrictions of conformity. While I had welcomed a uniform with open arms and loved how it made me feel, I'm sure the same could not be said about Ballantine.

I wanted to write my own note to ask a million questions. What had they done? How long were they destined to be in Siberia for? Had they worn the orange vest of shame too? Were they going to the beach after school?

*Okay, no need to be a creeper, Lexie.*

# Chapter Fifteen

By the time the bell sounded I had only managed to write my name on the top right-hand corner of my English homework.

*Awesome.*

Instead of turning over a new leaf and becoming the model student, I had spent every moment of the detention pretending to read while ogling Ballantine in my peripheral vision.

Ballantine frowning while reading.

Ballantine chewing on the end of his pen. MY pen.

Ballantine stretching in his chair.

Ballantine yawning, sighing and just being generally dreamy by doing the simplest things.

The bell had woken us all up. Jumping into action, the three of us packed up our books with enthusiasm.

Mr Anderson pulled out the earbud and quickly folded and wedged his newspaper in between his textbooks.

'You are free,' he announced.

Free as in 'go to your next holding cell'.

I grabbed my pencil case to find Ballantine holding my pen out in front of me.

'Thanks,' he said.

Amazing how such a simple word could make my stomach flutter. 'Aren't you going to need it?' I asked.

He shrugged one shoulder. 'Not for PE I won't.' He smiled. It wasn't the teeth-exposing kind, but it didn't matter. It was the dimple-dipping kind and that was the one I lived for. I knew my whimsical thoughts were ridiculous but there was just something about what Luke Ballantine did to me. Maybe I'd been isolated for far too long, sheltered from the reality of the world, but when I took the pen from him there was an insane stalker in me that wanted to encase the pen in a glass shrine simply because he had touched it. Mental thoughts like that made me want to run to Amanda and squeal. Yeah, well, that wasn't going to happen. Laura? Boon's sister: the link was too close and I didn't really know her.

'See ya round, Lex,' Ballantine said, backing away a few cool steps before turning.

'Yeah, and for Christ's sake, behave,' Boon said, laughing as they walked out of Siberia. It was then I realised the weight that was on me. I had no-one to talk to, no-one I could trust, no-one to confide in.

There was just me and my lustful thoughts about this mysterious Bad Boy Ballantine.

•

There were many things that surprised me lately. One of them was waiting by my locker at home time.

Amanda leant against the wall, her arms folded. I could never tell if she was actually ever in a good mood because her heavy eye makeup always made her look sullen. Maybe she was just always miserable. Who knew? All I knew was she was definitely the last person I wanted to see.

She stood to attention when she saw me closing in, pushing off my locker and standing aside for me to put my books away.

'Hey,' she said, adjusting the weight of her backpack over her shoulder.

'Hey,' I managed, not even bothering to look her way.

She stepped closer, tilting her head to the side, trying to get my attention. 'What did you do?' she asked in a low voice.

I slammed my locker shut hard, causing her to blink in surprise as I turned my darkened gaze on her.

'Really? I mean, REALLY?' I scoffed.

'You were only supposed to stick your head through the door,' she said, almost as if she was trying to blame me.

'Well, I didn't, and you know what? It wasn't the Year Twelve common room. In fact, there was no rainforest wall-paper in sight, but you know what was in sight? What I was faced with once I had made my way through the window? What I saw right after I face-planted into the carpet? What I saw was a table full of pissed-off teachers who wanted to chase me with sticks of fire,' I all but yelled.

Amanda rolled her eyes. 'Don't be so dramatic.'

My mouth gaped. 'Dramatic? I had to wear the vest of shame and spent most of my day picking up rubbish and chilling in Siberia with the Kirkland boys.'

Amanda's eyes flashed with interest. I stilled long enough to notice the definite change in her expression, the one thing that I could see had an effect on her. I, of course, recalled the one very interesting piece of information that I'd thought to file away for later, and now I was so mad and she was so dismissive, I couldn't think of a more perfect opportunity for me to use it.

I shrugged. 'Lucky I had Boon to keep me company.'

Amanda's eyes widened.

*Bingo!*

'Boon?'

I smiled dreamily to myself. 'If it wasn't for the notes he was passing me in detention, I think I would've died of boredom,' I said matter-of-factly, before shouldering my bag and walking off with a knowing grin. I didn't need eyes in the back of my head to know that what I had just said would've hit a nerve, and although there was a small part of me that felt kind of bad, there was also another part of me that thought very loud and clear:

*Good!*

•

True to form, Amanda went back to her snappy, snarly self. Maybe it was as a direct result of my casual name-drop of Boon, but there was no real way of knowing. From the day I'd arrived, she had displayed all the symptoms of Mad Cow Disease. I sat in the stuffy little alcove in our bedroom after dinner, attempting to finish off the English homework I had so miserably failed to complete during detention. If it wasn't the infuriating dancing bug that kept headbutting against the bulb of the desk lamp, it was the heavy banging and slamming of drawers, doors, basically anything Amanda could get her hands on as she pottered around the bedroom.

I ignored her.

I hoped by doing so the old adage of 'if you ignore it, it will go away' would come true. Well, not Amanda. Once she had finished loudly rearranging her CD collection, she obviously thought now was as good a time as any to put one on, turning the volume up so loud the bookshelves above my desk vibrated.

I clenched my jaw and continued to ignore her, hoping that Aunty Karen or Uncle Peter would come and intervene, but then considering they were probably tucked away in their insulated parents' retreat, they probably couldn't hear a thing. Instead, with no likely rescue in sight I focused all my energy on reading my paperwork, finally getting to the last page. I gathered up the pieces of paper, only to find a yellow sheet underneath the stash. An A4 leaflet that had been tucked into my folder from English. My eyes narrowed to see the bold heading: Paradise High Newsletter. With today's date in the corner. My head was pounding from the music I was so desperately trying to ignore, but as I lazily read down the columns of the newsletter, stifling a yawn, I froze. Right there in another bold heading: 'School Social'.

I read on. Was it too early to start planning my outfit? I couldn't pinpoint the date – maybe this headache was a lot more serious than I thought. My heart sunk as I stared at the yellow leaflet; taking in the date my eyes had now found. Maybe it was some horrid mistake, but the school social – a real school social – was weeks away. I turned, hooking my arm around the back of my chair, yelling above the music.

'Is there really a school social at the end of term?'

Amanda was lying on her back, her legs pressed up against her bedhead, jigging to the beat of the music. Her eyes strained upside down to look at me. 'Why? Can't you dance?'

'Of course I can,' I defended a bit too quickly.

I had visions of me doing the 'Time Warp' only to be shunned by the cool kids and their disgusted, cringing stares.

A shiver ran down my spine, the thought far more humiliating than any vest of shame. I didn't know what was wrong with me; with each passing day came a new obstacle, a new dilemma, but of all the things I had been faced with, this was by far the most terrifying. I could now see that having been isolated from a normal teenage population for so long had done damage. Hopefully it wasn't irreparable. I felt out of my depth in all social interactions, and didn't understand the rules of teenage interchange. I felt angry. Angry at who, though? My parents for their choice to live in such a remote place? Amanda for being such a bitch? Myself for not realising life in Paradise City could be so complex? It was just so confusing.

# Chapter Sixteen

I lay there, staring at the reflected glow of the streetlight that illuminated my ceiling. I closed one eye, opened it, closed it, then switched eyes in a series of blinks that turned my vision into a lightshow before growing bored and sighing into the night. Eleven minutes past eleven and I couldn't sleep, and neither, it seemed, could my roommate, who was suddenly rustling around in the dark. I rolled over, squinting across the room at the silhouette gently opening and closing her cupboards, before walking around the bed and stubbing her toe.

'Shit,' she said, falling back onto the end of her bed.

I leant over, clicking on my bedside lamp and flooding the room in a shadowy light, causing us both to squint at the adjustment. Amanda looked like a rabbit caught in the headlights, flinching against the unexpectedness of it. I pulled myself into a sitting position.

'Going somewhere?' I asked with a curious curve to my brow.

'Shhh,' she glowered, before standing and limping to her drawer, rummaging around and slipping some money and lip balm into the pocket of her jeans. 'Turn the light off.'

Without fuss I clicked it off, watching on as Amanda stepped onto my bed and, without so much as a sideways glance, worked on sliding the window open.

'Take me with you,' I said all too quickly and all too loudly.

Amanda's head snapped around. 'Shut up,' she growled, her face thunderous. 'This doesn't concern you.'

'You owe me.'

'I owe you nothing.'

'Really? Because a week in Siberia tells me differently.'

'I didn't tell you to climb through a bloody window.'

'No, you just asked me to lie to your parents about being daughter of the year.'

'And you got your note, we're square.'

'Not even close.'

We stared, or rather shot laser beams, at one another with our glowering death vision, unmoving, almost unbreathing we were so still. It was obvious she was not going to give an inch, not one bit, so I was forced to take the lead.

'Amanda, where are you going?' I yelled out.

She dived on top of me, slamming her hand over my mouth. 'All right, all right,' she said, freezing and tilting her head to the side to gauge if my loud question had caused any movement from upstairs; there was nothing. She blew out a breath before glancing down at my wide-eyed stare and flared nostrils. Her look was chilling and I wondered if she was going to lash out at me, smother me with my own pillow.

Instead, she pushed off me. 'Get dressed,' she bit out.

And even though she could be utterly terrifying, I couldn't have leapt out of bed quick enough.

•

'Where are we going?' I puffed, trying desperately to keep up with Amanda's long-legged steps. She was so furious I half expected her to start breathing fire.

My question was met with silence; it was clear that my sole mission tonight was just to keep up and shut up. We were nearing the end of our street, leaving suburbia behind as we stepped off the bitumen road and made our way across a walking path and onto the sloping grass. My heart pounded, the wind whipping my hair into my eyes as we stepped over the pine-posted barrier and down through the darkness, our way lit by the dotted lamps leading down to the beach below.

When I first arrived, I had wanted a taste of everything Paradise City had to offer. I wanted to blend in with the crowd and inhabit the true essence of living here. So far I had experienced cover stories of deceit, note forgery, lunchtime detentions, and now I was sneaking out on a school night. I could have squealed with delight, although Amanda probably would have killed me if I so much as made a peep. My first few weeks and I had already experienced so many firsts; my stomach flipped at the thought of experiencing so many more. For my parents it was about me assimilating into the education system in preparation for Year Twelve; for me it was so much more than that.

As the path finally flattened out and our feet began to sink into the sand I saw a group of shady figures up ahead, some standing, some sitting. I could hear their laughter echo into the night. The sky was dotted with sparkly pinholes, the wind warm and whipping against my skin. My eyes flicked briefly from the group ahead, to momentarily marvel at the surging ocean that roared over the sand, so loud, so incredibly intimidating in the night.

'Speak of the devil!' a voice cried out.

'And what's this, the devil has an assistant?' said another.

'Piss off.' Amanda shoved at the boy with woolly blond hair, snatching the beer out of his hand and sculling it down.

'Woo, chug-a-lug, Burnsy,' pierced Boon's voice.

'Yeah, baby.'

The chorus of wolf whistles only urged her on to finish the can, finally coming up for air, and with a wince crushing it and chucking it back to its owner.

I looked away, rolling my eyes, and in the process locked onto a familiar set across the group. I stilled, my heart stalling as Ballantine stood watching on, his hands in his pockets, the light of the moon bathing him in a muted white glow.

His eyes slowly broke from my gaze before he turned towards his mates sitting in the sand. 'Let's go.'

Any moment of exhilaration I felt was now replaced with bitter disappointment as I watched him walk away. Amanda was busy swearing and trying to big-note herself to those that remained and I wanted to scream at her, to kick and shout and ask why we weren't following the others that disappeared into the night, along with any hope I had of hanging out with Ballantine. It wasn't lost on me that the only actual interaction we'd had thus far was:

'You're in my seat.'

'What's your name?'

'Can I borrow a pen?'

They were probably the most memorable of our deep and meaningful exchanges. It was then I wondered what had me so desperate to be around him. What was it about *him*, more than anyone else, that intrigued me? He was just one boy. One boy who would never be interested in someone like me.

I knew there was no chance that Amanda would make a move to follow when Boon was left behind. I wondered where Ballantine was going: further along the beach, perhaps? Would it be weird to follow? Or was my fate to be near Amanda, watching on as she took another beer from the boys' stash. I stood to the side, my expression thick with disapproval as I witnessed Amanda become a massive try-hard in front of the boys. If I thought the Amanda I lived with was a stranger, then this socialite Amanda was even weirder.

Leaving the huddle of the group I stepped my way towards the frothy edge of the ocean's line, grateful that the wind was blowing my hair back over my shoulders as I faced the expansive spread of water that seemed to go on forever. Laughter and jeers sounded behind, probably another sculling competition with a few obscenities flung around as terms of endearment. I recognised the two other Kirkland boys from school. Amanda seemed to be showing off deliberately for Boon or maybe this was just her being her obnoxious self. Whatever it was, it bothered me. Bothered me because, well, I wasn't sure what I expected to find as I climbed out the window, but standing down at the beach drinking wasn't exactly what I had in mind. And then I felt foolish; was I such a prude? Was I that much of a dork that I was shocked this was happening on a school night? Didn't I want to infiltrate, to blend in? And just as I was about to psyche myself up to return to the group, to make an effort, I felt the presence of someone beside me.

'Gemma told us you thought you were breaking into the common room.'

I spun around, the wind catching my hair and snapping it into my eyes. I pulled it away to see Boon standing next to me, hands in his pockets, looking out to the great nothing.

'And then I wondered, why would the new girl be so desperate to see hideous wallpaper?' His lips pressed into a cheeky grin as he eyed me side on. It was a look that said that he actually knew a secret and was waiting for me to confess all, so I did.

'I was trying to get your football back,' I said.

So when Boon said 'I know', it was my turn to offer a cheeky side-glance.

'How?'

Boon shrugged. 'Laura keeps her diary in the worst hiding place known to man.'

My mouth gaped. 'You read Laura's diary?'

'You'll be pleased to know she feels really shitty about putting the idea into your head.'

'I'm not pleased, not pleased at all. Stop reading her diary.'

'It's usually filled with bat-shit boring stuff. What mundane crap goes on in home ec, what new dress she wants to wear to the social, her vomit-inducing, undying love for Ballantine,' he said, shuddering at the last word.

My head snapped up. 'Undying love for Ballantine?' I repeated, mostly to myself.

'Of course, if you repeat any of this I will just deny it.'

I blinked, troubled by information overload. And definitely not the information I had wanted to know. I took a deep breath, grateful that I'd never confessed my lustful thoughts about Ballantine; now I knew this was a definite no go.

'Well, what are you doing reading it, anyway?' I asked.

'Oh, I don't know,' he said, moving to circle around me, causing my head to crane to watch his movements until he walked in front of me. 'Thought there might have been some interesting information about the new girl.'

Boon's eyes locked onto mine; the seriousness of his gaze caused my heart to skip a beat, but not in the way that it did with Ballantine. This was a 'holy shit I'm in deep trouble' feeling.

I laughed, attempting to lighten the mood. 'What could you possibly want to know?'

*Stupid! I was so bloody stupid. Way to walk into a spider web, genius.*

Boon smiled, stepping forward, so close I wanted to take a step back. My heart was pounding, worried about where this was headed and the look he was giving me. *Oh God, was Amanda seeing this?* Was she watching her crush step close to me? Could she see him staring at me? My breaths were shallow; I glanced down at my feet, breaking eye contact from Boon, but it didn't stop him from reaching out and tucking a wayward strand of hair behind my ear, instantly causing my eyes to widen with the unexpectedness of it.

'Do you have a boyfriend, Lexie Atkinson? Or is there a broken heart somewhere in the wastelands of Oz?'

His voice was low, hypnotic, and had it been under any other circumstances – Amanda not being madly in love with him and my own thoughts not being elsewhere – I could surely have appreciated how gorgeous Boon was, especially this close. He wasn't much taller than me, but he had sparkling blue eyes and a cheeky, sexy smile – perfect and starkly white against his dark skin. Always full of yap, and the regular class clown, so to see him looking at me with serious, questioning eyes made my insides churn in panic. None more so than when his thumb brushed slowly against my bottom lip.

Oh God, was he going to kiss me? Right here, in front of all these people from school, in front of Amanda? Laura's brother, Ballantine's best friend? My heart was racing, the beats drowning out the roar of the ocean. I had to look for an exit, a clear-cut exit to shut down the look in his eyes, to stop this from happening. Why was Boon trying to kiss me? Me? Did I want Boon to kiss me? Shit, this was so confusing. And just as Boon worked on cupping the back of my neck and went to close the distance . . .

'Amanda likes you!' I blurted out.

Boon froze, his brows lowered in confusion.

'What?'

'Amanda. She's crazy about you,' I said quickly.

Oh God, I was a dead girl.

Boon's hand dropped back to his side, he even stepped away a little. 'Amanda? As in Amanda, Amanda?' he asked, looking even more perplexed. 'Your cousin Amanda?'

I nodded. Watching as his troubled eyes flicked over my shoulder, back to the group.

In Boon's moment of shock I took the opportunity to break away, but not before leaning in with some parting advice that I whispered into his ear: 'Of course, if you repeat any of this I will just deny it.' I patted him on the shoulder and made my way back to the group, back to face the music.

# Chapter Seventeen

'What do you mean, she's gone?'

When I returned to the others I half expected to be met with a death stare from Amanda. For her to come charging at me with an Amazonian war cry and tackle me to the ground, trying to gouge my eyes out. I even had visions of our reunion turning into a Michael Jackson video clip minus the switchblades and eighties-style choreography. So when I came back to find Amanda had left, actually left me behind, I didn't know what to think. Had she seen Boon and me? I glanced back to Boon. His silhouette was barely visible until he neared what was left of the group. I doubt she would have been able to see clearly enough to know if anything had happened.

'Where is everyone?' Boon directed his question to a couple from school who were obviously not very impressed with us interrupting their private make-out session. The girl with a disturbing amount of regrowth rolled her eyes.

'Aren't you supposed to be heading to the Wipe Out Bar?'

'That's where Ballantine was headed,' said the boy.

My interest piqued at the sound of Ballantine's name. I glanced left to see my reaction had not gone unnoticed by Boon, who was staring at me with interest.

*Shit-shit-shit. Subtle as a sledgehammer, Lexie.*

I cleared my throat, looking away and adopting my best casual, whatever, who cares attitude.

'It'll be shut by now,' said Boon, slowly tearing his gaze from me back to the couple.

'But Dean's pretty cool, yeah? He'll let you stay on, won't he?' said the boy, who was trying his best to move us on.

'That all depends what mood he's in and I don't intend to traipse over to the other side of the city to find out.' Boon sounded annoyed. 'Come on, Lexie, I'll take you home,' he said, tilting his head and walking off in the same direction Ballantine had earlier.

The couple sitting on the sand just stared at me, and it took me a moment to gather my thoughts before jogging after Boon, who was marching a quick, determined line down the beach.

'Boon, wait.'

He didn't.

Instead, I had to try to dig my heels into the collapsing sand, wondering how they managed it on *Baywatch*. Maybe the scenes weren't in slow motion at all, maybe that was just them really running; it was near on impossible. I was such a weakling. It wasn't until we hit the base of a wide concrete staircase that led up from the beach to higher ground that I ignored the burn in my legs and skipped every second step to gain some ground, managing to beat Boon to the top so I could stand in front of him, blocking his way.

'Home?' I breathed out heavily, leaning over with my hands on my knees, trying to catch my breath. 'Really?'

Boon, whose breathing wasn't even uneven, just looked like he had been for a stroll in the park as he folded his arms over his chest, eyes roaming over me as if I was the most pitiful thing he had stumbled upon.

I swallowed, repeating myself. 'You're really going to take me home?'

'Well, that all depends; your place or mine?' he said, flashing a boyish grin.

I rolled my eyes. 'Shouldn't we be looking for the others? What's the Wipe Out Bar?'

*And more importantly, how do we get there?*

I followed Boon, stepping over the pine barrier that worked as a divider from the grass to bitumen and into a narrow stretch of concrete car park with only a few lonely cars up ahead. Under a row of streetlights, Boon delved into the pocket of his shorts, pulling out a set of keys as he closed in on an older model Holden ute, old as in my grandpa's era. It was shiny and well maintained, a little bit funky even, just like my mum's knee-high boots and flared jeans were when they came back into fashion. But it wasn't the immaculate baby blue paintwork or the nostalgia that had me surprised as I came to a standstill beside the passenger door.

'You drive?'

Boon stilled, my question appearing to confuse him somewhat. 'I'm eighteen,' he said, almost puffing his chest out in challenge.

Oh, yeah, I kept forgetting I was a year below everyone. Still, a smile spread across my lips.

'So cool,' I said, mainly to myself.

'Hop in and I'll take you home,' Boon said, unlocking his door and sliding behind the wheel. He leant over and pushed the passenger door open. I didn't move.

'Umm, you do realise I can pretty much see my house from here. It's literally just over there.'

Okay, so a slight exaggeration but it was still really close, too close to warrant a lift.

'Get in and I'll take you to the Wipe Out Bar.'

My head quickly jerked up. 'Really?'

Boon's answer was to turn on the ignition and fire up the car. I as good as jumped into the passenger seat, fear coursing through my veins at the thought of being left behind. I had already been ditched once tonight; well, twice if you included Ballantine. I eagerly clicked my seatbelt into place, readying myself to be taken to where the others had headed. This was more like it. This was how I'd hoped the night would end, a local hotspot with the surfer boys, an insight into their world away from school rules.

Boon flicked the lights on full beam, highlighting the navy sedan in front of us and the couple that were pashing in it, only breaking apart in agitated, squinted stares towards the beams.

I blanched, looking away, embarrassed.

Boon laughed, taking in my unease. 'You sure you don't want to stay here, this is where all the action is,' he said, taunting me.

'I'm sure.'

He shrugged. 'Whatever.'

He backed up a little, changing gears and spinning the wheel expertly with one hand. He plunged his foot on the accelerator, which had my body whipping back in my seat, thudding my head and causing my heart to jump at the unexpectedness of it. The V8 of Boon's engine thrummed in the night as he steered around the corner, speeding up the hill. I was smiling so big, so goofy, thinking that what my aunt and uncle didn't know wouldn't hurt them. The sound of this loud, thumping ute would probably have them turning in their beds as the noise disturbed their sleep. Little would they know that I was a part of the crime. I was jolted out of my smug thoughts when Boon stepped on the brakes and brought the car to a stop. Outside the front of my house? My head snapped from the shadowy two-storey building to Boon, my eyes alight with confusion and then betrayal, taking in his cheeky smirk.

'What are you doing? I thought we were going to the Wipe Out Bar?'

Boon scoffed. 'I'm not going there.'

'But those two said it would be fine, that Dean would –'

'Dean Saville!' Boon burst out laughing. 'Dean is likely to be waiting for me with a shotgun if I rock up at this time on a school night. Dylan and Morgan don't know what they're talking about.'

Dylan and Morgan? Their names sounded like they were characters on *Beverly Hills 90210*. And whoever this Dean Saville bloke was I was starting to get really pissed off with him, but not as pissed off as I was with the traitorous Boon, who yawned and stretched in front of me.

He gripped the steering wheel, looking me over with interest. 'The party doesn't have to be over, new girl.'

'Pfft. In your dreams.' I opened the car door, slamming it in anger before wincing at what a stupid idea that was. My eyes flicked up to the unlit second storey, waiting for the lights to turn on and for Uncle Peter to come charging out with a shotgun, in his undies. But there was no sign of life and I breathed a sigh of relief before turning to give Boon one last death stare. I made to storm my way back in through my bedroom window.

'Hey, Lexie.' Boon was leaning over the passenger seat, motioning me to come back. Irritated, I stepped closer, leaning down to the opened window.

'Shhh, you're going to wake the entire neighbourhood.'

'Shit. Sorry,' Boon winced, quickly turning off his engine.

I tapped my foot impatiently, thinking maybe he felt bad and would take me to the Wipe Out Bar after all.

Boon shifted in his seat, picking at the seam on his leather steering wheel. He went all quiet and thoughtful like a little boy.

I sighed in impatience. 'What, Boon?'

'So . . . like . . . what has Amanda exactly said about me?'

I laughed. Was he for real?

'What?' he said defensively, straightening in his seat. 'What's so funny?'

I mock yawned. 'Oh, Boon, it's far too late to be chitchatting. It's a school night, remember?' I folded my arms, lifting one brow as if to say:

*Lexie – 1, Boon – 0*

That would teach him for bringing me home.

I waited for his response, for a counter offer to get back into the car and he would take me wherever I wanted to go if I would spill about Amanda. Not that I knew anything other than second-hand information from Laura.

He nodded as if accepting his fate. 'Fair enough.' He started up his car again; the roars of the engine so painfully loud.

'It's a shame, though,' Boon said, causing me to look back at him.

'Oh, yeah, and why's that?'

Boon smiled so wide I thought I might be blinded by it. 'Because I thought you might like to know what a certain mate of mine thinks about you.'

I paused. My world dropping away, nothing audible, nothing real to me other than the erratic beats of my heart.

'What mate?' I asked, my eyes wide as I failed to play it cool, to keep myself from wanting to fling my body across the car bonnet and beg for more information.

Boon stretched, yawning and then looked at the dashboard clock. 'Oh, is that the time?' He feigned surprise. Every action was so overacted, you could tell he was completely loving this.

'Boon.' I said his name as if it was a warning. A warning to not do this, to not drive away and leave me hanging.

But Boon pulled into gear and threw me a winning smile. 'Better get to bed, Lexie. It's a school night, remember?' he said in a chastising tone, before giving me a cheeky wink and speeding off down the street sounding a series of ear-piercing honks that had me cursing him and scurrying back to the house before a Mexican wave of outdoor lights flicked on.

My heart was thumping, my breath short and shallow, as I quickly made my way around the side of the house back to the bedroom window. Fast and silent was not easy and with each step I cursed Boon. Cursed his entrapment on bringing me home, cursed his sexual innuendo, cursed his infuriatingly loud car, and cursed how much glee he showed as he got the upper hand.

*What a certain mate of mine thinks about you.*

The sentence rolled over and over again in my head on a continual loop as I slid the bedroom window across and hitched myself onto the sill, the aluminium of the frame digging into my hip bones. I let gravity pull me forward, my squeal luckily muffled by my mattress. I flopped onto my bed. Home free, out of breath, and my thoughts blazing a trail through my mind as I dared to wonder.

*Which mate?*

# Chapter Eighteen

I was woken by the slamming of an elbow between my shoulder blades, the piercing pain only outdone by the heavy dead weight pinning me to the mattress, crushing all the breath out of me. My cries were muffled by my pillow. I was getting used to being woken up in the most random of ways, but this was ridiculous.

'Wake up! Wake up! Wake up!' singsonged Amanda, who was now jumping up and down on my bed. Was she drunk?

I winced, crawling myself upright, glancing at the clock which read three a.m.

'What the hell?'

I pushed aside the curtain of hair that covered my eyes, squinting at the still-open window, the very one Amanda had obviously just crawled through.

Amanda bounced up and down on my bed before letting her legs give way and bouncing onto her butt, breathless and laughing.

'Oh my God, Lexie, I wanted to kill you. Like seriously maddening homicidal tendencies and then . . .' Amanda broke off with a deep, dreamy-eyed sigh.

I wearily crossed my legs into a sitting position under my covers, not feeling warm and fuzzy about her rather light-hearted confession.

'And then?' I asked, with a curve of my brow.

Amanda's lips spread into a blinding, if slightly unnerving, smile. One I hadn't seen since I arrived here.

'And then he kissed me.'

I stilled. My breath hitching in my throat, a fear stabbing me in the pit of my stomach.

'He?'

Amanda sighed again, snatching up one of my pillows and hugging it to her chest like a child. 'Boon,' she said.

My shoulders slumped in relief.

*Oh, thank God. Boon.*

'Wait, where did you meet up with Boon?' I asked, confused.

Amanda shrugged, manoeuvring herself to mirror my cross-legged position. 'The Wipe Out Bar.'

*Bloody traitor.*

So Boon ditched me and headed to the last place he said he had intended to go. My insides burned by his betrayal. He was so full of crap. I wondered if he was just trying to get a reaction from me by insinuating that one of his mates had said something about me, assuming of course that whatever they had said was something I wanted to hear.

Before I had the chance to ask who else was at the Wipe Out Bar, a pillow thwacked against my face.

'Boon told me you said I liked him.' Amanda held the pillow above her head ready to lash out for round two when she paused. 'But . . . how did you know I did? I never told you.' Amanda lowered the pillow, genuinely perplexed.

Oh, great, way to go, big mouth Boon! And it wasn't as if I could betray my source as Laura, so I went with what came to mind.

'It's kind of obvious.'

Amanda bit her lower lip. 'Oh God, is it really?'

'Only to me. I guess I just know you better than anyone else, that's all,' I offered lightheartedly, even though it wasn't entirely true. The Amanda of old I knew. The Amanda that I had met in Paradise City was a complete stranger to me, and yet there was something in the Amanda I was looking at now, the very one that sat with her legs crossed on my bed. The light of excitement that sparked in her eyes, the way she looked as though she was about to share a thousand secrets with me. It was the same look we shared when we were young; my heart clenched at the memory, hoping it would last.

'So, Boon, hey?'

Amanda's smile spread wide, lighting up her whole face. 'Daniel Boon,' she crooned, before throwing herself on her back and muffling her elated squeals with her pillow.

I leant against the bedhead, folding my arms. 'Wow, that good, huh?'

She yanked the pillow from her face, regaining her breath once more. 'Oh, you have no idea.'

A moment flashed in my mind – Boon stepping closer to me, surely about to kiss me until I blurted out Amanda's secret. I'd seen the lines of confusion etched in his brow as he slowly registered what I'd said. Then it obviously registered on a deeper scale as he made his way to the Wipe Out Bar where Amanda was and, well, the rest was history. I just hoped that by morning Amanda wasn't also history. She was completely smitten. I had only experienced a small sample of serious heart palpitations over Ballantine so I totally got the hysteria.

Amanda rolled onto her side, leaning her head on her hand. 'I have liked Boon for so long. I can't even think of a time when I didn't. It's like he is the sun and the world is just so grey and dull, and then he comes along and changes everything.'

I sniggered. 'That's how I feel about Paradise. Red Hill was so mundane and bloody awful. Then I came here and it's like I have seen the sun for the very first time, and that's just geography.'

Amanda's brow rose. 'Wow, if you feel that way about a location I hate to think what you'll feel about a boy.'

I smiled. Oh, I think I knew how I felt about a boy, a particular boy.

'I'm sorry I've been so mean to you.' Amanda's words surprised me; she blurted them out so randomly I froze. 'I just worried maybe you'd be such a square you might tell on me for my midnight window hopping or something. I thought you'd be this lah-de-dah little miss; instead, here you are breaking and entering, getting detention and planning lunch-time escapes. They really should have put you in Kirkland.' She nudged my leg with her foot.

I took in what was a real-life apology, shaking my head, and revelling in the absurdity of it all. I was completely humbled and relieved that she had, in her own little way, begun clearing the slate.

I burst out laughing.

'What?' Amanda asked, straightening from her recline. 'What's so funny?'

My laughter subsided into a sigh of contentment, as I looked my cousin in the eyes. 'You should kiss boys more often.'

•

Maybe it was all a dream? The adrenalin-pumping antics of my first sneak-out to hang with the cool kids hadn't exactly been anything to write home about. A fluttering, heart-stopping moment of eye contact with Ballantine and he was out of there, not to be seen again. But in terms of something worthy happening, sharing a moment with my cousin, laughter, giggled gossip in the night, well, that meant more than anything. It was a feeling of such familiarity, I never wanted it to end. But like all things, inevitably the night lifts and the sun rises. I turned fitfully in my sheets away from the window that would no doubt be shining a new day onto my face. But instead I received a whack to the face by a pillow, again and again, until the final blow was stopped by me clutching it and yanking the pillow from Amanda's hold.

Had she woken up with a change of heart? Or was her icy facade slamming back into place while she bludgeoned me with her pillow?

'What are you doing?' I croaked, squinting through sleep-encrusted eyes, half expecting to see her glaring down at me. So when I was met by a blinding grin my surprise was marked by my eyes opening further.

'Wake up, bitchtits!' she chimed.

Amanda was fully dressed in her school uniform and ready to go. I glanced at the window, confused by the fact that it was still dark outside. Would this night never end?

'Am I getting a sense of déjà vu?'

'It's morning, you idiot, early morning.'

The clock read 5.30 a.m. and, quickly calculating my lack of sleep, I flung myself back down, covering my head with my pillow; if this was some kind of sick joke I wanted no part of it. 'Ugh. Go away,' I mumbled.

'Okaaaay, but I just thought you might want, oh I don't know, to go watch the boys surf?'

I ripped the pillow off my head, flinging it comically fast across the room as I sat up to attention, quickly gauging if Amanda was telling the truth or not. But she was deadly serious, despite the grin she was sporting.

'Get dressed.'

•

My dad, the early-rising farmer, always told me you haven't lived until you see the sun come up, that it was the best part of the day. But I could claim even better than that. You haven't lived until you've sat on the beach with an apricot Danish and a coffee, watching the sun come up and glimpsing the distant flecks, the silhouettes of surfers, outlined against the glow of a tangerine horizon. In tireless surges they paddled their way out, straddling their boards, laughing and chatting but ever watchful of the building waves, judging them, waiting and then positioning themselves. Reading not only the rolling water but each other, yelling words of encouragement.

'Yours, Boppo; take it, mate.'

I inhaled a breath of crisp morning air, almost holding it for ransom until the surfer was up, positioning himself to stand in one fluid motion, slicing across the path of the tumbling masses. He teased it, flirted on the edge, taunting to the point where I was certain he'd fall, and then he violently twisted his torso, pushing his board out and in, riding, riding until inevitably the wave caught him. Peaking and barrelling out of his momentum, he was collected and recycled as nothing more than the ocean's debris. I was of two minds. Firstly, fear. I breathed out in relief that it was over and that Boppo had broken through the surface. Stomach on his board again and being pushed back inland with what was left of the dying wave he had just tried to tame. I knew it was just a means for him to reposition, turn around and do it all over again. So, yes, first and foremost I thought them mad. But more than anything, as the sky lightened and the ocean's surface reflected the glittering gold of the sun, I sat transfixed, unable to take my eyes off the black specks that dotted the horizon, playing with mother nature. This was the other part of me that thought them simply magnificent.

No-one more so than when Ballantine paddled into motion; faster and faster he glided his way into the rising wall – it was an angry power that intimidated me from the shore, but not him. He was fearless. Even knowing nothing about surfing, as an outsider looking in, Ballantine rocked. I knew it wasn't just bias that convinced me that he sliced through the waves effortlessly, and owned the barrel in a way that seemed longer and larger than anyone else. Believe me, I was paying attention. Watching him skim along the horizon in a series of twists and turns had the word magnificent whisper from my lips.

'Yeah, he's pretty bloody good,' said Amanda, sipping on her coffee and shielding her eyes against the rising sun. She laughed. 'Did you see Boon's wipeout?'

I laughed, not wanting to admit that I was really only watching one person out there – one person who caused the hair to rise on my arms, tingling sensations to run down my spine, and my lower lip to indent in anxiety wondering what each ride would bring. The ocean was such a foreign place to me, it was not anything I would want to run into and do battle against. The very feel of the sand slipping away underfoot and the force of the waves rushing over my ankles was enough for me.

Nope, I would be just fine here, watching and waiting for them to do what they had to until enough was enough. And just when I thought I could watch on forever, to my surprise, one at a time, they rode into shore. Ballantine was one of the first, planting his feet and scooping up his board under his arm. My heart started racing knowing that he was headed our way, towards the boys' towels we were sitting near. Did he know we'd been watching? Could he see us from out in the waves? Did he even think to look or was he in his own world? Boon was not far behind him; carrying his board at a run he raced past Ballantine, closing the space between us before coming up short, unwrapping the strap from his ankle and wedging his board in the sand. Not sure if he was going to bid us any notice, I almost felt sick for Amanda, hoping that she wouldn't suffer humiliation at the hand of the boy she so desperately liked. But in true Boon fashion he turned to us, smiling boyishly as if he was happy to see us, then walked over and stood over us, ruffling salty drops from his shaggy, sopping hair.

'Dooooon't!' we shrieked in a series of squeals and giggles.

Boon laughed loud and goofy, taking sheer delight in making us squirm. He stepped back, taking us in with his mischievous eyes and shaking his head. 'Chicks, man. We're out there riding the waves, busting our rump, while you eat pastries and down lattes.'

'It's a tough job, but someone has to do it.' Amanda tilted her head, opting for flirty-adorable.

'You should be out there instead of us, burning off those calories, hey, Ballantine?'

By now, much to my heart-stopping delight, Ballantine too had unstrapped and wedged his board in the sand. He now stood tall and impressive next to it, his wetsuit peeled down to his narrow waist. He was lean and muscled, corded in all the deliciously right places. His skin looked brown and smooth and his dimple flashed as Boon posed the question to him; he turned towards us as if seeing us for the first time. His eyes landed on me before he shrugged one shoulder, slow and casual.

'Oh, I don't know,' he said, wrapping up the cord to his board. 'I can think of better ways to burn calories.'

His gaze was dark, his smirk cheeky, and the heavy insinuation only encouraged his fellow surfing mates to call out in howls and laugh in a way that said they more than agreed.

My cheeks tinged with heat, glancing away from his eyes, which had landed squarely on me when he'd spoken. I don't know if he was deliberately trying to unsettle or embarrass me but it had worked. I shifted uneasily, my stomach flipping in delight. In a way he had acknowledged me, even if it was in reference to a joke, a notch on his belt to be the hero among his mates; well, two could play at that game.

I lifted my chin, looking him directly in the eyes so that he couldn't mistake my meaning. 'And what way would that be exactly?' My eyes were devious, challenging, as I arched my brow in innocent wonder.

Ballantine saw it immediately for what it was; the sniggers from his mates and their watchful gazes didn't go unnoticed. He stared at me for a long moment, trying to stare me down or, in fact, thinking of a comeback. 'Well, seems like you're not accelerated in all subjects.' He smirked.

It was like a war waging between the two of us. I could sense Boon's and Amanda's heads flicking between us like a tennis match. The tension crackling between us with each exchange.

'Well, if I need tutoring in cryptic innuendos, I'll be sure to seek you out.'

Ballantine snaked his towel over his shoulder, before flashing me a brief crooked grin. 'And if I need further schooling in having the last word, then I'll be sure to find you.'

I smiled sweetly. 'Please do.'

Ballantine wedged the board under his arm before laughing and walking away.

# Chapter Nineteen

I didn't know what was more unbelievable, that I was amicably walking to the bus stop brushing shoulders with Amanda, or the fact that we were following the Kirkland surfers? Sure, we were following them at a respectable distance, but nonetheless, we were walking in their footsteps.

'You're staring.' Amanda's voice broke my thoughts.

'Excuse me?'

'Stop ogling their bums.'

'I am not!' I shoved her off the path.

'Hey, it's okay, I don't blame you, I'm just surprised. I didn't take you for a bum looker.'

I rolled my eyes. 'As if. I'm just trying to put names to faces.'

'Names to faces or names to bums?'

'Seriously, how old are you?'

I had desperately wanted Amanda to tell me every detail about where she had gone last night. What was the Wipe Out Bar? Where was the Wipe Out Bar? Who was Dean? Was he mad? Did they make it inside? Was Ballantine there? So far all I had gathered was that Boon had a wicked mouth and magic fingers and I really didn't need to know more about either of those things. I didn't quite know how to feel about me rejecting Boon's advances and then him getting with Amanda. I know that's what boys do; well, I think that's what they do. But still, I would never tell Amanda about it. He was more than likely just mucking around. He seemed to be a giant flirt.

'Okay, Kirkland boys 101,' Amanda began. 'There always seems like there's a big cluster of them, but the originals, the only ones of any real notability, are Boon, Ballantine, Boppo and Woolly. They're the real deal, the others are just hangers-on, but they're not what anyone classes as anything.'

I listened on with interest, watching the wall of boys up ahead; they walked shoulder to shoulder. Ballantine was actually in shorts today, exposing his bronzed legs. They were nice legs too. His school bag slung over his shoulder, his hair still damp from his surf. Next to him was a boy who was just as tall, but with shoulder-length, spiralled honey-coloured hair, the kind of hair most girls would kill for.

'Let me guess, that's Woolly?' I asked, nodding towards the boy.

'Geez, whatever makes you think that?' Amanda replied, laughing.

Which meant the boy on the far right of Boon was Boppo. He seemed just like any other boy, except he had the most interesting hazel eyes. They were quite hypnotic set against the tan of his skin, with his brown hair lightened by the sun.

'I know what you're thinking,' Amanda singsonged in a taunting fashion.

'What?'

Had Amanda suddenly gained the power of telepathy? What was she talking about? And before I had a chance to question her, she winked at me.

'Don't worry, cuz. I'll hook you up.' And just like that, she sprinted ahead, causing my heart to plummet to my feet watching on as she ran towards the boys.

*Surely she wasn't . . .*

But she merely pushed past them, and latched onto her BFF Gemma, who was sitting at the bus stop. The reunion was squealy and over the top, punctuated with the usual swapping of insults.

I clearly had a lot to learn. I couldn't imagine myself running up to Laura Boon at recess and saying, 'Hey, you dirty skank.' And I was quite relieved we hadn't reached that point in our friendship.

The boys fanned out to stand on the edge of the kerb by the bus shelter, joking, pushing and laughing as they talked about the morning's surf; you didn't have to listen to get that that was exactly what they were discussing. I watched on as Ballantine's hands danced in conversation, miming the crest and then slapping one palm on the back of his other hand, laughing. I sat down next to Amanda, shrugging off my backpack and clamping it between my legs.

Gemma's surprised eyes didn't go unnoticed. Her 'what the hell is she doing here?' expression was not in the least bit subtle. After a moment Gemma's bored stare broke away from me and instead shifted to Amanda. 'So what did you get up to last night? You never texted me back.'

'Sorry, my phone was on the charger,' she said with a pout. 'I probably wouldn't have heard it anyway, I was zonked by ten, and had a killer headache.'

I did a double-take. Was she serious? Was she not going to relay the story of how she snuck out and hooked up with Boon? Was she not going to relay every single detail to her supposed best friend?

'Wow! Sucks to be you,' Gemma sympathised.

'Yeah, hey,' Amanda replied with a sigh, subtly kicking my ankle and throwing me a warning look.

*Don't say a word.*

I broke away from staring at my cousin, who was scarily good at lying so effortlessly. I didn't have to force my focus elsewhere because it was the sound of 'Hey, Ballantine!' that caused all our heads to whip around in the direction the high-pitched yell came from.

Out of nowhere a petite blonde in a formal black-and-white uniform jumped onto Ballantine's back, giggling as he caught her legs and swung her around before letting her go. She pushed into his view, playfully slapping him across his chest.

'I'm mad at you, Luke Ballantine,' she said, loud enough for the population of Paradise to hear. She crossed her arms and pouted her lips, as she looked up at him with a 'come shag me' expression. I felt sick.

'Who is that?' I asked, my face pained as if I was watching a traffic accident.

'That's Lucy Fell,' said Gemma with as little enthusiasm as I had.

'If only Lucy fell off a cliff,' added Amanda, clearly not a fan either.

I would be happy if she simply fell on her face. Her infuriatingly perfect face. She had big doe eyes, shiny blonde hair, and perky big boobs. She was clearly from another school as she wore an elitist uniform with an embroidered logo on her blazer. She had broken away from the next bus stop over, leaving behind her giggling, whispering friends. By the look of them, it was clearly an all-girl school.

I swallowed my unease, trying to ignore the taste of bitterness.

'So what, is she like Ballantine's cousin or something?' I asked, hopeful.

Amanda scoffed. 'Do *we* look at each other like that? Definitely not cousins.'

'She used to go to our school, she was one of our best friends until last year when she started going to St Sebastian's,' said Gemma.

'Yeah, and then she started thinking she was a little bit better than everyone else,' added Amanda, her scornful eyes glaring at Lucy, who playfully pushed Boon, causing him to lose his balance in the gutter.

'Well, she doesn't seem to think she's better than the boys,' I said.

Amanda scoffed again. 'She's only trying to big-note herself in front of her friends. She's such a fucking parasite.'

My eyebrows rose at the venom in Amanda's words; I had never seen her so angry, not even at me. But I couldn't bring myself to care too greatly about Amanda's past. All I could care about was the present, about what was unfolding before my eyes like a nightmare. A painfully loud laugh, a flick of her hair, and was that a double blink?

I watched for Ballantine's responses. His hands deep in his pockets, his feet kicking against the kerb as he spoke, casually glancing up at her. Oh, Christ, how could a glance be so sexy? No, not now, please don't be sexy now. Lucy fell-on-her-face said something to him that caused him to smile, the dimple-exposing kind, the one that usually had my heart pumping with adrenalin, only now it felt like it would splinter into a million pieces. Oh, how I wished the bus would come along and run her over. Was that too much to ask, universe?

And just as if I had willed it, turning the corner and sweeping into the bus lane it came, pulling up at the girls' school stop, unfortunately doing so with no fatalities. Still, it had all the girls clambering to line up for pole position.

Lucy squealed, 'Gotta go!' while dancing on the balls of her feet. She pulled Ballantine down, reached up on her very tippy toes and planted a quick, chaste kiss on his cheek, leaving a visible outline of pink lip balm that caused the boys to cheer and wolf whistle as she skipped away, glancing back with a pointed look of hot promise. She sashayed her way over to her waiting friends, high-fiving one who was holding her bag before stepping on the bus.

I looked away. Enough. I had seen enough. I felt so stupid thinking how amazing it had been that he had asked to borrow a pen, a freaking pen; big bloody deal. The way I had revelled in our verbal sparring match on the beach, only to remember how Boon had taunted me the night before with insinuations. That's just what boys do, Lexie. They flirt and like to watch you blush and squirm with their innuendos: these boys more than any others. They were in Year Twelve, eighteen, and legally of age. What better way to pass the time than to entertain themselves with a funny mousy girl from the country? Taunt the likes of me while they bedded girls like Lucy. I had been kidding myself, kidding myself all along that Ballantine would even so much as think about me in that way. I'd instead over-analysed the big amounts of nothing, and weaved them into something – romanticising every minute action. What. An. Idiot. What would I know about a boy like him?

I made a promise to myself. No more time wasting, no more staring or swooning over Ballantine. Not only was he obviously trouble, but he was a direct route to a broken heart.

I could already feel the frayed edges of disappointment at seeing him just talk to a girl. Enough was enough. I breathed in deeply, resigning myself to take one last look at him, as if to get some closure before sticking with my decision.

*One last look and then move on, Lexie!*

So when my eyes finally shifted to where Ballantine stood, my breath caught in my throat. The universe was playing one last dirty trick on me, because my eyes had locked directly with his. He was already staring at me with an amused expression. I was tempted to look behind me, wondering if he was looking at someone else, but instead my eyes narrowed in question, eliciting a boyish grin from him before he stepped up on the kerb and glanced towards the sound of our bus nearing. It was a brief yet most direct connection, of that I was sure. I know because I made a clear note to make sure it was in fact real and not imagined, but Ballantine had definitely been looking at me, he had definitely smiled and I didn't know what kind of game he was playing, but my head told me I didn't want any part of it.

If only my heart would bloody listen.

# Chapter Twenty

Boys were stupid, and for a brief moment the idea of an all-girls school seemed genius, until I remembered Lucy and her cheer squad. Okay, definitely a bad idea.

I chose to distance myself from Amanda and co. at recess, instead taking in the quiet surrounds and leaning against a paperbark tree chewing a raspberry roll-up with Laura cross-legged in front of me.

I wanted to tell her about my late-night sneak-out (minus her brother's involvement) and my reconciliation with Amanda. I wanted to blab about how crushed I'd been over Ballantine disappearing and then have a giant hate session on Lucy Fell-on-her-face. But of course I didn't dare, knowing she would probably write my confessions in her bloody diary, and more importantly, recalling Boon's words about Laura crushing on Ballantine. I only hoped that that diary entry was old, really old, and that she no longer felt that way. You know, for her sake, I thought, because I wasn't going there anymore, remember?

*Yeah, right.*

None of those thoughts sounded in the least bit believable. Still, I had impressed myself by making the decision to sit on the side of the school that would have me nowhere near the Kirkland boys.

And just when I was thinking there was hope yet, I heard a distant yell.

'HEADS!'

A football came sailing through the air, ricocheting off the trunk of the tree, oh so close to my head. I squealed, protecting the back of my head with linked hands, remaining that way for a long moment, until I slowly lifted my gaze to check if the coast was clear.

'Sorry, ladies.' Ballantine jogged over, laughing at the near miss.

'Bloody hell, Ballantine, you almost took off Lexie's head,' said Laura, joining in on the laughter. Ballantine leant down, a whoosh of his aftershave swept over me, as did his mischievous look as he picked up the footy.

'Well, we wouldn't want that, would we?' he said, winking at Laura as if letting her in on the joke.

Laura was blushing profusely, probably over-analysing that very wink. Ballantine backed away before turning and thumping the footy across the field to where a cluster of boys played in front of us. Where Ballantine played in front of us. I sighed. Try as I might, there was no escaping him and, more disturbingly, I didn't really want to.

•

For the most part, the sound of the lunch bell elicited fist-pumps and whoops as everyone clambered for freedom. I wished I could enjoy that feeling; instead, I slinked my way to Siberia. If I had a rock and a chisel I would engrave a second line on the wall. I was deliberately the first one there, even ahead of whatever poor teacher had drawn the short straw and had to watch over us. I slid the door closed behind me, making my way towards the very back today; might as well mix things up a bit.

The next to arrive was a boy I hadn't seen before, with spiky hair that was a bit too long. I think he was going for punker-rock-badass with a dog chain hooked on the hip of his jeans. He wasn't quite pulling it off – something about the smattering of freckles across the bridge of his nose didn't exactly intimidate, somehow.

The door flew open and I saw an arm point into the room before I followed it to a familiar elbow-patched jacket and moustache.

Mr Branson. My heart stopped, thinking – no, fearing – that he was the teacher who would be watching over us, but instead he merely stood in the doorway, pointing to the front row. 'Sit,' he bit out, as if commanding a disobedient animal.

'But, sir!' came a long, pained whine from the hall.

'Now, Erica Yatesby, I will not be telling you again!' His face was flushed; I could tell he was on his last ounce of patience before exploding.

There were heavy footsteps as a girl with unnaturally blonde hair and unnaturally tanned skin (both a result of a bottle) sighed and slunk her way into her seat, pressing her head against the tabletop. 'It's not fair,' she whined.

'No, it never is, is it?'

'It wasn't my fault,' she exclaimed, tears of frustration causing pale lines to streak through her foundation.

'No, it never is, is it?' Mr Branson repeated. He reminded me of an unenthusiastic Willy Wonka who would like nothing more than to send all the naughty children to the boiler room.

He switched his focus to across the room. 'Got plenty to do I hope, Robbie Robinson?'

My head snapped to the spiky-haired boy.

*So that was Robbie Robinson, definitely not a badass.*

Before he could reply, everyone's attention shifted to the two figures that appeared in the doorway.

'Mr Branson.' They both nodded, but with an air of cheekiness as they rather miserably attempted to stifle their grins.

'Well, well, it wouldn't be a complete detention without Boon and Ballantine, would it?' Mr Branson said, shaking his head.

I couldn't help but wonder if Mr Branson was this bitter all the time.

Ballantine and Boon made their way into the class.

'How about we sit apart, boys, wouldn't want you to be distracted now.'

The boys stilled, looking at each other with guarded amusement.

Boon broke off down the middle aisle, throwing his books onto a desk and taking a seat. 'Yeah, Ballantine, stop distracting me.'

Boon had slunk in his chair much like the overly dramatic Erica Yatesby had, but my amusement was short-lived when Ballantine continued down the aisle, all the way to the back row. His steps closed in and his silhouette appeared in my peripheral vision as I forced myself to read my textbook, concentrating not so much on reading the words but on keeping calm and breathing evenly.

His books crashed down next to mine, the scraping of the chair legs across the floor shrieked as if someone had run their nails across a blackboard. A shiver ran down my spine, but for all the wrong reasons, as he took a seat next to me. The smell of his cool, crisp scent washed over me; I wanted to lean into it. Instead, I busied myself by foraging through my pencil case and without a word, pulled out the black ballpoint pen from last detention and held it out to him.

Ballantine's eyes flicked from me to the pen with interest. He reached out his hand and clasped it over mine. His fingers were soft and warm; they slid over my skin in a fleeting caress. I wondered if it was just a matter of me overthinking everything, but there was no overthinking the devious look in his eyes when he took the pen from me. It was like he was toying with me, much like a lion would prey on a wide-eyed gazelle. I wished he would stop. But, in other ways, I hoped he would continue. Were boys always this confusing?

Boon raised his hand. 'Mr Branson, I thought you didn't want Ballantine to be distracted,' he said with a cheeky backwards glance.

Ballantine laughed, scrunching up a piece of paper and turfing it in Boon's direction. Boon ducked too late, causing it to bounce off his shoulder blades.

'Mr Branson, Ballantine threw paper at me,' Boon whined like a small child, or like Erica Yatesby.

Mr Branson pinched the bridge of his nose and sighed deeply. He paced across the front of the room, placing his hands casually on his hips.

'This is not a summer camp, and it sure as hell isn't *The Breakfast Club*. There will be no teachers periodically leaving you to your own devices so you can open up about each other's lives or wreak havoc in an eighties montage. There will be no Judd Nelsons.' He pointed at Ballantine. 'No Molly Ringwalds.' Pointing at me. 'And no Emilio Estevez.' He pointed the finger at Robbie. 'Capeesh?'

Ballantine leant over to me. 'He knows way too much about that movie,' he whispered, causing me to snigger.

Boon was lost in thought, as if he was deeply troubled by what Mr Branson was saying. He raised his hand.

'Yes?' Mr Branson snapped.

'Can I be Emilio Estevez?'

# Chapter Twenty-One

As if by some divine intervention Mr Clarkson, the PE teacher and designated detention monitor, stepped into the room, distracting Mr Branson before his head imploded in fury.

'I've got it, John,' said Mr Clarkson, whacking him on the shoulder with a friendly smile.

Mr Branson grunted something under his breath before storming out; Mr Clarkson's brows rose as if he was equally relieved he was gone. He turned to take in the faces, his eyes moving from Boon to Ballantine.

'Well, nice to see you are consistent in some things, boys,' he said dryly.

Ballantine nodded his head in acknowledgment. 'Clarko.'

Mr Clarkson, or 'Clarko', just shook his head; his demeanour was nothing like Mr Branson's. I didn't know if it was his casual Adidas tracksuit pants and runners that made him less intimidating but I actually think he was just a laidback character, the Yin to Mr Branson's Yang.

'Okay, folks. Just think of this as like ripping off a Band-Aid: do it without fuss and it will hurt less.'

Such wise words. Even Clarko nodded as if he was proud of his own analogy, taking a seat behind the desk.

Everyone fell into silence. It seemed the presence of Mr Branson brought out the worst in students, whereas Clarko's calm ways earnt respect from Boon and Ballantine, who readied themselves with their books and work. Well, 'work' being Ballantine doodling inside his exercise book. A myriad of waves, swirls and circles made up an inky mural that was both intricate and beautiful. Drawn in red and blue ink, he now added flecks of black from my pen and there was a happiness inside of me that bubbled to the surface, a ridiculous satisfaction knowing that my pen was participating in some small way.

*Dear God, get over yourself, Lexie.*

I shut my overactive thoughts down.

*Don't think about the boy, the hot boy who, for some reason, out of all the chairs in all of Siberia, chose to sit next to you.*

I tried to not get too excited about that. I had been surprised at the time but now I'd had a whole hour to reflect and think and basically be tortured by his presence, by his mind-numbing scent. I wondered if swooning over a boy was a legitimate cause to be admitted to the sick bay?

My thoughts were distracted by the jigging of Boon's leg in front; his short attention span would be hard work for him, especially with no-one to pass notes to, no-one to taunt.

It had me thinking, and then, before I knew it . . . doing.

There was one way to pass the time and I slowly tore out a lined piece of paper from my book. I watched as Clarko was busying himself, marking papers.

I scribbled on the paper, smiling a small smile and feeling a little giddy at what I was about to do. I was going to break the ice with Ballantine. Treat him just like any other boy, strip back the fact he was ludicrously hot; let's just be two normal people in detention.

I slid the paper over to him, causing him to still from his masterpiece. His eyes flicked up to Clarko. Ensuring the coast was clear, he pulled the paper over to him, which shot an unexpected thrill through me.

He read my slanted writing, short and sweet.

*Where did you go last night?*

If he was surprised by the question he didn't show it, or maybe he was just using that poker face again. He looked at the note for a long while, so long that I thought he wouldn't respond, that he would just leave me hanging and feeling mortified. But then he committed pen to paper. Printing in neat, clean writing, and with the same care with which he'd received the note, he slid it back to me.

*Home.*

Talk about short and sweet. I frowned, looking at the one-word reply.

He went home? He didn't go to the Wipe Out Bar?

I scribbled a reply and slid it back.

*No Wipe Out Bar? Isn't that the place to be?*

I watched intently for his reaction; he breathed a laugh and shook his head, writing his reply.

*There's so much more to see than Dean's crusty old tourist bar.*

There was that name again. It seemed that Dean was very much the character behind the Wipe Out Bar, and with what I had gathered from the bits and pieces of conversations, I hadn't made up my mind yet whether he was a hero or a villain, but I was looking forward to finding out.

I could've asked more, but the note exchange wasn't exactly riveting stuff; still, I folded the sheet up and tucked it away. I felt a little sad knowing that I would probably moon over it later, like some pathetic pining woman wandering helplessly through the English moors fixating on a love that would never be.

Clarko stood up, stretching. 'I'll be back in five minutes, guys. I expect the room to be as I left it, okay?' He said it more as a joke, and I laughed, not because what he had said was particularly funny, but I remembered Mr Branson telling us how teachers would not periodically disappear, leaving us to our own devices. Guess in the real world though, even teachers need a toilet break.

Mr Clarkson had no sooner left the room than Boon rested on the back of his chair, his mischievous eyes flicking from me to Ballantine and back.

'Eyes forward, Emilio,' I said, cutting him off before he had a chance to say something smart.

Boon laughed.

'You heard Molly, eyes forward,' Ballantine added in mock seriousness.

Boon shook his head. 'This Breakfast Club sucks.'

•

There were no more notes passed. Ballantine kept working on his masterpiece and I kept rather unsuccessfully trying to work on my Maths pyramid project; trying to problem-solve was not a smart idea. Maybe I should just read some *King Lear* instead.

The bell sounded, ending another hour of misery. I couldn't tell who was faster at packing up their gear, Erica fake-tan or Boon. It was like they had something amazing on their agenda. I had to hand in a Maths project. Surprisingly, though, Clarko was out the door before anyone else. I took my time, slowly packing up, holding off zipping my pencil case until Ballantine returned my pen. But when he moved to stand, having packed up all his gear, I looked up to where he stood, or rather lingered, looking down at me.

'Are you going out tonight?' he asked.

I stilled from pushing my chair out.

*Did he seriously ask me a question?*

I blinked, trying to think of something to say. I had no idea, I hadn't planned on going out last night; in fact, nothing in my life was planned *ever*. I wanted a comeback – something smart, something witty and confident. Like, 'Yeah, just heading down for a few at the local. Wanna come?'

Instead: 'Any suggestions for a school night?' I asked.

Ballantine seemed to be amused by whatever was running through his mind. 'Some say that the Wipe Out Bar is the place to be,' he said, repeating my very own words.

'Really? Because I kind of heard that there are far better things to experience than that,' I said, gathering my books and standing. Even on my feet I still had to look up at him, into those dark brown eyes that glinted with trouble.

'I guess it depends on what experience you're after?' he said in all seriousness.

'Oh, yeah? And what experience would you give me?' I blurted it out, quick and unthinking, and just when I hoped he might take it the wrong way, Ballantine's brows rose in surprise, his eyes ever watchful as I blushed and squirmed under their scrutiny.

The bell sounded for the last time, and I prayed that it might break the awkward moment between us. But it didn't. So before he had a chance to reply I did what I did best. 'Um, better get going,' I said, brushing past him, trying not to think about how good he smelt or the feel of his eyes boring into me even as I walked away, thinking it was probably best he just keep the pen.

# Chapter Twenty-Two

'I know something you don't know,' Amanda tauntingly whispered into my ear as she passed me on her way to beat me to the front seat of the car where Uncle Peter waited for us.

Unlike the jovial array of questions about our day Aunty Karen would hit us with, Uncle Peter was too busy talking to himself, or rather the phone glued to his ear. Our laughter was cut off by a rather deep scowl and a finger to the lips for us to be quiet. Do you know how hard it is to close a car door quietly? Near impossible. Aside from Uncle Peter's business dealings, the commute home was a silent one. Still, it didn't stop Amanda from torturing me in the rearview mirror. Making kissy-kissy faces and hubba-hubba expressions. My insides were giddy with excitement; I just wanted to scream. What did she know? What did she have to tell me? Wasn't it enough with Boon's cryptic message about what a certain 'mate' of his had said about me? Was this related? Oh God, would this car ride ever end?

We finally pulled into the driveway. Uncle Peter was still deep in conversation about building permits when we dived out of the car, caring little about being quiet. I chased Amanda up the garden path and through the entrance, dumping our school bags just inside the front door. We ran down the hall into Amanda's room, her beating me by a clear mile, she was so bloody fast.

Amanda launched onto her bed, laughing so hard she could barely catch her breath; I was trying to catch my own as I slumped in the doorway. She clawed herself into a sitting position on the edge of her bed, her eyes wild with excitement. 'Shut the door,' she said breathlessly.

I didn't hesitate; I closed it and dived onto my own bed, ruffling up the immaculately made sheets. 'What do you know?' I bounced on my bed like an eager child on Christmas Eve.

'Sixth period was woodwork with Boon,' she said with a smile.

'How romantic,' I mused. Trust Amanda, who didn't strike me as the crafty type, to choose woodwork for Year Twelve – the things you do for love. I tried to appear all casual, but my heart skipped a beat at the thought that maybe Boon had said something to her.

Amanda sighed. 'He sanded my birdbox for me.'

I snorted. 'Wow. Is that what they're calling it these days?'

Amanda blinked at me, before my words slowly registered. 'Oh gross!' she said, throwing a pillow at me. 'And here I thought you would be the biggest prude.'

I dodged the pillow, laughing. 'What made you think I would be a prude?' I asked, genuinely intrigued by what her answer would be.

Amanda's head canted, as if it was obvious. 'Well, let's face it, playing with waterbombs at the Red Hill Field Day is a little less advanced than what you'll find here.'

My attention piqued. 'Oh?'

Amanda pushed off from her bed; walking over to her dresser and pulling her lip balm and loose change from the pockets of her school dress, chucking them into the glass bowl next to her perfume stash. 'Let's just say the boys in Paradise City will only hold hands for so long.'

It hadn't gone unnoticed. Year Seven girls wearing foundation, the senior boys having to shave their five o'clock shadows and driving. I didn't know if it was something in the water but everyone seemed so much more advanced in every way; well, except academically. That's where I could hold my own.

*How depressing.*

Even Amanda walked with an air of confidence: her hips swayed, her head was held high as she lazily applied lip balm before chucking it back into the dish. I could pretty much guarantee that she wouldn't be a virgin; she seemed too street smart, overly confident and super comfortable in her skin. Even though she blushed like mad at the mention of Boon's name, I had no doubt that she was doing more than hand holding, and here I was over the moon that Ballantine had used my bloody pen. Amanda was right; she had me pegged as tragic from day one.

*Well, that was about to change.*

I was here for a good time, not a long time, and if it meant experiencing every pleasure this city had to offer, then so be it. The last thing I wanted was to have any regrets or wasted opportunities. Now, with Amanda by my side and in good spirits, I would have to think of a plan. Even though I was not wholly comfortable with having to hang with Amanda, Gemma and Jess, she was the link to the Kirkland surfers, to Ballantine.

I straightened my spine, trying not to focus on the waves of anxiety overtaking me. 'So, what do you know that I don't?' I tried not to make out like I really cared, asking it with a nonchalant attitude, knowing that the more she thought I cared, the more Amanda would string out the information. I had to play this cool.

'Let's just say that a little birdy told me something *very* interesting in woodwork today.'

'This wouldn't be the same little birdy that sanded your birdbox, would it?'

'Lexie, please, I simply cannot reveal my sources. But, yes, Boon told me.'

I laughed. 'Remind me never to do a bank job with you.'

Amanda shrugged. 'Hos before bros.'

I grinned fiercely; I was loving this new connection with Amanda. I clasped my heart. 'That's the most beautiful thing you have ever said to me.'

'Yeah, well, if we're going to be double dating we're going to have to get along.'

'What?' I barely breathed out the question.

Amanda beamed. 'Boon told me someone likes you.'

My heart pounded wildly in my chest; all I could do was stare wide-eyed at my deliriously smug cousin.

'Who?' I managed, swallowing deeply. *Oh God, I'm going to be sick.* Suddenly every interaction with Ballantine ran through my head: the times we had made eye contact, the times he had sat next to me in detention, our first real playful display on the beach . . . My heart soared with hope and with the disbelief that something I wanted so badly could possibly be true, that my time in Paradise was going to turn from shit-ordinary to absolutely magical.

Amanda moved to sit next to me, her eyes alight with excitement. She bit her bottom lip and grabbed my hands, forcing me to turn towards her as she looked me in the eyes.

'What do you think of Woolly?'

*Wait. What?*

I blinked. Twice. I could literally hear a record player scratch in my mind, right before the bone-jarring feeling of disappointment plummeted down to my feet.

Amanda must have read it all over my face. 'Oh, that much, huh?'

'I– I don't even know him.'

'Of course you don't, you don't know anyone, dummy.'

I blinked again, the true weight of the situation washing over me.

Amanda rolled her eyes. 'Relax, he wasn't offering a marriage proposal; he just thinks you're cute. Trust me, you could do a lot worse than Woolly. He's actually one of the better Kirkland boys.'

Perhaps he was but I really didn't care, he could be a saint for all that mattered. I wasn't interested. Nope, I had hoped beyond measure that Amanda would speak of Ballantine's undying infatuation with me. I dreamed of him knocking on my window of a night, me flinging my arms around him at the bus stop, passing love notes to one another in detention, me holding his towel for him and waiting for him to emerge from the ocean like the Adonis he was. Okay, yeah, maybe I had given all these thoughts way too much attention. But I couldn't help it. Try as I might to forget about Ballantine, each and every day seemed to have me crossing his path, and it did strange things to my insides. When I thought about experiencing new things in Paradise, what I really wanted above anything was for Ballantine to be a part of it, not Woolly.

'Well, that was anti-climactic,' said Amanda, her shoulders slumping. 'I had it all worked out, someone to talk to on our dates while the boys talked about surfing.'

'Are you and Boon going on a date?' I asked.

'Well, not exactly, that shit only really happens in the movies. Still, a girl can hope, yeah?'

She certainly could, I thought. She. Certainly. Could.

# Chapter Twenty-Three

I thought I was dreaming when I heard the tap on the window.

A delicate tap-tap-tap that, at first, in my half-asleep state, I thought was a tree branch tapping against the glass, but of course I knew better when I felt the pressure on my bed and heard the sound of curtains flinging apart.

The window made its painful slide across the aluminium track, causing me to bury down in my covers. I had little to no interest in another late-night sneak-out; the last thing I wanted was a forced hook-up with Woolly. No, I think I'd enjoy some much-needed sleep. But instead of the hushed voices getting quieter, and the pressure lifting off my bed, the voices got louder and it felt like a stampede.

'Shit, be quiet.' Amanda giggled. 'Come on. Watch out for Lexie.'

The weight lifted off my bed and I burrowed deeper into my doona, forcing sleep onto myself as I tried desperately to ignore the whispers that were now in the room. Ugh, I didn't even want to know. With a sigh and a determined attitude to get back to sleep, I felt another dip on my bed, as if two feet were planted on my mattress top near my legs.

*Oh my God. Oh my God.*

Someone else had climbed into our room. I lay deathly still, squeezing my eyes shut, praying that Boon hadn't brought Woolly with him, that this wasn't him playing Cupid setting up the double date from hell. Just stay asleep, I told myself, slip into a coma until they take the hint. But worse still, the legs on my bed moved and I could feel the whole weight of a body now sitting on my bed. There was a boy on my bed – an unwelcome boy – and dread swept through me.

*Don't move, Lexie. Don't. Move.*

'Is she breathing?'

My eyes whipped open, I sat bolt upright in bed at the sound of Ballantine's voice. Holy fucking shit, Ballantine was sitting on my bed with a devious smirk on his face. I blinked. Was this a dream? A very real dream.

'Expecting someone else?' he said, curving an inquisitive brow.

'NO!' I said a bit too loudly, a bit too quickly.

'You sure about that?'

'I– I wasn't expecting anyone.'

'Sure you weren't dreaming about a certain woolly-headed surfer?' Boon eyed me knowingly, as he crashed on Amanda's bed, linking his hands behind his head.

'I don't *think* so,' I said, making it perfectly clear that that was never going to be the case.

'That's a shame. Woolly really needs to get a root.'

'Boon!' Amanda's head nearly spun off her shoulders.

'What? I'm just stating a fact; he's such a grumpy prick these days. Isn't he, Ballantine?'

Ballantine rested his elbows on his knees, nodding sombrely. 'That he is.'

'Yeah, well, sorry about that.' I sat in my bed, clutching a pillow to my chest, wishing I hadn't worn my skimpy summer PJs tonight. Although it wasn't like I'd had any way of knowing boys would be infiltrating our bedroom.

Boon sat up on the bed and turned to Amanda. 'Wanna come for a ride?'

Amanda smiled. 'Sure.'

'Sa-weet.' He stood, pulling Amanda up off the bed and planting a chaste kiss on her lips. 'Let's go!'

It wasn't until this point that I realised Amanda was fully dressed – she must have known about their arrival and prepared for it. She was like a ninja getting dressed in complete silence: impressive if not a little scary.

Ballantine scooted across, letting Boon and Amanda climb out the window without so much as a backwards glance. He then stood, stretching his arms up to the ceiling, causing his tee to lift slightly, exposing the toned wall of his stomach. His arms fell to his sides as he began to climb back over my bed, working to hook a leg over the windowsill, then he paused, looking back at me.

'You coming?' he asked.

I fought not to smile. 'Woolly isn't out there, is he?'

Ballantine laughed. 'No, big bad Woolly is not with us.'

'Okay.' I threw my doona off while jumping out of bed to head to the wardrobe, only to pause and spin around to Ballantine. 'Wait, where are we going?'

He didn't answer me straightaway, he simply looked – looked at me in that way that shows a boy appreciates a girl. In my eagerness to move I had momentarily forgotten I was wearing my short-shorts and sheer top. I stood in the middle of the room feeling completely exposed, more so with the way Ballantine's eyes were resting on me. He coughed, quickly looking out the window, squinting up at the moon.

'Ah, nowhere fancy. Meet you out the front.' And just like that he climbed out through the open window.

*What was that?*

I know my mind often played tricks on me but I hadn't mistaken that look, no way. The heat in his eyes as they'd dipped to my rather skimpy attire, the way he'd seemed to shift awkwardly, as if almost embarrassed for being caught staring. A thrill shot through me just thinking about it. Regardless of whether a boy like Ballantine could be interested in a girl like me, I saw that look for what it was. He was, after all, a male, and an experienced one, no doubt. If I wanted to see that look again I was going to have to stand out, be noticeable. I grabbed for some denim cut-offs, and a spaghetti-strap singlet top; the evenings were warm enough to be wearing such things. I quietly opened the bedroom door, pausing for any sign of life from upstairs before creeping to the bathroom. I vigorously brushed my teeth, combed my knotty hair, applied a light dusting of powder and lip balm before spraying some of Aunty Karen's expensive French perfume and walking through it.

I climbed out the window, making sure to slide it closed, leaving a little gap so as not to lock it shut. I crept along the edge of the house, under the cover of the shadows as I tiptoed around the front, where I came to a complete stop.

Ballantine waited near the tree in the side yard. The moonlight made only his silhouette visible, but I knew it was him. Even in the shadows his tall, lean physique was unmistakeable.

He turned, straightening from his casual recline against the gum tree.

'Hey,' I managed. As if we hadn't seen each other five minutes ago.

'Hey,' he replied.

Yeah, there was nothing weird about our exchanges.

I closed the distance between us, unable to stop myself from staring at him as he became more and more visible with every step. Gone was the school uniform, replaced by a casual navy t-shirt that accentuated every muscle. I tried with all my might not to let my eyes linger too long on the hypnotic landscape. His tan, frayed boardies looked like they had seen better days. My eyes flicked past his shoulder, noticing a canary yellow HJ Sandman near the driveway. My stomach fluttered, thinking how incredibly hot it was that the Kirkland boys had their licences – like, legally had them – not like the boys I knew who puttered around on the family farm in a rusty beat-up ute. No, it was nothing like that: sleek, shiny yellow with black lined trimmings, perfect to cart surfboards in, no doubt.

Ballantine followed my eyeline with interest. 'Oh, yeah, she sticks out a bit,' he said with a boyish smile.

'I love it!' I said without thinking, noticing how Ballantine's head turned my way to see if I was telling the truth. I absolutely was. It was so incredibly cool, so him. But I would keep those raving thoughts to myself.

'Where are the others?' I asked as we neared the car.

Ballantine sighed. 'One guess.'

•

This wasn't a double date, nowhere near it. Boon and Amanda were in the back of the Sandman, the divider curtains closed as Ballantine and I sat awkwardly in the front seat, silently looking out over the vast spread of ocean in front of us at Wilson's lookout. Well, silent aside from the rustling, laughing and kissing sounds coming from the back of the van.

Ballantine moved to turn the radio on in an attempt to drown out the noises but it still didn't alleviate the awkwardness much. He rubbed his palms along the steering wheel, wincing into the night. 'Do you wanna go for a walk?'

'Yes!' I replied quickly, and before we knew it, Ballantine shut off the radio and both of us were out of the car comically fast. The burst of salty air blowing in my face was like a cleanser after the stuffy car. The outdoor elements liberated us. Ballantine leant on the bonnet, slid out a strip of gum from a packet, unfolded the foil, and placed the spearmint strip on his tongue. He silently offered me a piece. I took it, marvelling at the simple pleasure of such an exchange.

'This way,' he said, delving his hands deep into his pockets as he led the way down the sloping sandy path towards the beach. I trudged after him, wincing at the sensation of sand in my thongs. I wanted to say 'Wait up' as he expertly made his way along the track, but I knew that would sound lame, so I just did my best to keep up. It got easier as the angle evened out and Ballantine walked closer to the shoreline, where the water made the sand firmer. I did as Ballantine did; he shucked off his shoes and threw them aside, walking closer into the waves, but when his shirt came off and he threw it back to land on his shoes, I paused.

'W– what are you doing?'

He frowned, genuinely perplexed. 'Aren't you coming in?'

My wide eyes darted from his naked torso, his perfect, smooth chiselled body, to the dark foamy waves.

'Umm, I don't think so,' I said, stepping back so no part of the water was touching me.

Ballantine watched me with interest. 'Are you afraid?'

I shrugged. 'I don't much like being part of the food chain.'

'You are not going to be eaten by a shark, Lex.'

My resolve melted just a little when he called me that. It was a dirty trick even if he wasn't using it as a ploy to get me into the ocean. Still, if he said my name often enough I feared I would follow him anywhere.

'So you can guarantee that I won't be eaten by a shark, can you?'

Ballantine sighed into the night sky. 'Look, I am eighty-five per cent sure that nothing bad will happen to you if you come in with me.'

'Eighty-five per cent!' I repeated, my voice a bit too high.

Ballantine laughed, taking a step towards me. 'Okay, ninety per cent.'

I shook my head. 'No way.'

He took another step. 'Ninety-five per cent?'

This time I took a step back, but it was too late. Ballantine reached out and grabbed me by the wrists, holding me captive.

'A hundred per cent,' he breathed, looking down at me with absolute certainty. I could do nothing to squirm away from him; his hold was like granite.

'Don't,' I bit out, my eyes pleading, my head screaming inside that I didn't want to go in, even if my body was completely betraying me by leaning towards him.

He began to pull me forward, my feet skidding on the wet sand. 'No wait, stop. STOP!' I cried.

He stilled for a moment, a devious gleam lighting his dark eyes. 'Famous last requests?'

'I don't want to get my clothes wet.' There, that was a good enough reason. But just as I realised what I'd stupidly said, something sparked in Ballantine's expression.

'No, can't have that,' he agreed. Ballantine's right hand slid down to the hem of my top, gathering the fabric with his fingers while he still held me prisoner with his left hand.

I gasped when I felt the brush of his knuckles against my skin, as he slowly lifted the material. He smirked. 'Arms up!'

Like a mindless zombie, I complied, lifting my arms above my head. Ballantine had even let my wrists go so I could. He didn't need to physically hold me, not when his heated gaze kept me in place. For as long as his eyes bore into me like that, I wasn't going anywhere. I blushed deeply at my wanton thoughts, at the way he was controlling me. He peeled my top off with one swift movement, chucking it aside. My eyes broke away briefly to see it land perfectly on top of my shoes.

I swallowed, looking back into his eyes. There was no humour in his expression, no smug tilt of his lips, nothing. All I was aware of was the way his fingers lightly grazed down my sides, causing goose flesh to prickle my skin. My breath hitched when his hands slid down to rest on the top button of my jean shorts. Without so much as an eye blink, he popped one button after the other. Expertly working his way down, loosening my shorts until they became baggy around my hips. The only thing that made him seem anything but the perfect vision of calm was the heavy rise and fall of his chest – the way it mirrored my own. He aided me by pushing down the denim, down, down, sliding over my hipbones until the shorts fell to my ankles so I could step out of them. Ballantine picked them up, and threw them aside to join my singlet and thongs. I held my arms across my chest, conscious that I was standing in front of Ballantine in nothing but my bra and undies. White cotton with little pink bows. My cheeks were burning with mortification, but Ballantine didn't flinch at my lack of attire. At a guess he had seen it all before.

He had probably seen Lucy Fell-on-her-face in far less, I thought bitterly.

'You ready?' His voice snapped me out of my depressing thoughts.

'No,' I replied.

He smiled broadly. 'Well, that's just too bad.'

# Chapter Twenty-Four

He was fast. So fast. Scooping me up and over his shoulder as if I weighed nothing at all.

He ploughed into the waves, his legs expertly lifting over the crests so he could gain traction. He paid no attention to my pleas and squeals, and before the true shock set in and the realisation that my world had quite literally been turned upside down as he carried me over his shoulder, he flipped me over and plunged me into the icy black ocean. The shock of it caused me to gasp, inhaling a salty mouthful of water. I broke the surface, scrambling to find my feet. The strong current of the water didn't make it easy but Ballantine broke through the surface next to me, reaching out to help me stand and get my bearings as I coughed and spluttered: a stark contrast to Ballantine's laughter.

'Refreshed?'

'No!' I snapped, shivering against the coolness of the temperature. Actually it wasn't that bad, quite warm now my body was adjusting, but I wouldn't admit that.

Ballantine dipped his broad shoulders under the water before standing fully, running his hands through wet tendrils of hair. He stood with the waterline nipping at his navel; he looked even more gorgeous wet.

I cowered, keeping myself concealed by the water, hiding my near-naked body, and was happy to stay that way until I felt something tentacle-like brush against my legs. I screamed, leaping towards Ballantine, seeking refuge near his body. 'Oh-my-God-what-the-hell-was that?' I yelled, breathing erratically.

Ballantine laughed. 'It's probably just seaweed.'

I felt it again, causing me to claw and scream at Ballantine. If he had been a tree I would have climbed him. Oh, yes, in the movies people walk romantically into the ocean, basking in the warmth of the water and getting lost in each other's eyes. But no, hell no.

'Let me out! Let me out,' I screamed, fear carrying me through the water as I bolted towards the shore.

I could hear Ballantine howling with laughter but I didn't care, the ocean and me were never going to be friends. I scooped up my clothes – struggling to gain traction in the sand – and made a determined beeline for the path that led up to civilisation. The sooner I put distance between me and the water, the better.

'Lex, wait!'

But I didn't, I kept forging on: woman on a mission. I started to run and just as I thought I was nearly free, a pair of arms wrapped around my waist and whipped me to the ground, landing me with an oomph.

Ballantine pinned me effortlessly to the ground, drops of water dripping off his body onto mine. I squirmed underneath him but it was futile.

'I don't want to go back in,' I pleaded through my laboured breaths.

'You're not going back in,' he assured me, 'but I think you should probably put your clothes back on.' His eyes dipped to my chest. I followed his gaze, horrified to see my white bra had turned completely see-through, the pebbled, pink discs of my nipples clearly visible through the cotton material. I gasped, instinctively wanting to move my arms to cover myself, but Ballantine was unmoving. His hands imprisoned my arms on either side of my face, caging me in. His damp torso pressed against mine; our breathing hard and heavy from running. Or maybe from something else. I knew it wasn't just the running that had me feeling the tingling sensation over my skin, between my thighs. Ballantine could undo me with a look – one simple look. If this is how I felt already, what would happen if he actually touched me? His dark eyes lifted from my chest to my face, and judging by his stormy expression, it was almost as if he might have been wondering the same thing. What would happen if we did, if we went there? I knew I had over-analysed so many ridiculous scenarios when it came to Ballantine, but there was absolutely no mistaking the hard feel of him pressing against my hipbone. A thrill shot through me in complete and utter satisfaction that I, in some way, had excited him in *that* way.

He seemed lost, completely frozen, unsure about what was to be done with the wet, half-naked girl beneath him. So I made it easier for him.

'Luke,' I whispered, my eyes searching his face, searching for an expression I could read.

He blinked, looking down at me as if seeing me for the first time.

I bit my lip, terrified that I had broken the trance for good, that in some way he might come to his senses and let me go. But as soon as I said his name it was like a trigger – like he now knew exactly what he had to do. His hands let go of my wrists, his right hand sliding down my arm, the sweep of his skin along mine causing a tingly sensation. He swallowed. As his eyes followed the trail he blazed with his palm, sweeping down across my collarbone, tracing it delicately, he touched me as if I were made of glass, so gentle, so delicate as his fingers ghosted over the centre of my wet bra. A gorgeous smile tugged at the corner of his mouth when he flicked at the little pink bow, causing me to giggle. I was amazed how I wasn't embarrassed, that I was open and eager, almost arching myself into his touch, urging him on. I didn't want to stop, not ever.

And he didn't. His hand continued down, his palm playing over the tender, ticklish part of my belly. I inhaled a steadying breath, causing him to smile again. This time he wasn't looking at me; his eyes were following his hand as it trailed over my skin as if he was fine tuning an instrument. It wasn't until his hand skidded upwards along the edge of my bra that he looked up, as if silently asking a question. When my silence told him everything he needed, he slid his hand under the material of my bra, cupping my breast and maddeningly brushing his thumb over my nipple. I gasped.

*Oh my God. This was happening, this was really happening.*

With no sense of mortifying thoughts or second-guessing, I let my body succumb to the pleasure. My legs shifted for Ballantine to lay snugly and hard up against me, the thin, damp material of his shorts and my knickers the only barrier between us. My head pushed back in the sand as I arched into his touch, rocking into him as he rocked back, building a delicious friction between us. His right hand moved to slide the strap from my shoulder, peeling it slowly down until my breast was exposed to the night – exposed to him.

I could feel the heat of his breath across my bare skin and I thought I might die from happiness. Then I definitely knew

I would when he spoke against my neck, his lips grazing the lobe of my ear.

'Is this what you want?'

His strained voice was hoarse, dark . . . promising. He asked the question just as his fingers pinched my nipple; it gave him an unfair advantage that left me gasping, 'Yes.'

He smiled, pleased by my answer.

His hand moved from my breast, skirting over my belly, lower and lower, breaching the elastic barrier of my knickers. I felt a brief moment of panic, a panic that was soon obliterated when Ballantine lowered his mouth onto mine. Soft and sure, his lips slanted against mine, slowly opening me up to him. His tongue plunged in just as he slowly pushed his finger inside me. I moaned into his kiss, greedily accepting all he had to give. As my hands flew up to tangle in his dampened hair – my mind circling in disbelief that this was happening – thoughts became unintelligible as soft, tentative kisses soon turned into fierce, needy kisses as I rocked into his hand. I felt alive everywhere. Every spot on my skin he touched raised goosebumps. My heart was racing. This felt so surreal yet so welcome. And oh, this boy could *kiss*.

My whimpers were captured by his mouth. I was on fire, my insides twisting and clenching with the building pleasure.

'That's it, Lex, let go,' he whispered against my mouth, and just as I was about to shatter into a million pieces and scream Ballantine's name into the starry night, I heard the distant calls.

'Leeeeexie! Ballantine?!'

We froze. Panic stilled my racing heart as we looked at each other.

'Come out, come out, wherever you are,' Boon's voice taunted from above, closing in.

*Shit!*

Ballantine rolled off me as if he had been electrocuted; I pulled up my strap, positioning my bra back into place as I scurried to find my top and shorts.

*Shit-shit-shit.*

Ballantine had been so busy chasing me down that he'd left his clothes by the shoreline. We stood, running back into the shadows; Ballantine motioned for me to go in the opposite direction. 'There's a set of steps up that way about fifty metres. Keep in the shadows and double round back to the car,' he said quickly.

I laughed and said, 'Okay,' and did exactly as he directed, keeping to the shadows and watching as Ballantine casually walked out onto the beach to collect his shirt and shoes.

'There he is!' called Amanda, spotting him from the walking track. I took the opportunity, as Ballantine distracted them, to somehow – some way – get my boneless legs to move me further along the beach and towards the steps. But this time, a newfound adrenalin carried me and had me smiling like a fool, skipping every second step out of the darkness, into the illuminated streetlight.

# Chapter Twenty-Five

I was the first one back to the car, which gave me a bit of time to straighten myself out. My hair was a half-dried, sand-infused, frizzy mess. I felt as though I'd rolled in dirt, which I kind of had. I checked my reflection in the side mirror of the van, taking in my flushed complexion with a cheeky smile, trying to stifle my giddy laughter.

*Oh. My. Fucking. God. What just happened?*

I wanted to do a little jig of happiness. I could still taste Ballantine on my lips, the spearmint flavour of his tongue. It seemed like it took forever for him to kiss me and then when he finally did, my mind exploded with sheer elation. It wasn't like I hadn't kissed boys before, but this was in a totally different league. I wanted to laugh hysterically at the memory. I paced back and forth in front of the car until I finally heard the distant sounds of voices coming up the path. Boon spotted me first.

'There she is,' he called.

Amanda sighed in relief. 'Bloody hell, Lexie. Where were you?'

I glanced back at Ballantine. His face was . . . completely expressionless.

I shrugged. 'Just went to wash the sand off my feet.'

'Well, don't just wander off. You never know who might be lurking in the dark,' Amanda chastised.

I snorted, quickly turning away from their concerned looks. I stood by the car door, waiting for it to be unlocked, trying as best I could not to burst out laughing.

Much like the ride to the beach, we travelled back and pulled up out the front of our house in silence.

Amanda and Boon hopped out of the back, languishing in their passionate goodbyes. I knew there would be no passionate farewell for me, although I did at least expect a 'see ya later'. But when I turned to smile knowingly at Ballantine, revelling in our little secret and how we nearly got sprung, I was met with his stoic profile and not so much as a smirk. My elation slipped away. I sat there for a moment, waiting for a change in his demeanour, but it never came. I didn't exactly know who was sitting next to me but it certainly wasn't the boy from the beach.

'Wow, that was fast,' I said.

Ballantine's eyes shifted to look at me. 'What?'

I breathed out a laugh. 'I thought it would take until at least tomorrow for regret to set in.'

His gaze darkened, as if he didn't like what he'd just heard. He gripped the steering wheel with a white-knuckled intensity, perhaps readying himself to retort, but I didn't give him the chance as I flung open the car door, swung it closed, and trudged a determined line across the grass with not so much as a backward glance.

•

No matter how hard I scrubbed, I still felt the remnants of sand against my scalp. It was infuriating, almost as infuriating as the anger I felt towards myself, *and* at Ballantine for ruining my night. He could have at least been a man and given me the 'I'm not looking for anything serious' speech. I wasn't exactly after a proposal of marriage. *Bastard.* I didn't know what I wanted; I just didn't want to be treated like the plague, to feel like such a reject. Should I have been so surprised to learn that Ballantine was just one of the boys, that getting with a girl was no more than a cheap thrill, get your rocks off and see you later? Perhaps that's all it was. Play with the new thing just for the fun of it. See how far she will go. And stupid me fell for it. I felt embarrassed. I felt ashamed.

One in the morning and I was in the bathroom violently combing the knots out of my hair, thanking the Lord above that Boon and Amanda had come along and disturbed us; there was no telling how far I would have gone, even though I knew in my heart of hearts I wouldn't have wanted him to stop, ever. My body reacted to him in a way that kind of scared me; even now, when I was so angry at him, if he came knocking on my window pleading for forgiveness my heart would spike in approval. Not that that was going to happen. I just had to wipe him and the night from my mind – if that was possible. If I couldn't shake him from my thoughts when we had barely done anything except sit next to each other in detention, how on earth was I supposed to forget him now that he'd had his hands down my pants?

I sighed, flicked off the bathroom light, and dragged my weary butt to bed. The lamplight guided me into the room where Amanda was lying in bed, smiling like the Cheshire cat. For a moment, seeing her so happy, so open about her relationship with Boon, a dose of resentment surged inside me, and I wanted nothing more than to plunge the room into darkness and not have to witness the sheer bliss that radiated from my contented cousin.

I crawled into my bed, my body aching, my mind alert but exhausted, and closed my eyes.

'Can you turn off the light?' I asked.

Amanda leant over, clicking off her lamp, and in the comfort of the darkness I let the tears pool under my lids.

*No-no-no-no . . . Don't be such a baby. You're just tired. Don't be stupid. You made out with Ballantine, you fooled around. So what? You weren't friends before, so nothing will change now. Just go with the flow, Lexie, just go with the flow.*

I did go with the flow all right – the involuntary flow of tears. Amanda's voice pierced the darkness; she happily went on and on about Boon and how amazing he was. I rolled away from her, answering in one-word responses to make out I was listening, even though I wasn't. I was too steeped in misery. I desperately wanted to feel the way I had felt with Ballantine – that thrill and excitement even before we had done anything, when he was merely sitting on my bed, looking at me. I feared he wouldn't look at me again, and my chest ached with the thought. I would sooner have moments of something, than a whole term based on awkwardness. I guess only tomorrow would tell.

•

With a new day came new clarity, indeed . . . it slammed me in the face the moment Laura Boon bounced up to my locker.

'Hey, Lexie.'

In all my moments of self-obsessed misery, a memory flashed, a memory I didn't need and one I couldn't believe I had forgotten. Looking at Laura's expressive, kind eyes and bouncing giddiness, I had somehow, some way, forgotten what Boon had told me that night on the beach. Laura had a massive crush on Ballantine. My self-entitled rage and self-pity was instantly wiped away with shame.

'Hey,' I said, trying my best to smile.

'Did you watch *Neighbours* last night?'

*No, actually, I was too busy dry humping your crush on the beach.*

'Um, no, I didn't. Was it good?'

'Ugh, so good!' she said, turning to her locker.

I was a shitty person. A shitty, shitty person who deserved all the cold shoulders in the world. From now on I would be a model student, a model friend, niece, cousin, and all-round decent human being. I couldn't believe I had done what I did last night, without even a thought for poor Laura and how it would crush her. I suddenly thanked God for Ballantine – if he didn't want to acknowledge what had happened then neither would I.

Nope, it never happened.

•

Paradise High was a big enough school to get yourself lost in if you wanted to, and that Thursday was definitely one of those days. But I knew that no matter how much effort I put into avoiding Ballantine, we were always going to be thrust together for detention. At least we didn't have to talk to each other. This time I made a point of deliberately being several minutes late. My theory: if Ballantine was already seated I could at least choose not to sit next to him. The ploy was really motivated by fear. If I was seated and he came in and chose not to sit near me, well . . . I really didn't want to have another hole punched through my chest. No, I would definitely give myself the upper hand here. I was a good ten minutes late and I could completely handle the fury of the teacher for the sake of salvaging my pride. When I coyly slid open the classroom door I was met by the steely grey stare of Mr Hooper. His eyes peered over his glasses as he made a point to crane his neck and look at the wall clock, accentuating how late I was.

I winced. 'Sorry.'

'Take your seat,' he said, unenthusiastically.

I made my way fully into the classroom, my eyes flicking across the tables at the few new additions to detention but, rather alarmingly, the lack of a few regulars.

No Boon. No Ballantine.

I made my way slowly to the back of the class, choosing the very last row again.

Maybe their detention had finished? I never actually asked what they had done or how long they were in for. Could there really be a God after all? One that would grant me a reprieve?

A smug smile lined my face as I took my seat, relaxing in a way I hadn't ever felt in detention. But that was shortlived as the classroom door slid open quickly, and Ballantine stood in the doorway.

*Shit.*

Mr Hooper did the same routine. Glare, turn to clock, glare.

Ballantine didn't look sorry though. 'Daniel Boon is away sick,' he said, making his way down the aisle.

I focused with all my might on my textbook, reading over the contents again and again before turning the page. I could feel myself holding my breath as I heard his footsteps getting closer. This was exactly what I didn't want to happen. I didn't want him to sit close to me, but I knew that if he chose to sit elsewhere that would be even worse. We would be doomed to ignore each other, with probable awkward exchanges if we ever had to be in close proximity. And as much as last night had initially been amazing, if it meant *that*, then I wished it had never happened.

I was snapped out of my thoughts when Ballantine slammed his books down.

Next to mine.

I blew out a breath. Shifting in my seat, I could feel relief flood through me in unexpected waves, and I hated that I felt so grateful he didn't sit anywhere else. His chair scraped along the floorboards as he took his seat. I didn't look at him, I didn't acknowledge him. I simply flipped through my textbook, reading but not taking in a single word.

'Now that's the last of the stragglers, heads down,' Mr Hooper said.

# Chapter Twenty-Six

The room was eerily silent, maybe because Boon wasn't there to fidget and sigh and throw paper. Instead, all that was really apparent was the slow, agonising sound of the wall clock: tick, tick, ticking each second that passed. That and the scratchings of the pen Ballantine used as he worked on colouring in his mural – the only form of work he tended to do in detention. I wondered if he ever handed in any homework? I couldn't exactly imagine him sitting down at a desk at home studying by lamplight before sneaking out and knocking on girls' bedroom windows. *Don't follow through with that thought, Lexie.* Ballantine was probably a regular at girls' windows. He didn't even come to see *you* last night. He tagged along with Boon.

He still had my pen – that much I could see in my peripheral vision. It was hard to comprehend that those same hands had touched me so intimately last night. My cheeks flamed at the memory and I forced my eyes forward, studying the wall clock once more.

There were no notes passed this time, no exchanges other than a momentary accidental brush of our legs that caused my heart to jump into my throat. I prayed this torture would be over soon, that the bell would sound and I could walk away, maybe ditch tomorrow's detention by saying I was sick like Boon had done. Genius.

When the bell did blare through the speakers, Ballantine and I, in synchronised desperation, packed up our things quickly, eager to put an end to what had been a super-awkward detention. One of the certain drawbacks to being at the back of the class was that we were always the last to leave – might have to rethink that next time. And just as I moved to walk behind Ballantine and go our separate ways, the worst thing possible happened.

'Hold on a minute, you two.'

Mr Hooper finished up packing his papers and putting them in his briefcase, something I didn't know people used anymore. Most teachers opted for man bags, but Mr Hooper was old school.

Ballantine and I paused in the doorway, glancing at each other briefly before stepping back into the classroom.

'Seeing as running on time for detention isn't such a priority for you both, maybe you could practise showing up on time at, say, 3.30 p.m. after school.'

'Sir?' Ballantine queried.

'You heard me, don't be late,' he said, snapping his briefcase shut with an air of finality as he picked it up and left us standing there in stunned silence.

•

For the second time that week I found Amanda leaning up against my locker at home time.

Unlike last time when she'd seemed her usual bitter self, today she looked, well, to put it bluntly . . . like death. And it wasn't just because of the heavy, black eyeliner.

I approached her with guarded interest, falling short just before my locker. 'You okay? You don't look so good.'

'Of course I'm okay,' she snapped, her brows etched in the grim-grey canvas of her clammy skin, her tired eyes painting the real story of fatigue. Her usual slick, straightened hair looked dishevelled and dull. Amanda folded her arms across her chest as if to ward off a chill, a chill that didn't exist in the stuffy, overcrowded hallway. She was obviously in denial.

'So, what do you know?' I reached past her, dialling the combination of my lock, only getting her to move reluctantly once I pulled at the door.

'Boon didn't come to school today,' she pouted.

'Too many late nights, maybe?' I tried to lighten the mood but there was nothing that was going to obliterate the dark cloud that had settled over Amanda. I only hoped she wasn't slipping into her old hateful ways. I didn't know if I could bear that. Having my old cousin back felt really good. I hadn't felt so alone.

'Worst. Day. Ever,' she said, thudding her head on my neighbour's locker door.

'Tell me about it, I have after-school detention.'

'What? What have you done now? You are out of control.'

'I guess so. Hey, can you tell Aunty Karen that I have some kind of practice after school or something?'

'Practice? Like what? Basketball, netball, band? Because I don't think they're going to buy it.'

'Okay, fair point. How about I'm using the library to study?'

'That's far more believable.'

'Cool, wish me luck,' I said, grabbing some books.

'Hang on a sec, you didn't tell me what you did.'

I sighed. 'Ballantine and I were late to detention. Mr Hooper's teaching us a lesson on punctuality.'

Amanda cocked her eyebrow. 'You and Ballantine, huh? Quite the partners in crime.'

*Oh God, no I didn't want her to look at me like that, to read something into it. I could barely meet her eyes as it was.*

'I'm going to have to get you to stop hanging out with him; he's a bad influence on you.'

I smiled weakly, turning to head towards my ominous after-school detention, thinking, *If only she knew.*

'Well, if Ballantine drove in, at least get him to drop you home,' Amanda called after me.

'I'll be right, I'll just walk.'

'Don't be ridiculous, he has to go that way anyway.'

I paused by the locker room door, confused.

Amanda rolled her eyes. 'Trust me, you wouldn't be putting him out, he lives around the corner from us.'

For the second time that day I stood in stunned silence. 'Around the corner?'

Amanda shrugged. 'On Sherwin Drive. You can literally rock his roof from our balcony.'

Ballantine had been this close all along and I had no idea. I'd just assumed that a delinquent troublemaker would live on the wrong side of town, that he was tortured in some way and was therefore rebelling against the clutches of civilised society; and yet, here he was. Poor little rich boy with a concrete driveway and an automatic garage door.

'Promise you'll get a lift, it's too far to walk,' said Amanda, the light of genuine concern in her bloodshot eyes.

'Sure,' I said sweetly. 'After all, it's the neighbourly thing to do, right?'

Amanda looked at me with guarded interest as if she couldn't quite put her finger on the reason behind my crazy eyes. Had she been feeling one hundred per cent she probably would've quizzed me, but she didn't, and I took the opportunity to make a run for it.

'See you later,' I said quickly, spinning on my heel with a new determination and a clear-cut thought.

I did not want to be late!

•

After-school detention seemed a lot more casual. I had guessed as much the moment I walked into the classroom and spotted Ballantine lying on a tabletop, hands casually clasped over his stomach, eyes closed as if he was in a meditative state. My eyes shifted to the vacant teacher's desk, wondering what the penalty for a late teacher would be.

I slowly and quietly made my way to stand beside Ballantine, staring down on his rested face, his dark hair in its usual tousled mess. I desperately wanted to reach out and brush a curl from his forehead but thought better of it. He looked so peaceful, so serene, hardly the appearance of someone who was hanging out in detention or worried about some teacher walking through the door at any second. I took the uninterrupted moment to look at Ballantine – really look at him. He seemed so young, like a little angel who could do no wrong. You would never guess that he was actually the devil. And then of course one eye opened, and he caught me standing there gawking at him. An infuriating smirk pinched the corner of his mouth. I wanted to push him off the table and might have done so if he hadn't interrupted my thoughts.

'Anyone tell you it's rude to stare?' he said, closing his eye again and folding his hands behind his head.

My brow curved incredulously. 'Social etiquette? I hardly think you're an authority on the subject.'

Ballantine's smile broadened across his face. 'Ooh, I love it when you talk dirty.'

I sighed. He was so bloody confusing. He had gone from flirting, to silent, to a smart-arse again. Moving across to the middle table and taking my seat, I said, 'I wouldn't get too comfy if I were you, Mr Hooper can't be too far away.'

Ballantine sat upright, swinging his legs over the edge of the table. 'You think this is my first stint in after-school detention?' He shook his head. 'Ye of little faith.'

'Oh, I don't doubt it's not, but if you want to be in a state of perpetual detention, go for it.'

Ballantine laughed. 'Perpetual detention? You're a Gilmore girl through and through, aren't you?'

'And you're a Kirkland meathead,' I snapped, hating how I was letting him bait me, hating how right he was in pointing out how nerdy I truly was.

Instead of taking offence, Ballantine appeared to be openly delighted about me snapping back, raising his brows in intrigue. 'Wow, kitty got claws.'

I sighed, canting my head at him. 'Please shut up.'

'Shut up?'

'Yes, shut up.'

'You want me to stop?'

'Yes, just stop.'

'That's not what you said last night.'

My eyes snapped up. I could barely contain my anger. My frustration was palpable and he bloody knew it. If this was some kind of cute game he was playing then it was wearing very thin. My eyes flicked impatiently to the door,

willing Mr Hooper to step inside and force silence upon us.
Ballantine followed my eyeline.

'He's not coming.'

'What?'

'They're not as vigilant after school as they are during
lunchtime. Trust me, that's a good thing.'

At this point in time, stranded in a class with Ballantine
and no supervision, I wasn't so sure about that. I straightened
my spine. 'So how long are we expected to be here for? Seeing
as you're the expert.'

Ballantine rolled his shoulder in a devil-may-care shrug.
'Halfer? I take the cleaner coming in lifting chairs up as a
sign that God wants us to move on.'

My eyes flicked over Ballantine; a small smile tugged my
lips as I took in the boy before me. Now I no longer saw the
wrong-side-of-the-tracks, hard-done-by misfit. No, now I
took in the white, crisp, ironed shirt, his dark cargo shorts,
and navy Converse shoes. Definitely a well-kept rich kid from
the coastal suburbs, probably a mummy's boy, too.

He looked back at me, matching my stare. 'What?'
he asked.

'Nothing, you just don't strike me as the religious type,
is all.'

'Oh, I don't know. I think it's safe to say I moved heaven
and earth last night.'

I rolled my eyes. 'Oh puh-lease! Spare me the caveman
innuendo. You don't have to big note, there is no-one here
to listen.'

'You're here,' he said, a devious sparkle in his eyes, causing
heat to flush my cheeks.

'So, you don't have to relive the moment with smart-arse
insinuations. Save it for your mates,' I scoffed, knowing that

he had probably already relayed the mortifying details of last night. It was no doubt a rite of passage for most girls to at least be humiliated in some way, with nothing being sacred, not even late-night fumblings with a hot boy, but I had desperately wanted to relay the news to Amanda myself. I know I was all about experiencing things I had never done before, but somehow being the butt of the Kirkland boys' jokes at the bus shelter was not one of the experiences I was after.

I could feel myself getting angry thinking back to the way I had felt the night before: from sky-high elation and disbelief that a sex-god surfer had kissed me, wanted me, when he could have chosen anyone in this school and the next; to the embarrassing humiliation of nearly being caught, then blatantly cast off. Yet, he could have forced one of his mates to accompany *him* to knock on Lucy Fell's window, but instead he chose to tag along with Boon. Probably as a way of distracting the mousy cousin while Boon wooed her cousin. *Oh shit.* The thought slammed into me; the very foundation of the prospect twisting my gut in a way that made it hard to breathe. Ballantine must have noticed the workings of my mind, his interest showing as he watched me in stony silence.

'Was I the decoy?'

'What?' he asked quickly.

'You know, the girl you had to distract while your mate hooked up with her friend.'

*Or cousin.*

Ballantine looked genuinely shocked. 'Where did you get that idea?'

I read it in a *Cleo* magazine, but I wasn't about to reveal my sources. I squared my shoulders, forcing myself to look him dead in the eyes. 'Was I?'

Ballantine obviously didn't like what he was hearing, he looked so mad I almost broke eye contact. But I didn't. No matter how much I wanted to. Instead, I lifted my chin, challenging his stare yet dreading the answer.

Ballantine shook his head, lifted himself off the table, and headed for the door. 'I'm out of here,' he scoffed.

I stared incredulously at his retreating back. 'Coward.' I said the word mainly to myself, but Ballantine had most certainly heard me; I knew that the second he paused, turned towards me, and shot death-ray beams at me.

I swallowed, almost wanting to slide under my desk at such a look. Then he stalked his way, in a long, determined line towards me, rested his knuckles on the surface leaning over, and looked down at me with a wicked spark in his eyes.

'Coward?' he repeated.

My eyes burned into his. 'You heard me,' I said coolly. 'Avoid the question if you want, I know the truth.' I looked away, feigning boredom when all I really wanted was to disguise the raw emotions I felt – the hurt.

My moment of interest in my textbook was cut short by sudden and unexpected laughter from Ballantine. My eyes flicked up, troubled as I took in the mad man before me, trying not to be wooed by that bloody heartbreaking dimple that flashed as he laughed.

He shook his head in disbelief. 'You want to know the truth?' he asked.

I didn't respond, I couldn't. Who wanted to know it? I sure didn't.

All humour fell away from Ballantine, disappearing as quickly as the laughter had come. He leant forward, lowering himself to lean on his elbows, yet maintaining his intimidating stance. 'The truth is, if I'm with a girl, in the sea, in the car, in a bed or on a beach,' he said, a wicked grin flashing, 'it's because I choose to be. Trust me, Lex, if my hands are on you, or *inside* you, it's because I want them to be.'

'But you could be with anyone.' The words tumbled from my mouth without thinking, and I wanted to slap myself for letting them out. They hung between us in the awkward silence, a long, lingering silence until he spoke.

'And, Lex? I wanted you.'

# Chapter Twenty-Seven

My head was spinning.

I could almost feel it rotating three-sixty degrees on my shoulders while my mind screamed: HOLY SHIT!

There was nothing to be said, no time to do anything other than openly gape at him and observe his devilish smirk. He had meant it. I knew beyond all else that he had. And even if he didn't, it meant little right at that moment because he had delivered his words with such conviction. The directness of them sparked the same fire inside me . . . and the smug bastard knew as much. It was infuriating, and so very, very hot.

I wanted to clear my desk dramatically, pull him across the table, and kiss the bejesus out of him, but this was not Hollywood. This became even clearer when the classroom door slid open and a man with an industrial vacuum cleaner strapped to his back walked in, smiling politely at us and well and truly breaking our trance.

'You're free to go,' he said, yelling above the hum of the vacuum cleaner.

It was music to my ears! (His words, not the vacuum cleaner.) I stood, gathered my things, feeling the weight of Ballantine's eyes on me. I ignored him until I moved around the table, coming to stand beside him. I pushed all the butter-flies, tingles and good-God hot flushes aside. I didn't know if it was his admission that had me feeling more confident, but I looked up at him, a small smile lining my lips.

Ballantine matched my smile, as his knowing eyes ticked over my face. 'You want a ride home?'

My first thought was yes, but that wasn't all I wanted from the boy. I wanted his smiles. I wanted his kisses. I wanted him.

•

Ballantine led the way, opening the car door for me in what I thought was a gentlemanly gesture, only to discover he actually had to work quickly to clear a space on the passenger seat – previously covered in papers and empty Solo cans that he grabbed and chucked into the back of the van. He brushed down the black leather, casting me a sheepish smile. 'Sorry about the mess. It's mostly sand,' he said, wiping his hands on his shorts.

'That's okay. Occupational hazard,' I said. A little bubble of pride fluttered in my chest at the way he smiled in response, a feeling I quickly pushed down, deep down.

*Don't get carried away, Lexie.*

Ballantine stood aside, allowing me to slide into the passenger seat. He shut the door behind me, walking a path around the front of his car, seemingly as uneasy about our soon-to-be commute as I was. Ballantine slid behind the steering wheel, pulling the seatbelt to click into place.

*Seriously, how could putting on a seatbelt be so hot?*

I snapped out of my daydreaming and grabbed for my own. Ballantine turned the key, pushed the accelerator, and brought the Sandman to thunderous life. The engine purred powerfully in a way that rattled my bones. The sound, the feel of the leather underneath my legs – this was sex on wheels. Ballantine lifted his hand up to the sun visor, flicking it down so a pair of sunglasses fell into his lap. He slid on the Ray Bans before shifting into drive and pushing the pedal down.

A fifteen-minute car ride isn't really long in the scheme of things, but when you're sitting next to a smoking-hot boy in awkward silence, it feels like an eternity.

The affluent houses of the surrounding neighbourhood whizzed by in a colourful blur as we sped through the streets, veering past a marketplace full of shops. I watched on with glee as I took in the yellow Sandman reflecting in the shop windows. If only my friends at Red Hole could see me now. I caught my own smiley, goofy reflection as we pulled up at a red light. My smile quickly dissolved as I straightened in my seat, sobering, and instead leant casually on the opened window for that, yeah, cool, whatever attitude, the whole time screaming inwardly at the thought of sitting next to a boy who had chosen me last night, not because he had a sense of duty to Boon, but because he had wanted to. In no time, the silence, other than the music of Nickelback on the radio blaring out of the sound system, had us turning onto my street and snapping me out of my thoughts. I turned my head around, wishing I had been paying attention as we neared my neighbourhood, *our* neighbourhood. Had I missed his street sign? Had we gone past it?

*Damn it.*

I was lost in my own inner monologue as Ballantine's Sandman thumped its V8 engine up the street, slicing through the peaceful suburban neighbourhood. There was nothing delicate about our arrival as he spun out wide and, much to my horror, turned into our drive. Gone were the midnight runs where he would have parked out front and slightly up a bit to shield any potential curious peeking through the windows. No, there was nothing subtle about it, and there was certainly nothing subtle about the unimpressed death stare we were receiving as Uncle Peter stood in the front yard, watering a line of agapanthus with the garden hose.

Colour drained from my face as I took in the sight before me.

*Oh God.*

Ballantine, unfazed, tilted his head, with a casual lift of his hand from the steering wheel to acknowledge my uncle. Uncle Peter did not return the courtesy, only the continued alpha stare of death.

I smiled weakly. 'Thanks for the lift,' I said sheepishly, wishing that the ground would open up or Uncle Peter would crack a smile or something? I liked my chances of a sinkhole spontaneously forming way before the latter happened.

Ballantine picked at the steering wheel, his eyes still shielded by his Ray Ban sunglasses. 'I really want to kiss you, but somehow I don't think that's a good idea,' he said, a boyish grin spreading across his face. He peered over to look at me, taunting me.

I thought my heart would break out of my chest, my eyes flicking questioningly to where Uncle Peter still stood.

I cleared my throat, before laughing nervously. 'Um, yeah. I don't think so,' I said, even though I had never wanted anything so much. It was hard to tear myself away, to force myself out of Ballantine's car knowing that somehow I'd have to make it past Uncle Peter's Judgey McJudgement eyes. Of course, telling Ballantine to reverse out of the drive and elope with me was probably not an option. So, with a deep breath, I hopped out then shut the passenger door to the Sandman and waved goodbye, before turning to face the music or – in this case – the firing squad.

•

I pressed my back against the front door, sighing with sheer relief. I felt like Indiana Jones must have after he'd just run through a death-defying gauntlet of booby traps. Skipping over the damp grass, dodging the garden hose, making sure not to fall into the hedge, all the while avoiding the laser beams no doubt protruding from my uncle's eyeballs.

*Don't make eye contact. Don't make eye contact.*

I had made it. I knew as much as soon as I hit the porch at a run and nothing had been said. It was a small mercy. I really didn't want a lecture, I really just needed time to process what the hell had happened in after-school detention: a detention I should be thanking my lucky stars for. I wanted to run upstairs to the second storey, step out onto the balcony and see if I could spot any sign of Ballantine's roof line in the next street over. But at the risk of being caught in the parental wing, I decided to do something even more important for now.

*I was going to tell Amanda about Ballantine.*

Dropping my bag at my feet, I pushed off from the door, bolting into a full sprint down the hall and bursting through the door of the bedroom.

'I know something you don't . . . Oh my God!' I came to a skidding halt, taking in the sight before me.

Amanda was vomiting into a bucket next to her bed.

I grimaced, stepped back, and turned away. 'Oh God. Are you okay?'

Amanda answered with another heave.

The room was desperately hot and it was no wonder, seeing as it was basically summer and Amanda had the heater cranked up.

'Bloody hell, Amanda.' I made a beeline for the window, sliding it open to let some fresh air in, and moved to switch off the heater.

'I'm cold,' Amanda croaked, wiping her mouth and clutching the doona to her chin.

Dodging the sick bucket I placed my palm on her forehead. 'You have a fever,' I said. Her skin was on fire.

'I'm sick, Lexie,' she sobbed.

'You think?' I said, looking at her pale, dishevelled state, and the disgusting puke stain on her t-shirt. 'You're a hot mess.'

'Go away,' she moaned, turning away from me.

'Does Uncle Peter know you're sick?' I asked gently, rubbing her back.

'I want Mum,' her voice was muffled as she lay face down in her pillow.

I pressed my lips together, completely understanding the feeling. It was how I felt whenever I was sick, or feeling upset. This week my emotions had been up and down like a yo-yo, and I had on more than one occasion wanted to pull the 'I want my mummy' card.

'Okay, hang on,' I said.

I bypassed Uncle Peter altogether, partly because I was selfishly worried that I might get another dose of death stares, but also because I quickly convinced myself that I was respecting Amanda's wishes.

*Yeah, sure. That's what it was.*

I picked up the phone and dialled Aunty Karen's work number.

•

The clicking sound of Aunty Karen's heels along the path outside the house had never sounded so good. I'd tried my best to help Amanda, given her aspirin to help break her fever, fetched glasses of water to help keep her fluids up and provided a cold compress for her brow. I mean, I even emptied her spew bucket. That's love.

Even though I was genuinely concerned and sorry for Amanda, it didn't take long for me to grow weary of her diva-like demands.

'I'm thirsty.'

'I'm hot.'

'I'm cold.'

'Shut the door!'

'Close the window.'

She snapped every order, the underlying evil Amanda resurfacing like the days of old. It chipped away at my empathy bit by bit. And when I tried to lighten the mood by suggesting maybe her and Boon had caught some kind of kissing disease off each other, her screamed response of 'Shut up!' was like the final nail in the coffin for caring. I calmly placed the face washer down and left her to feel sorry for herself.

'Hey, where are you going?' she called after me, her voice tired, her vague eyes squinting at me.

'Oh, I'm just going out here for a sec,' I said.

*Praying for the strength not to smother you with a pillow.*

# Chapter Twenty-Eight

Heaven was in the form of a sleeping Amanda, and the angel on earth was Aunty Karen.

I tentatively popped my head into the bedroom, as if I was entering the lair of a fire-breathing dragon – which was not too far removed from reality. 'How is she?' I whispered, creeping into the room.

Aunty Karen smiled. 'Much better. I gave her something to settle her stomach and she's kept down all her fluids which is good.'

Amanda was in clean PJs, settled between changed bedding, and had a clean, empty bucket by her side. She was definitely in better hands with Aunty Karen than she was with me.

Aunty Karen yawned, her eyes flicking to the bedside clock. 'Oh my gosh, is that the time?' she asked, standing to leave.

It was nine o'clock. I was aware of this, as I'd been forced to sit silently across from Uncle Peter at the table as we ate dinner, the clinking of our cutlery the only sound. At least he fed me, I guess. I had avoided his knowing eyes by calling Laura after dinner to kill some time. It was a rather interesting conversation. I found out that Boon was just as sick as

Amanda, and apparently there was something going around. This was not the glamorous Paradise I had envisioned.

I'd ended my conversation thinking that I would've felt better having spoken to her; that somehow I would've approached the subject of her diary, and told her that she should keep it in a safe place because of Boon's wandering eyes. I'd also wanted to ask her about Ballantine, to get her to confide in me. But of course I left all those things unsaid. Instead, we laughed about Mr Branson tripping over in the corridor between classes; I confessed to her my after-school detention with Ballantine, waiting for her to confess her undying love for him at the mere mention of his name. Instead, I heard her mum call from the other room that it was time to get off the phone.

So, yes, the irony was not lost on me. The very thing I had accused Ballantine of being, I was being myself. A coward.

I had two choices: 'fess up to Laura or stop kissing Ballantine.

And as I readied myself for sleep, laying down nestling against my pillows, I thought the decision would be simple enough.

I couldn't do that to Laura. Hos before bros, remember? I never wanted to be one of those girls who would end a friendship over a boy, and even though it was a new friendship, it was one of the only ones I had managed to form at Paradise High. So, as I closed my eyes, I nodded with finality.

Simple: no more Ballantine. No more verbal sparring, flirty looking, or car rides. Nothing.

And just as I cemented the decision well and truly in my mind, I heard a tapping on my window.

*Oh crap!*

•

I propped myself up on my elbows, looking over at Amanda's sleeping form under her covers, wondering if she had heard it. But she was unmoving. I heard it again.

*Tap-tap-tap.*

I leapt towards the window. Kneeling on my mattress, I flung the curtains aside, attempting to still my heavy breaths that were misting the window in front of me. Dazed and confused I pulled focus on Ballantine standing on the other side of the glass. I blinked. Moving to slide the window aside, I peered past him into the dark looking for his sidekick. I turned to Amanda who was still deep in slumber.

I turned back to Ballantine. 'Um, Amanda's sick,' I said.

Ballantine's eyes shifted to where Amanda slept, nodding. 'Yeah, so's Boon.'

My eyes widened in alarm, so much so Ballantine broke into a cheeky grin as he leant casually against the window frame.

'But there's nothing wrong with me,' he said. 'You?'

Inwardly I cursed the sexy boy before me, the way his dark eyes flicked over my face, the muted shadows and the subtle glow of the streetlight illuminated us just enough for me to be spellbound by him. But more so, I cursed myself. Just like I'd done on the beach confessing Amanda's love for Boon, I should have done the same for Laura: told Ballantine about her affection, then maybe he would think twice about coming to my window. But then something lodged in my chest and the sudden thought of him going to anyone else's window made me feel ill.

'I feel fine,' I lied.

Ballantine laughed, pleased by my answer. 'Enough to dance with the devil in the moonlight?'

My heart pounded so fast and loud – I was certain he would hear it – and when, against all my instincts, all my good intentions, I heard myself breathing out, 'Yes,' I delighted in the response of his smile.

'Then let's go,' he said, pushing off the windowsill.

I watched on as his silhouette was swallowed by the shadows, knowing that wherever he was going I was going too. It was at that moment I knew I was in deep, deep trouble.

•

The last rays of the sun had dipped well and truly, and the streetlights cast a rich orange glow. It was the same image I had seen in tourist catalogues. Now I was actually living inside those postcards, cruising down the congested streets that were flooded with life, music, smells of eateries, and death-defying pedestrians who were out for a midweek good time. I never fully relaxed – my body tense – as Ballantine zigzagged, expertly manoeuvring through the traffic. He was so comfortable behind the wheel. His right arm perched casually on the open window of the car, his fingers tapping impatiently on the steering wheel waiting for the traffic lights to turn green. On and on we drove, stopped and started on every block, catching every red light. Not that I minded. In the intense silence of the Sandman's cabin I felt goose flesh pucker my skin. Not from the warm, thick breeze that filtered through my open window whipping my hair around, but because I was travelling in a car, with a boy, through the heart of Paradise City.

Even if it was nothing more than simply driving, I wanted to live in the moment, ignore the finer details, and enjoy, just for the next however long, that I was riding in a hot car, with a hot surfer boy. That all the people walking along the streets, or passing us in their cars would think nothing of us – just a couple cruising the streets of Paradise, like young people do. My dreaming led to the thought of Ballantine pulling up in a car park along the beach, a secluded spot picked especially for the purpose of what people drive themselves there to do. I imagined him turning off the engine, the only sound the distant slamming of the ocean against the shoreline, and the beating of my heart. He would look at me, with silent questioning eyes – look for the longest moment – before taking my silence as the answer he was after. Slowly he'd reach across me, his arms would lightly graze my breasts as he leant closer to unclick my seatbelt, letting it slowly slide back into place. I'd feel the heat of his breath across my neck, he would be so close he would be able to feel the erratic thrums of my heart, know the effect he was having on me. But the way his dark eyes would flick to my mouth and then back up again, a ghost of a smile appearing as he revelled in me biting my bottom lip – indenting my flesh – with the need, the want of him. Wishing he would just close the distance. Closer, closer until the final . . .

Ballantine came to a sudden stop, jolting me out of my lustful thoughts. I blinked back into reality, taking a deep breath and attempting to clear my head. I hoped against hope that the muted lighting would disguise my crimson cheeks. I sat up straight, embarrassed by the fact I had been daydreaming the entire trip, amazed at how fast time went when you were having fun. He turned the engine off, and I looked out the window expecting to see Amanda's two-storey house. I froze, my breath catching at the sight of what was very much *not* my home, or street, or anywhere that resembled my destination. Confused, I turned my questioning eyes towards Ballantine. Who watched me with a wicked glimmer in his eye. 'Welcome to the Wipe Out Bar.'

# Chapter Twenty-Nine

All the tourists swarmed along the streets, looking over menus from local restaurants as maître d's tried to lure them inside with the seafood platters or a pot and parmi from the night's specials.

We made our way from where Ballantine had parked in a car park behind a bottle-o. Turning the corner, I was blinded by the bright lights that brought the city streets alive. Making our way down the narrow paths, every now and then our arms brushed against each other. Oh God. I hoped we saw someone from school, someone who would witness me walking down the street, on a school night, with Luke Ballantine. Let their minds go wild with the scandal of it . . . and then I thought of Laura finding out and how that would make her feel. Now my eyes shifted around not in awe, but in paranoia and fear of being spotted by someone we knew.

The road veered off to the right, but Ballantine led me straight ahead. Walking down the path we continued into a large arcade, an expansive sweep of open, flat, concrete flanked by surf shops, eateries, game zones, open bars, and a tattoo parlour that was strangely wedged next to an ice-creamery. There were no rules to follow walking among the crowd, no direct path that would not have you dodging people. The flashing lights from a games arcade, the ear-piercing loud music that blasted out of speakers, and the mumbled voices of all the people jostling around me: I felt like the silver ball in a pinball machine. It was all so over-whelming as I stuck close to Ballantine, who walked along with careless ease, showing he wasn't fazed in the slightest by his surroundings. If anything, he appeared a bit bored by it all. A typical city boy: not even flinching at the clattering, weaving skateboarders nearby.

I couldn't believe that it was like this on a week night. The biggest wow factor in Red Hill during the week was the real-life stories about horrific hoarders on TV.

A cluster of boys walking in our direction broke away from their conversation of insults and pushes, the redhead boy spotting us first, before elbowing his acne-skinned mate.

'What you got there, Ballantine?' the redhead boy grinned, his beady eyes shifting over me. Their gazes followed us as we walked past them. Ballantine paid them no attention, unlike myself, who caught their mimed hip thrusts and booty slaps, their crude laughter.

I turned to Ballantine. 'Friends of yours?'

Ballantine seemed almost shy as a line pinched the corner of his mouth. 'Not exactly; Lance is Lucy's younger brother.' He shrugged. 'You don't know her.'

My head snapped up, my mind whirling at the mention of her name. 'Lucy Fell-on-her face?' I blurted out so fast, and with no edit button.

Ballantine's head swivelled, his eyes narrowing, causing me to break away from his gaze, cursing my big mouth.

'What?' he asked, a small laugh accentuating the word.

'Oh nothing,' I said quickly, brushing away my words, my mind shifting to how Lucy and her younger ginger-haired brother looked nothing alike.

I could still feel Ballantine's curious gaze on me as we continued to walk on. Oh God, what must he think of me? I tried desperately to come up with something to say in order to change the subject and get him thinking about anything other than me bagging out his beloved Lucy. But then it had me thinking, hoping, that Lance would run home and tell Lucy all about the mysterious girl he saw Ballantine walking with down the arcade. A small bubble of approval formed in my chest.

'Here it is.' Ballantine's voice broke me from my thoughts, as he came to a standstill.

I don't know quite what I'd expected, but of all the grand visions I'd had of the Wipe Out Bar, this was not one of them. We stood in front of a sprawling two-storey corner building, bustling with an alfresco eatery, where families and tourists were dining. Music pumped out from above, causing the beams of the balcony to vibrate. A menu was attached to a giant surfboard next to the entrance. Above it, scrawled in blue letters were the words, 'The Wipe Out Bar', on a sign so big and bright, I'm pretty sure it could've been seen from space. The building was painted with bright yellow and blue stripes like it was right out of *Alice in Wonderland*.

'Wow,' I managed. 'I didn't expect it to be so –'

'In your face?'

'Tacky.'

Ballantine burst out laughing, deep and rolling just like that first night outside my window.

'What?' I asked.

He shook his head, laughter ebbing as he looked down at me. 'Lex, you ain't seen nothing yet.'

My heart soared when he called me that, as no-one called me Lex but him. It was like he had sole rights to the name and it sounded oh so sexy. I wanted him to say it again.

'Are we going to go in?' I asked, trying not to seem over-eager.

Ballantine glanced up at the roofline, wincing. 'You don't really want to go in, do you?'

'It's the place to be,' I said with a shrug.

Ballantine laughed, small and quick this time. 'You really still think it's the place to be?'

'Never judge a book by its cover,' I said, sidestepping to the entrance.

'Lex, wait.'

I stopped. Not because he said my name in that smoky-hot voice of his, but because he grabbed my arm. That instantly stopped me in my tracks and my eyes flicked to where he held me. Skin on skin, burning me like a hot brand. Obviously this wasn't the first time his hand had been on my body, and to be honest, I don't know why I was reacting so much, considering what his hand had been doing last night. But, damn if I didn't enjoy his warm hands on me. *Any* part of me.

Ballantine followed my gaze, no doubt reading the instant blanch of my cheeks. Still he didn't let go, he held onto my arm, touching me still as a devilish smirk spread across his beautiful face.

'This way,' he said, tilting his head in the opposite direction and pulling me away. I followed. I would follow him anywhere. Just as I could almost feel the heat of his hand seep through to the bone, he dropped my arm, and I felt the edge of disappointment plummet to my stomach as he severed the connection.

I followed close behind him; his eyes were watchful, each step purposeful, as we walked around the corner of the building, to the back.

Where was he taking me?

We walked along the side of the bar, where the budget for painting didn't seem to extend – the blue and yellow stripes coming to an abrupt and messy halt. Now all that was visible was grey, rendered concrete covered in bold, thick graffiti.

Ballantine took a sharp left, leading us into an alleyway. My breaths were quickening in the effort to keep up with his long, confident strides. Being taken into an alley with a boy like Ballantine was probably most girls' dream, but there was nothing romantic about our destination. The bitumen underfoot was wet, as if there had been a flash flood or, more likely, someone had taken to it with a hose. We passed a series of skip bins and with them the unmistakeable smell of rotting food. We passed a stray cat chewing on something unidentifiable next to the bins; it made me shudder a little.

Ballantine glanced back. 'You right?'

I dropped my hand that was shielding my nose from the stench, quickly dismissing the wincing by putting on a forced bright smile. 'Yeah, totally,' I said with confidence.

Ballantine's eyebrows rose as he kept walking down the lane.

*Okay, maybe that was a bit OTT, Lexie. Fine would have been more appropriate. Is he going to see how totally lame I actually am? Will I be a disappointment after tonight?*

I found myself second-guessing everything that came out of my mouth these days. I'd gone from someone who I liked to think was once pretty apt at stringing together intelligent sentences, to a bumbling idiot, no thanks to the smoking-hot, fine specimen in front of me.

Ballantine came to a stop at a railing; clasping onto it, he turned to me. 'Ready to enter the snake pit?' he asked, glancing towards a set of steps that led down to what looked like a basement door, lit by a dim, bug-infested bulb above.

'This looks like a nightmare,' I said mainly to myself.

Ballantine's smile was broad and smoulderingly sexy; I loved that I could make him smile. 'You still convinced this is the place to be?' he asked in mock seriousness.

I inhaled. 'Okay. Why is it called the snake pit?'

Ballantine pushed off the railing and brushed past me, but he leant into my ear on his way and whispered, 'You'll see.'

# Chapter Thirty

My expectations of the Wipe Out Bar had been of juke-boxes, booths, glossy checked tiles, milkshakes and girls wearing rollerskates waiting on tables. But what I saw was definitely not a scene out of *Happy Days*. I seriously doubted that if Fonzie had bumped his fist on the jukebox that Nirvana would have blasted out from the speakers like it was now.

Before me was a huge room filled with pool tables, the overhanging pendant lights the only thing lighting the space, which smelt of stale beer and smoke – a far cry from the tacky bistro area street side. It seemed that the Wipe Out Bar had many faces and I wondered, was this the one that Ballantine and Boon belonged to? There was no secret door-knock for entering, yet by the way everyone looked up and casually greeted Ballantine with fly-away insults and pats on the back, it was clear he was no stranger to this place. It was even more clear that I was the only girl in sight.

'You dining in our fine establishment tonight, Master Ballantine?' yelled one of the pool players as he straightened from his shot, a cigarette pack jammed up his sleeve. 'Nice place to bring a date,' he added with a wink.

I expected Ballantine to deny it, to be embarrassed by the insinuation, but he didn't. Instead, he simply flipped his mate the finger as he grabbed my hand and pulled me deeper into the room, making his way to the back where there was a couch set up along the wall. I wondered if this was where the Kirkland surfers hung out. Okay, so I wasn't exactly the only girl in the room; there was another who had her arms snaked around some guy on the couch, making it kind of awkward for anyone who wanted to sit there.

Ballantine didn't move to sit down; instead, he watched me, waiting to see what I wanted to do. I tried not to look at the couple, who were basically dry humping. I blushed crimson, glancing in the opposite direction.

'Um . . . is there a bathroom nearby?'

'Sure. Through that door, up the steps to your right.' He pointed, casually sitting on the arm of the sofa, turning his back on the couple, his attention focused on the nearest pool game; he didn't seem the least bit fazed by the gyrating that was happening inches from him. What a sheltered life I had led.

'Back in a minute,' I said, heading towards the door with the hope that upstairs led to fresh air. The acrid stench of smoke was making me lightheaded and I wanted to do a spot check in the mirror. I wasn't exactly prepared for bar hopping tonight. I couldn't believe I was actually at the Wipe Out Bar with Ballantine; I hadn't a clue how I was going to explain this to Amanda. If she woke up in the night and found I wasn't there, what would she think?

•

Pushing my way back out of the ladies' toilets, which were also decorated in a rather tacky nautical, surfing theme, I stood on the carpeted landing and noticed a sign opposite saying 'Bar'.

The thought of a refreshing, cold Coke made me instinctively lick my lips. I didn't know if it was the dank, smoky basement but I was parched. Maybe if I bought Ballantine a drink it would break the ice somewhat. I pulled out my Roxy wallet, counting enough coinage and a note for a couple of drinks as I quickly made my way in the direction of the main bar.

Now this was more like it. A circular bar divided a massive room lined with booths against the outer windows. There was still a distinct theme of surfing that screamed tourist hotspot, but there was something about the high ceilings and open space that made it seem more appealing than the snake pit. A few patrons were seated at the bar, a couple of men enjoying Oysters Kilpatrick and a beer as they watched a M*A*S*H rerun on one of the big screens. I decided to make my way to the far end of the bar where no-one was sitting, so I wouldn't get the passive whiff of anyone's Fisherman's Basket. Plus, I'd hoped I might get served quicker so I could get back to Ballantine.

I smiled, looking over the plastic laminated drinks menu on the bar, thinking how downstairs the hottest boy in school was waiting for me. He wasn't the only one waiting for me as I heard a distinct cough from in front of me. My eyes flicked up from the menu to rest on a tall figure, his hip cocked casually against the bar, as his steely stare locked on me curiously.

My lips parted in an inaudible gasp as my focus involuntarily roamed over his arms, which were crossed over his black tee. He looked hotter than sin and madder than hell, and I felt my heart pound heavily in my chest as his heated gaze refused to break away from mine.

'Thirsty?' His voice was like a crackle of thunder, the kind that made the hair on the back of your neck stand up and had you hiding under a blanket. How could such a simple one-word question be so intimidating? And what kind of business sense was it to hire a barman who would no doubt either scare the customers away, or make the girls gaga over the green of his eyes: eyes that dipped to the cocktail menu I still held in what were now my clammy hands.

I blushed, glancing at the rather lewd names of some of the cocktails and thinking how the party girls would just love to lean over the bar suggestively and ask this hottie for 'Sex on the Beach'. Yeah, that's a cocktail. I, for one, would never, ever have enough nerve to ask for anything like that. I was stumbling to voice two Cokes.

'You got I.D?' he asked.

*Oh shit.*

A student I.D. saying I was seventeen was not going to be looked upon favourably. I went to protest that I was only wanting two Cokes, but then I wondered what the laws were in the city? Was that why Ballantine had brought me in the back entrance? Was it illegal for me to be in a bar underage? I glanced around, failing to see any families or young people in this section and I began to panic. I imagined myself being locked in an interview room, being held captive until my irresponsible aunty and uncle were called to come and collect their disgrace of a niece. I would be shipped home faster than you could say . . .

'Hey, Dean. How's it going, mate?' a man sporting a Hawaiian shirt called out as he came up to the bar to get his beer jug refilled.

*Dean?*

My eyes widened as I watched tall, dark and deadly nod his head to the patron. A bar girl from the other end moved like lightning to take the jug and refill it without so much as a word from Dean. She was obviously well trained or too fearful to let a customer go thirsty for even a moment.

I swallowed hard. So this was Dean, a name I had heard on numerous occasions. In fact, seeing who Dean was and assuming he was the owner and operator of the Wipe Out Bar made it perfectly clear why you might not want this to be your local. Sure, he was nice to look at but he had the most shocking aura of anyone I had ever met. At a guess Dean was twenty, twenty-one maybe, still young enough to be deemed attractive but old enough to intimidate if needed, the perfect blend for a barman.

He sighed wearily, looking at me with a bored expression, as if his patience, what little he had, was wearing thin. 'It's a simple enough question. Do you have any I.D.?' he repeated.

My mouth gaped. 'Umm, yes but . . .' I struggled to say what I wanted; the weight of his stare turning me into a jabbering idiot. I wouldn't have been surprised if he personally escorted me from his establishment if I didn't answer his question in the next breath. And just as I became even more flustered and feared that that was exactly what was going to happen, I heard a voice from over my shoulder. 'She's with me.'

# Chapter Thirty-One

Y ou would probably expect that my heart would flutter, or my knees go weak at the sound of Ballantine's voice, but when I found myself caught in the crossfire of a serious alpha male stare-off, well, it wasn't so great.

Dean was the only one who seemed to be amused, his attention fully settled on Ballantine over my shoulder.

'Who's the jail bait?' Dean tilted his head, talking as if I wasn't even there.

'Lexie,' I snapped before Ballantine had a chance to answer for me. Maybe it was Ballantine's presence or the fact that Dean was being a dick, but I had somehow found my voice and I felt quite good about it, until Dean's cool gaze rested on me again. I wanted to recoil but I stood my ground, trying not to think about how truly scary he was. Helping me steady myself was the feel of Ballantine's hand on my lower back.

'She speaks,' Dean mused.

Ballantine interrupted by slamming a twenty-dollar bill onto the counter. 'Just two Cokes, if that's not too beneath you.'

Dean looked at the note as if it was some kind of squished bug on the counter. He stepped aside. 'Sherry,' he called over his shoulder, 'can you grab the kids a couple of Cokes?'

His eyes washed over us with an air of smug amusement.
'Excuse me, I have some business to tend to. Check the board
for your shift, Ballantine. You're pulling a double tomorrow
night.'

Dean unhooked a set of keys from near the cash register
before stalking towards the back of the bar and out of sight.
I glared after him, a burst of anger rising in my chest, disbe-
lieving of how arrogant some people could be. I mean, who
the hell did he think he was? I was just about to voice that
thought when it dawned on me.

*Wait a minute.*

I turned to face Ballantine. 'You work here?'

'Yeah, go figure, huh? Thanks, Sherry.' Ballantine winked
past my shoulder at the girl who had worked with impressive
speed to ice a couple of pots, fill them up with Coke, dump
them on the bar, and hand Ballantine back his change without
spilling so much as a drop.

I shifted, annoyed at the way they seemed so familiar
with each other. Did they work together behind the bar? Did
they do *more* than just work together? Oh, hell. I looked over
Sherry's womanly shape with her black, skin-tight jeans and
black tank top. Her long black hair lent a rebellious edge to her
with the odd matted braid highlighted throughout. She looked
so street smart, exotic and fierce the way she worked the bar,
owned it. She didn't even flinch in Dean's presence, even
when he barked orders. I wished I could be that confident.

Ballantine grabbed our Cokes, nodding his head towards
one of the empty booths. 'Might as well kick back in here,
now the big bad wolf is gone.'

'Yeah, what the hell is his problem?' I asked, glancing back
to where Dean had just disappeared as I followed Ballantine
to the table.

'Oh, he's a charmer, isn't he?' Ballantine said, laughing as he slid into the booth.

'Well, that's not exactly the word that springs to mind, no.'

'Don't worry about Dean, he was born with bastards' disease.'

I choked mid-sip of my Coke, spluttering and coughing. My eyes watered as I laughed through catching my breath.

'Bastards' disease? That sounds serious,' I managed.

'I'm afraid it's terminal,' Ballantine deadpanned, which only made me laugh more.

'But seriously, who gets away with running a business like that? I've never known anyone to be so –'

Ballantine grabbed my hand, which was resting on the table; the warmth of his touch and the unexpectedness of it caused me to break off mid-sentence. He turned my hand over, exposing the soft skin of my palm.

'Now, I didn't bring you here to talk about Dean Saville,' he said quietly, tracing my lifeline with his finger.

I swallowed, trying to keep my rampant mind focused, even though the workings of Ballantine's fingers were doing strange things to me. 'Why did you bring me here?' I asked, causing Ballantine's eyes to flick up, breaking his intense study of my palm.

He shrugged lazily, taking his hand away and leaning back against his seat. 'It's the place to be, isn't it?'

I placed my hand into my lap, disappointed at the break of contact. 'Well, not if you work here, too. I'm guessing this is the last place you want to be on your night off.'

'You guess right,' Ballantine said, a smirk lining his face.

'You should've said. I would've been happy to go anywhere.'

*With you, I would willingly go anywhere with you.*

'What, and miss all this? The snake pit? No, it's every new person's rite of passage to experience Arcadia Lane,' he said.

'Arcadia Lane?'

'That's where we are. It's kind of like a cesspool of activity for all the local delinquents and ignorant tourists. You have the boardwalk at the end leading out to the pier with more hideous attractions to behold.'

'Wow, sounds awful.'

Ballantine leant forward, resting his elbows on the tabletop. 'Trust me, you'll love it, everyone who doesn't live here does.'

I leant forward too, placing my elbows on the table. 'You sound rather jaded, Mr Ballantine.'

He smiled, broad and heart-stoppingly gorgeous, as his finger traced a bead of condensation that dripped down his glass. 'Maybe I am. Tell me, new girl, is Paradise everything you thought it would be?' His eyes lifted to look at me with interest, waiting for me to answer the million-dollar question.

I thought for a long moment. It was a simple enough question, but one I didn't quite know how to answer. In many ways the place exceeded my expectations, like sitting in a bar opposite a gorgeous surfer late on a school night, and the amazing feeling of having the beach at your disposal. School was most certainly different, as was my relationship with Amanda. These were the things I should probably be vocalising but didn't quite know how.

'It's not exactly how imagined it would be, no.' I chose my words carefully.

'What's been your biggest misconception?'

*Amanda.*

But I really didn't want to open that can of worms. Plus, when it came to Amanda, there was no answer to that problem.

'Well, things like surfers.'

'Surfers?' Ballantine repeated with a frown.

'Yeah, well. I kind of imagined that you would all have long blond hair, and say things like "gnarly, dude" and "cowabunga".'

Ballantine squinted. 'I think you're mistaking a surfer for a Teenage Mutant Ninja Turtle.'

Again I choked mid-sip, realising that my stereotyping of a surfer was in fact quite off.

'Really? You never find yourself screaming "cowabunga!" when you catch an impressive wave?' I teased.

'Never.'

'Oh, see? Illusion shattered.'

'Sorry about that,' Ballantine said. He was trying to be serious but was failing rather miserably as his lips curved involuntarily and a lightness lit his eyes. He shook his head and took a sip of his Coke.

'What?' I asked.

'You're a funny girl, Lex.'

'Oh?' I didn't know how to take that. Was I funny ha-ha? Is that what he meant? 'Yeah, I ain't from around here,' I mimicked a southern drawl.

'You most certainly are not.'

'I know. I'm pretty tragic, huh?' I tried to lighten the tone, prove I could be self-deprecating, but when Ballantine didn't laugh, didn't even so much as smile, I wanted to slap myself for being stupid. Yeah, definitely not funny ha-ha, just funny in the head, more like it.

He thought for a minute, shaking his head. 'You're different and I like it,' he said, leaning over to grab my empty glass. 'Another?' He held it up in question.

I was still getting over the compliment as I nodded my head quickly. I watched on as Ballantine weaved his way through the tables back to the bar, back to the busy Sherry. But surprisingly, this time no jealous part of me stirred, because as he chatted to her, he was glancing back at me. I couldn't believe this was my life now, sneaking out with the hottest guy in school, hanging out at the hottest nightspot in Paradise. If we did nothing more than sit here, drink Coke and talk all night long, then I would be more than happy. I didn't know what would come after this, and a little piece of my insides twisted with the thrill of all the possibilities. Would we end up back on the beach? Parking at Wilson's lookout? Or would I be dropped back home with a hand-shake? No, I tried not to over-analyse: low expectations, never be disappointed – just like Uncle Eddie, remember? I laughed to myself. Way to go, Uncle Eddie. He knew what it was all about. I shook my thoughts aside because regardless of whatever was to come, I was here with Ballantine, and that was all that mattered.

Nothing was going to burst my bubble, I thought smugly, until of course I glanced towards the entrance of the Wipe Out Bar, and suddenly realised that my bubble wasn't going to burst, it was about to explode.

# Chapter Thirty-Two

I hoped I was seeing things, that it was some kind of trick of the lighting or a paranoid mirage, but of course it wasn't. Because the eyes locked on me from across the room with burning intent were Uncle Peter's.

*Oh God! Oh God! Oh God!*

My eyes flicked towards Ballantine, but he was already looking to the door. Uncle Peter's focus was clear. Me. And that was precisely what he made a beeline for. A straight, determined line to stand before our table. It was about that time that I stopped breathing. Maybe if I passed out I would avoid the humiliation that was to come: the shouting, the screaming, the public ranting that would ruin my reputation and ensure I'd never be able to show my face here ever again. And as I braced myself for the worst, Uncle Peter spoke quietly.

'Get in the car.'

It was still powerful enough to hit me like a physical blow. I blinked, stunned, and moved to stand without argument or question. I looked over at Ballantine, who stood across the room like a statue, holding two glasses of Coke as he watched Uncle Peter escort me to the door. Uncle Peter stopped under the giant surfboard sign, simply pointing to the Volvo parked outside.

'Now,' he said, delivering the one-word direction with enough emphasis that I wanted to run. But of course my mind wandered elsewhere, noticing that he wasn't following, watching as he doubled back into the bar.

'Where are you going?' I blurted out, my heart spiking in panic.

'Just get in the car,' he snapped, before disappearing back inside.

I wrung my hands, pacing anxiously, fearing that Uncle Peter, from whom I had never heard so many words in such a short space of time, was going to murder Ballantine.

It wasn't his fault. Sure he had driven to our house and knocked on my window. But I had opened it, climbed out. I was mortified; God only knew what Uncle Peter was doing or saying to Ballantine. To hell with more trouble. I threw caution to the wind and headed back inside, only to run directly into Uncle Peter who now seemed angrier than ever.

'Car. Now.'

I spun around, making quick work of the distance between me and the car. Heat flooded my cheeks, hot tears burned my eyes, and as if matters couldn't get any worse, walking in the opposite direction coming towards us was Dean Saville. I wanted to die.

•

I made a point of not making eye contact with Dean as I skimmed past him. The last thing I needed was a smug look from the likes of him. I also managed to avoid conversation throughout the car ride home, which wasn't too hard as Uncle Peter wasn't much of a conversationalist anyway, and even less so when he was furious apparently. And, oh, how he was furious. He gripped the steering wheel with a white-knuckled intensity. I wanted to ask what he had said to Ballantine, but on the other hand the last thing I wanted was to initiate conversation with a crazy man. He looked like he might nail my window shut and pull a nightshift on the porch with a shotgun. Typical, I thought, how often had Amanda snuck out over the years, and the one time to get caught it was just me, on my own. The devil child who was probably corrupting their sweet and innocent daughter. Pfft, what a joke.

The car pulled up into our drive; the dashboard clock read 00:37. I tried to slink my way out of the car but was stopped by Uncle Peter, who chose now to break the silence. 'I won't be telling Karen about this,' he said.

I stared at his profile for a long moment wondering if he was being serious. He looked serious; but then, he always looked serious.

My shoulders slumped in relief.

'I don't want you to see that Ballantine boy anymore.'

Oh God, relief short-lived.

'Is that the deal I have to strike? You won't tell Aunty Karen if I promise not to see Ballantine again?' I asked in disbelief.

Uncle Peter sighed. 'Either way, you're not to see him, so it's up to you. I can tell her if you want.'

'No! No, I mean, I would rather she not know,' I said. 'Thanks.'

'Don't thank me, I'm not doing it for you,' he said.

*Ouch!*

'I don't want this house to be turned upside down any more than it is. This time I keep the peace, next time –'

'I know, you'll tell.'

'Next time, you go home.'

That caught my attention. Go *home*? That was far worse than any other threat I could possibly face. I would be good. I would try to be with all my power. I would be.

'I promise this won't happen again,' I said.

'Well, make sure it doesn't.' And just like that, Uncle Peter slid out of the car and made his way towards the house.

It wasn't until then I realised that being good meant one thing.

No Ballantine.

•

Amanda was waiting for me, the lamp in our bedroom was on. She still looked washed out but she sat up quickly enough when I entered the room.

'Oh my God, where have you been?' she asked in a hushed voice.

My defences slammed down, a newfound anger rising to the surface as I pouted about how unjust the world was. Getting caught, humiliated in front of Ballantine, and Dean, and then the clincher: forbidden to see the one person who made my Paradise experience what it was.

'Did you tell your dad?' I asked, trying to keep my voice even.

'No, he woke me up. He came in to check if I was okay and you were gone. How could I tell him when I didn't even know where you were?' Amanda looked authentic in her claim. I didn't have the slightest clue how he managed to track me down, nor did I care. The damage had been done.

'Are you in much trouble?' she asked, concern marking her eyes, eyes that had dark circles under them.

I went to tell her that I was banned from seeing Ballantine, but thought better of it. She didn't have to know who I'd been with or that I'd been banned from seeing anyone. The last thing I needed was for her to ask a million questions or jump to any conclusions. No, I wanted Ballantine to remain a secret: my secret. It would make my future endeavours of not being near him easier. If such a thing was possible.

'Where did you go?' she asked.

I was in no mood to answer twenty questions. I moved to the lamp and clicked it off, plunging the room into darkness mainly to shield the tears that threatened to fall.

'It doesn't matter,' I said.

*Nothing mattered, not anymore.*

# Chapter Thirty-Three

For the first time, I set off to school on my own.

Amanda said she was still not a hundred per cent and instead was going to spend the day slumped on the couch, watching daytime TV. She channel-flicked without breaking away from the screen. 'Can you call me at recess?' she asked, briefly watching to make sure Aunty Karen wasn't listening.

At first I thought, of course. She probably wasn't feeling well and wanted me to check in on her, but when she eventually shifted her cautious eyes to me with an air of mischievousness, she leant in closer and whispered, 'I want to know if Boon is back at school.'

A black cloud settled over my soul. Tell her if Boon was back? Be her little messenger? I couldn't have cared less and my look would have told her as much if she'd cared to pay attention. However, she fixed herself back on the couch with her blanket and pillow, staring blankly at the TV without a care in the world. She didn't look sick at all today; she was obviously milking it for everything it was worth.

How could I look Ballantine in the eye after last night, getting dragged off by my crazed uncle who had no doubt warned him to stay away from me. Oh God, I wanted to hide away, even if it meant watching the midday movie with Amanda.

•

It's not like I expected Ballantine to be waiting at the gate for me. I'm sure he wouldn't want to risk it with Uncle Peter on the loose, but then he wasn't exactly the kind of boy who worried about risks. I tried not to think about that, or the fact he wasn't at my locker or in the yard at recess. But when he didn't show up for detention at lunchtime, I started to worry: deeply worry. When Boon sauntered in I sat up in my seat a little, looking past him with the hope that Ballantine would follow, but he didn't and a deep-seated feeling of dread seeped in.

*What the hell had Uncle Peter said?*

I stared out the window, lost in churning thoughts of all the worst-case scenarios.

'Oh, hey, Boon. How's it going, Boon? Feeling better, Boon? Oh yeah. Much better. Thanks for asking, Lexie.' Boon stood in front of me, causing me to focus on reality.

'Sorry?' I questioned.

'I nearly died, you know,' he said, pulling out the seat in front and plonking himself down with dramatic flair.

'You did not, you just had a bug.'

'Yeah, a killer bug,' he said.

'Well, you look all right to me.' And he did; he just looked like normal Boon: full of yap, full of crap and I really couldn't have cared less.

'How's Amanda?' he asked in all seriousness.

'She'll live.'

'I have to drop something over to Ballantine's tonight. I might drop in after school and see how she's going.'

My head snapped up. 'Yeah, yeah she'd love that,' I said quickly. 'Um, where is Ballantine anyway?'

Before Boon could answer, the teacher called us to silence. I wanted to write a note but it would probably be a bit weird just asking where Ballantine was, so I suffered in silence, thinking it was a sign from God that he was helping make it easy on me by Ballantine not being around. Then I could be the saintly niece that my Uncle Peter wanted me to be and we could all go on living miserably ever after. Things happen for a reason, right? I stared at the square cut of Boon's shoulders in front, thinking about Laura and where she stood in all this mess. If I ever saw Ballantine again, we had to stop playing games, set the record straight and just go back to the way things were. I would keep my distance and it would work fine. Then, of course, the memory of his mouth on mine, and the way his hands slid over my skin would arise, and I was consumed by misery. I wanted to be with him, even if it was just one last time. By the time detention had come to an end, I was adamant . . . and filled with confusion.

Was Ballantine avoiding me?

•

It was worse than I thought.

I sat on the edge of Laura's bed, legs crossed, head tilted sideways, staring at the spines of the books on Laura's bookshelf, and there, boom!, front and centre read 'My Diary'. She might as well have hand delivered it to Boon. Worst hiding spot ever!

Laura came in with two glasses of Coke, with ice cubes tinkling against the glass as she concentrated on not spilling a drop. Even with her intense focus her eyes followed mine.

'I have to be honest,' I said, carefully taking my drink from her. 'That is the worst hiding spot I have ever seen.'

Maybe with a little encouragement I could convince her to move it somewhere out of Boon's clutches.

Laura sipped on her drink, smacking her lips in appreciation as she laughed her reply. 'I know!'

*Wait. What?*

My head snapped away from the bookcase, taking in her clearly amused and highly composed manner as she smiled, arching her brow at me.

'You know? Why would you do that?' I blurted out.

Laura shrugged. 'It's a decoy,' she said.

'A decoy?'

'You don't honestly think I'd put my *real* diary on display like that, do you?'

'Because you think Boon would read it?' I asked, trying to pretend that I didn't know for a fact that he bloody well did.

'Oh God, I'm counting on him reading it!' she said, crunching a mouthful of ice cubes.

I sat, stunned. 'Why would you do that?' I asked, genuinely interested in her motivations.

'Because I like to see who I can and can't trust,' she said.

I shifted uneasily, wondering how she tested such a thing. 'And who do you trust?'

Laura plonked herself down in her swivel desk chair, turning herself from side to side as she licked the end of her straw in deep thought. 'It's been an eye-opening experiment, I must say.'

I suddenly felt uncomfortable hanging out in her bedroom, my eyes shifting around, paranoid that maybe one of the stuffed toy bears on the shelf had a hidden nanny-cam inside.

Was the invite over here about homework for Health or was it some kind of a test?

'And what have you found?' I asked.

'That sometimes, mostly everyone likes to gossip about the most ridiculous things, and I know that's only human nature, but seriously, some of the things I wrote in there were just crazy. And yet, sure enough, within half a day the rumour mill would be set alight and some crazy out-of-whack version of myself would filter back to me.'

'That sounds like a rather elaborate test to me.' One that I knew I had failed with flying colours. By all rights I should have gone straight to Laura and told her about Boon reading what I thought was her legitimate diary; instead, I'd been too hung up on Amanda being civil to me again.

'I've only been doing it for a few weeks, but, boy, if you want to plant a seed,' she said, walking over to her bookcase and pulling out the lilac and yellow book, 'this is the way to go!'

'I couldn't imagine there'd be many people you could completely trust,' I said, mainly to myself; I always thought of myself as a pretty decent person but in this instance, not so much.

'Not many,' she said, sliding the diary back into its front and centre position, 'but you know the one person I found out I could trust more than anyone at Paradise High, hell, in Paradise City?' She took my blank expression as an invitation to answer.

'The one person who passed the test was Ballantine,' she said with a nod of finality.

My heart stuttered at his name, my mouth ran dry. 'How so?' I croaked, clearing my throat and trying to keep calm.

Laura smiled to herself as if she had a secret she was thinking of sharing. 'I kind of put in this spiel about how hot Ballantine is, and how he's the perfect guy and all that, knowing that my brother would run to him and rib the crap out of him.'

I swallowed hard. 'S– so you made that up?'

*Oh, please say yes. Please say yes.*

'What, about me liking Ballantine?'

I nodded, eyes wide, my heart pounding, waiting an insanely long moment for an answer. But answer she did.

'Me? Like Ballantine? Oh God, Lexie, he's like a brother to me,' she said with a shudder.

My shoulders sagged in relief, air escaped from my lungs as I exhaled a breath I hadn't even realised I was holding.

'I mean, don't get me wrong, he is super hot! But I've known him my whole life and that would just be so wrong.'

'Yeah, that would be so wrong,' I agreed wholeheartedly, revelling in the fact that Laura didn't like Ballantine.

*Laura. Didn't. Like. Ballantine.*

I wanted to freakin' moonwalk, I was so happy.

I kept my cool, calm exterior, pinching my brows together in genuine interest. 'So what makes Ballantine trustworthy?'

Laura grinned big. 'Because the very day after I planted the diary in my bookshelf, Ballantine deliberately went out of his way to walk me home from school. At first I thought my plan had completely backfired, but when he sweetly suggested that I should hide my diary some place safe, I instantly knew two things.'

I now sat on the edge of her bed, listening to every word, my wild eyes urging her to continue.

'Firstly I knew my brother was the dickhead I always pegged him for, and secondly,' she counted on her fingers, 'that Ballantine is the sweetest boy I've ever known.'

I smiled, feeling my heart melt at the very thought of Ballantine doing the right thing, even if it meant betraying his mate; he wanted to protect Laura, and that was so incredibly sweet. I certainly hadn't seen the sweet version yet. Delicious . . . yes, but sweet?

Laura slapped her palms on her thighs. 'So, that's why I trust him, and that's why I think you should totally take a crack.'

I nearly spat a mouthful of my Coke out, it bubbled through my nose as I coughed and spluttered, pounding my chest with my fist.

'S– sorry?' I rasped, thinking maybe I had heard her wrong.

Laura moved to sit next to me, slapping me on the back as I continued my coughing fit. I turned towards her, trying to clear my blurry vision from the tears that had welled in my eyes.

'I think you should totally go for Ballantine,' she said, deadly serious.

It wasn't just because my throat was on fire. I couldn't mentally piece together what she was saying.

I managed a stupefied look, one that obviously amused her no end. I searched her face for a long moment, failing to answer her, frozen in place.

'What?' she asked, laughing.

If I didn't tell someone I would burst. I needed to empty the thoughts from my head and the burden from my heart. I needed to lift the weight, and as I took in the genuine concern in Laura's eyes, I inhaled a deep, steadying breath.

'I've got something to tell you.'

# Chapter Thirty-Four

'Oh. My. God.' Laura emphasised every word for dramatic effect. 'You totally dry humped Ballantine?'

'Out of everything I've said, that's what you take away from it?'

'I'm sorry, but that's what sticks out. Like, wow. Way to go, Lexie. The new girl just bagged the hottest boy in school.'

'I haven't bagged anyone. He's avoiding me.'

'Um, hell yeah, he is; your uncle's scary even when he's not trying to be.'

I cringed, throwing myself down on the bed.

'So, maybe Ballantine was sick today? Maybe that's why he wasn't at school. I mean, we know there's something going around, so maybe you're just thinking the worst.' Laura tried to pacify me.

'Boon hasn't said anything?'

She shook her head. 'No.'

We sat in silence. We had hit a crossroads about what to do, where to go from here. As much as it was a relief that Laura didn't like Ballantine in that way, it meant little if he was avoiding me. And it meant even less if my uncle decided to send me home.

'Well, we could plant a seed,' Laura spoke tentatively, wincing as if she was afraid of my response.

'A seed?'

Laura sprang to her feet, bouncing to her bookshelf. 'If you want something to get back to someone, you just have to plant the seed,' she said, holding out the diary with a huge grin.

Her enthusiasm was contagious. 'What do you suggest?'

Laura's arms flopped to her sides as she rolled her eyes in dismay. 'My God, Lexie, use your imagination,' she said, throwing herself on the bed next to me. 'We think Ballantine is avoiding you, so what could we write that will grab his attention?'

'Maybe nothing will grab his attention; maybe this all means way more to me than it does to him.'

'Oh, I don't think so. I know Ballantine, this is different. Trust me.'

As much as I wanted to believe Laura, I suspected she was just getting carried away with the whole idea of it. Still, my interest was piqued. 'So, how long does it take for a rumour to manifest these days?' I asked, peering over at the diary.

Laura smiled, as if she had snared me in her trap. 'Faster than you think. If Boon sneak-reads tonight, Ballantine will know about it by morning, deadset.'

*Oh God.*

'The trick is not to link yourself to Ballantine per se – it has to be more subtle than that.'

'As in?'

'As in I write about your potential hook-up with someone else, someone who is going to get his attention.'

My mind started to back pedal. 'No I don't think –'

'Woolly!' Laura clicked her fingers as if a light bulb had sparked above her head.

'What? No way. He would know that wasn't true, plus it's way too close, they're friends.'

'Right. Okay, so how about someone obscure, like Robbie Robinson?'

'Oh God, as if. It would have to be someone that was actually intimidating,' I said with a laugh.

'Well, I don't know. Who's intimidating? Mr Branson?' Laura teased.

'Oh, gross!' I said, shoving her, before the laughter fell away and a figure popped into my head.

In fact, I was pretty certain that if you looked up the word intimidating in the dictionary Dean Saville's name would be the definition.

'Dean,' I said, mainly to myself but Laura had heard. I could tell by the way her head snapped up comically fast.

'Dean Saville? Oh. My. God! Perfect!' She beamed, unhooking the pen from her binder and taking the lid off.

'Whoa, wait a minute, I was just thinking out loud,' I said, blocking the blank page with my hand.

'Are you kidding me? Dean Saville? I don't know why I didn't think of it, he's like Ballantine's arch nemesis.'

My heart started to pound furiously in my chest, my mouth felt dry.

'Lexie, do you want to get Ballantine's attention or not?'

I shook my head. 'Not like that; besides, what if he is sick or what if he was just waiting for things to cool down before he came and spoke to me. I mean, what if –'

Laura muffled a frustrated scream into her pillow. 'Bloody hell, what if? What if? What if? Find out, woman! Go talk

to him. Go see him, then you'll know. Go to his house, ring
him up, anything, but just decide.'

My mind flashed back to last night. 'I can't,' I said slowly,
remembering Dean telling Ballantine he had a double shift.
'I think he's working at the Wipe Out Bar,' I said.

Laura grinned. 'Perfect! Let's go.'

•

I should've felt a bit more confident; this time I had Laura
by my side and the light of day to carry me through Arcadia
Lane. It was still a frantic mix of activity but seemed to have
a different feel to it, or maybe it was just because I'd been
with Ballantine.

'I don't want to stay too long; I just want to have a quick
chat and then get out. The last thing I need is Uncle Peter
finding out about this.'

'Relax, he won't.' Laura waved my words aside.

We made a direct line towards the Wipe Out Bar. I looked
beyond the bustling streetscape of the arcade to where the
land met the sea, and saw there was indeed a long pier leading
out with the distant imposing structure of a Ferris wheel.
Ballantine was right: I would love it; I would want to roam
along the boardwalk and discover all the touristy things,
but I would love it more if he could show me. I wished that
was where I was headed now, instead of turning towards the
entrance of the decaying Wipe Out Bar, which looked even
tackier in the daytime.

'I haven't been here for ages,' said Laura, leading the way
underneath the giant surfboard.

We entered the bar, the large one with lots of open space
but not so many patrons, far less busy than at night-time, it
seemed. My eyes went straight to the bar, expecting to see

Ballantine behind it, pouring drinks for the tourists; instead, Sherry stood as if she hadn't moved from the night before.

*Maybe he was sick?*

I had never felt more like a stalker and wanted to back out and pretend that I had never come here.

Laura elbowed me, drawing my attention with a frown. 'What?' I snapped.

Her chin lifted to the second storey, a staircase swept its way upward to a boxed room, the front lined with mirrored glass, one-way glass, at a guess.

'The lion's den,' Laura whispered.

I knew exactly what, or rather, 'who' she was referring to. *Dean.*

I felt the hair on my arms stand on end with the thought of his deep-set glower upon us. I opted for a long, confident stroll to the bar, where Sherry glanced up between working the beer tap. If she was surprised to see me she didn't show it; in fact, apart from the good cheer she shared briefly with Ballantine last night, I hadn't seen her show any kind of emotion. Maybe that was the selection criteria for staff in this place: be as emotionally vacant as the industrious leader. And as if by speaking, or in my case thinking, of the devil, I heard the distant slam of the door from above, and footsteps descend the stairs.

Laura and I quickly glanced at each other.

Dean was reading a document with a heavy scowl on his face, as he blindly stepped his way down onto the landing of the bar area. It was like he had eyes in the top of his head, or a true sign that he knew this place too well.

I turned my attention to Sherry, who was standing by impatiently.

'Ah, two Cokes, please,' I said, causing her to spin into motion, her hands working in a blinding flurry to delve into the ice bucket and reach for the post-mix gun.

Dean came to stand right next to me; in my peripheral vision, I could see he was still silently reading the paper in his hands. Aside from the mere feel of his presence, I could smell the clean, crisp notes of his aftershave. It had me breathing in deeply; it was almost mouth-watering, and it felt like the temperature in the room had escalated. I desperately wanted to place the glass of Coke to my cheek to cool down. My thoughts were interrupted by a cough, and my eyes blinked to Sherry standing before me holding out her hand.

*Oh shit.*

I scrambled for my wallet, desperately counting out the coins as I tipped them onto the bar. Oh God. *Please have enough,* I thought. *Please, all the gods in the universe, don't humiliate me now, not again.* I glanced pleadingly at Laura, who shrugged.

'I used all my cash on the bus fare,' she said grimacing and sharing in the awkwardness with a sheepish look to Sherry, who was now crossing her arms and staring me down.

I counted out five-cent pieces with agonising precision, like some granny at a supermarket checkout. I could feel the weight of everyone's eyes on me, none more so than Dean's. He'd now put down his paper and was watching on with amused interest. I was getting flustered and annoyed, thinking about the sick delight he was taking in watching me squirm.

I was going to be five cents short – a measly five cents, that I had no doubt discarded on so many occasions. Now I would never, ever take that tiny silver coin for granted again. Before I announced what was clearly obvious, I heard Dean speak.

'Well . . . this is awkward.'

*What the hell?*

'Are you always such an arsehole?'

The entire bar went deathly silent.

*Oh shit. Shoot. Me. Now.*

My stomach dropped away as I took in the heavy-set glare from Dean's eyes. I could almost imagine Laura standing behind me, mouth gaping in horror, Sherry's eyes darting between the two of us as we glared at one another.

'I guess some people just bring out the worst in me,' he said before nodding his head at Sherry and walking towards the back door. It wasn't until he'd disappeared from view that I took a much-needed breath. My shoulders slumped, and a collective murmur filled the air.

'I'm sorry, I'm still short,' I said quietly to Sherry.

Sherry scoffed, 'Relax, they're on the house.'

'Look, I really appreciate it, but I really couldn't.'

'Don't thank me, it's not my choice,' she said.

I watched on, confused, as she wiped down the bar.

'You mean –'

'Yep, a head nod from the "arsehole" means the drinks are on him,' she said, giving me a pointed look. 'Word of advice, kid, don't judge a book by its cover.'

# Chapter Thirty-Five

I suppose a free Coke should have tasted pretty amazing, but it didn't. We sat in exactly the same booth that Ballantine and I had sat in last night, except this time, daylight shone through the windows highlighting the grubby drinks rings on the table. Ha! Looked like Sherry wasn't the amazing barmaid she thought she was.

'What are you waiting for? Go talk to him,' said Laura.

My head snapped around, my eyes hunting. Had I missed his entrance?

Laura kicked me under the table.

'Hey!'

'Not in here, dummy. Ballantine works out the back.'

I rubbed my shin, glowering across the table. 'Well, that kind of information would have been real handy, say, five minutes ago,' I said, thinking if I had known that I would have gone directly there and saved myself the encounter with Dean Saville and Sherry bitchy-resting face.

'Just go,' Laura urged, but I didn't need much encouragement. I had run through this scenario time and time again. What would I say? What did I even want from this? Did I go against my uncle and see Ballantine anyway? What if he didn't want to see me; what if Uncle Peter's little interaction with Ballantine was enough to convince him that I was better left alone? With every step I felt my palms become more clammy, and my stomach churn into a series of knots.

I turned down a long darkened corridor; it was the only direction to go as the landing either led to the toilets or the door that I knew for certain led down to the snake pit. I heard the clanging of pots, running water and echoed voices; the only slice of light came through a door with a circular window cut into it. I was halfway down the hall when the distant chatter and light became brighter and louder, and the door burst open as a girl pushed it backwards, laughing and carrying Fisherman's Baskets in both hands. As she turned into the hall her smile quickly evaporated, her eyes darting over me with disdain.

'You're not allowed to be back here,' she snapped.

It took me a moment to recognise her in uniform; short black skirt, white shirt and black vest, all hugging her petite frame.

*What the hell was Lucy Fell doing here?*

'You work here?'

'Well, I don't carry these around as a fashion accessory.' She held up the oily baskets, sneering at me like I was an idiot.

'Um, is Ballantine here?' I asked, my eyes darting to the circular window.

'Who wants to know?'

'I do.'

'Well, he's busy and these are getting cold.'

'Can I just duck in and see?'

'Staff only. Jesus, what are you, some kind of stalker or something? If Dean finds out you're back here he'll fire Ballantine on the spot and don't think he wouldn't.'

I didn't doubt it, not for a second. 'Look, can you just please go and tell him that Lexie is out here, and tell him it's important. If he doesn't want to see me then I'll go, but if he wants me to wait, I'll wait.'

Lucy sighed. 'I can't believe I'm doing this. What's your name again?'

'Lexie,' I said quickly, excited that Lucy was reluctantly moving away from her bid to get rid of me.

'Here, hold these,' she said, shoving the baskets into my hands, before heading back and pushing her way through to the kitchen. 'Oh, Ballantine,' she called.

I waited for what seemed like an eternity, just me and the Fisherman's Baskets oiling my hands. When the door opened, I straightened in anticipation.

Lucy had pushed her way through the door with less dramatic flair this time, her walk was less hoity-toity, and her demeanour had somewhat changed. She took the baskets from my hands, her gaze struggling to meet mine, until of course it did.

'Look, I'm sorry, but he doesn't want you to wait,' Lucy winced.

'What did he say?'

Lucy was beginning to look uncomfortable now.

'Did you tell him my name?'

'Of course I did,' she snapped. 'He said you were just some chick from school.'

'Maybe he doesn't want me to wait because he's working a double shift?' I was trying to voice the possibilities for his reasons, but when I looked into Lucy's face I didn't need to press any further; her eyes told the story, even Lucy Fell-on-her-face felt sorry for me and that was the most tragic thing of all.

I nodded my head, letting the reality sink in. I was numb. Numb and stupid to think that Ballantine was any different. He didn't want anything other than a quick one time feel-up in the dark, and come the time when things got tough, he bolted.

I scoffed. 'That's okay, at least he's going to make it easy on me.'

I turned, taking long, determined strides back to the landing.

'Hey, Lexie,' Lucy called after me.

I paused briefly, looking back to see her standing in the same spot.

'You're better off without him.'

Yeah, well, I hadn't picked that up from the way she had practically sucked on his face at the bus stop the other day. I turned around, continuing my walk of shame back to the main bar.

*You're better off without him*, she had said. *Yeah, tell that to my heart.*

•

I found Laura at the booth, tipping the dregs of ice into her mouth and crunching on the shards. She didn't see me at first but when she did, she straightened from her casual sitting position, her eyes alight with interest, until of course she saw the sullen, flushed look on my face.

'What's wrong?' she asked.

'Let's go.'

'What happened?'

'I'll tell you on the way out.'

'Did you see Ballantine?'

'Laura. Please.' My voice was shaky, I was on the verge of losing it, and I really didn't want that to happen here in front of Sherry, or Lucy, or a lurking-in-the-shadows Dean. I just wanted to get the hell out of the Wipe Out Bar and never come back again.

'Okay,' she said, sliding out of the booth.

As we quickly walked out, I could feel her watching me every step of the way, afraid I was going to lose my shit at any moment. Maybe I was? I sure felt like there was something building inside me, something that even scared me.

I knew it was killing Laura not to speak, not to continue assaulting me with one hundred and one questions, but somehow she knew better. We walked briskly through Arcadia Lane, towards the bus stop for the long journey back to the 'burbs. Laura struggled to keep up with me as I worked on putting distance between the bar and us. Well, between Ballantine, arsehole extraordinaire, and me.

We came to a stop at a pedestrian crossing, my mind working frantically as I shaded my eyes from the sun.

'Laura.'

'Yeah?'

I turned towards her, looking down at her wildly inquisitive expression. 'You put whatever you want in that diary; I have only one stipulation.'

'What's that?'

The pedestrian crossing gave us the go ahead to walk, but before we did, I looked Laura straight in the eyes. 'Make it bloody good.'

# Chapter Thirty-Six

A good rumour has a general gestation period of around twenty-four to forty-eight hours to take effect. In this instance, where information is as good as hand delivered to Boon, you give it two point five seconds before the first whispers begin.

Today was Friday, last day of school for the week, last day of detention, last day of the most turbulent week of my life. I had no real expectations that Laura's diary entry – whatever she had decided to write – would generate such an instant-aneous stir. But I felt it the second I got out of Aunty Karen's car. The atmosphere seemed different, the air was thick with a sort of speculation, a certain murmur. I thought perhaps I might have been paranoid, yet I know Amanda felt it, too.

We walked through the gates, side by side, the crowd that hovered before us, parted with whispers and stares. This was exactly the kind of grand entrance I had hoped to make on my first day, but now it was happening: like, really, really happening.

*What the hell had Laura written?*

We lingered at the bottom of the steps to the main building. I casually adjusted my school bag with a devil-may-care attitude until I caught Amanda staring at me.

'What?' I asked.

'What have you done now?'

I shrugged. 'I don't know what you mean.'

I had decided against telling Amanda about anything to do with Ballantine. The only people who knew were Laura . . . and Uncle Peter. I was still seriously pissed off with him for ruining what could have been, but then I wondered if I should be grateful to him for preventing me from going God knows how far I might have gone with Ballantine. But at the core of it, if Ballantine was only after one thing, he was messing with the wrong girl.

'Fine, be like that. I doubt it'll take me long to find out,' she said, breaking away from me and heading up the steps into the school building.

*Ha! Hanging with Boon, I had no doubt either.*

It was an interesting thing being the centre of attention. It was something I thought would be cool, something I had craved – being that new mysterious girl in school – but I now realised I'd sooner be the under-the-radar girl who simply snuck out for a night with bad-boy Ballantine. My heart ached at the prospect that I had been lusting after a lie, an idea of who Ballantine was. All unwelcome attention aside, I had never felt more miserable.

Just one more day, and then the weekend would hit and I could put some distance between myself and them.

*Them.*

As I stood on the highest point of the concrete steps I could see them, seated and standing Kirkland boys under the shade of a tree near the bike shelter. They seemed their usual boyish selves, laughing and fidgeting, pushing and shoving at one another. And there was Ballantine. I couldn't see his face as he was standing with his back to me. His hands were thrust deep into his pockets as he kicked the edge of a pine sleeper while he listened to Woolly, who held centre stage, miming wildly with his hands and talking about surfing, no doubt. I had hoped that they would all be whispering and speculating about me, that Boon might be consoling Ballantine maybe, but instead they all looked . . . normal.

I couldn't help but feel disappointed by that.

•

I swear that even the teachers were looking at me differently; even the resident Goth kids were staring at me with their crazy eyes.

I didn't have first and second period with Laura so I made it my life's mission to track her down at recess before she was engulfed by the canteen queues.

I came up quickly behind her, grabbed her arm and dragged her into the girls' toilets.

I pushed open every cubicle door, making sure we were well and truly alone before spinning around and facing her. 'What did you put in the diary?' I asked.

'Well, you said to make it juicy.'

'Good, I said make it *good*. I never said juicy. Oh God, I didn't say juicy. How juicy?'

'Well, you said "bloody good" and in my translation, that means juicy.' She folded her arms in defiance.

I sighed, closing my eyes briefly and praying for patience. I had to work quickly; I needed a heads-up before someone came in and interrupted us.

'Like I said, it wouldn't take long for the word to spread at the hands of Boon, the little shit. He must have had a sneak read when I was brushing my teeth last night. Of course, I may have left it on the coffee table near the PlayStation remote, so I'm not totally surprised,' she said, looking rather proud of her efforts.

'Awesome, but what did it say?'

Laura shook her head. 'I knew you'd ask,' she said, as she delved into her pocket and retrieved a folded-up piece of paper, then handed it over to me. 'Here.'

My eyes flicked to the paper, uncertainty lining my face, and I gingerly stepped forward to take it.

Right at that moment a group of giggling girls burst into the toilets.

Instinctively I walked slowly to a toilet cubicle, closed the door behind me and sat on the toilet lid. Unfolding the lined page, my heart raced at a million miles an hour as Laura's neat, cursive handwriting appeared in blue ink.

*Dear Diary,*

*You're not going to believe this. I don't even know where to begin, all I know is that I have been sworn to secrecy, and if this was to ever get out I know that it would make things really difficult and I don't want that to happen. Despite the possible controversy I am actually surprisingly happy for them. I saw that first hand tonight, seeing them together and flirting like crazy with one another. (Talk about feeling like a third wheel.) Still, good for them, I say. I can't say I don't feel a little bit jealous. I mean, I don't know a girl with a heartbeat who wouldn't want to go there, and the fact that she actually did go there!! Well, let's just say she promised me all the details and I can't wait to find out if all the rumours are true: is he a complete horndog in the sack like they say, with the hottest lips in Paradise City? Okay, getting distracted here. But from an outsider's view, things look set to be pretty serious. Not sure where to from here but all I can say is, even if I am secretly chanting it, I am a hundred per cent Team Lexie and Dean. One week in and she has hooked up with the hottest of them all.*

*Not bad, not bad at all.*

*L*

*Oh my God.*

By this time I hadn't even been aware that the voices had come and gone from the toilets; all I was interested in was slowly opening the door and stepping out to an eagerly awaiting Laura, who looked rather apprehensive at my reaction. I blinked, looking up from the paper.

'Do you think Ballantine knows?' My voice was a tiny whisper as there wasn't much air left in my lungs.

Laura stepped forward, taking the paper from my hand before refolding it back into her pocket for safekeeping. 'Oh, he knows all right,' she said, grinning from ear to ear.

'How do you know?' I asked quickly.

'Because I was watching from a sneaky, safe distance when my brother told him before school,' she said, laughing at her genius.

My heart slammed against my rib cage; I could feel my skin become clammy. I swallowed.

'And?'

Laura was smiling so brightly I thought I might have been blinded by it. 'Oh Lexie,' she giggled, 'he was fucking furious.'

# Chapter Thirty-Seven

wandered through the halls, my binder clutched to my chest, lost in my own thoughts. An eternal line of worry seemed to be creased between my brows these days.

*Did I want Ballantine mad at me? Wasn't I supposed to be mad at him?*

'Don't look so serious, Lexie, it may never happen.'

I blinked towards the voice.

Clarko, the PE teacher, was directing traffic in the halls today, dressed in his silky-green Adidas tracksuit, with impossibly bright white runners and fetching accessorised stopwatch draped around his neck.

He smirked, thinking his little wisecrack rather amusing; I feigned a small smile and kept walking, choosing to pick up the pace and head directly to detention. At least it was Friday.

*Friday.*

Thank God! One more day, one more detention, one more . . .

I yelped. Feeling an unexpected hold on my left arm as my whimsical, daydreamy walk turned into a full-fledged march.

I was being escorted – no, make that dragged – down the hall as if I weighed nothing. Trying to shake free from the iron-like grip and flashing a murderous glare at my assailant,

I couldn't actually believe Ballantine was smirking, actually fucking smirking, as he dragged me around the corner and towards a door, sliding it open, and pulling me inside.

'After you,' he said, stepping in behind me and sliding the door closed.

I could still feel the indentations in my upper arm so I rubbed vigorously. 'What the hell do you –'

Ballantine leapt forward, covering my mouth with his hand. Now I was even more pissed off. My eyes were wide and wild with outrage, my nostrils flaring, I mumbled obscenities into his palm.

'Shhh.' He frowned, cocking his head to the left, craning his neck to listen as shadows glided past the crack under the door. We stood there in silence for a long moment; well, mine was a forced silence. When he was sure the coast was clear, he slowly let his hand drop, letting down his guard just enough for me to push him away.

'Jesus, Ballantine. You're lucky I don't . . .' I paused, my eyes adjusting to the dull lighting of the room we were standing in. At first I focused behind Ballantine, then my gaze circled around me.

*No way.*

An incredulous smile ghosted across my lips, as I took in the hideous line of rainforest wallpaper, the acrid smell of paint and freshly laid carpet.

'Is this what I think it is?'

'Year Twelve common room,' Ballantine replied, clicking the lock behind him, a sound that echoed in the unfurnished space. The long line of windows was covered with sheets as a means to keep curious eyes from peeking in. It was, at a guess, in an effort to offer some grand-scale reveal, although, to be honest, there was nothing to boast about. The person who designed the room was obviously colourblind. Even though the light was dim you could still make out that every inch of the walls was covered in hideous rainforest wallpaper. I mean, really? Wallpaper? I gave it less than a week and the Year Twelves would tear this room apart.

Even with the overwhelming amount of wallpaper and black carpet – yeah, black – there was nothing else in the long, narrow room; as my gaze wandered around the space something occurred to me, my focus snapping back to Ballantine.

'Where are your balls?'

Ballantine's brows disappeared into his hairline. 'Excuse me?'

I rolled my eyes. 'You know, the footy, and stuff that gets confiscated.'

'Oh, *those* balls,' he said, smiling sheepishly. 'Who knows?'

'Yeah, well, thanks for the tour,' I said as I moved to push past him.

Ballantine stepped in my way. 'What's wrong with you?'

'What's wrong with *me*? What's wrong with *you*?' I snapped.

'Well, I do have two very important things on my mind.'

I lifted my chin. 'Oh?'

'One: a crazed uncle seems to be wandering the streets of Paradise.'

*Oh God!*

Every time I thought back to the other night I just wanted to die.

'And secondly, and most importantly, when am I going to see you again?'

*What?*

Okay, so that was not what I'd expected. 'Fucking furious' over the Dean rumour was what I'd expected, or maybe 'we should just be friends, seeing as your uncle is a psycho'. But this? This was definitely not what I'd been expecting.

'You don't need to look so happy about it, Lex.'

By this point I'd snapped my gaping mouth shut.

Ballantine sighed. 'Lexie, I don't care about your uncle. I know you're trying to push me away but it's going to take a lot more than that.'

My eyes flicked over his calm, sincere expression and I wanted to punch him in the face. 'Yeah, well, that's not what you told Lucy last night.'

Ballantine's eyes studied my face as if he was trying to solve the mysteries of the universe; it was a cross between that and a look that said I was insane. 'Lucy?'

'Don't pretend like you don't know,' I scoffed.

But when Ballantine's confusion remained, it was me who started to question myself. Thinking back to the sad, sincere look that Lucy had given me after she told me Ballantine didn't want to see me; she'd even looked like she felt sorry for me.

Ballantine sighed, wearily rubbing his hands through his hair in frustration. 'Lexie, what are you talking about?'

*Holy crap.*

Taking in his genuine confusion, it was all suddenly very clear.

'That bitch!' It was like my stomach plummeted to my feet. 'You don't know, do you?'

Ballantine threw his arms up in the air. 'What are you talking about?'

*Uh-oh.*

'I came to see you at work last night.'

'Work?'

'Yeah.'

'I wasn't working last night.'

'But didn't you work a double? I heard Dean say that –'

'I was feeling a bit crook so I switched.'

*Fucking Lucy.*

I could feel my temperature rising, my hands balling into fists at my sides. I didn't feel relief; I felt a deep-seated anger. I had made a fool out of myself, germinated a wild rumour that made me look like a slut . . . and all for nothing.

Forcing myself to breathe, my eyes flicked up to Ballantine who stood stoically, the lines of his face cast in a serious shadow.

'So you weren't avoiding me?' I said in a low voice.

'Avoiding you?' He laughed. 'Crazy uncle aside, Lex, I'm still crazy about you.'

My insides twisted, as if his very words had wrapped themselves around my beating heart, clenching it to a stop in that very moment.

*Luke Ballantine was crazy about me?*

I bit my lip, another very complicated thought sobering me. 'And what about the rumours?'

Ballantine clenched his jaw so tight I could see the muscle pulse in his temple. My heart raced in panic as I stepped forward.

'Nothing happened.' I blurted it out. 'It was just a stupid rumour and I didn't shut it down because I was mad at you. I wanted you to be jealous, I wanted you to feel as shitty as I did, and I was terrified that I was the only one who was feeling anything.'

*And now you've said too much, Lexie. Awesome.*

Ballantine's dark eyes bore down into mine, his entire body was coiled with tension; it was as if he was gauging if I was telling the truth, but when his eyes softened, the rigidness in his shoulders melted.

'I know.'

'What?'

'I know nothing happened between you and Dean.'

I frowned, confused, if not thrilled, by his certainty.

'How?'

Ballantine shrugged. 'I asked him.'

I swallowed. 'Y– you asked him?'

Ballantine looked bored. 'I rang him up.'

*Oh no-no-no-no.*

Ballantine asked Dean about our mythical hook-up, and now Dean knew! Oh God, this was out of control; I was beyond mortified. I would never, ever step back into the Wipe Out Bar as long as I lived.

I tried to seem cool, calm, as if what he had just said didn't have me wanting to claw off my own face.

'And what did he say?'

'He thought it was funny.'

*Funny?! FUNNY?*

I straightened my back. 'Why funny?'

Ballantine sighed, as if he really wasn't that emotionally invested in the conversation. 'He just said that that wouldn't happen in a million years.'

*A MILLION years? Ouch!*

Even coming from him, it was like a full-blown punch to the ego. Was I that hideous?

'He just said you weren't his type,' he added.

'Ha! Ain't that the absolute truth?' I scoffed.

'Make no mistake. If anything had happened between you and Dean he would have taken great pleasure in telling me as much.'

I cocked my brow. 'And I suppose you tell him with great pleasure about your conquests?'

Ballantine smirked, shaking his head as he stepped closer to me. 'No,' he said, reaching out his hand to push a strand of hair from my face. 'What I plan to do to you is between you and me.'

I swallowed deeply, my eyes flicking down to his mouth. 'And what is it you plan to do?'

Ballantine's wicked dimple puckered as he closed the distance, whispering his words across my neck. 'I'm going to finish what I started, and then I'm going to do it again, and again, and again. That okay with you?'

# Chapter Thirty-Eight

I closed my eyes, holding my breath, expecting Ballantine's lips to claim me. Instead, I felt his fingers lace between mine. I opened my eyes, before my attention lowered in confusion to where his hand held my hand.

He pressed a finger to his lips as he pulled me along to follow him. He led me to the only other door in the room, a sliding, bright red, high-glossed door. It clashed horrendously with the wallpaper, but right now that mattered little. I was too busy trying to control my heart as Ballantine slid the red door open. Pulling me inside he closed it behind us. It seemed pitch black until again my eyes adjusted, enough to see there was a strip of light piercing through the venetians of a high, narrow window. There were open shelves, a bench and a sink – it almost seemed like the new common room had been converted from an old science lab. I glanced around the poky space, turning around and smiling coyly up at the shadow before me. The room was small and somehow being cramped inside it in the dark made me very aware of how close we were and what we had come in here for. I suddenly felt hot, as if there was no air; my heart pounded fiercely as worry crept at the edges of my conscience.

I swallowed. 'W– what about detention?'

Before I had a chance to suggest maybe we best not be late again, Ballantine placed his hands on my waist, hitching me up onto the bench as if I weighed nothing. I yelped at the unexpectedness of it as I latched onto his shoulders that felt hot with rock hard muscle through the cotton fabric of his shirt.

Ballantine's eyes almost sparkled with devious intent. 'Fuck detention,' he said. Placing his hands under my knees he pulled me closer to him, stepping into the space between my thighs.

The abrupt jolt and feel of heat pressed against the thin material of my knickers made it hard for me to think – to breathe – as I stumbled to try to keep talking.

'You know, with us both not showing up for detention, that's going to start a whole new set of rumours.'

Ballantine's hands slid slowly up the outside of my thighs, trailing a hot line under my skirt and down again. A devilish smile across his face.

'Good,' he said darkly. 'When anyone looks at you,' Ballantine popped the bottom stud of my school dress open, 'when they whisper about you,' he popped another, 'when they imagine someone touching you,' and another, 'I want it to be my name they say.' He slid his hand inside the opening of my dress as his mouth lowered on mine, hotter and needier than ever. My fingers dug into his shoulders, desperately clinging onto him, revelling in the feel of him, the taste of him as his tongue delved to tease mine. His kisses were like a drug, clouding my anxiety. It was like a dance, a to and fro of maddening senses. His hand would slide along my skin, intimately pressing and squeezing my breast through the lace of my bra, causing my mind to spike in panic. But it would quickly ebb by the sweet press of Ballantine's lips as he kissed me passionately. I willingly opened myself up to him.

My conscience was an annoying, insistent little thing; with every moan or grind, I had a little voice inside my head telling me that I shouldn't be doing this, that we shouldn't be here, that it was wrong. I blinked and breathed and was haunted by the voice in my head as Ballantine trailed his lips down my neck.

It was a war between what I wanted and what I knew was right. Fucking consciences.

Ballantine took my hand and guided it down to feel him through his jeans.

*Oh God.*

Giving me little time for shock, he kissed me again – deep and hard – as if knowing that his kisses eased me into any wicked moment, and they did. I rubbed the long, hard line of him that strained against the material of his jeans, feeling the power of how my touch was affecting him. I captured his groan of pleasure with my mouth. My heart leapt with approval. Suddenly I cared less about right or wrong and instead just revelled in the wicked, lost in the pleasure of what Ballantine was doing to me, wanting more and needing more. As his hand slid underneath my bra, he broke our kiss, catching his breath. His eyes burned into mine.

'Please, don't stop,' I breathed, panicked by the thought.

Ballantine smiled against my mouth, his breaths as laboured as mine. 'Open your dress.'

I moved quickly. Grabbing the material still together at the top, I pulled what remaining studs were closed, clicking them apart in one blow, exposing my white bra underneath and the flat bare line of my belly.

A cocky grin curved the corner of Ballantine's mouth as his heated gaze raked over my body. 'This is so much better than detention,' he said. Leaning forward, he clamped his hot mouth over my nipple, sucking through the material and causing my body to melt.

'Fuck detention,' I moaned, pushing into his mouth, inciting a chuckle I felt vibrate through his chest. He pulled away, a devious glint in his eyes; his hands moved to bunch the material of my dress up and over my hips.

'Now that's more like it.'

I didn't know if he was referring to my change of heart over detention, or the fact his hand was moving to pull the elastic of my knickers aside, his finger breaching the material and ghosting over the most tender part of me. He stroked and teased so gently. I opened for him. Closing my eyes, I melted back onto my elbows, the tingly sensations robbing me of all thought, until he pushed his finger inside me. I gasped, my eyes snapping open as he pushed deeper. I could see shadows dancing on the ceiling. They flickered through the window above: the shadows of people walking, running, the movement outside from the yard. Talking about sports, TV, homework, canteen orders, sleepovers; and all the while I rocked into Ballantine's hand, legs wide open. He added another finger; I sat up, yanking his tie to pull him to my mouth, taking control and kissing him, grinding myself against him to match the rhythm of his thrusts.

'Ballantine?' I groaned it like a warning, almost frightened at what was building inside me, as his hand worked harder and my hips ground quicker. My body was greedy to release the pressure that was building – the almost unbearable pleasure – and relieve the too-sensitive area between my thighs.

*Oh God, don't stop, don't ever stop!*

Sensing my climb, he covered my mouth with his free hand, muffling my screams as I fell apart, my hands fisting into the fabric of his shirt, anchoring myself to him as he pushed me over the edge. Only when my body became languid and defeated did he slowly let his hand fall. With my chest rising and falling, I looked into his amused, warm eyes. It took a moment for his breaths to even.

*Was it always like this?*

Ballantine slowly took his fingers away, pulling the fabric of my knickers back into place. I averted my eyes, concentrating on snapping the push studs of my dress back into place, grinning knowingly as Ballantine watched on in silence.

*What do you say after something like that?*

This wasn't something that I had ever experienced before, a lunchtime hook-up in an abandoned room. I said nothing, hoping that Ballantine would break the silence. But he didn't. Rather, he simply helped me slide down off the bench, then lifted my chin up so he could look down into my eyes for a long moment, as if he was trying to read my mind before giving me a slow, lingering kiss on my lips that ended all too soon. My insides burned in recognition of his touch as if I could easily go for round two, so when he pulled away with a cocky grin I felt a twinge of disappointment hit me.

'There's no need to look so pleased with yourself,' I said.

He bit his lower lip to stifle a smile.

I shook my head incredulously. 'You're going to be so bad for me, aren't you?'

Ballantine circled his arms around me. 'You know what they say about being bad?'

I shook my head.

He pressed his forehead against mine. 'It's going to feel so, so good.'

I could feel just how so, so good it was going to be pressed up against me. I was still a little dazed and confused that this had simply been about me. We so needed to talk this out, but now obviously wasn't the time. I hoped he was going to be good for me.

•

The rest of the day, the agonisingly long, drawn-out fifth period Science and sixth period English were all undertaken with a big goofy grin. I tried to disguise it as I must've looked like a bit of a freak, smiling all the way through group discussions on *The Adventures of Huckleberry Finn*.

Scrawling love hearts in the margin of my exercise book, I listened less to the journey of Huckleberry and reminisced more about the screaming big 'O' Ballantine gave me in the Year Twelve common room.

When Ballantine and I had parted ways – him leaving a few seconds before me, turning right down the corridor, then me turning left – we didn't exactly have a grand exchange of numbers or make plans to catch up over the weekend or anything. At the time, our smug little act of escaping detention and getting out of the common room undetected was what occupied us.

But now, as the day drew to an end, I felt a small bubble of anxiety. I felt it grow as I walked through the halls, glancing around, wondering if Ballantine was still here. I took the long way around towards the back of the music room, walking up the path where the outside car park was, where all the Year Twelves with licences parked, but the yellow Sandman wasn't there, and the worry morphed into panic. I needed to see Ballantine before the weekend started, or the next couple of days would be filled with rampant paranoid thoughts and then a possible awkward Monday. I made my way to my locker, lost in my own thoughts, mindlessly turning the dial of my combination lock. I hardly even took in any of the giggles and whispers around me, as students speculated about the new girl hooking up with Dean. The falseness of the rumours meant little to me now, as all I cared about were the very real-life issues that were playing on my mind. I flung open my locker, and a folded-up piece of paper fell out to land on the top of my shoe. I reached down, picking it up, wondering where it had come from and who it had come from. My heart raced and I didn't know if I even wanted to open it. What if it was some kind of hate mail calling me a slut or something? But then curiosity got the better of me and I slowly unfolded the little square.

In my hand lay an A4 piece of paper covered in a black-inked mural, full of twists and circles; a large wave flowed through the centre crashing into a sun that splintered into a million tiny pieces. I recognised it instantly for what it was. It was the drawing Ballantine had been working on the entire week of detention. He had created it using my pen, and at a guess, I seriously doubted there would be any ink left in it looking at all the intricate details, with barely a white space to be seen. What did stand out was something in one of the corners – in red ink there was a faint calligraphy-styled 'L': an L for Lexie. I smiled so broadly my face hurt: I may not have had the chance to see Ballantine at the end of school but this, this very piece of paper I held in my hand, was enough. It was more than enough.

# Chapter Thirty-Nine

Basking in the solitude of an empty house, I ignored the English assignment that was due on Monday, putting that on my list of things for future Lexie to worry about. For now: first one home, first one to raid the cupboard. Not that there was really ever anything in it aside from fruit and a box of bran; um, no! I was going to need something a little stronger. Thinking I couldn't get into any more trouble than I was already in, I raided the forbidden shelf that housed Uncle Peter's Coke for his Scotch and Coke. I grabbed it with great delight. If he hadn't come into the Wipe Out Bar none of this would have happened. I pulled the tab, hearing the hiss as I punctured it open. Yum!

I slurped a big mouthful down, eyeing the flickering, flashing number on the answering machine on the kitchen bench. I pressed the play button, hoping it was a message from Mum. I really wanted to hear her voice, so when Principal Fitzgibbon's voice came through the loud speaker I almost spat my mouthful of Coke all over the kitchen.

*Hi, Mr and Mrs Burnsteen, it's John Fitzgibbons, principal of Paradise High here. Just wanted to check how Lexie was doing? She wasn't present at her lunchtime detention today and there is no record of her leaving the grounds. She might*

*not be aware of the rules when it comes to going home sick
but she has to sign out. I am sure it's all a misunderstanding.
Our main concern of course is that Lexie is okay. Please give
us a call back on . . .*

I quickly pressed the button.

Message deleted.

*Oh shit, that was bad: very, very bad.*

The walls were closing in on me: there was no un-opening
and putting back the Coke, there was no way of avoiding my
wagging detention and fooling around with Ballantine in
the common room, and the way that news travelled around
here, both Uncle Peter and Aunty Karen would probably
come home thinking I'd been knocked up by Dean Saville.
If even a sliver of any of this got back to my parents I would
be going home, first thing.

I heard the front door open and the unmistakeable sound
of a bag being dropped.

*Crap!*

I quickly tipped the rest of the Coke down the sink,
spinning around the kitchen looking for a place to hide the
evidence. I opted for the bread bin. I wasn't in the mood to
face Amanda . . . alone!

I readied myself for the inevitable onslaught of questions
about Dean Saville. I opted for light and casual, placing
one hand on the bench and the other on my hip, like 'Hey,
what's up? I'm just hanging in the kitchen, real casual like.'
I felt about as casual as an eighties model in a knitwear
catalogue.

Amanda appeared from around the corner looking every
bit as pissed off as I had ever seen.

'Hey,' I said, light and airy, my attempt to set the tone.

'Oh, you're here.' It was more of an accusation than a statement as she walked past me and went straight to the fridge. 'Oh goody!' she said sarcastically.

I couldn't help but wonder what her actual problem was. I thought maybe if I explained the full story to her she might be less mad at me and just see it for the colossal mistake that it was.

'Amanda, what's wrong?'

I expected to be met with her usual cagey silence, so when Amanda slammed the fridge door and spun around glaring at me, I wanted to run and hide under my bed.

'What's *wrong*? What's wrong is you are embarrassing me! The whole school is talking about my slutty cousin who is fucking Dean Saville!' she screamed.

*Whoa.*

*I had expected one hundred and one questions, but not this.*

'I am not doing anything with Dean Saville,' I deadpanned.

'Oh, really? Because that's not what your BFF Laura is saying.'

It suddenly occurred to me that above all else there was a far bigger crime being committed here, something that everyone failed to see. Boon was reading Laura's diary, albeit a fake diary. Still, he had no right and someone had to point this out.

'Did she tell you this directly?' I probed with interest.

'No, but Boon said that –'

'So Laura told Boon?'

'What? I don't know,' she snapped.

'So how does Boon know?'

Amanda glowered at me; it was like this was all she could manage because I knew she couldn't pinpoint the blame directly onto Laura, and by saying any more she'd be incriminating her boyfriend.

'How strange,' I said, smirking to myself.

'If you don't go home, I'll make you wish you had.' A chill ran down my spine. Amanda could be so venomous when she wanted to be, and I could hardly believe I'd ever managed to tap into any kind part of her personality. She was a complete stranger to me.

'Why would I want to do that, when staying here and torturing you is so much more entertaining?'

Amanda laughed, folding her arms across her chest. 'You know what? Stay; knock yourself out. It's not like I have to do much, you're already destroying your own reputation. Face it, Lexie, a few weeks in and you're already the laughing stock of Paradise High. And no-one is talking about you in any other way than in utter disbelief that someone like Dean would be interested in someone like you,' she scoffed, her eyes roaming over me as if I was something she had scraped off the bottom of her shoe.

It was then that Ballantine's words echoed through my head.

*Not in a million years.*

But Ballantine liked me, he had said as much, showed as much. I wanted to rip out Ballantine's drawing and ram it into Amanda's face, tell her all about my secret times together with Ballantine, the coolest, sexiest boy in school, but I didn't dare. I was grateful that Ballantine and I were a secret. Let them speculate about Dean. What did it matter? As long as Amanda didn't know, she wouldn't be able to hold anything against me. I glared back at her. Gone was any understandable longing for what was once between us when we were young. Now I had proven that I could cope on my own, she could go to hell for all I cared. I could've been really cruel and told her that Boon had tried to crack onto me the same night they hooked up, but no matter how angry I was, or how harsh Amanda's words were, I could never bring myself to stoop so low.

Like my dad always says, it takes more courage to just walk away. So that's what I did, as much as it killed me to hear Amanda smugly snort as if she had won the argument, and had the last word.

There was no time to think as the front door opened, and the well-known key drop on the hall stand caused the hairs on the back of my neck to rise. The house filled with upbeat chatter, mostly coming from Aunty Karen.

I stilled from storming towards the bedroom – instead, I lifted my head and plastered on false bravado. I didn't want to make myself look visibly guilty so I psyched myself to greet my aunty and uncle instead.

'Hey,' I said, which was always more than what Amanda could manage, even on a good day. I went to continue to the bedroom, aiming on getting there before Amanda could lock me out.

'Oh, hey, Lexie, can you wait a second?' asked Aunty Karen. 'Peter wants to call a family meeting.' She glanced at Uncle Peter, who, if surprised by the notion, didn't show it. His serious, yet bored gaze fixed on me. It was like he saw straight through me. That's when I began to panic.

Family meeting? A family meeting was usually announced in my house for either good or bad news, and somehow the grim lines of Uncle Peter's face suggested good news was unlikely. Oh God, maybe Principal Fitzgibbons had tracked them down, told them about my week-long detention and me skipping the final day. I felt sick. What would be my explanation? Kissing the one boy I was forbidden to see? Oh God, help!

I glanced towards Amanda, who seemed equally wary as she headed towards the dining-room table.

I sat at the glass-top table staring down at my hands. With Aunty Karen sitting opposite, Amanda sitting to my right, it was going to be a 'family meeting' from hell. Uncle Peter sat at the head of the table, gloomy as usual. I couldn't decide if I was more worried about why he was home so early from work, or about what he had lurking deep within his mind.

Just what I needed – another complication. It felt like I was on trial for murder. Maybe this would be a chance to plead my case, to put forward my defence, to clear my name. Of course, if Uncle Peter was going to make his witness statement of me sneaking out to the Wipe Out Bar – of all places – it was going to be a tough one to win. I had already mentally packed my bags. If the betrayal of the late-night sneak-outs wasn't bad enough, all they'd have to do was talk to Principal Fitzgibbons to check out how my first few weeks of school had gone and I'd be shipped back to Red Hill quick smart. There was no way of escaping it anymore. I would come clean, talk before anyone else had a chance to; I would put everything on the table and then maybe I'd be able to sleep at night. No doubt I would anyway, back home in my childhood bed, that is – minus any sexy boys knocking on my bedroom window.

Uncle Peter rubbed his chin in thought, before placing his hand on the table and drumming his fingers on the glass. It felt like I was about to be cross-examined, torn to shreds on the stand.

*I want the truth!*
*You can't handle the truth.*

Uncle Peter leant forward, clasping his hands together. 'So . . . where do you ladies want to go for dinner?'

*Wait. What?*

Amanda's head and mine snapped around comically fast, instinctively glancing at each other, no doubt wondering if we were dreaming.

'Dinner?' Amanda sneered.

Uncle Peter shrugged. 'Yeah, why not? It's Friday night, let's go out.'

Aunty Karen beamed with approval. 'Oh, Peter, where should we go? The Club? Alfredo's? What about Donovan's?' She rattled off names like an ecstatic teenager.

Even I was getting excited by Aunty Karen's enthusiasm; and so unbelievably relieved that I was not getting sent home.

'How about the Wipe Out Bar?' suggested Amanda. I turned to see her raise her brows at me, taunting me. I kicked her under the table but I think it hurt me more than it hurt her.

The Wipe Out Bar was the last place on earth I wanted to be. I couldn't imagine having to face Dean knowing he knew about the circulating rumours. I knew it was just a way to entertain Amanda, to allow her to watch on with her beady little eyes. God, I hated her. But it mattered little, there was no way Uncle Peter would agree to take us to the Wipe Out –

'Okay,' he said, pushing himself up from the table. 'The Wipe Out Bar it is.'

*What?*

My eyes widened in horror as I watched Uncle Peter walk out of the dining room.

Aunty Karen's enthusiasm seemed to dim somewhat. 'Is that down Arcadia Lane?' she asked, as if the very idea was too unsavoury to even contemplate.

'Yep!' said Amanda, leaping up from her chair then, as she moved behind me, she grabbed my shoulders and whispered in my ear, 'At least you'll get to see old Deano. You can even introduce him to the family. No need to thank me.' She seemed to delight in my misery, slapping me on the back as she moved her head away. 'Better get ready,' she said, bouncing on the balls of her feet as she skipped out of the room.

Aunty Karen smiled. 'I'm so glad you two are getting along so well.'

*Yeah, like a freakin' house on fire.*

# Chapter Forty

I wondered if I pushed my foot on the back of her kneecap, would she collapse to the ground? The thought of a blood-curdling scream and perhaps even the sound of a bone snapping made the fact that Lucy fucking-fell-on-her-face was leading us towards a vacant booth in the family bistro section a little less sufferable. Of all the waitresses in the entire world, she had to serve us? She smiled at me, all sickly sweet, but I knew what it meant.

*I'm going to spit in your food.*

Although, I did wonder if she had seen Ballantine yet. If so, she might know that he and I had talked, and that he was aware of her pretence the night before. Time would tell.

Aunty Karen and Uncle Peter were trying to humour us, but they were obviously massively out of their comfort zone as we slid into the booth. Aunty Karen awkwardly shimmied herself around, her expensive gold jewellery clinking all the way, her ample bosom bouncing, and the leather underneath her made farting noises as she scooted along. Her eyes strayed to the rafters; the fishing net that draped from the beams with an inflatable shark wedged in it caused her to frown. No, this was most definitely not the Ritz; this was going to be a struggle for her.

Uncle Peter, on the other hand, maintained his poker face. He had an air of 'let's get this over and done with'. But that was pretty much how he went about everything in life. There was a definite feeling of unease between Uncle Peter and me, thinking back to the last time we had been here together. It was somewhat dramatic, to say the least. I glanced to Amanda opposite me, who offered a super-sweet smile that was about as genuine as Lucy's. She too had metamorphosed in and out of character. Guess the apple didn't fall too far from the tree, I thought as my attention flicked between Uncle Peter and his daughter. I had huge sympathy for that inflatable shark trapped in the netting – I knew exactly how it felt.

The hostess with the mostess, Lucy, appeared at our table with an armful of menus that she lovingly placed down before each of us as she chirped away, listing the specials off the top of her head. 'Would you like any drinks while you decide on your meals?' Blink, smile, blink.

*God, I hate her.*

She was one of those 'memory' waitresses: didn't need a notepad because she had some kind of bullshit perfect memory.

'All right then, back in a jiffy.' She tilted her head like an angel.

'That's Grant Fell's daughter. Lovely girl,' Uncle Peter said, straightening his cutlery on the table.

I looked away, disguising my eye roll. I could see that even Amanda was almost gagging on that one. Then I paused. *Oh hell.* Weaving his way through the tables towards us: Dean Saville.

*Oh no-no-no-no-no . . .*

He paused between tables, laughing and joking with the customers, as if he was some kind of schmoozer from back in the fifties. I hadn't seen this side of him before, and it seemed . . . weird.

I could feel Amanda watching me as he neared.

'You guys right for drinks?' he asked, warm and friendly as you like.

I instantly saw my uncle's demeanour change – straighten into proud family man.

'Yeah, we're right thanks, mate.'

*Mate?*

'Great! Well, if you need anything just let me or my staff know and we'll fix you up.'

Who were these people? It was like body snatchers had invaded their bodies.

'It's a lovely place you have here,' said Aunty Karen, in her typical bright and bubbly manner.

Dean laughed, and smiled that same roguish smile. 'Oh, that's very kind of you. I see you've met Hank.' His eyes lifted to the inflatable shark.

Aunty Karen followed the direction of his eyes, laughing and clutching her necklace like a school girl. 'Oh, yes, we have met.'

Oh my God, was Aunty Karen blushing?

Amanda was openly sneering at her mother, equally as embarrassed as I was.

'Well, I'm afraid Hank's days might be numbered. I plan on doing some extensive renovations, so if you know anyone who's interested, I'll be looking for a new home for him.'

He winked at Uncle Peter – as if he was in on the joke – knowing that somehow an inflatable shark in Aunty Karen's living room was not exactly to her taste.

Aunty Karen's smile wavered. 'Oh, um, well, I'll keep my ear to the ground, see if I hear of anyone who's looking,' she said, nodding with sincerity.

'I appreciate it. Well, I better let you get back to it; enjoy your night.'

I tried to make eye contact with Dean before he left but he merely glanced my way, treating me no differently from the others. I was relieved. He seemed to just let it slide. Ballantine had said he had thought it was funny, like it was a huge joke that someone like *him* would be interested in someone like *me*, just like Amanda said.

I watched his tall, lean frame, dressed in his usual all-black attire, drift out of the bistro and back towards the bar. I hated where we were sitting, away from the main area, unable to see the comings and goings. All I could see was Lucy bitchface making her way back to us with a tray of drinks that she expertly carried with one hand.

*Oh yeah, so clever.*

'Here you go!' She put the tray on our table, placing drink coasters out before each of us.

'One house white, one Carlton Draught, and two Cokes for the kids.' She winked at my uncle, who smiled.

Oh, how I wanted to wipe that smile from her face.

Kids? We were the same age as her. *Bitch.*

•

So far, so good. I watched my aunty and uncle relax somewhat, melting into the booth, accepting that this wasn't fine dining, but that the atmosphere was good enough: family friendly with an over-the-top sweet waitress and a personal welcome from Dean. I, of course, didn't melt into my seat. I was nothing but a livewire, fidgeting, and thinking about

Ballantine. I desperately wanted to know if he was working tonight. Was he in the same building right now? My leg jigged impatiently under the table as I cursed the fact I had no-one to ask. Amanda? No. Lucy? No way! Curiosity was killing me.

'Um, I'm just going to the ladies before dinner gets here,' I said, moving to stand. 'Does anyone want a non-alcoholic beverage while I'm heading that way?'

Amanda's glass was empty. 'No, thanks. I think I'll wait for Lucy.' She smiled defiantly at me.

*Whatever.*

If she'd rather be looked after by that skank – after all, I knew what her friends thought of Lucy – then so be it.

Aunty Karen countered, 'Thanks anyway, Lexie.'

Rounding the corner through the double doors, the room was bustling with Friday night celebrations, but I looked past all that. My eyes skimmed over to the end of the bar, to the corner where Dean was moving his pen over a clipboard, an intense frown lining his face.

I walked over to him, his eyes failing to lift as I stood before him.

'Hi honey. Did you have a good day?' he asked.

I knew he would deliberately make me squirm.

I sighed, taking the vacant stool next to him. 'You're going to torture me, aren't you?'

A smile spread broadly across his face, as his eyes glanced up from his clipboard. 'Every chance I get.'

'Now listen –'

'Oh, don't worry, I'm listening. In fact, I'm quite fascinated to recall the details of our hook-up,' he said, chucking the clipboard on the bar and crossing his arms across his chest, giving me his full attention.

I swallowed. 'Our hook-up?'

'Play. By. Play,' he said.

I cringed. 'What exactly do you know?'

If I knew how much Dean knew I could at least determine how much damage control I had to do, and how much information to share. I wasn't going to unnecessarily dig my hole deeper if I didn't need to.

Dean shrugged. 'Apparently I fucked you on a pool table.'

I gasped, my eyes widening in horror. I could feel the heat climbing up my neck. I don't know what shocked me more: the brash words or the sheer delight he was getting at watching my horrified reaction.

'I *never* said that –'

'I gathered as much.'

'What I mean was, that kind of thing, well, that wasn't even part of the plan.'

'The plan?' Dean looked straight into my eyes, something I really wished he hadn't done, as they were distracting, the interesting greeny-brown of them. They were so unique, so unusual. But then again, nothing about Dean Saville seemed usual.

'It was just a little joke,' I said.

'To make someone mad?' he asked.

'Not exactly.'

Dean's eyes were unmoving. 'Or was it to make someone jealous?' he queried.

When I didn't answer he nodded.

'I see.'

I felt about two feet tall, and if the ground could open up underneath me it would be a blessing. A silly little high school rumour was never meant to gain such traction, or to get back to the very source, and with such X-rated details added to the mix. I felt like an idiot, and cursed Laura and her diary.

'So is your plan working?'

My eyes lifted to his.

'Is he jealous?'

I shrugged. 'I don't know.'

He had been angry, was that the same thing?

'Anyway, I'm sorry you got involved and thanks for letting Ballantine know it wasn't the truth.'

*Not in a million years. Yeah, that still stings a bit.*

If I hadn't witnessed the jovial, charming Dean moments before, I would have thought him arrogant, like my original impression, but I dug deep and searched for that good part of him, the one I knew lurked beneath the black clothing and bad attitude – the Dean behind the businessman.

'And thanks for acting normal at the table before. I owe you one.'

A smirk lifted the corner of his mouth. 'I'd watch what I said if I were you, some people might misconstrue that as something else entirely.'

I blushed. 'Yeah, well, all I'd need is someone like Lucy to overhear and that would be it.'

'Ah, yes, young Lucy,' he said as if bored by the topic.

'Please don't let her spit in my food,' I said in all seriousness.

'If she does that, she's out on her arse.'

'Just promise me she won't.'

Dean sighed, 'If I do, that's two things you'll owe me for. You prepared for that?' he asked with a mischievous gleam in his eyes.

*Oh, great. Add mischievous to the sexy, dark-lord look.*

'It would be worth it,' I said, moving to stand.

'Ballantine wants to see you.'

I stilled, looking at Dean, gauging whether he was serious. There was no humour in his expression, none at all.

'Really?'

He shrugged. 'He's out the back. I told him you were here.'

I shook my head, trying to calm myself so I'd avoid the instinct to throw my arms around Dean's neck and hug the crap out of him. 'You are a saint, Dean Saville.'

Dean scoffed, and that cocky, gorgeous smile reappeared. 'Well, that's something I've never been called before.'

'You are; I would totally date the shit out of you,' I said with a laugh.

Dean's eyes rested on me, serious and penetrating. 'Is that so?'

I cleared my throat, cursing my poor effort at a joke, another one that had backfired; I really just needed to shut the hell up sometimes. I squirmed under his heated scrutiny.

'Well, I was . . . just saying that I . . . was trying to –'

'Construct sentences?'

I glowered. 'Funny.'

'Wow, a funny, dateable saint: I really should change my business card.'

'Yeah, change it from smart-arse.' I smirked, ready to leave this time for real.

'So I'll tell Lord Ballantine that you seek an audience with him then?'

Oh my God. I spun around so fast I almost knocked the stool over, much to Dean's amusement.

*Shit-Fuck-Ballantine! How could I have forgotten?*

'Yes!' I said, a bit too high-pitched. 'Absolutely.' I nodded, my chest filling with air as I resisted the urge to dance on the balls of my feet.

Dean grabbed his clipboard. He stood, towering over me, but seemed somehow less intimidating than he had in the past. 'All right, I'll get Sherry to let you know when he's on a break,' he said, his no-nonsense businessman facade slipping back into place.

This seemed to be his normal modus operandi: stern, aloof, distant.

'Wait.' I reached out, grabbing his upper arm – his solid, muscled arm. His brows rose as he looked down at my hand on him. I flinched back, blushing at how hot his skin felt.

'Um, do you think you could do me a favour?' I grimaced, biting my lip.

Dean turned, his full focus on me now, a spark of amusement in his eyes. 'Another favour?' he asked, shaking his head. 'So needy.'

I really hated to ask what I was about to, hated to reveal my petty side, but what the hell.

'When Ballantine takes a break, can you get Lucy to come and let me know?'

I waited, and instead of walking away, he laughed, actually deep-bellied, earnestly laughed.

'What? What's so funny?'

Dean rubbed at his stubble, shaking his head in disbelief. 'I thought you didn't want her to spit on your food.'

'Well I don't but –'

'All right, I'll happily pass on to Lucy to let you know. But remember one thing, Lexie Atkinson.'

*How did he know my last name?*

He stepped closer to me, so close I had to strain my neck to look up at him. I wanted to make a point of holding my ground, to not shy away from his smart mouth that creased into a smirk.

'What's that?' I asked, lifting my chin, attempting to stare *him* down.

'I always call in my favours,' he said darkly, a heat lighting his green-brown eyes, one that was full of promise – or something.

I hated how my chest was visibly rising, giving away how not in control I was.

Instead of letting him get to me, I smiled sweetly. 'Saints don't call in favours.'

Dean smiled, his eyes searching my face. 'Maybe I'm the devil in disguise?'

# Chapter Forty-One

I splashed water onto my face, flooding my cheeks with the coolness I so desperately craved. Clasping the edge of the basin, I took in my flaming complexion, praying the dull lighting in the bar would hide it from the others.

I ran my fingers through my hair nervously – excited Ballantine was here and wanted to see me. I made my way back to the bar. I was relieved that Dean was gone – probably up to his lair, I thought, as I glanced up to the office with the one-way glass. I pictured him sitting on a throne-like chair, watching his minions.

Sherry swooped in, silently raising an eyebrow. She wasn't much of a communicator.

'I think I'll have a raspberry tonight, I'm feeling kind of dangerous.'

'Can you pay for it this time?' she deadpanned.

I smiled. 'As a matter of fact, I can.'

She nodded, plunging a glass into the icy recess.

I wondered where Ballantine was. He was obviously out the back in the kitchen doing . . . what? Chef's apprentice? Dish boy?

'Hey, Sherry, what does Ballantine do here?' I asked.

She looked at me as if she wanted to be anywhere else than here exchanging small talk. She had a rather intense 'kill me now' kind of body language. 'He's a dish pig. Two-fifty,' she said in a no-nonsense manner.

I scoffed, totally unsurprised by her answer. 'Thanks,' I said, taking my drink and handing her a five-dollar note. 'Keep the change,' I said, giving her my own deadpan expression as I made my way back to the bistro.

I had just sipped the bubbly excess off the top so it wouldn't dribble over the edge. Which didn't help in the slightest because I didn't see the upsweep of a set of menus until they hit me, dumping raspberry lemonade all down my white top.

I froze, arms outstretched as I looked down at myself, stained like there had been a massacre. My eyes locked with Lucy's, who stood before me with her hand covering her mouth in feigned horror.

'Oh, I am so sorry, I didn't see you coming.' She blinked innocently. 'Boy, I hope that doesn't stain,' she said, grimacing.

'Oh my darling.' Aunty Karen's heels could be heard a mile away, clicking quickly towards me. I appreciated that she saw it for what it was – an absolute fucking disaster of biblical proportions. She dabbed at my top with a scrunched-up serviette.

'Oh, we need to get some club soda right away.'

'I think it's too late for that,' I said, pulling out my shirt, trying to prevent it from sticking to my skin.

'I am so sorry, Mrs Burnsteen, I just didn't see her coming,' added a fake, yet still visibly upset Lucy. Oh she was good, really good.

Aunty Karen turned to Lucy, and for the first time ever, I saw the bright sparkle dim in her blue eyes. 'Oh, make no mistake, Miss Fell, I saw exactly what happened and I know what a nasty piece of work you are.'

A shiver ran down my spine, partly because I was wearing my drink but also because when Aunty Karen turned on her badass, wow, she really turned it on.

Lucy's cheeks reddened as deeply as the raspberry I was wearing.

'I'm sure Grant would be very disappointed in you, Lucy,' came my uncle's voice from next to my aunty.

'I–I'll get some soda water,' she said, quick-stepping out of the room, tears visible in her eyes.

'Don't bother,' Amanda called after her, before cutting me a pitiful look. 'Can't take you anywhere.' She shook her head.

'Oh, honey, do you want to go home?' Aunty Karen's eyes took in my dismal state; it was then that I glanced around the restaurant and noticed every table was looking at me.

I breathed. 'No! We're here for a nice, family dinner. I won't let someone like Lucy Fell-on-her–,' I paused. 'Um, I mean I'm not going to let her get the better of me.'

'Good! Because I am freakin' starving,' said Amanda, heading back to our booth.

I smiled at my aunty and uncle. 'It's okay, there's a hand dryer in the toilets,' I said. 'Back in a minute.'

I had a sense of déjà vu heading back past the bar, and funnily enough, there was no Lucy fetching me any soda water. She was nowhere to be seen.

'Hey, you!'

I stalled, looking to where Sherry was standing behind the bar. She looked over my drenched clothes with disdain, before pointing towards the stairs. 'You've been summoned.'

My eyes glanced up at the one-way glass window.

*Oh great.*

'What does he want?'

She shrugged, going back to serve a customer.

I sighed. He was probably worried I was going to sue him or something, and then I thought how quickly news travelled in this place. As I made my way up the stairs, feeling sticky and gross, I was in no mood to have to explain the reason why Lucy was a massive bitch – and why he clearly hired staff who had zero personality, except Ballantine, of course.

I made it to the top of the landing and knocked on the door, deciding that if he didn't answer within five seconds, I would be hightailing it back down the stairs.

'Enter.'

*Damn.*

I twisted the handle and gingerly pushed it open.

There wasn't a vulture on his shoulder, or even a throne; instead, he sat behind a very normal desk, in a very normal office, with a couch, filing cabinet and little kitchen area. It all looked very civilised. He even had a framed black-and-white poster of The Beatles mounted on his wall. My eyes drifted out the window through the glass, which had an impressive view over the bar, but did not extend into the bistro. My eyes wandered to a wall of monitors that covered all of the other parts of the building as well as one showing the bar. BINGO!

No wonder news travelled so fast.

Dean leant back in his chair, taking in my attire. 'Red suits you,' he said.

'Yeah, well, who should I send my cleaning bill to?'

'I'll trade you,' he said, getting up out of his chair, heading towards the top drawer of his filing cabinet, opening it and pulling out a black square of material. He then threw it over and I caught it clumsily.

'What's this?' I asked, unfolding the material to see it was a black tee with 'The Wipe Out Bar' scrawled across the back, and the same insignia that was on the beer coasters printed on the front.

'Am I being inducted as a staff member?'

'I don't think so,' he deadpanned.

'Oh, do you doubt my skills?' I asked, interested in his disinterest. Surely I could do what Lucy Fell could do: be fake and pour drinks on customers.

'Trouble seems to follow you wherever you go, Lexie Atkinson.' He brushed past me, reaching for the door handle, amused; my gaze followed him.

'How do you know my last name?' I asked, curving my brow.

Dean shrugged. 'Apparently some chick called Lexie Atkinson is shagging the owner of the Wipe Out Bar,' he said, grinning as he opened the door.

I tilted my head. 'Ha ha.'

'Get changed in here if you want; sink's over there.'

I turned to see where he was referring. 'Oh, umm, I don't know. I'll just –'

'Relax, I'm leaving.' He paused for a moment. 'Don't touch anything,' he said with a pointed look, before stepping out and slamming the door closed.

I breathed out, taking a moment to lift up the shirt, knowing it would be too big, but what did I care? Free top! Although, with Dean Saville, maybe nothing was ever free. I smelled the fabric: clean and crisp. I made my way over to the sink in the corner. Setting the t-shirt aside on the back of the chair, I washed my hands and arms with hot, soapy water, removing all traces of the sticky mess. I glanced at the screen, noticing that Dean was behind the bar, no doubt ordering his staff around. Knowing he was safely downstairs, I made quick work of removing my top. Plunging it in the sink and dowsing it with water and soap, I knew that there was no salvaging it. I looked at my reflection, grimacing at the pink tinge in the middle of my bra. I glanced back to the bar on screen before removing my bra and adding it to the sink. I took no chances, grabbing for my new top because somehow being half-naked in Dean's office didn't seem right at all, and just as I draped the material over my head, pulling down and turning myself into a piece of walking merchandise, I froze, hearing the door screech slowly open and a tentative cough.

I was no longer alone.

# Chapter Forty-Two

I saw him in the reflection of the mirror first, but I didn't truly believe it until I spun around to see Ballantine, standing in the doorway of the office. He stepped in, closing the door behind him, leaning against it, folding his arms and looking all cool and calm. The only giveaway was the deepset intent of his eyes that flicked from my bra hanging over the sink and then back to me.

This was not ideal.

Standing in Dean's office with my bra and top in his sink, wearing his t-shirt. It was a definite mood killer. I scrambled to push them deeper into the sink and added more cold water to the pale pink mess.

'I'm just trying to salvage these,' I said, glancing at his still form in the mirror. 'Bloody Lucy spilt my drink all over –'

'I heard.'

I stopped scrubbing. 'You did?'

Ballantine pushed off from the door and started towards the monitors, his eyes flicking over the black-and-white security screens. 'News travels fast in this place.'

I abandoned my clothes to soak in the sink, brushing my hands on my jeans to dry them as I came to stand next to Ballantine.

'I get it, but aren't all these monitors a bit over the top?'

'You'd be surprised what goes down in Arcadia Lane; it's a full-time job dealing with all the freaks that can wander in at any given moment.'

'And that's not including the staff.'

Ballantine laughed. 'Especially the staff.'

'I mean, no offence,' I teased.

'No, you're absolutely right. Why do you think I'm kept out back, chained to the sink?'

'Why don't you work in the bar? You're old enough and I think you'd make a great barman.'

'Because of my immense charm and irresistibility?'

'Well . . . there isn't a whole lot of that happening behind the bar right now,' I said, focusing on the grainy black-and-white image of cyclone Sherry working the bar, expertly pulling a beer, dumping it in front of a patron, scooping up the money, then whizzing around Dean, who was standing in the way. He seemed intently focused on listening to a tourist couple at the bar with great, if not faked, interest. It amused me no end: he was trapped, trying to edge his way out politely but then the husband, who sported a snazzy-looking bum bag and trusty knee-high socks, pulled out a map, unravelling it over the bar. I watched on as Dean gathered patience and morphed from owner of the Wipe Out Bar to Tourist Information Guide; it was hilarious and I suddenly wanted a bucket of popcorn and to pull up a seat, the view was so entertaining.

I pointed to the bistro screen to where the image flicked onto our table. 'Heads-up: avoid table twenty-two, my uncle's here.'

I was trying to make light out of the insanity of the situation but Ballantine didn't look amused, his serious gaze was set on the bistro screen.

'What did my uncle say to you?' It was the one thing that had haunted me since that night; as much as I'd like to think that my uncle had simply stormed back into the bar and ordered a tequila slammer to calm his nerves, I seriously doubted that was the case.

Ballantine breathed out a laugh. 'Let's just say he made his point very clear.'

*Oh God.*

I grimaced. 'I'm so sorry.'

'So, at a guess, I'm thinking he would not be very happy to know you're up here talking to me.'

I watched on as our meals were delivered to our table, and interestingly enough, not by Lucy.

'Um, no, he wouldn't.'

I felt bad. I felt bad that Ballantine was probably being judged for leading the sweet, innocent farm girl astray, but I had discovered that anytime I was around Ballantine, I wanted to be anything but sweet or innocent. Maybe he brought out that side of me? It was a side I had never met before and it scared me. Actually, it excited me.

Ballantine sat down in Dean's chair, setting his elbows on the armrests and linking his fingers together. 'So, am I to be your dirty little secret then?' he asked, a devious spark in his eyes as he swivelled from side to side in what was like a chair fit for a Bond villain.

'Yeah. You don't mind, do you?' I teased.

'Ignore me by day and have your way with me by night?'

'It doesn't have to be like that.'

'What way can it be then? Tell me.'

Once again I glanced towards the screen. I studied the serious lines of my uncle's face as he salted his plate, the scornful way Amanda ignored her parents by playing on her phone, the way Aunty Karen chatted, oblivious to everything that surrounded her. How could I fit Ballantine into my life? I didn't want Uncle Peter watching me like a hawk or handing down ground rules so early on; I didn't want Amanda to blackmail me or use my time with Ballantine as a bartering tool. Sweet Aunty Karen would probably be quite carefree and liberal about it all, but I'd give her less than a minute until she accidentally name-dropped Ballantine to my mum and then it would be game over. As much as I liked to think I had some control over my life, I really didn't. I had one more year to ride out after this one – my last year of school – and then I was free, free to do and *be* with anyone I wanted. The very thought gave me hope.

My silence pretty much answered Ballantine's question.

'See? It's the way it has to be.'

As much as I wanted to shout from the rooftops and be public and loved-up like Amanda and Boon were, I understood that we could never be like that; well, not right now anyway.

'How depressing.' I sighed, looking down at Ballantine. 'Living a lie.'

Ballantine smiled broadly. 'Believe me, there will be nothing depressing about it.'

I turned my back to the screens and leant against the lip of the desk. 'So you'll make it worth my while then? You know us country girls get bored very easily.'

Ballantine stood from his seat, placing his hands on either side of my hips, caging me in as he looked down at me with a cocky grin. 'I'll make it worth your while,' he whispered against my mouth, before brushing his lips against mine, grazing my bottom lip playfully with his teeth, causing my insides to churn with excitement.

'Come on, you better go. Your dinner will be getting cold.'

'Let me guess: you leave, then I leave?'

'See, this is going to be easy,' he said, backing away to the door. 'Watch the bar screen and as soon as I'm around it, head out.'

I straightened. 'Luke.'

He paused midway out the door, his eyes flashing with a heated interest, the same way they always did when I called him by his first name. I would have to remember that.

'Thanks for my picture.'

Something happened then. It was an unexpected shyness I had never seen in him before, as a boyish grin spread across his face. 'No worries.'

'Hey, do you want to try something different next week?' I asked. 'Do you want to try actually having a lunchtime instead of detention? I hear it's pretty good.'

Ballantine laughed, warm and tender, until his eyes dipped to my t-shirt; it served as a trigger to wipe away his smile. He had said he believed that there was nothing going on between me and Dean, but the sudden coldness that swept over him said otherwise. I stepped forward, tilting my head to get into his line of vision, bringing him back to me. He blinked in confusion, which softened the hard lines of his face.

'It's you, Ballantine. It's always been you,' I said, taking his hand. 'You have to ignore the rumours because that's exactly what they are: rumours.'

Ballantine's eyes ticked over my face, wide and taken aback. 'I trust you, Lex.'

I gave him a small, sad smile. 'I don't think you do.'

Ballantine stared down to where our hands joined, thinking for the longest time. 'I trust you,' he said, lifting his eyes to mine. 'It's him I don't trust.'

Ballantine had never hidden his disdain for his boss. I'd seen Dean the boss. He didn't say much to his staff, and he ran the place with almost military precision. Had he and Ballantine fought over the way he was treated? I knew he wasn't happy. Surely Paradise City was big enough for Ballantine to find employment somewhere else. There was nothing between Dean and me. Ballantine had to know that.

'Well, you're going to have to get over it,' I said in frustration. 'You can't go living your life filled with all this anger towards him. Stop working with him, find a new job, a new hangout. Sever the bloody cord. Simple!'

A small smile curved the corner of his mouth. 'Simple,' he repeated.

'Simple.' I nodded with a sense of finality.

'If only it was that simple.'

Now I was getting mad – mad and more frustrated – at the stubborn, gorgeous boy who stood before me. I folded my arms. 'And it's not, because?'

He sighed. 'Because even if I quit my job, found a new haunt, or moved towns, it wouldn't change things.'

'Why wouldn't it?'

Ballantine's expression sobered as his dark, serious eyes looked down into mine. 'Because he'll always be my brother.'

•

*Whaaaaat?* Brothers? They were *brothers*?

With nothing more than a peck on the forehead and a devious little smile, Ballantine had dropped the bombshell and left me in Dean's office – no, wait, make that left me in his *brother's* office – mouth agape, stunned.

*What the hell?*

I had no real recollection of going down the stairs; all I recalled was turning my dazed expression towards Dean as I walked past him at the bar where he was pouring a drink for a thirsty patron.

*Fucking brothers?*

I slid back into my seat, wearing my oversized Wipe Out Bar t-shirt. My heart sank as I took in the soggy plate before me. Parmi and what chips were left. I threw a knowing look to Amanda, who refused to look my way.

'That's better,' said Aunty Karen.

I pulled at the baggy tee. 'Yep! I'm a local now.'

But not local enough, it seemed, to be in the know about certain facts . . . they were brothers? How had this not been mentioned? I felt like a giant mug. I remembered Laura's eagerness to use Dean to make Ballantine jealous, but she never mentioned they were brothers.

I tried to be upbeat and cheerful, but after the Ballantine bombshell, well, I was a bit distracted.

'You're not hungry?' asked Uncle Peter.

It was then that I realised that all of their plates were empty, and I was the one who was holding everyone up.

'I just don't feel very well.' It wasn't a complete lie.

'Oh, sweetheart, I hope you're not letting what happened get to you?' Aunty Karen responded.

'Yeah. No need to cry over spilt raspberry. Jesus!' added Amanda, rather unsympathetically.

'No, it's not that; I just have a really bad headache.' Okay, so that was a lie.

'Well, we can go if you want?' suggested Aunty Karen.

'What! And miss dessert?' said Amanda, pouting like a small child.

'There's ice-cream at home.' Aunty Karen was grabbing her bag, ready to move, and Uncle Peter glanced at his watch. They had fulfilled their duty in pacifying us teen-agers in a place they would otherwise not step foot in, so their eagerness to leave was not a surprise. I was relieved I wasn't going to be forced to eat my food, as I really just wanted to get out of there. The only one who was put out was Amanda.

'So precious Lexie wants to go home so we go home? Typical,' she scoffed.

'Amanda, we'd do the same if you felt unwell,' said Aunty Karen.

'Maybe it's just the place that's given Lexie bad vibes. What do you think, Dad?'

She was teetering on the edge of hinting at something more when Uncle Peter cut her a dark look, one that had her instantly falling quiet and storming out in front of us.

Aunty Karen sighed. 'I don't know what's wrong with that girl lately.'

Uncle Peter guided Aunty Karen out of the bistro, placing a hand on the small of her back while I lingered behind, hoping to catch a glimpse of the bar. I wanted to make eye contact with Dean before we left, but he was nowhere to be seen. I was never more curious than now to look at Dean, really look at him, and see if I could detect any kind of family resemblance between the two of them.

I looked to the office upstairs, wondering if he was watching us leave. Before I knew it, our bill was paid and we were out the door, weaving down the arcade.

I blew out a long, steadying breath. Uncle Peter and Aunty Karen let go of their hand holding so I could pass them and walk in front with Amanda.

'What's wrong? Did you forget to give ol' Deano a kiss goodbye?' Amanda teased.

My head snapped around to her. 'I didn't know Ballantine and Dean were brothers.'

Amanda scoffed. 'Yeah, duh . . . everyone knows that.'

'They look nothing alike, they don't even have the same last name.'

*I mean, how the hell was a girl to know?*

Amanda rolled her eyes. 'Different dads, idiot. Jesus, and they put you in accelerated classes?'

'Shut up,' I said, glowering at her. I forged forward, hating the fact that home meant more time spent with her and her moods. It was like living with a child, a spoilt child. Seriously, had my aunty and uncle ever thought about boarding school? Or a convent or something? A Tibetan monastery where she would have to take a vow of silence? It would be considered a community service.

At least by the time we got home, I could excuse myself in a believable enough way that had me fake-pop some Panadol and go to bed, while Amanda stuffed her face with ice-cream. I lay on my bed, unfolding the drawing that Ballantine had created. The inky magical world he had built made me smile, calming me with the knowledge that we were good, that we would make the effort to be together, even if we had to fly under the radar. I regretted not asking him what he was doing on the weekend, or where he would be, at least. I really didn't want to have to hang out with Amanda socially if I could help it. Still, if it meant seeing Ballantine, I would suck it up.

I folded the paper and stuck it inside my pillowcase, covering myself with the doona, and wondered if I would get a knock on my window tonight or tomorrow night. When I started to drift off to sleep I smiled, thinking about the events of the day. From the way Ballantine had made me feel, it was no wonder I was exhausted. Then, inevitably, I thought back to Dean's office and Ballantine's revelation and it played over and over in my mind.

# Chapter Forty-Three

Time flies when you're ignoring someone . . . or at least trying to.

With seemingly little drama – a.k.a. no detentions to speak of – aside from a hundred lines of 'I will not forget to turn up to detention', no really serious retribution for skipping that Friday's detention occurred. It was a pretty lenient punishment from the easy-going, softly spoken art teacher, Miss Parker, and it certainly made for a better start to the week. A week that quickly bled into another, and before I knew it weeks had passed and I wasn't known as the new delinquent kid on the block. Sure enough, even the rumours of Dean and me subsided, helped by Gemma and Boppo hooking up. All was well with the world and I welcomed the change with open arms. I never thought I would be so deliriously happy to have studying for end-of-year exams as my main worry.

I was just enjoying the drama-less aspect of my life, which meant no Dean Saville, and no Wipe Out Bar. I was keeping out of trouble and staying focused, except when Ballantine was anywhere in my eyeline, then all rational, logical thought seemed to fly out of my head. Aside from Dean, and a suspicious Uncle Peter, Laura was the only other soul who knew about Ballantine and me, and therefore the only person I could sigh and share things with, important things like:

'Did you see Ballantine's new sunglasses? They really suit him, don't you think?'

'Did you see the way Ballantine put Boon in his place about that history assignment?'

'Did you see how Ballantine shot that empty can in the bin from like fifty metres away, as if it were nothing.'

'Did you see how Ballantine –'

'Lexie, shut up!' Laura snapped one day.

It took me by surprise, and I almost tripped down the path. I blinked down at her.

'Shut up?'

'Yes! Please shut up. All we ever talk about is Ballantine. Ballantine parked his car under the shade of a tree; Ballantine smells incredible; Ballantine has the heart of a poet and the grace of an earthbound angel.'

'Okay, I never said that,' I corrected.

'You might as well have. It's all you talk about. Ballantine, Ballantine, Ballantine!'

I didn't know what to say. How could I deny it? I probably didn't speak about much else – okay, anything else, ever – but . . . Oh God, I had turned into one of those girls, the ones that I had always despised. The revelation was not a good one.

Laura took in a calming breath. 'You know, maybe if you two just acted like normal people who like each other instead of all this bloody cloak-and-dagger stuff then you wouldn't have to share so much with me.'

'But it's going so well, flying under the radar. You've seen how Gemma and Boppo have been copping it; they can't go anywhere or do anything without a running commentary.'

Laura rolled her eyes. 'It would die down and then something else would come up and you'd be old news.'

'Yeah, well. No-one has a cousin like Amanda, or an Uncle Peter to deal with.'

'They probably don't have a best friend like Laura either who is seriously contemplating climbing a bell tower if we don't start talking about normal stuff, like what are you wearing to the social next week?'

My eyes lit up; now that was something worthy of discussion. The school social was next Friday, my first social ever, and I could almost jump out of my skin I was so excited. It was going to be a bittersweet way to end the school year. As much as I tried not to think about it the term was drawing to a close. Everything was moving so fast and the Year Twelves were finishing up their last week. Exams were now finished for all seniors so the social was a big deal for more than one reason. It was a funny feeling to be looking forward to and dreading something at the same time. I had never hated being in Year Eleven more and for the life of me I couldn't think beyond that, to next year, a year with no Ballantine, no Boon, even no Amanda. Every time it popped into my mind I had to quickly shake it from my thoughts.

'I have no idea. Do you want to go down to Arcadia next week sometime and we'll go shopping?'

'What about now? We could hit Priceline and get some fake tan for your legs.'

'Okay, firstly, I am going to pretend I am not offended by that offer, and secondly, I can't tonight.'

'Oh, and pray tell, why not tonight?'

'I would tell you but you'd probably climb a bell tower,' I said tilting my head.

'Don't tell me you two are doing something normal, or are you wearing disguises?'

'Nope, we're not going anywhere public. Ballantine isn't working so I'm going to watch some movies at his place.'

Laura's expression darkened. 'And let me guess . . .'

'Can you please, please cover for me?' I clasped my hands under my chin in prayer.

'Do you promise not to give me the rundown tomorrow about how cute Ballantine was at loading the DVD player?' she said, curving her brow in amusement.

'I swear, you will not even know what we watched, what we ate . . . nothing.'

'Unless it's sexy in nature, I don't want to know anything.'

'Well, you are definitely not knowing any of that,' I said.

'Aw, come on, you are so cagey about that stuff. Best friends tell each other everything; come on, how big is he?'

'Laura!' I snapped, looking around the suburban tree-lined street we were walking along, hoping there wasn't a stray grandmother watering her garden within earshot.

'Come on, I want details!' She bounced on the balls of her feet alongside me.

'Well, he's a great kisser.'

'And?'

'And that's all you're getting,' I said with a laugh.

The truth was, after the common room and the occasional stolen make-out session, there had been no sexy times to speak of. We were both hoping to rectify that tonight, and because of the sexy wink Ballantine had given me as he'd passed me going out the school gate, I suddenly felt nervous.

'Unless you haven't done the deed there is no excuse not to tell.'

I fell silent, concentrating on the cracks in the pavement as we walked.

'Oh my God. You haven't done it?'

'Laura,' I warned.

'You and Ballantine haven't made the beast with two backs?' She looked aghast.

'That's none of your business.'

'Listen, Lexie. I'm sorry, I just thought that you, well . . . it's Ballantine.'

I stopped, spinning around to face her. 'And what? He's a horndog surfer who usually beds every girl he sees?'

'Well, yeah, kind of. Don't get me wrong. I'm just surprised, that's all.'

Laura's words only made me feel worse.

We hadn't really spoken about sex with each other. Maybe he wasn't as interested as I thought he was? Why was he waiting? Was I going to end up dying a virgin?

'Well, how about you stop worrying about it? If you're not interested in the mundane then don't sweat it over anything else.' I stormed ahead, wanting to leave Laura and the conversation behind.

'Lexie, wait!' Laura grabbed my arm, pulling me up short.

'I'm sorry, really. You're right, it's none of my business and I have no right to pry.'

I nodded. 'Okay.'

'Can I just offer some words of advice? As a friend.'

I let my silence urge her on.

'I don't know how things are in Red Hill, but here in PC, things move a lot faster. You know boys will only hold hands for so long, and boys get bored . . . and then the new girl comes along and –'

'What are you saying? If I don't seal the deal with Ballantine his eyes might wander elsewhere?'

'Well, that's kind of what happened with Lucy Fell.' Laura cringed.

My blood ran cold, which was a normal reaction to anything to do with Lucy, but to do with Ballantine *and* Lucy, it made my stomach turn as well. I could have guessed from what had happened at the bus stop, and from Lucy's particular hatred of me that it was because they did share a past. I just wasn't sure it was a past I needed to know about.

Laura stepped forward, tilting her head to grab my attention. 'Lexie, you have . . . done it before, right?'

Okay, now I *definitely* wanted to leave this conversation well and truly behind.

'Look, I've got to go and get ready, so I'll see you later,' I said quickly, turning and walking fast. I might be able to look Laura in the eye and confess that Ballantine and I hadn't 'done it yet' but I drew the line at telling her I was a virgin. Although, by the way I was running away from her, I was thinking she would have guessed. And now, instead of looking forward to our movie night, I was bloody well dreading it.

# Chapter Forty-Four

'd made up my mind.

After tonight I was no longer going to be a virgin. Ballantine would not get bored with me and I would not be the only freak at Paradise High that still held her V-plates. I had wanted to come here for experiences, and it didn't get any more real than this.

The warm wind made my eyes water. I had to continually blink my vision clear as I ran down the long concrete footpath, mindful not to scratch myself along the less manicured fence lines where bushes invaded the walkway. For the first time ever, I turned into Ballantine's street. I steadied into a slower jog, attempting to gather my breath. I paused for a moment, leaning over with my hands on my knees, breathing in through my nose and out through my mouth. Wow, I was so impossibly unfit; still, the adrenalin that was coursing through my body carried me on and towards a large, two-storey home on the right, with a silver Lexus parked in the drive. Number fourteen. Just like he had said. I had hoped that Ballantine would be waiting out the front for me, but he was nowhere in sight.

*Crap!*

I crossed the road, making my way towards Ballantine's house, anxiety growing with each step. Maybe I was pushing my luck? What was I thinking? After the promise I'd made to my uncle about staying away, here I was at Ballantine's house, under the guise of watching movies with Laura, having raided Amanda's jewellery box for a condom.

*I'm turning back.*

I made that decision as soon as I reached the letterbox with number fourteen on it. That was too much of a reality check for me and just as I was about to turn, I felt something grab my arm and pull me into the thick of a bush. I screamed, but only a muffled yelp managed to escape as a hand clamped across my mouth. I struggled against the iron grip, my heart racing, my legs working to kick out as I tried without much success to break free.

'Lexie, it's me.' A voice laughed in my ear, shaking me to my senses. It was then that I felt the grip around my wrists loosen enough for me to spin around to see the darkened silhouette of a figure I would recognise anywhere. I breathed out in relief as I threw my arms around his shoulders and buried my face into the hollow of his neck.

*I don't want him to get bored. I don't want him to be with anyone but me.*

I had one more week until school was over, and then I'd be heading back to Red Hill. I couldn't even stomach the thought.

He seemed surprised at first by the force that I used to wrap myself around him, but then I slowly felt his arms circle around me, enclosing me in the sweet-smelling warmth of his body. I was so desperate to be in this place, to be in these arms, I never wanted to leave. I was completely happy in the shadows with this boy who I had been enamoured with from the first moment I saw him – also in the shadows. Ironic? As happy as I was, I could still feel a tightness in my chest, a lingering feeling that this was the edge of goodbye. This is why I had come here, this is what had led me into the night, consequences be damned. I had to know, had to experience the very thing that drove me to want to come to Paradise City. The final week of school was like a ticking time bomb; once it was over, what then? I had to give him something that would have him coming back for more.

In such a short time, with the ups, the downs and all the untruths, I had managed to experience so many things, things that both excited me and terrified me. It was the same feeling I had now being in Ballantine's arms.

'So what are you doing lurking around my neighbour-hood? Stop being so creepy.'

'Creepy?'

'Yeah, besides, my bedroom's upstairs, so there'll be no knocking on my bedroom window. You'd best leave me to the late-night house calls.'

'Do you share a room?' I asked.

'No.'

'Well, there you go; I think your upstairs bedroom trumps my downstairs room-share.'

Ballantine tilted his head. 'Lexie Atkinson, are you trying to get into my bedroom?'

I could feel the heat flush my cheeks as I let my arms fall from him. 'No! I'm just saying that if I had a choice I would sooner –'

'Relax,' he said with a laugh. 'Do you want to hear something crazy?' He stepped backwards and led me out of the bushes. 'At my house, we use the front door.'

•

My anxiety lessened a bit when Ballantine moved towards the back of the house; he almost seemed nervous himself as he paused by the door at the very end of the hallway, giving me a small smile.

We entered a large rumpus room that was designed as a home theatre. With its large, reclining suede couches, an enormous television, a coffee table set up with bowls of popcorn, lollies and chocolate, as far as a secret rendezvous went this was pretty spectacular.

My ear-to-ear grin probably said as much. 'This is amazing.'

'You approve?'

'Ah, yeah!' I said, making my way across the room to plonk myself onto a seat, then settling into the comfy contours of the soft cushioning, all my worries instantly melting away.

Ballantine appeared beside me. 'Here, check it out.' He pulled a lever on the side of my chair that flung my legs up and my body backwards; I squealed at the unexpectedness of it.

'S–sorry,' Ballantine said through a fit of laughter, which only added to my giggles as I tried to get over the shock of the Transformer-esque couch.

'This is dangerous,' I said, trying to adjust my position. 'Seriously, you need a licence to drive this thing.'

Ballantine tried to shift the lever and press down on my footrest to get me back into position, but it wasn't too easy because he was laughing so hard.

'Well, someone sounds like they're having a good time,' came a voice from the doorway.

Ballantine stood, taking his weight from pushing my footrest down; I flung backwards again with a yelp.

'Oh, shit. Sorry, Lex.' He grabbed my hand and helped me scramble my way – rather inelegantly – out of the chair, helping me stand to face the voice, the friendly, feminine voice of the bemused-looking woman standing in the doorway with a drink tray.

'Don't mind me, I just thought you might be thirsty.'

'Ah, yeah. Thanks, Mum,' Ballantine said, rubbing the back of his neck and grimacing. 'Just, um, put them down there.'

'Oh, don't look so worried, Luke, I'm not staying,' she said with a knowing little smile at her son's embarrassment.

All I could think of when I looked at Ballantine's mum was how he must have taken after his dad. She had shoulder-length, blonde hair, with big blue eyes, and a bold shade of red lippy that she was really pulling off. Her skin was fair, and she wore beige Capri pants and a white linen top. She was, in a word, classy.

She placed the clinking tray down next to the popcorn before straightening and turning the full weight of her friendly blues on me. 'You must be Lexie,' she said, stepping forward and taking my hand. 'It's so lovely to meet you. I've heard so much about you.'

'Muuum,' Ballantine groaned.

'What? I want to meet the girl who inspires my son to go to school every day.'

Ballantine pinched the bridge of his nose as if summoning strength.

'For a boy who went from wagging every other day to now having perfect attendance, I am one very happy mother.'

'Mum, we've got to make a start on these movies.'

'Okay, okay. I'm out of here. Nice to meet you, Lexie.'

'Nice to meet you, too,' I said, as Ballantine ushered her to the door.

'Thanks, Mum.'

She pinched his cheek, deliberately embarrassing him. 'You're welcome.'

•

The room was plunged into darkness, true theatre-style. There were even drink holders in the couch . . . drink holders!

*So fancy.*

The light and movement from the screen danced in front of us, illuminating Ballantine's transfixed face, which I found myself watching more than the movie. My elbow was pressed next to his on the armrest; the warm skin-to-skin contact did strange things to me. I found it hard to concentrate, and all I could do was think about the hot boy next to me: the rise and fall of his chest, his perfectly proportioned profile, and his ludicrously good-looking bone structure. I could hardly believe I was sitting here with him. Just Ballantine and me.

The couch was great, cosy, comfy, but there was one irritating factor that I caught onto pretty quickly: those fancy drink holders that folded down out of the couch acted as a barrier between us, making that elbow press over time more and more frustrating. It was, like, so close yet so far. And then of course I reminded myself –

*Just watch the damn movie, Lexie.*

I'd just settled down and resigned myself to the idea that I would at least try to concentrate, when Ballantine moved. 'Back in a minute,' he said, leaning over.

He made his way to the door, closing it behind him and leaving me to watch a convoy get blown up after the hero smugly delivered some witty catchphrase. Next movie will be my choice, I thought. *Pretty Woman* or something. It was only fair.

By the time Ballantine returned I was actually starting to understand what was happening in the movie. Some guy had kidnapped the hero's daughter, hero was pissed off and started to blow things up – surely there was a better way to deal with the situation – but apparently the hero was a trained marine in another life so looked like he just wanted to cut some corners. Fair enough.

Just as it looked like the hero was about to get ambushed by the villain's henchmen, the screen went black, and the room was plunged into darkness. For a moment I thought the power had gone out, but then I saw the darkened silhouette of Ballantine with the remote control in his hand, then heard him put it on the table.

'And they all lived happily ever after,' he said, grabbing for another remote and adjusting the room into a very delicate low light. Moving next to take the drinks out of the holders and place them on the table, he flipped the impressive feature back into place and returned it once more to a couch.

Ballantine sat next to me with no annoying divider between us, just Ballantine and me.

# Chapter Forty-Five

This was it. This was what I wanted.

I didn't want Ballantine to get bored; I didn't want to be the mousy, prudish farm girl. I was going to take control and now that we weren't on a sandy beach, or wedged in an alcove of the Year Twelve common room, now that we were at Ballantine's home, it seemed right. Ballantine moved to kiss me first, slowly, gently teasing with his soft lips. He cupped the edge of my neck, tilting my head to gain better access to my mouth, but I wanted more. I placed my hand against his chest, pushing him back into the couch, lifting my leg over to straddle him. 'Where are your parents?' I breathed past my kisses.

'Asleep,' he whispered, as he hitched the edge of my denim mini over my hips so I could sink down more snugly on his lap. I felt the heavy press of him against my now damp knickers. Would this ever be enough? This feeling? I crossed my arms, peeling my top up and over my head with Ballantine's help, letting it fall to the side. Between tongue, teeth nips and moans, we feasted desperately on one another, full with the need to release and enjoy each other's bodies. Ballantine had fulfilled me in the common room all those weeks ago, and now I finally had the chance to do the same for him. I didn't let the voices in my head or the knots of anxiety in my stomach control me. I just wanted to get lost in his touch, engulfed by the pleasure I was feeling as I ground my hips against him.

Ballantine pulled down my bra, baring me to the light and his lips, as he grabbed and pressed the tip of my breast into his mouth, and then moved to taste the other. It was the sexiest thing I had ever seen, running my hands through his hair as he groaned, pressing his head into me. I could feel myself building, my hips were grinding harder, faster. I opened my eyes, catching our reflection in the mirrored cabinet across from us. I didn't recognise myself – wanton, needy, desperate.

'Don't come,' Ballantine whispered against my skin, as if I had a choice in the matter as his fingers dug into my hips, trying to stem my movement. Giving up the battle, he moved, flipping me onto my back on the couch. I could have cried if he hadn't followed me down, filling my mouth with his hot tongue to sate my need. This was it, he was going to take my virginity. There was no going back and I didn't want to. This felt so good. So right. I felt Ballantine hook his fingers into the elastic of my underwear, edging them down until I lifted for him so he could slide them down over my thighs and off completely. My skirt was all twisted and hitched up to my belly button, which meant I was exposing myself entirely to him; his eyes raked over my body, his chest was heaving as his dark eyes rested on the most intimate part of me. He leant back, grabbing my legs, hooking one over his shoulder. I readied myself for him to undo his zipper, but instead, he bent down and kissed my belly button, eliciting a shocked gasp at the unexpectedness of it. He glanced up, flashing me a knowing little smirk.

'If that's how you react to your belly button being kissed, I can't wait to see what you do next.'

And before I could question him further, he lowered his head, kissing a slow, agonising trail, down . . . down, kissing me in a place I would never have thought I could possibly give to someone, but I gave it to him. He pushed my thighs open, my hands flew up to entwine in his hair, urging him to go deeper with his tongue . . . and he obliged. I was a writhing, panting mess, arching into him. I had thought I had felt the throes of pleasure by his clever, wicked hands, but his mouth was something else, to the point of pushing away from him as I felt I couldn't take any more. My heart was racing. My skin had goosebumps all over. I could hardly get a breath. *Oh God.* His fingers dug into my legs, holding me in place and making me take the unrelenting pleasure of his mouth. Without the aid of his mouth or hand to quieten me down, I grabbed for a cushion, pressing it over my face as a muffled scream escaped me, until my body was spent and his mouth lifted from me. I lay there boneless, my chest heaving, my flushed face still hidden by the cushion, a cushion I didn't want to remove as my senses slowly returned to me and I realised what the hell had just happened.

'You okay?' he asked, lifting the cushion from my face and looking down on me. I wasn't the only one that was flushed – Ballantine looked most pleased.

And then it occurred to me, judging by the noises he had made as he'd made me come: Ballantine was all about making me happy, putting me first. Doing that time and time again, he'd probably lose interest and with that thought in mind, I bit my lip as I slowly sat up. Ballantine looked at me warily. 'Lex, you okay?'

I didn't want to speak; I didn't want to break my intent, so instead I showed him. I pushed him back into a seated position and slid to the floor between his legs; he never asked again. Instead, with a heated stare, he watched me as I held eye contact with him while I worked on the top button of his jeans, then the zip, pulling it slowly down. I had never done this before, and I had no idea what I was doing. I pulled him free from his pants, running my hands up and along the hard, smooth length of him. I revelled in the way his entire body tightened as I touched him. He felt so soft, yet he was so hard.

I laughed. 'If that's your reaction when I touch you, I can't wait to see what you do next.'

I took him in my mouth. Slowly and gently at first I tasted him, holding the base of him. I groaned when his hands threaded through my hair.

'Lexie,' he breathed, his head falling back against the couch as his hips involuntarily bucked. His hoarse voice guiding me through only excited me more as his hands on the back of me directed my speed. 'That's it, Lex, take me deeper, all the way.'

He wanted it faster so I went deliberately slowly, teasing the tip with a swirl of my tongue. I smiled up at him as he looked down on me like I was the devil, or maybe even an angel – it was hard to tell.

'You keep doing that and I'm going to come,' he breathed.

I hesitated a bit, not knowing whether to pull away now or keep going, so I let instinct take over and took him deep, drawing him in and hollowing my cheeks.

'Fuck me, I'm going to come.'

And just as I went to repeat the trail with my mouth once more, there was a knock on the rumpus room door and muffled voice spoke through.

'Lexie, you have a phone call.'

•

'Abort! Abort! You have to go home right now,' Laura's voice whispered down the phone.

By some act of God, there was a phone extension in the rumpus room. Ballantine yelled out to his mum that I would take the call in there. We madly scrambled to make ourselves decent; it was safe to say that the close call took ten years off our lives.

'What are you talking about?' I snapped, flustered and still in shock, more so when Ballantine handed me my knickers with a smirk.

'Amanda is here hanging out with Boon.'

'So?'

'So, you're supposed be here, too. Yes? That's the cover story?'

*Shit!*

Ballantine stood beside me, looking on in concern, and mouthed, 'What?'

'Okay, no worries, I'm leaving now. Thanks for the heads-up,' I said, before hanging up the phone.

*Fucking Amanda.*

•

Ballantine walked me home, both of us smug in our silence and exchanging knowing sideways glances on how bloody lucky we were not to be discovered.

'You okay?' he asked for the hundredth time.

I laughed. 'Never been better.' And I did feel good. Liberated somehow. Proud of myself for being able to elicit such a raw response from Ballantine.

A response that had seemed to please him.

When we said our goodnights in the shadow of the neighbour's tree, Ballantine looked down on me, tracing my bottom lip with his thumb; the look and his touch felt so tender, like there was something different to us than there had been before. I grasped the hand at my face and turned his palm up to the sky, highlighting the lines underneath the streetlight we stood near, the same one that shone through my bedroom window. I was studying the braided strips of leather bound around his wrist when I noticed something of interest. There, underneath the knotted threads that had slipped down his wrist, was a marking. I lifted his arm to the light and gazed in amazed wonder.

'I didn't know you had a tattoo,' I gasped.

Hidden beneath the bracelets on the inside of his wrist was a tattoo of the sun; it was something I couldn't believe I had missed. Even if not openly on display, seeing it now for the first time was like seeing Ballantine for the first time.

I smiled, looking up at him. 'How appropriate,' I said.

'What? That it's black and twisted?'

I rolled my eyes at his reference to the blackened ink. 'You are the sun, Luke. To me, you are all the things Paradise City is about.'

'Ha! It depends on your definition of what Paradise City is; some might not think that a compliment.'

'Well, I can only tell you what my definition is,' I said, lacing my fingers with his.

'Oh, yeah? What's that?' he asked, cocking his brow.

'Warm. No, make that hot!' I grinned. 'Unpredictable, exciting, beautiful . . . life-changing.'

Ballantine's face sobered. I worried I might have gone too far, but when he lowered his head to kiss me sweetly on the lips, I knew I hadn't.

He smiled, as he backed away. 'Now that is one hell of a character reference,' he said, winking at me. 'Goodnight, Lexie Atkinson.'

'Goodnight, Luke Ballantine.'

I felt really bad that Luke hadn't finished. After all, in terms of orgasms, I was way ahead in the tally. It was so hard to reconcile the myth to the actual man. How could someone so cocky, so self-assured, so *experienced*, be happy to simply make me come without getting any for himself? It didn't make sense. For the times we had spent together and talked, I felt like I could see past the facade presented to the rest of the world. What Laura had seen in him was true. But, he was still a boy and must have a serious case of blue balls right about now. Yet he'd smiled and kissed me so sweetly. He was the definition of a paradox. I only hoped I would continue to be enough for him.

# Chapter Forty-Six

I didn't regret not sleeping with Ballantine. I had later asked myself the question: did I really want my first time to be on Ballantine's couch in his rumpus room? I didn't exactly expect for it to happen in a canopied, four-poster bed with candles or anything. In fact, I didn't know how or when it would happen, I just knew it would and really soon. At least, that's all I could think about, morning, noon and night. If I wasn't obsessing about every aspect of all the wicked things we had done, then I was daydreaming about Ballantine and when I would get the chance to do it all again. Flying under the radar was getting more difficult to maintain. The more I kept away from Ballantine the more brazen he seemed to become. Deliberately standing behind me in the canteen line, albeit minding his own business, but I could still feel the warmth of his breath on the back of my neck. He stood so close. Or how he would brush past me in the corridor with a knowing wink that would make me blush. I even went as far as pretending I wanted to learn how to surf after school. It seemed like a legitimate way to spend time with each other.

*Desperate times called for desperate measures.*

We stood away from the others down the beach a little but still in view. Ballantine let his board fall to the sand, squinting against the sun with a broad smile.

'What?' I asked, wondering what he found so amusing.

'You're so pale,' he said with a laugh, his eyes wandering over the pink-and-white striped bikini I wore.

'I'm not that pale,' I said, frowning at my shoulders and examining my lily-white legs.

Yeah, okay, standing next to Ballantine, I looked like a milk bottle.

'Shut up!' I snapped, trying to disguise my smile.

Ballantine chuckled, moving to stand beside me, clearing his throat. 'Okay, you see this line here?' He pointed to the board. 'You want this line going right down the centre of your body; your toes should be touching the back here. That's called the sweet spot.'

'Oh, I like the sound of that,' I said, lying face down on the board, smiling up at him.

'Settle down,' he said, trying not to smile as he kneeled in front of me. 'All right, when a big wave comes I want you to pop up. Now I'm going to show you four steps. You're going to put your hands down right next to your chest, push all the way up, go back to your knees, bringing your front foot forward.'

I moved in every position he described, concentrating intently.

'Now your back foot's already back there so we're going to leave it there, because you're going to stand up on it. All right, stand up.'

I stood a little shakily on the board that rocked on the uneven sand. Ballantine stood to move next to me. 'Okay, stand exactly where you are. You see this line? You want

this line to go down the middle of the arches of your feet.'
He placed his hands on my waist, guiding me over the line.

'Now bend your knees, arms out like a gnarly surfer dude
and shoot the waves screaming "Cowabungaaaaaa".'

Through fits of laughter and trying not to fall off the
board, I screamed, 'Cowabungaaaaaaa!'

'*Yeah!*' Ballantine clapped, laughing and moving to high-
five me. By now, the others were looking at us as if we were a
pair of freaks, probably not helped by the double thumbs-up
I gave them. Yeah, so I was excited. Sue me.

'Very good. Okay, in the water.'

My head snapped around, my laughter quickly dying.
'What?' I asked, my eyes wide with fear.

'You didn't think that would be it, did you?'

'Umm, yeah, kind of.'

'Lexie, Lexie, Lexie,' he said, shaking his head. 'If you're
with me, it's nothing but all the way.'

Well, that had my blood pumping.

I curved my brow with interest. 'Are we still talking about
surfing?'

Ballantine laughed, like really, really laughed. 'Bloody hell,
Atkinson. Get your mind out of the gutter, we have waves to
ride.' Even though he said that while laughing, I could see
the definite lusty interest my comment had created.

*Does he want that too?*

In some ways, I wasn't sure. But then he would look at
me like that and I would melt a little bit more.

•

The next day marked so many things: the last day of school
for the Year Twelves (yeah, I didn't want to think about
that), and my parents arriving to take me back to Red Hole

for the summer holidays (yeah, I *definitely* didn't want to think about that). I was completely and utterly miserable at the very thought of being taken home for 'family' time. I had tomorrow night for it all to count, to tell Ballantine how I felt about him, to show him what he meant to me, that he was the one, the one I wanted to give my all to. We hadn't been able to have any decent alone time together since the night we nearly got caught. Tomorrow night had to be the night; only then could I go back to Red Hill for Christmas and feel as though I had something to come back to in the New Year – finish off Year Twelve and come back to Ballantine. I felt all giddy inside just at the thought of such a future. Me, Ballantine, and Paradise City.

My thongs made suction cup sounds against the glossed tiles as I squelched a path to the bathroom, blissfully singing the Easybeats' 'Friday on my Mind'. My hair was a matted heap of salty tendrils. I marvelled at the fact that, yes, I had stood up on a real-life surfboard (for two point five seconds) and secondly, I had lived to tell the tale. I had surfed! I was as good as a local now. Red Hole was a distant memory, I thought, towelling my hair dry as I pushed through the bathroom door, flinching at the unexpected sight of Amanda at the sink.

'Bloody hell! You scared me,' I breathed, clutching my heart. 'Sorry, I didn't know you were –' I paused.

She tried to avert her gaze, wiping her cheeks, but the sniff kind of gave it away.

'What's wrong?'

I moved to stand beside her, taking in the streaks of mascara running down her cheeks and her bloodshot eyes; she was so upset she couldn't even swallow her sobs long enough to tell me to leave her alone. Instead, she did something that really scared me; she threw her arms around me and cried even harder.

'I'm in so much trouble, Lexie.'

My hands slowly lowered around her, feeling the shuddering vibrations of her frame. I caught the reflection of my troubled eyes.

*This is bad. Really, really bad.*

•

At first I thought she might have done a bank job, spilt red wine on Aunty Karen's Axminster carpet, scratched the Volvo, or maybe cheated on Boon? I was trying to equate what would mean 'trouble' to Amanda, and what would elicit a meltdown of such epic proportions. As I sat next to a very shaken Amanda, rubbing her back, waiting patiently, I gave her time, to the point that she literally had no more tears to cry. She leant forward, cupping her face in her hands for the longest time, so long that I thought she'd forgotten I was even there. Just when I was about to break the silence, she beat me to it.

She straightened, inhaling a deep shuddery breath. 'I think I'm pregnant.'

'Whaaaaaaaaat?' I breathed out.

Okay, that was probably not the reaction she needed. Her face crumpled.

'Oh, no, no. Please don't cry. I'm sorry.' I patted her quickly. Apparently she had a lot more tears to shed; hell, I even felt like donating to the cause. 'Are you sure?'

'Yes, no . . . I don't know.'

'Well, what makes you think that –'

'I'm late! Really late!'

Watching Amanda's despair was enough to make me want to wear a chastity belt and join a nunnery. I didn't need to know the details. They wouldn't change the fact.

'D– does Boon know?'

Amanda's eyes snapped up, wild and alarmed. 'No! God, no and if you tell *anyone* –'

'Hey,' I said, reaching for her hand. 'This is between you and me, okay?' I looked her dead in the eyes, refusing to break the contact until I felt with no ounce of uncertainty that she believed me. It took a long moment but she finally conceded, nodding her head.

I breathed deeply, rubbing my clammy palms on my thighs.

*Okay, think, Lexie, think!*

'All right, well, I have read a few *Cleo* magazines, so I think I am pretty much an expert in these situations so –'

'Lexie, please, now's not the time to be funny,' she said.

'I'm not, I'm deadly serious. We're going to have to go to a doctor, find out if –'

'NO! No way.'

'Okay, okay. But we need to know . . . for real. Okay?'

'I'm not going to a doctor, Lexie. No way.'

'All right, then, we have a plan B.'

'Plan B?' she asked, wiping her eyes.

'We'll get a pregnancy test, lock ourselves away while the parentals are out, and just find out. They're like ninety-nine point nine per cent accurate, right?'

'Oh God! I feel sick.' Amanda's face disappeared into her hands again. 'What if I am, Lexie, what will I do?'

'Let's cross that bridge when, and if, we come to it. Now, come on, we'll go and get a test and get this over with.'

I moved to stand but was stopped by Amanda's white-knuckled grip on my arm.

'No! I can't. What if someone sees me? Peter and Karen Burnsteen's daughter up the duff. Great,' she scoffed.

I canted my head, wondering how small bloody suburbia really was, but her fear was reasonable enough. She was fairly well known here.

'All right. Stay here, I'll go.'

Amanda's eyes flicked up. 'Really? You'd do that?'

I shrugged. 'It's not my preferred way to spend the afternoon, but that's what family's for, right?'

Amanda's chin trembled as more tears welled in her eyes. 'Thank you.'

My lips pressed into a thin line. 'No sweat.'

# Chapter Forty-Seven

had always wanted to go to the Imperial Shopping Centre in the heart of the central business district. A multi-level shopping mecca, a treasure trove of escalators, food courts and retail shops as far as the eye could see. It was only a fifteen-minute bus ride and just opposite the junction that led into Arcadia Lane. I was becoming quite familiar with my city surrounds. Sure, I had wanted to come here, to shop for a new bikini or get a pedicure perhaps, but I'd never imagined myself wandering into a chemist perusing the pregnancy test section. Somehow I had thought that by going to a bright, clean, classy chemist such as this one, the success rate for the test results would be more reliable. Even the assistants in the makeup section wore white coats. This was world class.

Normally I would be liberally spraying myself with a Dior perfume tester and checking out the sunglasses section, but today I was on a mission. I stalked through the aisles, declining the helpful queries from the shop girls and eventually found the section I needed. I wanted to do this fast, which meant scanning the section as fast as possible, spotting that magical wording: 'ninety-nine per cent accuracy', and that would do me. I grabbed a packet, holding it between my arm and my tummy. Eyes down, I walked a direct line to the back, thinking I must look like a shoplifter.

Mercifully there was no-one in my way as I hit the counter almost at a run, sliding the box towards the assistant and digging in my bag for money. 'Just this one, thanks,' I said.

The box slid away from me; the cash register sounded painfully loud as it rang up the total. I thumbed out a twenty and then paused, lifting my gaze with that uncertain feeling that something was wrong, very, very wrong.

'Lexie?'

My world dropped away, spinning and tumbling as the colour drained from my face. My unblinking eyes stared ahead as there, right in front of me, standing with the pregnancy test kit in her perfectly manicured hands, stood Ballantine's mum.

Her vibrant red lips parted in shock as her eyes flicked from me to the box and back again.

*Oh. My. God.*

Without a word, and without taking her horrified gaze away from me, she lowered the box to the counter.

*Say something, Lexie. SAY SOMETHING. Anything! Tell her it's not for you. Tell her.*

My inner voice screamed at me. *It* was always so logical and smart thinking; it was just a shame *I* wasn't. Instead, the girl who had been so brave, so noble to go in batting for her cousin, was about to do the most cowardly thing of all. Without a word, I slid over the twenty, grabbed the box and walked away, not looking back, not caring about the change, not caring about anything. I just wanted to die!

•

I ran. I ran so fast I thought I would be sick, or maybe that was just the feeling of my gut spasms. The look on Ballantine's mum's face flashed in my mind like a horror movie. Had I imagined what just happened? Seriously, of all the chemists in the entire world? It felt as though the gods were against me. First Lucy, now Mrs Ballantine. What's with that?

I finally slowed down, leaning against a building, running my hands through my hair and clenching my scalp, wanting to scream, pull my hair out – something.

I pressed my back against the brick wall, feeling defeated. I glanced around, envious of all the carefree skateboarders rolling up the arcade without a care in the world; it was when I blinked at the ice-creamery opposite that I realised where I had run to. I turned, frowning up at the illuminated sign of the Wipe Out Bar.

God, was Ballantine working? I had to get to him first, I thought, pushing off the wall and dodging my way through the crowd.

*Oh, please. Be working. Please be working.*

The bar was quiet save for a few couples dotted around eating. I clasped the edge of the bar, breathless, trying to gain some composure as Sherry glanced at me with little interest.

'Is Ballantine out the back?'

She shook her head. 'He's not on tonight.'

*Oh no-no-no-no . . .*

I tried to remain calm. 'Do you know when he's working next?'

Sherry shrugged.

I slammed my hand on the bar, frustrated to the very core of my being for not having asked him myself. I wanted to kick and scream and basically have a meltdown that would make Amanda look like a girl scout.

'Well, can I at least use your phone?'

'Sorry, business use only,' she said, raking over me with her dull eyes.

It was enough for me to see red.

I lifted my chin. 'Is Dean here?'

'No.'

'You sure about that?'

'Check for yourself.' Her eyes flicked up the staircase as if daring me to.

*Well, maybe I just would.*

I backed away from the bar, managing to give Sherry a parting filthy look as I stomped my way up to his office, a determined move I hoped would pay off. If she wouldn't let me use the phone I would go to the very person who just might. When I got to the top of the landing, I knocked in a series of thumps.

'Dean?' I called out, turning the handle to find it locked. I felt my heart sink. I didn't dare look down to where Sherry was no doubt watching me with her smug expression.

*I'll show her.*

I delved into my bag, searching for something to write on. I definitely didn't think ripping off a piece of the pregnancy test box was appropriate, so I settled for the back of a brochure that had a price list for manicures. I found a pen at the bottom of my bag, leant on the door, and started writing on a blank space on the paper. It was about time someone gave Dean a first-hand account of just how bloody unhelpful his staff could be.

*Dean,*
*I need to speak to you ASAP.*
*Lexie*

I printed my home number underneath, a seething rage bubbling beneath the surface – if I didn't get to Ballantine before his mum did I was going to kill Sherry. I slid the brochure under his door before heading back down the staircase, casting Sherry a departing death stare.

*Thanks for nothing.*

•

There was nothing I could do; over an hour had gone by since my disastrous run-in with Ballantine's mum, plenty of time for her to contact him, grill him about his knocked-up girlfriend, and then enrol him in military school in Alaska.

As the bus pulled away, I found myself at a crossroads: I could turn towards Ballantine's street and see if he was home, explain to him the funny story behind the whole thing and problem solved – well, except maybe for Amanda, who was now potentially not going to get off so lightly.

I bit my lip, looking down into the depths of my tote bag. Surely another ten minutes of waiting would be okay. I'd be quick, really quick, I thought, already making my way towards Ballantine's street at a run – the fastest run of my life. Hope pushed me forward, had me turning the corner and tearing up the concrete path with the sole intent of preventing impending disaster. But just as quickly, I came to a sliding halt. I could almost feel my heart explode inside my chest as I stared on in wide-eyed horror. There, across the street in Ballantine's driveway, was Ballantine's mum's car.

It was too late! I. Was. Screwed.

# Chapter Forty-Eight

I wanted Amanda to be pregnant with triplets. I wanted her to be walking down the aisle in the most scandalously arranged teenage wedding of the century. Instead, we stared down at the stick that sported a very clear minus sign.

Amanda checked the box for the hundredth time. 'Oh my God! I'm not pregnant, Lexie! I'm not pregnant!!' she screamed with elation, dancing around the room like she had been called down for *The Price is Right*.

She encircled me into a bone-crushing hug on the way. 'Oh, thank you! Thank you! Thank you, Lexie!'

I tried to smile, but I felt like a woman on the edge.

*All for nothing. It was all for nothing.*

I closed my eyes, breathing deeply, and summoning the patience to put up with Amanda, who was now spinning around the room like Julie-fucking-Andrews.

•

There was no word. Nothing. I had hoped that there might have been a phone call, or maybe a tap at my window in the middle of the night demanding an explanation, but nothing. After a sleepless night, the day lay before me with an epic number of new challenges. My parents would be here by lunchtime and as much as I had missed them and couldn't wait to see them, all I could think about was getting to Ballantine.

Amanda woke up in high spirits, chirping away and picking out her outfit for the last official day of school. She was so happy and carefree I just wanted to punch her in the face. 'Don't worry, Lexie, I won't water-bomb you,' she said, smiling at me in the reflection of her mirror as she smoothed down her hair.

'What?'

Amanda swivelled around in her chair. 'Today's muck-up day for the Year Twelves,' she said, her eyes alight with excitement. I sighed. I already had egg on my face; I really didn't need that to be literal.

•

The schoolyard vibe was filled with an electric buzz; everyone walked around with an air of guarded amusement, half expecting to be ambushed by a Year Twelve with a bag of flour or a water bomb.

There was no sign of anything untoward, which only built the anticipation. By recess I still hadn't seen Ballantine, but I tried not to panic because on the whole there were very few Year Twelves in sight and rumours began circulating that muck-up day had been cancelled. All this seemed semi-believable . . . until lunchtime hit.

The sound of screams and the thudding of feet along concrete paths rung out through the schoolyard. A stampede of squealing girls rounded a corner near the library. They ran, screamed and laughed as they blindly rubbed away the caked-on flour in their hair and smattered across their navy uniforms. Two Year Twelve boys dressed all in black with balaclavas to disguise their identity followed behind; they looked like ninjas and were only two of the many others who started infiltrating the school from all angles, dressed in identical outfits.

'Shit-shit-shit! Lexie, let's go.' Laura grabbed my arm, dragging me into motion as the ninjas closed in. As much as Amanda said she would leave me alone, that didn't account for anyone else, and Laura and I sprinted into action, only to run into a group shaking cans of whipped cream.

We screamed, turned on our heels and bolted towards the girls' toilets, thinking maybe we could find some kind of shelter there; unfortunately for us I didn't have telepathic abilities to communicate with Laura who kept running when I turned left. I skidded to a halt and watched on in horror as Laura, while looking back for me, ran into the direct path of a hooded Year Twelve, who grabbed her as another dumped a bag of flour smack-bang over her head, followed by an egg smashed on top.

'Boon! You dickhead, piss off!' Laura screamed and kicked her assailant who was most definitely Boon, not only completely obvious from his height, but also from his distinct muffled laughter. I couldn't help but find myself laughing at poor Laura who was now chasing after her brother, trying to attack him with the excess egg and flour she was dripping with. My humour was short-lived when I spotted a figure coming my way, with what looked like an industrial-strength water pistol in hand.

*Oh shit, oh shit.*

I turned to run the other way only to blindly slam into the chest of another Year Twelve who caught me in his grip. I was a goner. I attempted to pull myself free, but it was no use; the more I struggled the stronger the hold was, and as bad as flour, egg or cream might be, I was to suffer a far worse fate. I was being dragged into the girls' toilets.

*Oh my God, I was going to get flushed!*

Instead of any of the screaming, cowering girls that were hiding in the safety of the toilets coming to my aid, they scurried out like rats from a sinking ship.

Every man for themselves, I guess.

All I could do was put all my weight into the back of my heels as I continued to be dragged along.

'Please, please don't do this; you can do anything else, anything!' I screamed, as I was flung around like a rag doll to stand in front of him. Before I could let out another series of incoherent pleas, the boy in black before me peeled off his balaclava, revealing a beautiful, familiar face.

Ballantine.

A devious smile tilted the corner of his mouth as he fought to catch his breath. 'Anything?' he asked.

I didn't get a chance to answer as he leant down, taking my mouth in a hot, passionate kiss that ended all too soon.

'See you tonight,' he said, winking at me as he backed out of the toilets. He pulled the balaclava back in place, readying himself for war. I couldn't see his mouth but I could tell he was smiling when he glanced back at me. 'Stay here,' he said, his voice muffled through the black knit, before leaving me alone, standing in the middle of the girls' toilets in a flustered daze.

I lifted a shaky hand to my kiss-swollen lips.

He definitely didn't know.

# Chapter Forty-Nine

You would think that I would have been filled with relief on learning that Ballantine hadn't been ignoring me, or by the fact that his mum had obviously not confronted him, giving me a chance to explain what had happened with the pregnancy test disaster. Yeah, not so much. Aside from Ballantine's toe-curling kiss, I went around the rest of the day in a state of confusion, as the world around me was bombarded in eggs, flour, cream and water, turning students into walking pancakes. I couldn't help but be burdened with a much worse problem as my thoughts plagued me.

*Why hadn't she told him?*

•

Sure, I'd been lucky not to be attacked at school, but when it came to arriving home I was to face an ambush of a different kind.

Emotional parents!

Don't get me wrong, I welcomed the familiarity of my mum's arms wrapped around me and my dad's hideous jokes, but regardless of how glad I was to see them, their arrival started the clock ticking.

*Tick-tick-tick.*

Having already had the pleasure of completing my accelerated exams with the Year Twelves, it turned out that I was free to go. For the most part, my fellow Year Elevens were seething with jealousy that I got to start my holidays early; I, however, was less than thrilled.

*One night to make it count.*

I would explain everything to Ballantine and lose my V-plates once and for all. It was the perfect plan; only then could I feel better about the way I would leave Paradise City.

'School social?' piped up Dad. 'Surely you're not abandoning us to go to a school social.'

'It's the final one of the year,' I said, pacing in the lounge room, waiting for Laura to arrive.

'And this is what people wear to school socials, is it?' asked Dad, who was looking over my outfit with uncertainty.

'What?' I said. A suede brown mini with knee-high boots. What was wrong with that? It had taken me and Laura hours to find the perfect outfits.

'Oh, leave her alone, Rick. You look lovely, honey, just ignore him,' said Mum, but it was too late. The seed had been planted and I was already on edge. I was seriously contemplating getting changed when I heard the doorbell ring.

*Laura, thank God!*

I ran towards the front door, my boots clicking on the glossed tiles, never so relieved to be saved from my parents' running commentary. I ran so fast I overshot the door, sliding sideways rather inelegantly, barely saving myself from toppling over by latching onto the front door handle, and then whipping it open.

'Thank God you're he–' My words fell away as I stilled, my mouth agape as my eyes locked onto a dark figure on our doorstep.

Dean Saville.

Tall, dark and wicked, he flashed a wolfish grin as he flicked his Ray Bans up onto his head.

'W– what are you doing here?' I whispered, moving forward and closing the door behind me, before grabbing his arm like a small child and dragging him away from the window.

Dean looked down at me as if he was offended by the action. He glanced back towards the front door.

I pulled at his arm, drawing his attention back to me. 'Hey, what the hell?'

Dean's eyes narrowed; he went to speak but then paused and stepped back a little, taking in my outfit with interest.

'What?' I frowned, once again fidgeting under the scrutiny, cursing my skirt which I now realised was too short. 'Stop looking at me like that.'

Dean's eyes lifted. 'Like what?'

'Like you're judging me like a bitchy teenage girl would.'

Dean laughed, way too loud.

'Shhh.' I placed my finger to my mouth to emphasise the point. 'What's so funny?'

'Believe me, I was not looking at you that way,' he said, moving past me and picking a leaf absent-mindedly off one of the bushes near the porch.

I wanted to ask what way he was looking at me, but I really had to shut this down.

'Look, as much as I would love to chitchat . . .'

'So what's the occasion?'

'What?'

'Well, I'm guessing "come fuck me" boots aren't exactly casual after-school wear.'

I gasped, horrified. Which only seemed to amuse him all the more.

'Not that it's any of your business but I'm going to a school social, and you're making me late.'

Dean grinned. 'Wow, a school social. Good to see Paradise High has progressed.'

'Oh, right, and when did you graduate, Grandpa?'

'Grandpa?'

'That's right, I'm assuming you are Ballantine's *older* brother.' I folded my arms; it was now my turn to let my eyes roam over him in assessment.

Dean smiled slowly. 'The better brother.'

'I seriously doubt that.' My patience and time were running out. 'What do you want, Dean?' I sighed.

'You wanted to see me,' he said matter-of-factly.

'What?'

He reached into his back pocket and pulled out the folded brochure I had slid under his office door. Dean flicked it open; clearing his throat, he squinted at the handwriting.

'Dear Dean, I can't stop thinking about you and your huge –'

I snatched the paper from him. 'It doesn't say that,' I snapped, crumpling it up and shoving it into the safety of my own pocket. 'Seriously? You could have called, you didn't have to come here.'

'Well, you were looking for me. What gives?' he asked, as he plunged his hands into his pockets.

'I just wanted to use your phone.'

Dean's expression darkened; his eyes flicked over my face for a long moment. I almost felt like stepping away but I held my ground.

'Is that all?' he asked.

'What do you mean, is that all?' I replied.

'That's all you wanted to see me about?'

I shrugged. 'Yes.'

*Okay, so maybe I had wanted to get Sherry into trouble, but I didn't really have time to go through that right now.*

He laughed, shaking his head and rubbing the stubble on his chin. 'Fair enough. Tell me, how is my baby brother dealing with our love affair? Still jealous?'

I didn't answer. Instead, my eyes bore into his. I didn't know what the story was between the two brothers, why there was such venomous hatred, but I wasn't buying into it anymore. Using Dean to get back at Ballantine was not an option any longer, nor was it necessary.

Dean stepped closer to me. His gaze pinned me in place, the multi-coloured hues of his expressive eyes changing in the light. Now they seemed almost clear, with yellowy-brown tinges in them. I was locked onto them in an effort to anchor myself as I remembered to breathe. He was so close. I wanted to step back but realised I was already too close to the door. He looked down at me, his eyes on my face, amused and silent.

*What is he doing?*

I felt like prey, like he was the lion, taunting his supper. His eyes roamed over me as if he might devour me whole.

I felt lost, completely powerless as the rest of the world fell away. He leant forward and whispered, 'Let me know when you get tired of school boys, Lexie.'

Pulling away, flicking his shades back into place and offering a cocky grin, he said, 'Have fun at your little disco.' He moved away and headed across the grass towards his car, before pausing at his door and spinning around. 'You'll have to swing by some time, you left your bra in my office,' he called out for the whole neighbourhood to hear.

I wanted to die, but more importantly I wanted to murder Dean, who lifted his shades again and flashed a departing wink as he slid behind the steering wheel. Not wanting to risk another unpredictable outburst I moved to head back inside when I was stopped by Amanda standing in the doorway, her eyes staring in the direction Dean had just left.

I waited for her to say something, anything, but in true Amanda fashion she simply stared at me, judging me like a bitchy teenage girl.

Perfect!

# Chapter Fifty

All the Year Twelves were still riding on the adrenalin of the last-day-of-school shenanigans; muck-up day had been a complete success. No-one was mortally wounded, maimed or expelled. An excellent result.

The annual end-of-year school social was being held at the local town hall; apparently heels on the indoor basketball courts wreaked havoc one year, so now it was an off-premises arrangement – a fascinating history lesson courtesy of Aunty Karen who sat chatting to my mum up in front. I sat in the back wedged in between Laura and Amanda, praying Aunty Karen wouldn't drop us off right out front.

She did.

It wasn't easy to manoeuvre quickly across a leather back seat in a mini skirt; how do celebrities manage an elegant entrance onto the red carpet? There was no red carpet here, though, not even close. The height of Paradise High décor was the helium-filled balloons in the school colours adorning the entrance. Navy and white.

'What time do you want to be picked up?' Aunty Karen called from the open driver's window.

Amanda looked as though she might die of embarrassment. 'Mum, I told you, we have a ride home,' she said through gritted teeth.

'You never told me that,' Aunty Karen insisted.

'I did tell you, you weren't listening,' Amanda snapped.

Aunty Karen wouldn't have it, and so the back and forth between mother and daughter continued. So much for a grand entrance; this was just embarrassing.

'Well, how are you getting home?' asked Aunty Karen.

Amanda rolled her eyes. 'Ballantine's mum is picking us up; they live just around the corner.'

My attention snapped towards Amanda.

'What?'

Aunty Karen tilted her head. 'Oh, that's lovely of her.'

'Happy now?' Amanda asked, turning away and heading towards the glass doors.

'Yes, I am!' Aunty Karen called out. 'Have fun, girls.'

A blind panic clawed at my insides as I chased after Amanda, catching her arm before she disappeared inside.

'Why wouldn't the boys drive here? Why will Ballantine's mum be taking us home?' My eyes were wide with horror, surely it couldn't be true.

Amanda's gaze darkened as she pulled her arm away from me. 'Oh my God, you are so lame. I was lying, unless you really want to be picked up by our parents,' she scoffed, before turning and heading through the doors.

I stared after her, breathing a deep sigh of relief. Laura stood by me, bringing me out of my stupor.

'Come on,' she said, dragging me into the hall, squeezing past a group of boys loitering out the front dressed in their casual best and doused in enough aftershave to deem them highly flammable.

As we walked through the dimly lit foyer, my heart pumped in time with the beat of the muffled music coming from the hall beyond the double doors. Mr Branson stamped the back of our hands and told us to be good as we were edged forward from the push of the impatient people in line. All this onslaught of sight and sound would have made me giddy with excitement if I had not been totally consumed by skimming the crowd.

I had to find Ballantine.

As Laura dragged me through the double doors, the blinding strobe lights and deafening beats of Spiller's 'Groovejet (If This Ain't Love)' hit me. It took me a minute to adjust and adapt to the multicoloured bodies that were busting moves on the dance floor. Laura led the way. Dancing through the sea of people, she never let go of my hand as she guided me to the other side of the hall. Aside from making sure I wasn't hit in the face by a flailing arm, I was intent on looking around for Ballantine.

*Is he here? He did say 'see you tonight'. I hadn't imagined that.*

Maybe I'd been lulled into a false sense of security; just because Ballantine's mum hadn't told him about the pregnancy test kit yet, didn't mean she wasn't going to. One thing was for sure, I wouldn't be at peace until I got it off my chest and explained myself.

'Bloody hell, Lexie, you look terrified. Don't they have social gatherings in Red Hill?' asked Laura.

'Not like this,' I said, my eyes skimming around the perimeter of the hall. Amanda wasn't plastered to Boon's face, which was a definite indication that the Kirkland boys were yet to arrive.

'Hey, do these stamps on the back of our hands mean we can go in and out of the hall?' I asked Laura, shouting above the music.

'Going somewhere?'

'I thought I might wait for Ballantine.'

Laura looked at me like I was deranged. 'Um, wouldn't that look a bit suss?'

I shook my head. 'I'm not hiding it anymore, I don't care who knows about us.'

It had hit me the moment Ballantine kissed me in the girls' toilets, the way his cheeky smile appeared when he removed his balaclava. He'd looked at me, really looked at me; a spark lit his eyes as he'd pulled away from me. The memory of Ballantine breaking away tugged at my chest, as if the mere action of him leaving caused me to physically ache. What if people knew about this boy, what if I shouted from the rooftops that I, Lexie 'no middle name' Atkinson, was head over heels for the hottest boy in school? What did I have to lose?

Laura smiled brightly. 'About time.'

My smile mirrored Laura's. I felt determined in my pursuit, ready to take charge from this moment on. As this would be my last night then I would have to go out, guns blazing. Weaving through the dancers I felt every bit confident until the crowd parted and my gaze locked with a familiar set of deep brown eyes. There Ballantine stood in the doorway of the hall, flanked by Boon and Woolly, their eyes skimming over the crowd. Heat crept up my neck; my heart pounded more violently. Blue, red, green hues flashed across Ballantine's beautiful face, the light from the foyer backlighting him as if he had a glowing aura around him; seeing him there stole my breath away. His stony exterior gave nothing away. The heat of his eyes was unnerving; I could feel my heart thunder, my pulse race as a new anxiety over-took me. I was ready to turn and run back to Laura when something unexpected happened.

Ballantine smiled.

That sweet, sexy, dimple-forming smile that had dominated my every living, breathing memory from the first night I saw him. Just when I thought my heart might explode, he started to move across the floor towards me. A long, purposeful line. The world fell away with every step he took; it was as if the room had plunged into darkness, all that remained was him and me. Before I could work to steady my breath he stood before me; without saying a word he took the choice away from me – he cupped my face and kissed me so passionately I thought we might catch fire. Right then the entire world slammed back into the here and now: the deafening pounding of the music, the flashing disco lights, the loud whoops and hollers from shocked onlookers as Ballantine kissed *that* new girl from the country, as Luke Ballantine kissed Lexie 'no middle name' Atkinson.

Ballantine broke away slowly, looking down at me with a small, yet ever-so-cocky smile tracing his lips as I worked on catching my breath.

'I don't want to be a secret anymore,' I blurted out.

Ballantine laughed. 'Oh, I think we've established that.'

'You don't care that people know?'

Ballantine frowned. 'I've never cared.'

My heart swelled with a new emotion, a raw, unidentifiable emotion and I could have died from happiness. It was all I had wanted: to be standing here with Ballantine for the world to see. This was just how I had wanted my last night in Paradise to be – a declaration of us to the world and who cared what anyone would say: Amanda, Uncle Peter, Lucy, Ballantine's mum . . . *oh God*.

'Luke, I have something to tell you.'

'You're pregnant?'

I paused.

'W– what?'

Ballantine laughed, actually laughed. 'Do you honestly think anything can remain a secret in Paradise City?' He shook his head. 'Boon told me what you did, how you helped Amanda.'

My mouth was agape. 'You know? Oh my God, does your mum know? The truth, I mean.'

Ballantine laced his fingers with mine as he gently tugged me into a walking motion. 'She does . . . *now*.'

'Oh my God.' I felt the relief wash over me as I briefly closed my eyes and praised all the gods in the entire universe.

Ballantine leant into me, whispering into my ear, 'Don't think there won't be a safe sex lecture coming from her though.' Ballantine winced as he pulled away.

'I think I can handle that,' I said, laughing and thinking how things could have ended up so much worse. I would be forever grateful to Amanda for being honest with Boon, and to Boon for being the biggest mouth in the southern hemisphere; it really was a very handy combination. Even if Amanda didn't know what she had done, I still wanted to hug her. It would be priceless seeing her reaction to such a thing, even more priceless than the expression that was spread across her face now as Ballantine and I sidled up to the group hand in hand.

She looked confused, if not a little bit horrified, as her eyes flicked to our linked hands.

Boon stood next to Amanda, his arm slinked around her shoulders, grinning like the Cheshire cat.

'Well, well, well,' Boon said, shaking his head. 'And to think I tell you everything.'

Amanda elbowed him. 'Better not be everything,' she warned.

Boon simply held up his hands in innocent surrender, as if he didn't know what she was talking about.

'Christ, does this mean that I have to hook up with Laura?' added Woolly, who playfully nudged a less-than-amused-looking Laura.

Boon's head snapped around. 'You touch my sister and you're a dead man.'

Everyone broke into side swipes and digs about our loved-up group; it actually felt quite good, being treated in that smart-arse, innuendo-heavy, Kirkland-boy way. But the one thing that was very clear to me was that Amanda looked less than happy about it.

# Chapter Fifty-One

had never felt so alive, so happy as Ballantine spun me on the dance floor, flinging me in the air as if I weighed nothing more than a feather. Dragging me around he had me laughing and pleading for him to stop, but I didn't want him to stop, not really. The only thing that eventually ended our questionable rock 'n' roll dance moves was the sudden dimming of the lights and a change in tempo as Coldplay's 'Yellow' flowed from the speakers with its unmistakeable guitar-strumming start.

A slower song would usually banish all the serious dancers – they'd groan and leave the floor, opting to rest their legs, grab drinks or duck to the toilets. Instead, as the music started up, the opposite happened: there was an almost stampede-like effect. Some groups of girls linked arms in a circle, swaying to the melodic music, and then there were the coy, loved-up couples who took to the floor to join the out-there couples who completely ignored their surrounds entirely and spent the night slow dancing and pashing to every song, like Boon and Amanda. I looked away from them, blushing and feeling suddenly very exposed on the floor, until I felt Ballantine's arms slide around my waist, pulling me closer to him. I slid my hands over his square, broad shoulders and lifted my eyes to meet his, only visible with eerie flashes of red that swooped around the room – red for romance, at a guess – and then the smoke machine puffed out a surge of smoke, another means to build a sexy atmosphere or give the poor kid with asthma an attack. Ballantine laughed as I looked at it almost as if it were some kind of poisonous gas.

My eyes drifted up to see that Ballantine knew all the words; he sung and rocked me from side to side in the darkened hall, linking my hands around his neck, and I watched on with much amusement as he jokingly smirked and serenaded me. I couldn't help but get lost in him. As much as this moment made my skin tingle and my heart pound, every minute that passed was like a countdown to the inevitable: tomorrow would come, and I would go home. It seemed like an impossible ending to something as amazing as this; Ballantine must have read it on my face as he lifted my chin up to look at him, his questioning eyes looking down on me. I smiled weakly.

He leant forward, brushing his lips against my earlobe. 'Do you want to get some air?'

It was exactly what I wanted to do; it seemed the entire school was on the dance floor. With the heat of the lights, the smoke and the crush of swaying bodies, it felt like all the oxygen had been sucked out of the room.

Ballantine led me through the crowd, expertly dodging and weaving a line to the exit, both of us making sure not to make eye contact with Mr Branson on the way out. Our pace quickened as soon as we pushed the double doors towards freedom. Compared to the stuffy hall interior the fresh air felt cooler and welcoming on my skin as we ran into the night, turning around the concrete wall and down a path towards, well, I wasn't sure; I just ran after Ballantine, not an easy thing to do in a mini skirt and knee-high boots.

We crossed the main road and ran until the bright lights of the hall and the highway became faint and all I could see was his shadowy outline. We continued into a park, running along a dirt track and finally coming to a stop as Ballantine stepped up onto the top of a concrete picnic table, panting and slowly circling as he took in his night-time surroundings before looking down at me.

I leant against the tabletop, breathless. 'Can we stop now?'

Ballantine laughed, stepping down onto the bench seat and sitting down on the table, his dark eyes visible from the full moon that hung high in the sky. 'You really want to stop?' His voice was as dark as the night, sexy as hell. 'You tired of chasing me?' he asked, nudging me playfully with his leg.

*Tired of chasing Ballantine?*

I smirked, shifting to move around the picnic table, my hand skimming across the roughened concrete surface. 'Never,' I crooned, stepping up on the seat and sitting next to him, trying for my best seductive gaze; I hoped I wasn't giving him the crazy eyes.

Ballantine slid his hand across my knee, gliding up along my thigh and back down again in a gentle caress that made my mind go all blurry. His fingers brushed across the hem of my suede skirt, inspecting the fabric. He smirked. 'Nice skirt.'

I smiled. 'You like it?'

Ballantine nodded, his hand skimming down my leg, lifting it up as he cocked his head to the side.

'The "come fuck me" boots are a bit of a worry though.'

I burst out laughing, so loud Ballantine's eyes snapped up in question.

'Oh my God, that's what Dean called them.'

Ballantine froze; all humour slipped away as his eyes bore into mine, a heavy silence pressing down on us.

*Oh shit.*

I said it because it was true. I said it because it was an innocent enough statement. I said it because I was a bloody idiot who had no filter whatsoever.

Ballantine scoffed, shaking his head. 'Fucking Dean.'

I blinked, shocked by the sudden change in his demeanour. I had to say something to get the old Ballantine back, to make him see that Dean wasn't even in the picture – but how do you put a stop to what was no doubt an age-old sibling rivalry between the two?

He let my leg go. 'How is it his name always comes into things? Tell me that there is nothing between you and Dean, because I'm beginning to think there just might be.' He looked at me hard, his anger barely contained. I could see it in the way he clenched his jaw.

I slid off the table, moving to edge my way to kneel between his legs. I placed my hands on his thighs, hoping that the light of the moon made my eyes clear enough to him, so when I looked up at him he knew I was telling the truth.

'Tell me, Lex, tell me the rumours aren't true.' He said it as if challenging me.

My mind was reeling, panic building at the thought of Ballantine walking off into the night if he didn't believe me; he had to believe me, he just had to. My eyes searched the stern lines of his face, looking for a trace of the carefree Ballantine from moments before.

It took all my energy to keep my voice even. 'Right now I am confused about everything in my life . . . except you.'

Ballantine's eyes burned into mine, his body coiled with such tension it was palpable; I grabbed his hand, turning it over, exposing his palm to the moonlight. I studied the lines, biting my lip as I worked up enough courage to voice what I wanted to say.

'Luke.' I swallowed. I barely had enough nerve to look him in the eyes, but somehow I did. 'I want you to be my first.'

Ballantine's eyes flicked rapidly across my face as if searching, gauging whether I was telling the truth or not.

I felt my cheeks flush as I shifted uneasily under his surprised stare.

It was then that I felt the tension melt from his body; the uptight rigidness of his shoulders lowered as did his resolve, the hard lines of his face softened and I could once again be drawn into the deep, dark depths of his eyes, but it was only when he smiled, and that infamous dimple formed, that I truly felt at ease. Ballantine shook his head, breathing out a laugh as he pulled at my shirt. Bringing me near to him he wrapped his arms tightly around me, hugging me in a way that left me in no doubt as to how he felt about me. Even if nothing more happened tonight, I knew I could leave Paradise City feeling like he belonged to me and I belonged to him. Ballantine kissed the top of my head before lowering his lips to graze my earlobe.

'You're a bloody lunatic,' he whispered.

•

As for the rest of the school social, well, I didn't see much more of it; the closest thing to a light show was the streetlight Ballantine and I stood under at the top of our road. Our fingers laced together, we looked into each other's eyes as we stood on the highest point of the street. Under the light it was like we were on a stage, so the fact that Ballantine edged me back against the pole and slowly lowered his mouth to mine, capturing my breath in a slow, hot kiss, made me worry we might be seen by someone. I worried for like a second until Ballantine slid his tongue teasingly into my mouth; the minty taste of him on my lips made me forget the world around me. My hands splayed across the broad back of his shirt, working to pull him into me. Ballantine's hand lowered to skim down my thigh, gliding behind my knee so as to bend and lift my leg around his waist, as he pushed against me.

'You want me to be your first?' he whispered against my mouth, nipping at my bottom lip, tasting me, and taunting me with his wicked mouth.

'Yes,' I said, my voice shaking.

He took my hand, lowering it to touch him through the strain of his jeans. 'This is what you do to me.' His voice was uneven, his breaths laboured as he kissed me sweetly against the line of my neck. Ballantine was always intent on pleasing me, now I wanted to do the same for him. I kissed him deeply, taking control as my shaking hands clumsily unbuttoned his jeans and worked the zip down.

'Lex!' His voice was almost inaudible as I slid my hands inside his briefs, feeling the long, smooth, sensitive line of him as I pulled him free. I grabbed his hand and placed it over mine. 'Show me,' I whispered against his mouth; he didn't need any more explanation as his hand covered mine firmly, and began to pump slowly at first before guiding the rhythm into a more frantic pace that had us both breathing heavily. Ballantine let go, leaving me to finish the long, firm strokes as he grabbed onto the pole, anchoring himself as I worked him towards mind-numbing pleasure. I watched the vulner-ability on his face, the soft, raspy words of encouragement that I only just caught the edges of, but the one that pleased me most was the deep groan against my neck and his frenzied words: 'Lex, I'm coming.'

I felt a hot dampness pool against my thigh; Ballantine gripped the pole as his release ripped through him, moaning my name into the night. It was the sexiest thing I had ever heard in my life. After a long moment, Ballantine inhaled deep shuddering breaths as he regained his composure. He breathed out a laugh that flowed over the sweat of my skin.

'Jesus, Lex,' he said. 'You'll be the death of me.'

I smiled, pride bubbling to the surface; never before had I felt more powerful than I did right then.

Ballantine straightened, zipping up his jeans and doing up his button before taking off the outer dress shirt he was wearing over his white tee and using it to clean the stain off my now-ruined skirt.

'Shit, sorry, Lex.'

I laughed, grabbing his hand, stopping him from rubbing a hole in my skirt.

'Don't worry about it.'

Ballantine's dreamy, soft eyes looked down at me, a small smile lining his lips; he almost looked bashful.

Our trance was broken by the distant sound of a car engine, closing in on a crisp, quiet night.

'Shit,' Ballantine cursed.

He pulled me from the post and towards the shadows of a neighbouring grassy yard, shrouded by bushes. Sure enough, the car veered down our road, way too fast, before doing a wide turn into a driveway, the headlights illuminating Aunty Karen's house as it pulled up.

*Crap! Boon was dropping off Amanda.*

I sighed. 'I better go, if she goes in without me they're likely to send out a search party.'

I turned to Ballantine; he was still looking down the street at Boon's car.

'Will you come and say goodbye tomorrow?'

Ballantine's attention snapped to me, frowning as if I was crazy. 'Of course.'

'Uncle Peter will be there,' I warned.

Ballantine looked unfazed. 'I can deal with that.'

'And my parents.' I curved my brow, waiting for a tell-tale sign of fear. Ballantine just smiled. 'There's no crazy uncle or over-protective parent that could ever stop me from seeing you off tomorrow,' he said.

I smiled, standing on my tippy toes and giving him a chaste kiss on the lips. 'Don't you forget about me, Luke Ballantine,' I teased.

He grinned. 'Not likely; I'm not one to leave things unfinished, remember?' His eyes were heated, piercing.

I broke into a winning smile, fearing less about the future and wishing more than ever that I could skip forward a month or so to when I would return to Paradise City and back to Ballantine.

# Chapter Fifty-Two

I t was crazy, really. I knew I would only be gone for a month or so, but a month is an eternity in the scheme of things, and a month without Ballantine was something I couldn't think about, not even as I sat with Amanda in the gutter out the front of Aunty Karen and Uncle Peter's mansion.

The afternoon sun was high in the sky, blasting down its searing rays, requiring me to shield my eyes as I squinted up our street, expecting to see Ballantine turn the corner any minute.

'Why didn't you tell me?' Amanda's voice broke the silence.

My head snapped around, my squinty focus concentrating on Amanda's serious stare.

'How long have you and Ballantine been . . . a thing?'

*A thing?* She made it sound like it was unsavoury, as if it was something that needed to be treated with a shot of penicillin.

I shrugged. How could I tell her I didn't trust her? 'The night your dad found me at the Wipe Out Bar, I was with Ballantine; he wasn't really happy about that, and he made me promise that I wouldn't see him anymore.'

A crease formed across Amanda's brow. 'But you did.'

'In secret, yes.'

Amanda nodded. 'Wow! First Dean and then Ballantine. I'm impressed.'

'Dean was just a rumour,' I said, trying to defend myself.

'Okay . . . and he was on our doorstep last night because . . .'

'It's not like that.'

Amanda gave me a sceptical look, as if she wasn't buying anything I said. I guess I couldn't blame her, she wasn't exactly my confidante. Why would she believe me? But more to the point, she didn't have to. There was only one person whose opinion I cared about, and although I could just kick myself for using Dean at all to make Ballantine jealous, I knew with absolute certainty where my heart belonged.

'Ready to get this show on the road?' I heard my dad's voice travel up the drive as he carried the last of my bags to the car. I anxiously glanced down the street again. Ballantine would be here any minute now, I thought, as I stepped up from the gutter, brushing the back of my pants.

Usually I avoided goodbyes, but this time I would embrace them wholeheartedly, taking my time to say my farewells. I even awkwardly hugged Uncle Peter for a moment too long; he frowned as I pulled back, looking at me like I was possessed or something. The things you do to buy some time.

I gave Amanda a hug goodbye, her surprised limp arms circling around me. Our relationship had been the epitome of a rollercoaster ride: enemies one minute, friends the next. As for the terms we were parting on, well, she might have been glad to see the back of me, but there was no mistaking the gradual pressure that built in her hug, as if the ice queen was slowly thawing. As I pulled back, the same nondescript emotion reflected in her blue eyes and I almost smiled with the predictability that was my cousin Amanda. An unexpected emotion lodged itself in my throat when I was crushed by Aunty Karen's perfumed embrace; her teary farewell had me taking a deep breath.

*Hold it together, Lexie.*

Mum laughed at her highly emotional sister. 'You'll have her back before you know it.'

My heart leapt in approval; I hadn't received my exam results yet, but the fact my mum was talking this way, well, my heart definitely approved.

*I will be back*, I told myself, *I will definitely be back.*

My palms became clammy as I wasted as much time as humanly possible getting into the car, my mind flashing back to Ballantine pressing me against the very street post I was staring at now. The way he'd placed his mouth against mine, branding me so hot, so fierce, it was like he was making sure I would never forget his lips, so I wouldn't be able to even if I tried. He had told me he would be here, that he would see me off, he'd said even Uncle Peter couldn't keep him away. So where was he? Had he slept in? Surely he hadn't been called into work, today of all days, surely he would have let me know. My mind began to race as Dad started up the engine, his elbow leaning out the driver's side as he and Mum chatted to the others through the open window.

All I could do was look down the road, a bubble of panic rising in my chest.

*He's not coming, he's not coming to say goodbye.*

I swallowed hard as Dad's laughter filled the cabin, my heart stalling as he moved to shift the column into gear. It was then by some miracle I saw a silhouette at the top of our street.

*Oh my God.*

'Wait, Dad, stop!' I cried out. Scrambling to open the car door I slid from my seat, my feet connecting with the hot bitumen of the road as I broke into a run, caring little that my entire family was watching on. My heart soared and my lungs burned, a trickle of sweat ran down my back. I was smiling so broadly my face ached as I dashed towards the outline of the shadow, closer and closer, until my smile all but fell away, and my legs gave up their determined strides and slowed as my vision cleared to the figure before me, the silhouette belonging to a boy who was most definitely not Ballantine.

'Boon?' I panted, blinking as if unable to believe that it really was Boon, closing the last stretch between us.

'I thought I might have missed you,' he said, coming to stand before me with his hands plunged in his pockets.

My chest heaved as my eyes looked past him briefly, before focusing back on him in silent question. I could feel my insides burn with a raw anxiety as a feeling of dread surfaced in me. I was about to grill Boon with a million questions when he cut in.

'Oh shit, before I forget, this is for you,' he said, scrounging through his pocket and pulling out a crumpled bit of paper. 'Ballantine wanted me to give this to you,' he said, holding it out to me.

Without a moment of hesitation I snatched it out of Boon's grasp, unfolding it with a shaky hand. I would take any goodbye, any explanation. If something had come up and he couldn't make it, at least he had sent something with Boon, at least that was something, right?

*Wrong, so utterly, utterly wrong.*

My eyes connected with the paper. I paused; all colour drained from my face. 'Oh-no-no-no-no . . .' I whispered, my voice shaking.

Boon seemed puzzled by my reaction as he shifted uneasily from side to side, and even more uneasily as I lifted my horrified gaze to meet his uncertain one. Boon shrugged. 'He said that you dropped this last night.'

Boon was clearly unaware of what it said, but all I could think of was the insinuations of such a note. I closed my eyes remembering how I had plunged the paper into my skirt in a hurry before the social. I then pictured Ballantine, picking up this crumpled piece of paper that had fallen out of my infuriatingly impractical mini skirt; he would have unwrinkled it and seen clearly enough under the streetlight in my frenzied handwriting:

*Dean,*
*I need to speak to you ASAP.*
*Lexie*

After swearing black and blue that there was nothing going on between Dean and me, that Ballantine had no reason to think we were connected in any way, one single note would implicate me – such a simple, innocent line could appear so sinister. This was bad: very, very bad.

I swallowed. 'D– did Ballantine say anything?'

Boon shook his head. 'He just wanted me to give that to you.'

I read the smudged ink of my message, read it one last damning time before I crumpled it up in my fist, so tight, hoping to wipe it all away. My vision blurred as I plunged the twisted piece of paper into my pocket. My mind was reeling at a hundred miles an hour. *Why?* Why did he believe that stupid note over what I told him the night before? How could he accept that the pregnancy test had been for Amanda and not for me, yet couldn't see past this note? Why wouldn't he let me explain?

Boon studied the worried lines of my face. 'Trouble in Paradise?' he asked, nodding his head towards the paper that now lay in my pocket.

'Something like that,' I muttered.

From his uncomfortable stance, I could tell Boon wished he was anywhere else but here. But I wasn't going to let him off the hook that easily – what the hell did I have to lose?

'Boon, what's the deal with Ballantine and Dean? Am I missing something?'

Boon shrugged. 'He and Dean have a shit history.'

That did nothing to answer my question as to why he wouldn't at least try to learn the truth about me.

*Why did he believe the rumours?*

'So, will you come back to Paradise?'

That was now a very loaded question. Would I come back? Could I come back? Ballantine had made a very public display at the dance, openly declaring us a couple. But what would he do while I was gone? Why didn't he come and talk to me about this? I didn't even know what he was planning to do now that he'd finished school. Maybe he won't even be here next year?

*Will I be back?*

'I . . . I guess so, Boon. Maybe. I don't know.'

I didn't wait for a reaction, I simply turned and made my way back to the car, my heart growing heavier with each step that led me away from the very streetlight I had stood under with Ballantine just hours before.

*How quickly things can change.*

Avoiding my family's inquisitive stares, I made a long, intent line towards the open back passenger door. I needed to slip into the back seat, to hide away from the world, to avoid their questions and concern.

Head down, veering to the side of the car, my path was abruptly cut off as, without a word, Amanda crossed the small stretch of road to me, wrapping her arms around me so tight it knocked the breath from me. I stood there, stunned, taking a minute for my arms to fit around her. Amanda didn't say anything, and I didn't have to, she could read it all over my face. I inhaled a deep, shuddery breath. Just as I thought everything about my stay in Paradise was so utterly predictable, Amanda's comfort surprised me; the unexpected kindness tore away the last barrier I was so desperately trying to cling to. My tears fell, and a bubble of sorrow lodged itself in my chest.

Amanda pulled away. 'See you soon,' she said firmly, as if the point was non-negotiable. 'Okay?'

I smiled weakly. 'Sure,' I said, finally making my way towards the back door, sliding in just as Boon reached the kerb of Aunty Karen's house to stand next to Amanda and join in the farewell party.

I craned my neck to look out the opposite window, unable to bring myself to focus on anything besides the sun in the clear blue sky and the delicate hum of the car's engine.

Mum turned in her seat, offering me a thin smile. 'You okay, love?'

'Yeah, fine,' I lied. 'I just want to go home.'

Dad's eyes lifted to the rearview mirror. 'Now *that* we can do,' he said. He once again put the gear into place as he readied to pull away from Aunty Karen and Uncle Peter's house, accelerating with a friendly double honk of the horn and a wave.

A blur of colour passed by my open window as suburbia quickly melted into cluttered city landscapes with tacky palm trees and swarming tourists. I slowly took the scrunched-up piece of paper from my pocket, my eyes skimming over it for the very last time, before I extended my arm and held the note out the window. It fluttered around in my grip until eventually, and finally, I let it go.

I quickly turned to watch its fate, swirling and flailing until it was inevitably swallowed up by the city. A brutal, beautiful, gritty city that was far more challenging than I could ever have imagined.

*Will I be back?*

More than anything I wanted to believe I would be, but as Paradise faded behind me, I had to wonder if there was anything left to come back to.

Lexie's story continues in *Paradise Road* . . .

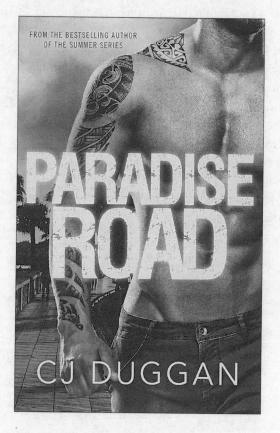

FROM THE BESTSELLING AUTHOR
OF THE SUMMER SERIES

PARADISE ROAD

CJ DUGGAN

# Acknowledgements

This book was born from great sadness, at a time when I didn't know if I could write again. It is a testament to each and every one of those mentioned directly and indirectly, for giving me the strength to not give up.

To Michael, for believing in and supporting everything I do with your unwavering love and understanding. For being patient with the stress I bring, and the deadlines and insanely odd hours. I know it's not easy, but you are the beautiful part of my reality. I wouldn't want to share it with anyone else.

To the entire Hachette family: it has been an absolute honour to collaborate with such a reputable and prolific publishing team such as yours. Fiona Hazard, Kate Stevens – I have said it before and I will say it again – you ladies are a class act. Your passion, support and encouragement make working with you a sheer joy. I will never forget how one email transformed my life; from the bottom of my heart, I thank you both. A special mention also to the people behind the velvet curtain: Louise, Justin, Josie, Kelly, Kimberley, Melinda, Anna, Nathan, Naomi and Chris.

To Sascha, Marion, Anita, Keary and Karen, for always pushing me and helping me to the finish line even when it seems impossible. Your friendships, patience and smarts are what help govern my success; I cherish each and every one of you.

To Chris Burgess, for believing in my work and transforming my career to new heights through your constant championing of my novels. A thank you seems so inadequate, but I will never forget your part in this, truly.

My beautiful Misfits. This industry would be impossible without you; my life has been enriched simply by having you three warm, wonderfully hilarious, crazy talented women in my life. Jessica Roscoe (Lili Saint Germain), Frankie Rose (Callie Hart), Lilliana Anderson: my love for you ladies is immeasurable; let's grow old together.

My amazing family and friends for putting up with my lockdowns and never-ending deadlines, for constantly reminding me of things I tend to forget; you remind me to live and be balanced. Your love is the best anchor I could wish for.

To all the readers, bloggers and reviewers of my stories, for taking something away from my words and for loving and embracing the characters; for wanting to read Australian voices, and get lost in a rich culture worthy of any local and international platform. In a world that is often dark enough, it is a pleasure to inject it with a little bit of sunshine and a whole lot of passion.

And of course to those who I've loved and lost while penning these novels – my beautiful Dad and mother-in-law, Brenda, your spirits are with me each and every day; I write to make you proud. Love you always.

C.J. Duggan is the internationally bestselling author of the Summer series who lives with her husband in a rural border town of New South Wales. When she isn't writing books about swoony boys and 90s pop culture you will find her renovating her hundred-year-old Victorian homestead or annoying her local travel agent for a quote to escape the chaos. *Paradise City* is C.J.'s eighth book, and the first in her new series of New Adult romance.

CJDugganbooks.com
twitter.com/CJ_Duggan
facebook.com/CJDugganAuthor

AUSTRALIA

If you would like to find out more about Hachette Australia,
our authors, upcoming events and new releases you can visit
our website, Facebook or follow us on Twitter:

hachette.com.au
facebook.com/HachetteAustralia
twitter.com/HachetteAus